# RAGGED GLORY

## Mark S Owen

### SMUGGLING, PRECIOUS LOVE, AND OUTLAW ZEN IN THE WILD AND TURBULENT 1960'S

Burning Bright Books Publishing
markowen4404@gmail.com

Cover Art Design by Rosa Tara Cortes
Back Cover Photo by Leon Currea

*For all of you who made the trip and arose.*
*You live in my heart always wild and free.*

*Salamina, Caldas, Colombia*

*July, 2018*

# PART I

*"Only those who will risk going too far can possibly find out how far one can go."*

~~T.S. Elliot

*"And all, like the diamond, is charcoal before the light."*

~~Jose Marti

# Chapter 1

BONES OSGOOD NODS as the air blows through the window vents, lifting the hair away from his lean cheekbones. He nods to himself, musing, steering with one hand and stroking his sparse beard with the other. The old Mercury flathead chugs along at fifty-five, about as fast as Bones ever wants to go. But today I'm not on my motorcycle, I'm riding shotgun, tuned to the wind fluttering in the hollow of my ear, those subtle nuances that the pure acid illuminates in my bloodstream. The wind carries audible messages and I listen as we cruise down the coast highway to the Mexican border. The beach towns pass by glistening in the sun-shot haze. San Juan Capistrano on the hillsides, avocado and orange groves, high horse tail clouds brushed on an infinite window pane. The blue ocean curves away like a sheet of stained glass. Bones and I are riding high and light in this holy summer of 1966, everything that happens, happens now.

For the past day and a half I've eaten nothing but a few handfuls of dried black figs, sipping strong black coffee with spring water, preparing myself for this mission. Before we left L.A., I slipped a quarter tab of pure Sandoz under my tongue and now a translucent energy ripples all through me. Whatever I look at is lucid and luminous, whatever I hear has layers of meaning. We believe in our luck like the thighbone of Jesus, but you never really know what's coming around the bend.

Glancing at Bones behind my shades, I point at the sun arcing into the shimmering Pacific.

He flashes me his affable smile. "Yeah, I dig it. But we'll make it by sundown, no sweat."

Tall and angular, sun-browned and skinny as only a protein-starved vegetarian can be, Bones weathered face has a benign groove. He hasn't eaten a bite of red meat in three years, not even a chicken drumstick. He believes that eating animal flesh makes people cruel and warlike, and gives them cancer. To me, with bloody Vietnam breathing down my neck, that hypothesis makes perfect sense. Something drives these political mother-fuckers to perpetrate an insane and criminal war on a tiny Asian country ten thousand miles from home.

Bones and I briefly touch hands in agreement. He's older than me by several years, a sort of laid-back beatnik turned hippie. Every morning, with honey-sweetened coffee and a joint, he consults the I-Ching by tossing bronze coins on a red cloth. Sandalwood incense rises in the air along with the fumes of Michoacán seer weed. As we smoke the pungent dope, he trips out on various philosophical tangents. "Dig, Jake, my brother. The only thing really going on is whatever happens to be happening. Doesn't really matter how much people want something else. It always is what it is. Karma rules the day."

"Karma rules the day?" I counter. "Maybe so, maybe not, but there's no existential guarantee for any of it. I still think we have a major say-so in our fate, otherwise we're at the mercy of whatever's going down."

Bones nods his head, considering how to respond, then tosses the coins. He's a fatalist at heart and it's his deep fatalistic streak that bothers me. I'm hip to karma, we both are. But I believe our intuition and conscious will are the real aces in our deck. We are creating our world through our thoughts and actions, every day, all the time. You don't need Tarot cards to figure things out, you don't need a special ritual. But Bones and I are solid, we are partners. Over these past few months we've shared one wild and crazy ride together. We have a strong trust.

Now, as we motor south toward the Tecate border crossing, the sun glints off the sea, making me squint. The freeway breeze rustles in through the window wings. The radio doesn't work in this old coupe, not that it much matters. Bones and I share a knowing glance, I light up a Canary Island robusto. You're never bored tripping and soon enough we'll be flush with hippie glory.

All that happens, happens now, always. Six weeks ago, under a pump-kin August moon, we limped back up the long Mexican road from sweltering San Blas to the Tecate crossing. Our '52 Mercury coupe was about done in from the bad gas, gaping potholes, and the patched and plugged retreads. We carried a small load of high-octane marijuana that we didn't dare smuggle across right away, knowing better than to push our luck. We'd been living way down in the mountains of southern Oaxaca in a village so remote that it didn't show up on most maps. But in those cloud forests and nights drenched in monsoon rains the sacred mushrooms grew, the magical fungi the Mazatecas called *the little birds.* This was why we came and we might still be there had Bones not become infested with the blood-sucking fleas that almost drove him mad.

Those vampire fleas drove us down out of the primitive sierra, then across the vast central plateau to the parrot jungles of the San Blas coast, obsessed with our risky scheme. Once we got back to the border our clothes hung on us like ragged flags, two gaunt long-hairs with luminous eyes, the old Merc sputtering like a tractor. On that journey we found miracles, we came to know what cannot be known, we lost, we scored, we endured. The nerve-wracking Federale checkpoints, machine gun toting, scowling guards, our illicit weed stuffed in the trunk, insufferable fucking heat, the bitter swarms of flies. Things seem to work out as long as you don't wimp out.

We made it back to the California border in one piece, hungry, thirsty and worn-out, and down to our last few bucks. On the sun-baked plaza of dusty Tecate we find a patio cafe with umbrellas and a juice stand. Sprawled in our chairs, we gulp tumblers of fresh-squeezed jugo de naranja and scarf chips with guacamole infused with chili, cilantro and lime. The dour waiter comes and goes, thinking to himself, two wild-eyed gringos, probably insane, we can read his thoughts. These border Mexicans are warier than their open-hearted brethren down in the interior, their eyes are hooded in distrust. Or is this just my paranoia at work? We have been out on the road a long time, trucking illegal contraband, we have been burned, we have been cosmically high for months. Who can trust anybody anymore?

Bones, I can trust. Clearing my throat, I say, "We need to plan this next move, amigo."

His slate-blue eyes are as shiny as glass. Rubbing the avocado pulp out of his mustache, he says, "Right on, I know it. We need to find a safe hiding place."

"Somewhere to stash the goods. Because first we need to get back to L.A. and regroup. Nothing too risky right now, we look too weird. We'll come back later and bring it across."

"Right on," Bones agrees, stroking his Jesus beard. "Let's just hang out here for awhile, eat oranges, drink cold beer. Tonight, later, after it cools off, we'll drive outta town and look for a cave to hide the bolsas in."

A cave? A pirate's cave on the Mexican border? Is he serious? I furrow my brows, trying to visualize this. A cave would almost surely be someone's hidey-hole already. But Tecate is surrounded by rocky desert hills and arroyos, so I nod my okay. There's no need to debate speculative details, old Mexico has already wrung us to the bone.

"All right, man," I smile, "let's drink some beer and let the world ease up."

"Don't worry," Bones says in an encouraging tone "We'll find the perfect stash place, nothing's gonna go wrong. Our karma is too good, Jake, our karma is good."

Looking in his eyes, I wonder about the condition of Bones' wits This is my friend, our bond has been forged out on that reckless adventurer's road. Still, a lot has gone wrong and after the ravaging fleas and the horrible dysentery down in San Blas, I wonder if he still has it altogether. Sometimes Bones reminds me of a Taoist sage. But at other times, he has the look of a man half-expecting an unseen blow. It's hard to really know anyone, we all have our hidden personas. But Bones and I are brothers in our denunciation of this racist, war-mongering society and in our zealous desire to wake up its stupefied denizens.

AFTER THE SUN goes down over the ragged hills, on a hilltop mesa strewn with large stones, we find our hiding spot. Notching the car in between two yellow-flowering Acacia trees, we roll a joint of the cosmic weed we scored off the back of a burro on a jungle beach. Hallucinogenic weed, it literally stops the world. Suffused and aglow, a giant moon rising over the hills, we spy out in the field a large jumble of pale rocks. The boulders seem almost white, maybe fifty yards from where we stand. If you sight between the Acacias back toward the lights of Tecate, that mound is dead-center. Using his long legs, Bones paces off forty-seven irregular steps. Stoned, in open-toed huaraches, it's tricky going. Cat-footing over the dim terrain across jagged stones, cactus, maybe scorpions, who knows what else? But in that pale mound of rocks we find a crevice deep enough to stash our two jute bolsas stuffed with mas o menos five kilos of the most psychedelic grass on the planet—resinous, golden-green buds wrapped in tubes of Mexican newspaper. The loop-handled jute sacks are dyed red, yellow and green. We shove them into the gap, plug it with stones, then stand back to appraise our work under the lambent full moon.

"Hell Bones, no one can tell what's here, that's perfect until the right time comes."

Lifting his palm, Bones intones, "Aiyee, our lips are sealed. And until that time comes, we're keeping a low-profile."

"A-fucking-men to that," I laugh, clasping his hand to seal the deal.

We amble back to the beige coupe and swig from a tepid bottle of San Carlos beer. In the eerie lunar light, the landscape seems to float and dance. Over on the California borderline we can make out the ominous silhouette of the American watchtower, about a half mile away. The border narcs are probably up there right now, scoping the terrain, their presence looming over the border. But we're a ways away in the night, confident that no one can decipher our movements. What would they even see at such a distance? Some drunken Mexicanos way over in a field, swigging tequila, hanging out, laughing and pissing, nada mas.

Leaning against the fender, we finish off the pungent roach, burning our fingertips. The moon-glow shifts shapes out in that field of pale stones, but our landmark remains visible. We feel at ease, nothing much to worry about. We have drawn our secret treasure map.

"We'll come back in a few weeks and smuggle it across," says Bones.

"Sounds good to me. And we make the run only when we feel it's right."

Sucking on the hot roach, Bones says, "What if we forget where we hid it?"

"No man, we won't forget. Don't even put out those vibes. No way, not after all this."

"Aiyee, Jake, we're gonna be in the money soon. Those rich potheads up in Topanga will pay top dollar for this ganga, they're gonna flip out."

Bones rocks at the waist, propped against the chrome grill, an apparition in the nebulous light. If some mescal-swilling local comes wandering along, everybody might freak out. Truth is, we've been out on our gypsy road way too long and it's time to go home. We back the car down off the bluff with the lights off, easy and slow. It's a magical night on the border, teeming with spirits, alive with omens.

About a half-hour before midnight, we cross into California without any hassles. The little-used crossing at Tecate is a one-horse operation, an ideal smugglers route. It closes at midnight and opens again at seven in the morning. At midnight, yawning time, the station is manned by a solitary bored guard, ready to split on home. He questions us, disgusted by our glass beads and long unkempt hair, gives the car a cursory once-over, flashlights the trunk, then waves us on through into the USA. It's so easy I almost feel a twinge of regret, as though, maybe, we should have done the deed right there? But no point in second guessing ourselves. Relaxed and elated, we cruise the canyons back into San Diego in a reverie of night wind and August moon light.

# **Chapter 2**

ONCE BACK HOME in Silverlake we gorge ourselves like famished refugees. We feast on the organic Indio dates, almond butter smeared on dark rye toast, black Mission figs, juicy green grapes and dry-roasted sunflower seeds, washing it down with unfiltered apple juice. Everything is so clean here in California—no flies crawling on everything, no DDT being fogged into the air, no putrid heaps of vomit and shit in the roadside latrines. The intoxicating sense of danger is gone, replaced now by a sense of balmy ease. I walk over the hill in the old Gypsy Boots neighborhood to the weathered garage that I rented months before and dial off the combo lock. This paint-peeling hideaway shelters all my valuable goods in the shade of some Jacaranda trees. Twenty-two lids of pretty good grass, a few hundred bucks in cash, around a thousand hits of purple Owsley and Sandoz acid sealed in amber jars. Acid of this quality, for me, is like money in the bank. I check the boxes in the shadowy garage, making sure it's all still here. Several pine orange crates of books and clothes and tools; a thick stack of typed and scribbled poems and short stories in manila folders along with a green Remington typewriter; leather gloves, a couple folding knives, a scuffed pair of Wellington boots. And my most prized possessions, two strong English motorcycles. I go over and pull off the dusty sheets, check the drip pans to see how much oil leaked, test and hook up the batteries. These Brit bikes are my babies. A burgundy and chrome teardrop BSA Lightning twin 650 and a black Matchless Typhoon 600 single with its flying M on the tank. The Matchless has a deflated rear knobby that I decide to deal with later. After connecting the ignition and adding a little oil, I roll my race-tuned BSA Lightning into the sunlight, swing onto the seat, open the choke, prime the carbs, and kick it over. The Beaser coughs to life on the third kick, spits, fires with a throaty snarl. Down in the Mexican wilderness what I missed the most was riding, I dreamed of riding, like a bereft lover.

Coasting the bike down one of the hilly side streets to a Gulf station, I add air to the tires and top it off for half a buck. Then I hit it, flying along, riding way out Sunset Boulevard clear to the ocean, past the SRF Lake Shrine, falling in love again with this quicksilver British bike. Stopping at Sunset Beach, I kick off my huaraches and wade into the foaming surf, glad and grateful to be back home. As much as I love deep Mexico, it's can be primitive beyond belief. In the teeming cities they rip you off and laugh, then charm you all over again in the coastal fishing villages. But traveling across that labyrinth of cultures has undeniably changed my life. Now I need to make it all count.

Standing to my shins in the swooshing surf, I know I have to make our border gamble happen. The draft board with their Vietnam noose has been hounding me for over two years, although at the moment they have no notion of where I am. The despicable bastards want me in uniform, want to cut my hair, want to brainwash me into killing other people in their loathsome, fucking, imperialistic war. The government has gone insane with its assumed license to ruin lives and wage death, and if I could, I'd burn the entire stinking system down to the ground. But what I need to do most is score a wad of cash and clear out of this fucked-up racist country for as long as it takes. Bones and I are brothers, but he doesn't have to sweat the draft, I do. But the first thing I want to do is find the dark-eyed girl I left behind here in L.A., Dawn Freitas. I let myself think of her for the first time in a while, now that the dangerous time is past, standing here in this wild and hissing Pacific surf.

TRACKING DAWN DOWN isn't all that hard. I look her up through our old mutual friends. She's in east Hollywood, living in a third floor studio above a beer and wine joint called 'The Dazed Door'. The bar is a seedy hangout for pill-popping bikers who guzzle tap and rub elbows with the losers that blink their way out of the all-nude, all-night strip club down the street. These sleazy dives, the way they smell, the twisted vibes, definitely not my scene. But Dawn's the daytime barmaid and these dudes lavish her with tips and imagine themselves being her stud. She's a half-breed wet dream and brings out the fool in lonely men.

The creaking old elevator takes me upstairs. I pad down the faded hall to her door and knock my knock. She opens up without a word, regarding me with her moody brown eyes, an incredulous tilt to her face. She's wearing black jeans and a yellow tee shirt with red letters that says, "No You Can't". Her long hair falls like jet-black silk. For a girl in her fourth month she doesn't look very pregnant; she's still quite alluring, Dawn gives me a knowing smirk, her eyes smile, she takes my hand, kisses my fingers, then pulls me inside and closes the door.

"I knew you were coming," she says, leading me toward her bed, her lovely lithe hips, fine round ass. This is the girl I fell quite madly in love with and who responded with a wildness of passion unknown to me.

She sits down on the rumpled bed and gives me her Lolita look, with a playful toss of her hair. "You hear what I said, Jake? I knew you were back, so I took a couple days off."

Sliding my hands in my pockets, standing, I don't doubt what she's saying. Dawn is not your usual girl next door. She communicates daily with her dead Iroquois grandmother and psyches out bullshit in an eye blink. She knows that I know this, but she likes to remind me. Looking at me, she opens up like a dusky rose, beautiful and breathless, hoping. But the disappointment is keen in her and this makes me wary. Guilt is a heavy drug, guilt is a trap.

"I'm glad you're still here, Dawn, where I can find you, I'm glad you didn't leave."

"You can always find me, you know how." She pats the bed beside her. "Come sit. Did you miss me down there at all?"

"All the time. You know I did. You got those letters I wrote you, right?"

"A letter. I only got one letter from you in three long months."

Settling beside her on the bed, I take her fingers in mine. "I wrote you three times."

"I wish I had gotten them. I've been all alone mostly and surrounded by dumb assholes."

We laugh together. Afternoon sun filters through the slatted blinds, illuminating specks of dust. Her presence in this room is evident. A red hibiscus floats in a chipped cup on the mirrored bureau; a poster of Maxfield Parrish unframed on the wall; a National Tattler open on the coffee table, proclaiming an infant has been born with a pig's tail; a pile of her favorite movie magazines. Not the least bit self-conscious, Dawn reads this crap and laughs out loud. She snuggles against me, warm and supple, my arm goes around her. Traffic noise rises from the street, you can make out the bar jukebox three floors down, pumping out sounds. This doesn't seem to bug her at all, it's just wallpaper. A black and white TV with rabbit ears sits on the table, but turned off. I detest the boob-tube in general, she likes to watch the soaps. The only plush chair in the room is strewn with her clothes, her blue plastic makeup case near at hand. A pad of paper lies on the coffee table with a scribbled message, "You need to do something about me."

Kissing her hand, I say, "Listen, I have some amazing things to tell you. So many times I wished you were there with me. It's another world, Dawn, it's like another century."

She pushes the crown of her head into my neck. "You're telling me? Jesus Jake, you look like you just dropped in from another planet. I hope you realize that."

"Actually, hah, I do," I reply, smiling into her fragrant hair. "And maybe I have."

"Did you keep your promise to me?"

"I can't even promise I remember my promises. What are we talking about?"

"Not funny, I wanna know. Just tell me if you kept your promise."

I don't want to go into these reckless and sordid details, so I say, "I'm back whole and healthy, does that count?"

"That's not what I mean."

"Well, things got a little weird but we made it through alive. We're good."

"Oh beautiful, meaning you got involved in some kind of dope deal?"

I don't answer. She looks at me with her brown, candid eyes. "I got that rambling letter of yours," she says. "It took three weeks to reach me, you could've been dead for all I knew. You should read it. It sounds like you were tripping out on God again, Mexican-style."

"Dawn, dig, I know what I wrote. And I was tripping out on God. It all came from the heart."

She moves closer, skin to skin, her lips near mine, wanting more. I breathe in her fresh scent. My lips graze her forehead, I love her dusky skin, her shoulders relax. We have never gotten over the intensity of our psychedelic love-making and maybe some things you don't ever get over. But a lot has gone down and we can't pretend otherwise. Sometimes I wish we could just take a match to memories.

She takes my hand and kisses my palm, presses it to her breast, moves it to her stomach. She slips her tongue into my mouth, sweet insatiable girl, wanting her way, knowing she can get me super-hard in a moment. She really doesn't give a fuck about my transcendental trip or my metaphysical aspirations. To her, that's all just part of the lsd carnival. She's the love-child of a Iroquois woman and a Portuguese sailor who shipped the Great Lakes on iron ore freighters, but skipped out and didn't return. None of this seems to bother Dawn. She's playful and girlish, a ravishing sensual creature. And there's nothing like ultra-pure acid and fast English motorcycles to ignite a love affair, ignoring everyone else, we fell wildly in love almost overnight.

She moves her hand to my lap, caressing my burgeoning cock, but I stop her. She looks at me from beneath her dark lashes. Compressing her lips, she starts to say something, then doesn't, then it blurts out.

"You gave me your word you wouldn't do anything risky down there. No smuggling, you promised me, Jake. You remember that?"

"Yea, I remember," I say with a poker face. "And I haven't smuggled anything yet."

"Yet?"

"Even apostles need some cool green cash."

"What do you mean?" she persists, suppressing a laugh. "What kind of trick are you up to now?"

"Trick? Come on, Dawn, lighten up. I didn't come to see you for this. It's been three months. I don't want any more arguments."

She puts her face against my chest, murmuring, "Sorry. It's just that I've been living too much in my head with you. I keep going over and over all that stuff."

Before I took off for Oaxaca she and I pretty much fell apart. We bick-ered for weeks. She was against the mushroom pilgrimage, although she knew what it meant to me. We've got a baby coming, I'm pregnant, she'd yell, like I'm supposed to change on a dime. I'd made it clear from the get-go that babies weren't in the picture for me, that I had zero interest in a domestic scene. Then out of nowhere, she's pregnant. And really, what did I know, after all that had gone down, my baby, whose baby?

"Oh don't be ridiculous, it's gotta be ours," she swore. "I haven't been with anyone but you!"

"Me, a father?" I retorted. "That's the last thing in the world I want to be, you know that. You told me you couldn't get pregnant again, no worries, your doctor said you'd always miscarry. So how come you're suddenly knocked up? And baby, you've been running around late without me for weeks."

Stung, she swore that this could only be mine. How could I even doubt her? Except I did have cause to doubt her and I'd just as soon forget the reasons. She resented my fascination with mysticism—how could someone be into outlaw bikes and dope be into yoga? She doesn't feel the need to transcend this deranged society or to even try and change it. To her it was too awful to change, so fuck it, and that sort of flippant cynicism pisses me off. But she says what do I really know about hardships? I'd never lived in a tarpaper shack on a cold water reservation.

So yeah, things got pretty weird between us. When I stopped eating her delicious chorizo omelets and went on the brown rice macrobiotic diet it really flipped her out. She took it personally, she thought I'd gone off the deep end with lsd. We stopped playing together, the way we loved to do, things got dicey. She stayed out late and then later after her bar shift, running with a pack of Dexedrine chopper hooliigans. That wasn't my scene and she knew it. We had a series of howling confrontations, she accused me of being judgmental and snide. She wanted us to go back to Illinois together to have the baby. I said no, no way in hell. She became furious and moved out.

Remembering all this, I let out a ragged sigh. You got to be true to you.

Shifting beside me on the bed, she says, "What's the matter?"

"Nothing. I'm just kinda worn out, it was a rugged trip back home."

Her hand caresses my thigh. "You're eyes are very green right now, Jake Acree."

"Dawn, my darling Dawn. I'm still doing what I'm doing."

"Oh, I get it. Still trying to live without sex and become like God? Still trying to make love to the universe?" She pulls away. "All that cosmic-consciousness crap, how can you buy into that? You, why you?"

Aiyee, the other shoe drops like lead. "Yeah, me," I reply with a twist of my lips. "Imagine that, Dawn. I just want to turn on all the lights up inside my head and keep them lit. And you know what's funny? It's what I'm really into doing, yet mostly what I get is flak from the people who know me. Why is that?"

"Because it's asinine?"

"But you don't know that, it's just your opinion. You don't know because all you do is put it down."

"Uh, maybe because I'm not interested in wasting my time?"

I almost point to the ridiculous National Tattler baby-with-a-pigtail story. But instead, I say, "Forget it. It's just a broken record, Dawn, and I've heard all this too many times. I'm doing what I'm doing, you do what you do, and I'm okay with that. Just be good with that where I'm concerned."

"Oh sure," she mocks, "mustn't waste that precious sperm of yours, right? But I bet you wouldn't mind me sucking you off right now, like I do?"

"Oh fuck off, will you? Look, I'm gonna split." I stand up abruptly, but she pulls me back down on the bed.

Propping herself up on the pillows, she slides her foot along my thigh. She gives me a sultry look, closes her eyes, cradling her breasts. She's twenty-two, passes for school girl, moody as a Siamese cat. I still adore her but I'm not giving in, but curious, I wait her out.

Blinking her eyelids open, Dawn says softly, "My mom wants me to come back to Joliet to have this baby. So does my grandma, my grandma says this is a very special child."

What am I supposed to say? Her grandmother is dead as a doornail, I'm not in on the seances. She studies my face, my mind is a lucid blank. Stroking my neck, I reply, "I don't know, I wish I had the answer. But you don't seem to like my answers much anymore."

"Because you are so fucking selfish," she retorts. "When we could get high and make love in the orange groves everything was hunky-dory, right? But now I'm pregnant and you can't be bothered."

"What? What the fuck, Dawn, I'm here. Stop wigging out on me, please. You knew from day one where I was coming from You said you didn't need the pill, didn't need an Iud, didn't want another kid. Now you want me to be someone I am not intended to be. That's crazy."

Silent for a moment, she says, "You're still a ruthless prick, as always. And my doctor did tell me that, he said it was because of the shape of my uterus."

"Whatever, the quack was wrong. And you say no to an abortion, so I'll do the best I can with the situation. I'll do the best I can. But I'm not changing my aims just to satisfy you and your grandma and your momma. I'm not moving into Squaresville with you. This is my life, okay? But when this Mexican deal pans out I'll be flush with cash, so at least that won't be a problem."

Dawn sniffs. "What Mexican deal?"

"We'll be able to take a trip out of this smoggy rat-hole if we want. Go live on a beach down on the Mexican coast, I'm telling you, it's paradise. Everything simple and beautiful, ripe fruit on the trees, parrots flying around, beer cold and super-cheap, that turquoise ocean."

She plays with her hair, avoiding my eyes. "I don't want to go live in Mexico, not with this baby coming. It's too backward. You wrote me about all the flies crawling on the meat, are you kidding? Besides, your pal Bones would always be hanging around. That asshole thinks he's the second coming of Jesus."

"I don't eat meat anymore and no goddamnit, he doesn't. He's a truth seeker just like me and we're partners, Dawn."

She frowns at my tone of voice, the wheels turning, then she brightens. "Hey, I hope you noticed something about me today. Something different?"

All at once I flash on it – she isn't smoking. No cloying fumes in the air, no foul ashtrays, no mashed Winston butts. "Wow," I say, smiling, "you quit! You actually kicked it? Baby, I am so proud of you!"

"It was no big deal, really. And I'm hardly drinking at all. Sometimes I get a craving at the bar, but I just don't. I think about our baby instead. I think about her."

"Her? How do you know it's a her?"

"It's a girl. I just know, Jake, and my grandmother says so too. She says we have to start living in a better way."

"I'm hip," I mutter half to myself, wondering what happened to the girl I fell for? Was she ever really there or did I just imagine her? It seems pointless to try and outwit a disembodied granny soothsayer.

For a minute we sit without words. She looks at me hopefully, her toes dig a into my thigh. "I should probably hit the road," I suggest, "got some things I need to do."

"No, don't go yet," she says, coaxing me down beside her. "I don't mean to be such a crabby bitch. I get sick in the mornings sometimes, I keep going up and down. Just hold me."

So I do, I fold her supple body into my arms. Her forehead feels like warm silk. She murmurs, "You're not ever gonna really change, huh?"

"I don't know whether that's true or not. I seem to be changing all the time, a mile a minute sometimes. But you're asking me to stop and be something I'm not, the thing I'm not cut out to be."

She relaxes into my chest. I kiss her eyelids, the crown of her head. I smooth her black hair down between her shoulder blades. She drifts off, feeling safe, even as my arm falls asleep. Down on the street an ambulance goes wailing by, the unholy siren of Los Angeles.

She stirs against me. "How come nothing ever turns out the way we want," she says in a child's mumble. "Tell me that."

My response catches in my throat. Because I don't and won't believe that is true. Because that means we're all just hopeless suckers, trapped in a maze of fake dreams. If that's the real low-down, then junkies are way ahead.

"You know how I feel," I murmur. "This life has whatever meaning we give it. We have to make it real or it doesn't really happen. We make it whatever it is."

She cuddles against my chest, her languid warmth stealing into me. Half-asleep, she says, "Even if I'd never seen you I woulda come looking."

"How so?"

"Your voice. A voice has a face all it's own. I woulda found you."

She drowses off in child-like slumber, her breath softening, I listen, I hold her, this precious girl, then I get up and gently stretch. She mumbles but doesn't wake. Gazing at her, my heart feels like it's secreting a substance I cannot name, because there is no name. There was a time not long ago when all we needed was each other.

I let myself out and walk along the musty hall to the ramshackle elevator, ride it down, walk into the smog-enriched daylight. The Stones are blaring out of The Dazed Door's jukebox – "Hey dude, get outta my dream! Don't be hanging around on my dream!" Two chopper hooligans in red bandannas slouch beside their panhandles, fixing me with hard-assed stares. But it's not like I give a flying fuck and they know it. They'd give their left nut to be with the chick upstairs but I'm still the one she wants.

I stroll over to my BSA Lightning, tie my hair back, and prime the racing carbs. My right wrist is wrapped with a sweat-stained leather band embedded with three turquoise stones. I wear flat-heeled cordovan Wellingtons. On the side plate of my bike is the white imprint of my palm and five fingers, with the words, *Mojo Hand.* I know and they know that anytime, anyplace, anywhere, this sleek limey motorcycle will blow their Harleys clean off the road. Make Love, Not War, is a slogan I take seriously. But don't let any asshole bring you down and no apologies are owed. I give them a nonchalant look, kick my motorcycle to life, throttle the raucous pipes, and ride off in the hazy L.A. sunshine.

# Chapter 3

L ATER, BACK AT the Silverlake abode, I lounge in a sidewalk chair and light up a Canary Island robusto. The rust-stained sunset bleeds across the Los Angeles skyline. When your intentions get bent so far out of shape, what can you do? I'm not sure. But I do know you can't indenture your life to a misstep, You have to live your purpose and stay true to your purpose. Maybe what Dawn says it true and maybe it's not, maybe I'm the father but maybe I'm not. Maybe one of those barflies did knock her up, as much as it pains me to say so. And until I know for myself I'm not going to brood about it. Guilt is the trap.

From inside the 1920's brick storefront, I hear Bones arguing with his chick Veegee. I'm not trying to eavesdrop. We're all living together in this corner store that Bones is fixing up in a deal with the landlord, where we only pay in sixty bucks a month in rent. It's a single-story building with plumbing and Bones is adroit with tools. He's installed a kitchen sink, a gas stove, hung wooden cabinets on the walls, now he's remodeling the bathroom closet into a redwood chamber complete with an ornate tub. We've draped Indian tapestries over the bare brick walls and thrown an Oriental rug on the concrete floor. We've slung a red hammock between two floor to ceiling posts and against the back wall Veegee has her antique brass bed. A rocker, a few stick chairs, a round barrel table, a frayed easy chair and ottoman fill out the room. No television, we don't want television programming, TV is for the automatons. We eat at the round table, play cards there, sift seeds and stems from lids, and throw the I-Ching for favorable portents. After all, hippie smugglers need all the help they can get.

My main contribution to this communal scene is a 33 rpm Hi-Fi player and stacks of 33 rpm records—Dylan, Miles, Ravi Shankar, Ali Akbar

Khan, Coltrane, Howling Wolf, Love, Dave Von Ronk, Muddy Waters, Butterfield and Bloomfield, Donald Bird, John Mayall and the Bluesbreakers, Nina Simone, Brubeck, the Stones and Jeff Airplane, Joan Baez, Jimmy Reed. But Bob Dylan is my main man, Dylan's lyrics struck a match that set fire to my whole world. And we have many, many books. Books stacked everywhere, shelves and boxes of poetry, philosophy, beatnik fiction, Zen, astrology, yoga, and metaphysic new age. Bones and I are voracious readers, these books are like food. My sleeping and meditation space is against the front wall, under the long window, on a bare mattress and unzipped sleeping bag. This is our groove on a shoe-string budget, and for the time-being it's perfect.

Bones' mulatto girlfriend, Veegee, hung in here while we were away in Oaxaca, keeping the scene together. But at the moment she's bitching again, half sport, half complaint, why I don't quite know.

"Look at that old bathtub," she sasses, gesturing at the clawfoot tub encased in cedar planks shaped like a rowboat with an unfinished bow.

"At least we have one," Bones cajoles. His hand work is precise and elegant, and he takes rightful pride in it.

"A tub that gives me splinters if I slip," Veegee parries, honing her edge. She tokes on the brass hash pipe, her eyes aglitter, nursing some grudge against Bones I can't put my finger on. Her moods seem to cartwheel all over the place. Still, Veegee gets up in the morning, puts on a straight dress and low heels, then hops a nearby bus to temp office jobs. Every week she brings home a paycheck, the only reliable money that we have, and Bones treats her with wary respect. He and I both know that dope money is unreliable because dopers themselves are notoriously unreliable. The only solution is to score big once and for all, to roll free in the high cotton.

Getting up from my chair, flipping my smoldering cigar into the gutter, I go to the front door and lean against the frame. In the red hammock Veegee is sagging into a Lebanese Blond dream. A poster of Viva Zapata presides over the room. A Few Of My Favorite Things moans on the turntable, Coltrane's magical vibes. Bones is hunched over the barrel table, rocking himself, reading one of Dane Rhudyar's far-out astrology books. All is so mellow mellow, except I am feeling more exasperated by the day.

Our primo-deluxe weed still lies buried under those rocks down on the Tecate border, doing us no good. Bugs could be devouring that precious cargo, stoned ants, wigged-out scorpions. I've never liked dawdling around. I want to get this show back on the road.

Bones bends in thought over his charts, making notations, seeking the revelatory aspects—Sun trine Jupiter, Mercury square Moon, Venus opposition whatever, Sun conjunct the nodes of life foretold. I suspect some crucial part has been left out of all this astrological divination, but I keep such thoughts to myself. We're always trying to make speculative stuff fit together, even when it doesn't hold water. Awareness is the only thing I'm banking on—lucid, intuitive awareness.

Twilight begins to paint the Silverlake hills. I twirl the purple and yellow god's-eye dangling from a rafter. In the flecked wall mirror, I study my own reflection: the handsome visage, high cheekbones, skeptical lips, Roman nose, the compelling green eyes. My pupils are dilated from psychedelics. I sport a dark bandido mustache and my long brown hair is swept back. We have the look of ardent apostles, Bones and me, we can't disguise it. To be who we really are, we have to live by our wits.

Bones is older than me, maybe thirty-two, thirty-three, the perfect age to be crucified, hah ha ha. But I don't buy into that nonsense that you can't trust anyone over thirty. Bones is a quirky hippie dervish who glides around in his congenial manner. He meets the world with open arms, whereas I am not nearly so trusting. I am a hunter, always with an eye out for what's being concealed. What's being concealed points to the unspoken truth.

Cocooned in her hammock, Veegee begins to snore, snores and mumbles. I share an amused look with Bones, toke on the joint in my hand and pass it to him, then nod at his ruler-drawn horoscope. "What's the word, brother-man?"

"The signs are turning green for us, no malefactors," he says, smoke trailing out his nostrils, "the vibes are good."

By malefactors, he means no bad trips. "Cool," I smile. "So let's pick a day, and put the wheels in motion."

Bones rocks back, his brain lit up. "Never hurts to get some perspective.".

"I agree, I definitely agree. But let's remember what old Will Shakespeare said."

Bones laughs. "What was that? What did he say?"

"The stars don't decide who wins and loses in this world. We do."

We touch fingers, Bones goes back to work with his colored pencils and ephemeris. The horoscope is his mandala, he tolerates my blasphemies in an amused way. But you don't win a race by drawing pictures of it. I step outside into the hibiscus dusk, breathing in the cooling air. I have my own strange trips going. My fascination with the yogic siddhi powers, which involves conscious celibacy, makes Bones' eyes glaze over. He cannot fathom not fucking for any reason under the sun, not even to become Godlike.

"Jake, bro, listen to me," he insists, "that celibacy crap is a total myth. Nothing ever comes of it, except you don't get laid anymore. You, a celibate? You'll just be frustrated and all stressed out. You'll become a eunuch man, dig, a eunuch. It's all a form of bullshit religious control."

"You think cosmic-consciousness is a myth? Seriously? You think all those enlightened swamis just made all that shit up? Come on, man, get real."

Bones eyes are opulent slits from the hash-hish fumes. "Believe me," he says, "celibacy is just another con invented by the control freaks. You don't have to put your cock in a sock to get cosmic, that's why we have psychedelics. Drop a thousand mikes of that Sandoz acid of yours, it'll do the trick."

Laughing, I say, "Yeah, I'm aware of that. But Bones, I'm not talking about an extraordinary, hallucinogenic trip, that's still just transitory. I mean a transcendent and transforming state of being – a permanent super-consciousness!"

"Permanent, whew, far out, I hear you. Okay, I'll admit that it might be possible. But I'm not giving up fresh pussy to prove it."

"Well, I intend to find out for myself. Because for me, that would be worth it. It doesn't mean you have to give up chicks forever. It's more like a special esoteric experiment."

Peeling an orange, my lanky friend shrugs. He's a Leo with an Aquarius rising, self-certain and proud. I'm a Virgo with Scorpio rising, strong-willed and visionary. And as usual, we leave it right there. Neither one of us likes to get hung up on our differences, we'd rather shake on our agreements. Truth is, Bones has turned me onto some heavy-duty insights. He's the one who persuaded me to get off the austere brown rice macrobiotic diet, my early food obsession that freaked Dawn out.

"Sure," he expounded in my kitchen that day, "macrobiotics are better than eating greasy burgers and chorizo omelets, but if you just eat rice and steamed root vegetables you'll be malnourished. Your ph balance will go out of whack and stress will devour your organs like battery acid. No man, you need dates, organic food, apples and figs and bananas, and big juicy oranges. It's all about natural vitamins and minerals and amino acids in an alkaline system. If we're not alkaline, we're breeding the Big C, so dig it."

This stuff was right up my alley. Recently, I'd begun to realize that pure foods and pure liquids, consumed with pure psychedelics, would gradually translate into an ageless body. Why turn old and decrepit if you don't have to?

I say to Bones, "Tell me more, man. This sounds like info I definitely need to know."

Beaming in a haze of Acapulco Gold smoke, Bones says, "The alkalinity of our bloodstream is the secret key. You have to eat lots of pure foods, raw foods, raw not cooked, especially fruits. Otherwise, the uric acid in meats and other garbage builds up and wipes you out. Aiyee, stress is the killer. Stress and toxins lay waste to our bodies before we even reach forty."

"Wow, far out, I can totally dig it and it's unacceptable. Fuck that, not for me, I won't allow that to happen to me. You know of any books where I can go deeper?"

"Oh, for sure, I've got some way-out books. I only wish I'd started earlier myself. But the secret is that even damaged organs can be fully rejuvenated, even the liver."

Actually, Bones look a little weathered and worn for his age, but I let that slide. I figure he's had a hard life. And during these confidential exchanges we strike up a brilliant friendship. We share the fervent conviction that what you put into your body has a profound affect on your awareness, and how you act. If you eat the meat of a terrified hog, you absorb those beastly vibes, dig? You become pig-like. It's all so obvious, but refuse to open their eyes.

Bones lays a massive book on me that literally changes my life. Back to Eden, a 600 page tome written by one of the pioneers of the health food movement, Doc Jethro Kloss, who coined the phrase, "You Are What You Eat". This axiom strikes my acid-refined sensibilities with the clarity of a temple bell. I am what I think, I am what I do, I am what I breathe, and I am what I eat, it's as simple as that. Old doc Kloss advised eating only organic raw or dried fruits, nuts, seeds, vegetables, and whole sprouted grains. If at all possible, grow your own. Pesticides and chemical fertilizers are lethal to our health. Never drink the poisonous fluoridated tap water and shun diary products like the plague. Cow's milk produces a clogging mucus inside the human system, you'll slowly suffocate in your own snot. Likewise, never eat red meat because animal flesh pollutes the blood and causes ulcers and myriad cancers. You want the big C? Okay then, chow down on you're juicy pork chops, hombre. And unless you want to rot slowly from ruined intestines, never eat fried anything. Pure water, pure food, pure air equals the Fountain of Life itself! And to that triad I add, pure psychedelics!

In no time flat Back to Eden becomes my daily bible. I devour its hundreds of pages of common-sense wisdom like an oracle. No one really needs to grow old and die, dig that. Death is for the stupefied ones, for those who won't listen, who won't learn, who won't change. Death is for those who refuse to stop doing harm to themselves and other living creatures. I munch the delicious Indio dates and sip bottled spring water, reading Patanjali's Yoga Sutras. The Shining Path opens before me like a lamp.

# Chapter 4

THE DAYS SLIDE on by. Bones is still not ready to go back to Tecate to collect our weed, he's still stalling. I take my motorcycles out for fast rides on the hilly Griffith Park roads, working my technique, honing my skill, honing my attention. Veegee comes home one day in a serious funk, almost comical in her navy business suit. A bohemian in disguise, she rolls up a finger-thick joint from our sifted shoebox lid.

"Goddamn that man," she fumes, "that sneaky fucker promised he'd stop messing around like that."

Veegee squints at me as she turns the joint into a burning coal. Bones isn't home to answer for himself, I don't want to get involved. But to be polite, I ask, "What's bugging you?"

"Bugging me?" She scrunches up her round chocolate face. "Well, number one, the asshole said he'd stop fooling around with that teenybopper twat up the hill, what's bugging me. That bass player's little cousin. Those freeloaders sucking up all the free dope they can, actually your dope, and don't even pay. Don't you have eyes?"

Freeloaders? What's she ranting about? I don't really know those people, their Bones' musician friends. Veegee's got a weird glint about her, and I don't want to get dragged into any dubious scene.

"Umm, is this something I really need to know? I've got my own hassles, Veegee."

Taking off her pumps, she sends one shoe clattering across the room. Joint still glued to her lips, she hacks out a blue haze of smoke. "Need to know," she coughs, "or should you might want to know? You tell me. Maybe you don't give a fuck."

"All right then, what the hell are you talking about? What's going on?"

"Maybe you don't notice but when he goes off up there, to get it on with those flakes? Bones loves to show off and pass around all this grass, Mr. Magnanimous."

"So what? What do I care if he gives away a little dope? He's probably just drumming up some business. I mean, you have to give a little to get a deal going sometimes."

Veegee rolls her big brown eyes. "Oh that's how it's done, huh? Okay, you so cool, you know. He goes up there acting up, turning on the underage chicks, and you guys are on the verge of doing what? Meditate on that when you're over there on your pallet next time."

An acute shiver goes down my spine. Veegee's barbed insinuation glues me to the spot. The girl is jealous, yeah, but she's also very smart. Veegee is no airhead. I stand there, chewing on my lip, considering what I don't want to consider. By temperament, I am already a little paranoid. And I know damned sure you can't trust these dreamy-eyed, patchouli-drenched stoners wandering around. That's a fool's game. But could Bones actually be blowing our cover?

With brazen insouciance, Veegee undresses right in front of me down to her peach panties and bra. She wriggles her smooth plump ass into a pair of tight bellbottoms, flashing her tits as she slips into an orange tie-dye tee. This is my partner's chick and she knows all about my yoga trip. Tumescence swells in my jeans, hot and urgent, mocking my celibate aspirations. Veegee glances at the bulge, gives me a tender smile, then flounces out the door to who knows where.

She leaves me with a massive hard-on; and worse, with the image of my garrulous partner letting the cat out of the bag. Suddenly I feel vulnerable. Tucked around our flat are a dozen fat lids, chunks of Afghani and Lebanese hash, with another half pound of Mexicano grass over in my garage. That doesn't even take into account the amber jars holding enough acid and mescaline to get hundreds of people high for months. Possession of acid isn't a felony yet but it's definitely on the cop's radar.

I sit down on my meditation-sleeping pallet and cogitate hard. The last thing we can afford to do is get lax. But wait a minute, Bones is my standup and road-tested compadre. Chicks can drive men crazy, they do it all the time, just listen to the blues. My own lovely, dark-eyed Dawn is driving me crazy right now. I can't even come close without her turning all weepy –

tears meant to reduce to a compliant smudge. Any day now she'll be pleading with me to cut my hair and get some real job, the baby's coming. But that's not gonna happen, fuck that. And I do wonder is this always the fruit of ravishing, soul-melting sex? Do we always get shafted?

To blow off steam, I fire up my BSA Lightning and go for a long wind-ripping ride up along the Malibu Coast, playing a tune on the gearbox, a voodoo song through my pipes, sliding in and out of traffic at 80 to 90, totally flashed in. The drivers are skittish, their eyes popping out, holy fuck, who's the long-haired freak on the motorcycle? But nothing can touch me. Far out past the coastal headlands the pewter clouds are shot with sun-spears and the ocean looks like a plate of glass. I wick my thrumming bike up past 90 and over a 100 mph, my eyes tearing behind my wraparounds, hair tied back with a rawhide cord, the heavy vibes blowing away in the wind. Be here now, be here now with me, there is no other place to be! The few cars on the road up past Malibu scatter like rabbits as I come tearing through the wind-splashed curves.

LATER ON, WHEN I get back to our Silverlake hideaway, Bones is standing in the doorway. He takes one look at my face and calls out, "Hola, rider. You feeling hungry?"

Yes, I am starving. We lay out a little repast on the barrel table, a platter of chips and home-made guacamole seasoned with garlic, lemon, green onions, and cayenne. I wash my face and hands, crack open a beer, and we fall on the delicious food like hungry wolves.

Amiable, Bones muses, "Yogananda says avocados are an excellent source of protein. That's interesting, when you think about all the junk the nutritionists recommend."

"Then I do not doubt it," I say, upending a jar of raw sunflower seeds. "But you'd have to eat so many avocados you'd be as fat as a bear. Yogananda was rolly-polly himself."

"But dig," Bones says, "they claim we need at least thirty-five, forty grams of protein a day. They say eat eggs, eat bacon and pork chops, fried liver, cheese, all that artery clogging poison. So people listen and then eat themselves to death. The toxins build up, the stress peaks, and boom, you drop dead of a heart attack. Aiyee, if you ask me, ten grams of protein a day is plenty."

My brows lift, I smile at my unusual friend. "I hear what you're saying, but I think that probably depends on individuals. I'm pretty sure my body needs more than a measly ten grams of protein a day. Bones, if that's all I ate I'd never get my Matchless single kicked over."

Bones squints, as if reading answers in the air. I tilt back and chug half the beer bottle down, our eyes meet in glancing amusement.

"Yeah, that sounds right," Bones concedes. "It probably does vary, and might even depend on our astro signs. But I'll bet you one thing. As long as we follow the Hunza diet, we're gonna outlive a whole lot of these nay-sayers!"

"Brother, I am all in there with you on that. Let's live forever—no reason not to."

Then the thing that's bothering me pops out. "So tell me, what's going on up the hill, anyway? Any action in that scene?"

"Naw, not really," Bones says, stroking his beard. "Same old stuff. They're making it day to day, doing a gig here and there. Deuce got his favorite bass out of hock, so he's stoked."

Those cats are old friends of Bones, club musicians living with their old ladies. But sometimes they practice so loud it shakes the whole neighborhood and that's not good. Loud blasting music always draws the heat, and the heat is what we don't need.

"Any hot chicks running around there?"

Bones, lascivious pussy hound, lights up in a friendly leer. "Hey Jake, dig man. There's some sweet young stuff hanging around that place. You really oughta come check it out."

"Yeah? Well, maybe I will, but not until our border deal is in the clear. Know what I mean? We need to be super-careful until we're home free."

Slightly insulted, Bones says, "I understand that, compadre, and don't worry about me. All I'm doing is priming the pump. When we get back I'll unload some primo dope on those cats. Just trust me to do my thing."

"I do trust you, Bones," I tell him, "just know that I do."

He gives me his most ingratiating smile, aspiring, as he does, to be only love. To be love. It's what we all really want, I suspect, and I dig how Bones openly goes about it.

We clean up the dishes and cups and get into our thing. Bones goes to the barrel table and starts fine-tuning his star charts. I go over to my pallet, sit down cross-legged, and reach for a couple of books. But before long a playful tap-tap-tap comes at the front door. Bones gets up, cracks the door, mumbles something jocular, then slithers outside. Curious, I saunter past the door to the water cooler, and as I go past, I glance out. Bones is in close chit-chat with a young honey-dripper in hip-huggers and halter top, a blond bare-bellied Lolita. She's so delectable she brings a lump to your throat. Her breasts pout like ripe pears, and she's cajoling Bones like she wants him to do her some favor. Bones is all but drooling on himself. Right on cue, vengeful Veegee flashes through my mind.

Fuck. I go over to my pallet, flop back down, and take some deep yogic breaths. I've been on this celibate trip a few months now and it can be a bitch. I disengaged from the frolicking free-love scene and dove headlong into these esoteric pursuits and I'm still diving. It's an ancient science of self-liberation. But cosmic-consciousness doesn't mean didley-squat to your adoring, orgasmic girlfriend. And I honestly can't say how long this trip might take. This transmutation of the seminal fluid up the spinal column in order to illuminate your crown chakra, how long, how long does it take? No one seems to have that answer. I don't want to be a new-age eunuch. Can I flash into Samadhi in six months, in a year, boosted along by elegant doses of psychedelics? Because I confess that is my wish, to seize the holy grail then plunge back into the joyous pleasures of life. I want super-consciousness, yes, fuck yes. But I don't want to deny myself these luscious little chicks running around half-naked, like the flirtatious teenybopper outside. I am not into unnecessary suffering.

Cross-legged on my meditation pallet, consoling myself, I open the slim red leather edition of Patanjali's Yoga Sutras to this passage:

*"Control those manifestations and you will be at liberty to manifest the real 'you'. First be master of yourself, stand up and be free, go beyond the pale of these laws; for these laws do not absolutely govern you, they are only part of your being. First find out that you are not a slave of nature, never were and never will be . . ."*

This resonates inside me like a luminous cello. Self-Realization, God-Consciousness, whatever you call it, it's not your everyday ho-hum religious blather. Back when I was fifteen in my journal I wrote "People ascribe to themselves their own limitations, and then they live them."

So unless we shatter the conditions of limitations we'll never realize anything new, we'll just keep repeating the same old shit in different guises. And if I can can consciously become a God, I want to be a God. Super-conscious beings don't have to put up with trivial bullshit.

Feeling better, I close the red book of yoga aphorisms. Bones ducks back inside. He slings his canvas kit bag over his shoulder, eyes bright with lust, saying, "I'm gonna hike on up the street to talk with her cousin. Catch you later."

Feeling a tad forlorn, I reply, "Right on, man. Good luck. Score something."

He flashes me his smile and splits. I stretch out on my sleeping bag and wriggle my toes. He's trying to make that blond nymphet and who can blame him? These girls have discovered exciting uninhibited sex, it's pretty wild. But for now I've taken myself out of that game. Closing my eyes, I breathe deeply, gliding in and out on the river of my breath. Behind my eyelids purple pools of light coalesce, dissolve, and coalesce again. Paramahansa Yogananda, in his little book, Metaphysical Meditations, says to visualize a radiant star in a circle of pure blue light, and I practice this. But usually I see this beckoning purple hue that coalesces, flows, and coalesces. Maybe it's all the acid and mescaline I've taken, I've lost count of all the trips and it doesn't matter. Only the weak go mad. As Jesus said, *Ye Are Gods*. The glowing purple light pulls me deeper into a floating, half-awake state of blissful relaxation.

# Chapter 5

Brimming with confidence, we finally light out for the border to go get our stash. We agree to not even smoke a joint until the job is done, although I do slip a quarter tab of Sandoz acid under my tongue before leaving. It'll make the snail's pace journey a lot more bearable.

The ocean towns on Route One glimmer past in the hazy September sunshine. The day is hot, wind flutters in through the craked windows. The luminous energy of the lsd has me on serene alert, even though this is mainly a paint by the numbers operation. A couple of wandering hippies drinking cerveza in a sleepy border town, meandering their way home. One tired border guard on midnight duty, ready to call it a day. We figure to be back home in Silverlake with the goods before daylight.

In the long shadows of the falling afternoon, we motor up to the barren Tecate crossing. A taut guard with a marine buzzcut steps out to greet us. Sizing us up, his eyes like flint, he says, "Where you fellows headed this evening, if I might ask?"

"Just over into the free-zone," Bones tells him, "grab a few cold ones, fool around a bit. Maybe drive on over to Tijuana on the Mexican highway."

"That so now?" the guard remarks. He squints into the hovering red sun, then back at us. His pale eyes are stoic, his jaw carved out of soapstone. "Well, just be careful you don't get squashed by those big Mexican semis, and don't fool yourselves into any trouble. Trouble along this border is a mean sonofabitch."

Turning away, he signals another man inside the concrete hut. The gate lifts, we ease the old Merc across the border. Bones whistles low, "Man, talk about bad vibes. I hope that dude isn't around later."

"They've got no reason to suspect anything. He's just another macho cop trying to spoil our day. But no shit. I'm glad he's on the dayshift."

At the Mexican checkpoint, a sweat-stained guard needing a shave saunters out, leans in. "Where you muchachos going tonight?" he asks in accented English. "Looking for las chicas?"

"No, no chicas, just a little fun," we reply, meeting his quizzical eyes. "Quiero cervezas fria. Muchas maybe!"

"Ah, cervezas!" The man smacks his parched lips. "Okay then. You go drink all the beer you want, only don't fall down. Because if you fall down over there they will take all your dinero, even your shoes."

Amused by his own wit, he waves us on into his drowsing, sun-baked country. Breathing easier, we chug along the road at twenty-five miles an hour. A skinny, rawhide steer ambles beside the tarmac, spooking as we go past.

We pass a tedious hour on the dusty plaza, nursing beers and sipping mineral water. The sun sets in ragged glory over the barren hills, spilling paint bucket colors across the sky. At twilight, the street lights blink on one by one. We pay up and leave. Driving out of town we go west for a ways on the rough highway, then pull over on the gravel and kill the engine A few trucks and jalopies rumble past as we wait for the dusk to settle. Then, with lights off, we lurch up the eroded ruts to our dry field of stones. A sliver of moon hangs in the ink-stained sky, Venus gleams off its horn. We park between the two Acacia trees and wait, listening to the chirring cicadas, watching and listening, dogs barking off in the distance. The subtle infusion of ultra-pure acid still washes my senses.

As night gathers we get out of the car, leaving both doors ajar, making no tell-tale sounds. We take a sighting between the two trees across the mesa toward the Tecate lights. But it's weird. Nothing seems the way it was before, the way we remember it. It's almost as though the terrain has been somehow rearranged. Our landmark, the jumbled mound of pale stones, is nowhere in sight.

"What the fuck," Bones says, echoing my own thoughts, "what hap-pened to the white rocks? This can't be."

"Too bizarre. But gotta be out there somewhere."

"Damn. Are we in the wrong place?"

"No, this is the place, Bones, this is our spot." But a trickle of dread stirs in my guts. What if we are turned-around somehow? But no, I have never been lost.

"Then where the fuck is that rock pile, Jake?"

We share a baffled look, then spit. Sometimes you got to slough off the confusion.

"Let's go check out that field, amigo. We'll find it."

We walk out onto that mesa of shadows and stones and poke around on the broken ground, looking here, there, all over, but keep stumbling into the same awful realization. Our pale mound of boulders, our hiding place, has vanished into thin air. Scrambling all around, we retrace our steps. Night is falling fast, we didn't think to bring a flashlight, didn't think we'd need one. Off in the desert scrub a lone dog keeps up a frenetic barking, as though sensing us. Gringos, gringos in the night.

"This can't be happening," Bones mutters in despair. "Somebody must've ripped off our dope, man. Somebody found our stash, some greedy pendejo ripped us off."

"That's insane, Bones," I say. "Nobody saw us, nobody even knows we've been here. Who's gonna dig up a pile of rocks for no reason?"

"But what if they saw us? What if they watched us bury it?"

"No fucking way. No one saw us."

"Then where is it? Where is it? You saying the rocks just walked away with our stash?"

"No, I'm not saying that. I'm saying I think we're a bit spaced out right now. Our weed's gotta be here somewhere. Because we buried it here. It's got to still be here, Bones."

Bones tugs at his beard, anxious and fretful. "But it ought to be right over there, except its not. I mean, it's like those white boulders got taken away. I'm telling you, some sneaky Mex burned us."

"That's bullshit, that's not possible. No one knew, no one knows, and no one saw."

My partner slumps down on a flat rock, mumbling, "Somebody must have been spying on us. Maybe that bastard Conrad to get some revenge."

"Conrad? That's insane, Bones. Conrad is back down in the San Blas jungles. That kraut swindler doesn't know shit, didn't have a clue where we went. Fuck him."

Squatting down beside him, I peer into the gathering darkness, worried myself. One thing not calculated into our sure-fire plan was not being able to find our bolsa stash. But I say, "Listen brother, boulders just disappear, know what I mean? We've got to be doing something wrong."

"Yeah, that's gotta be it. We need to start allover. Hah, let's pace it off again."

"Right on, let's do it."

Determined, we scrabble back over the rough landscape. We retrace our original steps as best we can in the darkness, but nothing changes—the mound of white rocks is gone. It's like the earth itself has swallowed up our precious kilos of weed. Desperate, my partner roams all over the field flailing his long arms, mumbling to himself. I have the bewildering sensation that hours have already passed out here in this Mexican field But I refuse to accept the unacceptable. Stubbing my sandaled toe against a rock, I yelp, then tenderfoot back to the car.

Something is completely out of sync out here, but there has to be an answer. No one stole our weed, the hiding place was invisible. Leaning against the fender, smelling the radiator seepage, I massage my bruised toe. I can feel the twisted mojo out in the field, it's alive, taunting us. That border station will be closing down soon, shutting for the night, which means we'll be stranded in Tecate for another day. A shiver runs through me. Rolling the dice twice seems far too risky.

I tilt my head back and tell myself to relax. I take some slow, deep breaths. I gaze up into the glimmering, star-strewn sky. The night is deep, a fingernail moon painted on a black ocean The luminous whisper of acid is still in my blood, and I wish now I hadn't dropped it. Staring up at the sliver of moon, the truth hits me like a ton of bricks.

Leaping away from the car, I shout, "Bones, holy fucking shit! It's the new moon, Bones, it's the moon! There's no moonlight!"

Out in the inkblot field, Bones mutters something unintelligible, then comes trudging out of the darkness. "What're you saying?" he says, an apparition in a pale muslin shirt. "What about the moon? The moon didn't steal our grass."

Taking his arm, I point to the scimitar moon in the dark sky. "The moon didn't steal it but the moon can conceal it, dig. Compare that moon with the full moon that was up there when we hid our dope."

Bones scowls into the heavens, then smacks his forehead. "Aiyee, fuck me," he moans, "fuck me. I cannot believe it."

"Believe it, man. Because there it is and there it ain't."

We slide back into the front seat, mortified by our colossal blunder. Reaching into the paper sack of dried Mission figs, we chew a few and swig from a bottle of mineral water. Back in August, when we came here and found our pale mound of stones, a huge pumpkin moon had lit this mesa with an eerie clarity. All the terrain had a stark definition. But the light from this new September moon is nebulous, the field shrouded in starlight. Far overhead the constellation Virgo turns in the glittering void, implacable, not in the least concerned with the foibles of idiots.

The desert air is cooling now, night is deepening, we get back out of the car. "It's out there somewhere, Bones. We've just got to find out where."

Bones gives me a cryptic nod. "Right on, partner. Let's go find our ganga."

Once again we cat-foot out into that mesa of cactus and stones, no longer looking for pale rocks, just for a jumble of rocks somewhere in the goddamn dark. Moving with intuition, psyching it out, we finally find it. A dim slot in a pile of ordinary rocks, the jute bolsas crammed where we left them. Dropping on the ground, we fondle the super-weed rolled in tubes of newspaper, almost panting in relief. But exhilaration soon gives way to somber recognition.

"Fuck, man, it's got to be pushing midnight. We've been out here for hours."

Remorseful, Bones says, "It might be after midnight for all we know. I royally screwed up. I spaced the full moon on my charts. But how? It was right in front of me in the ephemeris."

"No, it's not your fault. Neither one of were paying very good attention. It should've been obvious, the full moon. But forget it, I've got another idea."

"What kind of idea?"

"All right, dig. Remember when we drove across the last time, remember what they did, and didn't do?"

Bones gives me a puzzled look. "They nosed around, yanked the seats up, looked in the trunk. But what the fuck, Jake, we don't dare run it across in daylight. Too many guards on duty, way too risky."

"Maybe not. Because what's the one crucial thing they forgot to do?"

"Doesn't matter," Bones says stubbornly. "We can't chance it. Not in daylight."

Gesturing over toward the border, I stand up. "Listen to me. What they didn't do last time was look under the hood. They never even bothered to lift the hood."

I let that sink in. After a moment, Bones says, "Yea, that's right, man, they didn't. That guard completely spaced it. We even joked about that."

"Not only that, man. There's plenty of room beside that flathead motor to stash both our bags. Hell, we could get four or five bolsas in there if we had to."

"But the heat from the engine? The motor could cook our grass and they'd smell it."

"No, won't happen. It'll be first thing in the morning, it won't be that hot. We get across safe, stop up the road and stow everything in the trunk. We can do this, dig it."

Bones hunches his bony shoulders, cogitating, visualizing my plan. I figure he's coming around. But after a moment he gets to his feet, scowling. "No, it's too risky. We'll never get that lucky again."

"What are you talking about? We are that lucky. And it's not just a matter of luck, it's knowing we can, Bones, knowing that we can. Listen, in the morning I'll drive it over myself. You hop a bus on over to Tijuana, then another one up to San Diego. I'll pick you up there at the Greyhound station. I can pull it off, it's no big deal."

Bones gives me an incredulous stare. "No way, that's a crazy idea. Who are you all of a sudden – the invisible yogi? You'll get your ass busted, we lose our dope, and all because I spaced on the charts. No way, Jake. I'm gonna make good on this myself."

"Make good? What's that supposed to mean? We need to get our weed home, no one's to blame. We just need to get it done. Either that, or we just bury it again and come back next month. That's all right with me too. But I'm telling you, I can get it across and I'll be less suspicious by myself."

Bones turns and walks about ten feet away, his back to me. Looking over st the night-smudged border, he puts his hands atop his head. We have never had an argument like this before.

"Look," I say, "let's just rebury the shit, that's probably the smartest thing anyway. Come back when it's safer, come in from Tijuana next time. But one thing we don't want to be doing, Bones, is standing out here when daylight comes."

Bones stands like a statue, hands on his head. Then he replies, "I don't wanna have to do this all over again, Jake. We got people back in L.A. waiting for the goods. If we don't deliver, we'll look like fools. Like you said, we need to get this show on the road."

His words perplex me, our operation is supposed to be incognito. But I say, "So what, fuck 'em. They can all wait. It's not their asses on the line."

Bones turns and faces me. "No, I screwed this deal up and I'm gonna make it right. I'm gonna hike our stash across that border tonight."

"Say what? You're gonna walk our dope across that border? That's totally insane."

"No, no it's not. The Mexicans do it all the time. I can hike it across the line over there about a half a mile. There's a low fence that you can step right over."

I stare hard at him, mouth agape. Just a minute ago he was complaining about it all being too dangerous, now he wants to play superman? "Bones, dude, listen to yourself."

But he tunes me out. He looks out across the night-shrouded terrain, nodding as if in agreement with his own demented idea. The moonless arroyos, the jagged ankle-twisting rocks, the scorpions and cactus and maybe even rattlesnakes. I mean, we are wearing open-toed huaraches. Yeah, true, somewhere over there is the border fence. But over that fence looms the American watchtower, manned night and day by border patrol. We saw the tower before, that ominous silhouette in the full moon light.

Bones fills his chest with manly bracing breaths, energizing himself, a transfixed look on his face. I wonder whether he's lost his wits. "Bones," I plead, "it's not needed, you don't have to do this. Let's just step back. Dig, man, you don't even have boots on and you're going out into that scrub? Just forget it. Let's rebury the grass and drive over to Tijuana and go home and regroup."

Lifting his bearded face, Bones says, "No problemo, bro, the Mex smugglers do it all the time. I'll make like them, just like a coyote. I'll stay low in the gullies and sneak over the fence in the dark. Then I'll find the highway and hide out until morning. When you drive over, you gotta be on the lookout for me. I'll be there, Jake, I'll be there waiting."

"Aw, fuck me. Up in that watchtower, Bones, remember that watchtower? They got those Vietnam night goggles, they can see you in the dark. They've got infrared scopes and can shoot your ass at night. Forget this crazy idea. Let's bury the dope and come back later. That's the smartest thing."

But my partner has a weird glint in his eyes. "Nope, I'm hiking it on across. You gotta trust me on this one. This is our night, tonight's our night."

All at once I feel exhausted, spent. Bones wants to play the hero, that in itself blows my mind. He has always told me he's not into macho challenges, that confrontations are not his thing. Yet now he wants to hike across no-man's land carrying a load of prison dope? It doesn't make sense, and I'm acutely aware that we're running out of time.

"Tonight's our night," he repeats, hefting each bolsa for balance. "Just be sure to find me in the morning. I'll be waiting on that road, maybe in a culvert. Be on the lookout."

On the downslope of the acid flow, nerves frayed, I give in. "Okay, we'll do it your way. We sure as hell can't stand out here arguing all night."

We sit on the rocks and rehearse our flimsy, makeshift plan, we clasp hands in a soul shake. Bones starts picking his way across the broken ground, the night like an inkblot obscuring itself. He stops once, shifts the bolsas, glances back and maybe grins, then fades into the shadows. For a minute I can still make him out, a pale ghost, then nothing.

I walk back to the car and get into the front seat, knowing I have hours to kill. Closing my eyes, I try to meditate and visualize our way through the contradictions. I whisper to the One that is always present, always with us, merging with my breath, dozing, waking, then slip dreaming of the lost beaches and the sun-dusted La Mota, the burlap sacks of cosmic weed brought out of the jungles on the backs of burros. There at the booming surf, beneath the wild green cliffs, we trade for the sacred herb. We trade bourbon whiskey and American cigarettes, the swarthy traders laughing and praising the amber booze. I don't care for whiskey, detest the smell, and they won't smoke their own grass with us, loco, loco, they laugh. We all pass a good time, hermanos on the smuggler's trail. But there's something up on those cliffs, hiding in the tangled vines, something watching, something strange, that doesn't want us there and never will.

I come awake with a start in the faintest pale of dawn. I eat a few figs, swallow some water, take a piss, then maneuver the rust-bucket coupe down the slope and onto the pitted highway. The world seems deserted as I drive back into Tecate, wondering where Bones might be. Did he get waylaid or did he make it through? Lo malo, the bad thing is I have no way of knowing and this trip is already a crap shoot. I find an early cafe on the plaza, go inside and drink strong black coffee and eat salted peanuts, waiting for the sun to come up over the buttes. A rooster keeps crowing out back, behind the latrine. Nights in Mexico seem endless. Down in Oaxaca, in the lost sierras, I'd stay awake all night and barely move. Wild psilocybin mushrooms enable you to do that. Barely breathing, and yet infused with luminous life-force, you become the essence of anything you behold. You become the rock, the crawling insect, the message within a bird's call, rain drumming on the tile roof, the eye flickering in the candle's gleam.

There is this quote from Euripides that I've always liked—*'Danger gleams like sunshine to a brave man's eyes'*. But now, sitting here by myself on this strange morning, I'm not sure of anything. All I'm really trying to do is hold our luck together.

"Quieres más café?" The old waiter stands beside me, patiently waiting.

Smiling at him, I say, "No, no gracias señor, no más."

A rose-gold patina spreads across the broken rim of the hills. Rising, I pay the meager bill and walk outside into the keen dry air, whispering to myself. When you take a wild-ass gamble you go all the way. I sit in the car, watching sunrise flare over the desert bluffs. In a distant Asian hellhole called Viet Nam guys my age are paying with their lives and for what? Slaughtered like dogs to satisfy some rapacious old bastard's lust for power. Oh you pawnbrokers of war, Dylan sang. I'm up against it with the hounds of the draft board, my conscientious objector's claim has run out of appeals. Yet this is my life, it's my freedom at stake. It's about who and what I choose to serve, never mind their hideous false claim on my life. I reject their murderous intentions, I repudiate their criminal war. I won't surrender my body to some twisted fuck's idea of patriotism. I will not fight, nor kill, nor die in the bloody rice paddies of Vietnam. I'd just as soon hang every lying, traitorous politician first.

My reverie is broken by the clanging of a church bell, seven atonal clangs The sun is up over the sere barren hills, illuminating a pale blue sky. That border station will be opening for business right about now. I key the ignition and all ninety horsepower of the old Merc flathead shudders to life. The game is on and I need to play it right, play it with all my wits. But I sure as hell wish I had my motorcycle.

# Chapter 6

WHEN I STEER the rattling coupe up to the American checkpoint, the same dour ex-marine from the day before steps out. Same flinty expression, stiff brush cut, ram-rod up his ass. This dude has no love for me but I give him an affable nod and turn off the motor. It's not like I didn't half-expect him.

"Back so soon," he observes dryly, eyeballing me. "Where's your scrawny friend?"

"Him, he wanted to go on down to Guaymas for a few days and I don't have the time. I've got a job waiting back in L.A."

Narrowing his pale eyes, he says, "So you're just leaving him down here?"

The question is off-key. I just shrug, saying, "He'll make it back by bus sooner or later. He knows his way around."

"Whatever you say. You mind stepping out for a minute? Then we'll get you on your way."

I get out of the car and stand off to the side, watching him poke around, methodical. I visualize a white circle with a red dot inside my mind, I don't want him picking up on my thoughts. He prods under the seat, snoops into the glove box, pulls up the back seat, taps the door panels, burrows through the trunk. But there's nothing to be found, not even a stray seed. We cleaned every inch of the car before we left.

He turns to me with inquisitive eyes. "Everything seems shipshape."

"Right. I've got nothing to hide in the least."

"Good to know." Glancing across at old Mexico, he adds, "Let me give you a piece of advice, son. Don't be messing around this border, just go on home. People who mess around this border always end up in a pile of dog-shit."

Right, I think, nodding my understanding as I slide behind the wheel, drop it into gear and move on into California. What a bizarre pointed statement to drop on me. But what really blows my mind is that once again they never opened the hood. My plan would have worked to perfection and I'd be on my way to L.A. with the goods. But instead, some fucking how, I've got to find Bones hunkered down somewhere.

Driving slowly around the curve on the two-lane highway, I notice a dirt road veering off to the west, a road I didn't notice coming down yesterday. Is Bones out there hunkered down in a gully, praying I'd guess it right? Reacting to this image, I swerve onto the dirt track and follow my hunch into the desert scrub, dust billowing behind me. But it's smooth enough, running between sandy knolls and rock outcroppings until I come onto an arid flat and see a low wire fence running west, yep, low enough for a man to step over. But to my horror that's not all I see. Right ahead is that dreaded American watchtower rising up on metal stilts dominating the landscape, and I'm right out in the open.

"Muthafuck," I mutter, heart lurching in my ribcage.

Swinging a wide, bumpy turn in the billowing dust, I head back toward the highway, my head high with hope. Some days aren't as good as other days, but if you keep moving they turn out okay. But no sooner do I make it back to the asphalt then the same border cop screeches up in a black and white Ford, cutting me off. Glowering, the man leaps out with one hand on his holstered gun, pointing his finger at me as he approaches.

"You stupid shit," he barks. "Did I not tell you to clear outta here? Now get out of that car!"

Doing as he orders, I say, "Hey officer, it's no big deal. That road just caught my eye, I was kind of curious—"

"Shut the fuck up, go stand over there," he orders, jerking his thumb. "And don't so much as twitch, you hippie prick."

Struck mute by his ferocity, I oblige. I go over and stand in the shallow roadside ditch. He glares me down, then turns his baleful attention to the car. He yanks the seats apart, pries the door panels off, digs through the trunk, bashes the wheel wells, and finally pops the hood. He roots and snorts through the coupe, a predator on the scent, trying to root out the secrets of my life. Watching him, I swallow hard.

Red-faced, he slams the hood back down. "All right hotshot," he growls. "I'm not sure what you think you're doing but one last time, I'm telling you now—get the hell away from this border. Not gonna warn you again."

"Okay, officer, I got it," I tell him with a even look. "Sorry about that wrong turn. And no problem, I'm heading on home."

Fixing me with his bayonet stare, he replies, "Be damn sure you do that, son."

I get back in and key the engine, knowing now that things are stacked against us. This border narc means me real harm. I acknowledge him with a grim nod, drop the car into gear and move off at twenty-five miles an hour. But my heart is galloping. I've got to find Bones, got to ditch the weed, got to make tracks. There's barely room to breathe. Once around the next bend I punch it up to forty, scanning left and right for any sign of my partner, checking the rear view, sweat stinging my eyes. The road dips in and out of dry arroyos and rocky hummocks studded with desert scrub, leading toward the canyons. Black flags rip in my mind. But I maintain, following the narrow highway, all but willing Bones into existence.

All at once Bones leaps out of a ravine as I go past, waving his arms like a scarecrow. He's taken off his shirt, flapping it above his gaunt body like a flag. Pumping the brake pedal, I bring the car to a swerving halt, then jam it in reverse and back up with the gears whining.

"Hey man," Bones laughs, ducking his head in the window. "We did it, we've pulled it off, we're home free! It's right below me in the culvert!"

"No, Bones, we're not home-free," I rasp, knuckling the wheel. "I just got rousted by that mean-ass border cop. He tossed the car and flat-out threatened me to my face. They're on to us, Bones, I don't know how, but somehow they're on to us. We gotta split."

"On to us?" Bones gives me an incredulous look. "No, that's not possible. We're cool, Jake, the hard part's over. I humped it across, not even a flashlight went on. We're good, we're good."

"No, goddamnit, you're not hearing me! The hard part's about to be rammed right up our ass! Something's gone wrong! We need to ditch the grass and make tracks outta here!"

A confused scowl crosses Bones' face, then he pulls his shirt back on.

Looking up and down the road, he says, "That's ridiculous, they never saw me, there's no way they're on to us. You're over-reacting. I'm gonna jump back down in the gully and grab our dope. Be right back."

"No, Bones, no" I shout, pounding the steering wheel, "leave it, ditch it, ditch the shit! We got to hightail it, we gotta go now!"

But he's already ducked out of sight. Clenching my jaws, I sit with motor idling, trying to squash the panic rising in my guts. The seconds crawl by. Bones comes back, climbs in, stuffs both bolsas on the floorboard between his legs, then grins, "Righteous, let's head home, partner."

Pissed beyond words, I drop the car into gear and pull away, my eyes glued to the rear view mirror. All my instincts tell me we're caught up in a surreal desert clusterfuck.

"Jake, really my man, just relax," Bones is saying. "It's all cool, we're home free. You're stressing out for no good reason. This trip is gonna make us rich."

"For no good reason? You have no fucking idea." I relate to him what went down, the bad signs, the uptight border cop, how I feel certain we're stumbling into a blind man's bust – if not here, then somewhere up the road, cops have radios, cops set up roadblocks, cops have guns to blow your head off. Those grass-stuffed bolsas between his legs are jail bait.

But Bones laughs it off, telling me I'm being way too paranoid. All lit up with his daring, he tells me, "Don't sweat it, we're in the money now. Hundred dollars a lid, easy money, just imagine. We'll go back to San Blas and set up the pipeline, we'll live like hippie kings!"

What the hell, I want to believe him, an adobe hacienda in San Miguel de Allende with teenage maids? Fuck yeah, beautiful, if we can just make it out of here alive! Shot with adrenaline, I careen the lumbering coupe through the tight canyon, hugging the steep slope. Bones begins to grunt but I don't care. He hasn't seen the malicious glint in that border narc's eyes, the mean predatory lust. I drive hard, pushing the rust-bucket Mercury for all it's worth, yawling through the curves, cliff falling, birds flitting away chasing open daylight.

"Jake, Jesus, man," Bones pleads "please slow down, slow it down. We're cool, we're home free, man, we're home free."

Maybe not, I say to myself, fear panting down my neck. Still, I ease off on the gas and Bones stretches out, rambling on about how our karma is good, congratulating himself. He doesn't sense that dark furious shadow on road behind us, he isn't wired like I am. And then I actually see him, hunting us down.

"Fuck. Maybe not, Bones," I say tersely.

"Maybe not what?"

"Maybe not home-free at all. That same government Ford is coming up fast behind us. There's a red flasher going off on the roof."

Bones gapes at me, then swivels around to face the awful truth. He lets out a gasp, his eyeballs shrinking back into his skull. And in that instant I know we have only one fleeting chance. Bellying into the next curve, I stomp on the gas and the old car swerves so hard it almost goes off the edge into nothing, slamming Bones into the side door.

"Listen to me," I demand through clinched teeth. "We need to throw the shit out. Right around this next bend, heave it out the window, ditch it, both bags."

Bones mutters something incoherent in reply and slumps down. He just sags, as if all volition has left his body. The car skids into the blind curve, giving us a few precious seconds. "Now," I shout, "push it all out, Bones! Throw it into the canyon!"

But my partner goes catatonic on me. "No," he mumbles, staring straight ahead. "No, they might see us, they might see us and catch us."

"Catch us?" I scream, fighting the wheel. "You dumb fuck, we're already caught! We gotta ditch that weed, you dig? This next curve, heave it out the window!"

The beige coupe dives into the sharp bend like a wallowing hippo, tires squealing. My gambit is that our fiendish pursuer won't see the bolsas tumbling down the rocky slap, he'll run us down, yeah, but at least we'll be clean.

But Bones falls apart. In a herky-jerky motion he starts rolling his window up. He's kicking at the bolsas with the back of his heel, as if trying to stuff the fat bags back under the seat.

"Listen, Bones, listen to me," I plead, but he just stares straight ahead like a wooden Indian.

By now the black and white Ford is almost on my tail, red light flashing, its siren wailing. I see the man inside glaring at me, something ominous in his hand, I see his hard face. With a groan, I know we've lost. All I can do is drive on down out of this canyon and pull over.

"Maybe he won't look in here," Bones wheezes, still kicking at the jute sacks. I don't bother to answer.

Minutes later, we descend onto the mesquite flats and I slow down as my nemesis overtakes me. Looking over into his sneering face, I stare right into the bore of an army .45 automatic. Pull that goddamn car over, he mouths at me, stabbing with the muzzle. Slowing to a crawl, I pull onto the shoulder and stop, my heart sinking like a stone. Nabbed, fucking nabbed.

"Dues to pay," I say to Bones, "some serious dues to pay now."

But he doesn't respond, he just sits there breathing through his mouth, staring. At least he's stopped kicking at the marijuana-stuffed bolsas.

The enraged border narc comes to my window, shoves the automatic in my face. "I told you, asshole," he snarls, "but you're too smart to listen. Now get the fuck outta there with your hands where I can see."

He yanks the door open and menaces us out, making Bones slide past the steering wheel. He spread-eagles us across the trunk and frisks us down. He makes us squat in the red dirt behind the car, telling us to stay silent and not move. Then he goes to the passenger door and tugs the bolsas out one by one, tossing them on the roof. Breaking open one of the newspaper tubes, he sticks his nose into the buds, snorts in glee, then leers over at me.

"And I guess," he cracks, "all you got here is a little hippie catnip, right?"

There's nothing to say. We sit cross-legged in roadside dirt, stunned and rueful. I went against my own intuition, and when the shit came down my partner froze up on me. The peerless blue Pacific sky spills over the rugged hills, offering no solace.

Next to me, Bones moves his cramped legs. "Fucking unbelievable," he mutters.

"No shit. This is some really fucked-up mojo."

The border cop shouts over at us, "I told you fuckers not to talk! That means don't move and shut up!" The hard-barked narc carries the bolsas over to his government Ford, stows them in the trunk, then makes a call on his radio. He watches us over the car roof, his gun hand clearly visible. A riff from the Buffalo Springfield comes to my mind and I feel like all the strength has left me.

Bones slumps back down, whispering, "They're gonna ask us where we got the shit. Make sure we don't tell 'em in Mexico."

"No problem," I whisper back, "so where did we get it? We need to be on the same page."

Bones blinks a few times, then says, "Say we bought it from a wetback at Crystal Pier."

"Where's that?"

"In San Diego. It's an amusement park, like Pacific Ocean Park."

"Okay. So we scored it from a Mexican on Crystal Pier. But why'd we bring it with us over here?"

"Right on, right on. Just say we hid it in that culvert on the way to Tecate. We didn't want to take any chances."

Glad that he's recovering his wits, I whisper, "Man, that's pretty far-fetched."

"I know it, but fuck. What else have we got to work with?"

The car radio squawks, the border cop talks into his handset, glaring at us. "Nothing really," I admit, "and it does make a weird kind of sense."

"And the main thing is we didn't smuggle anything in from Mexico, nada."

The buzz-cut narc bellows over at us. "Shut the fuck up! Button it up! Don't talk, don't even twitch, motherfuckers, your ride is on the way!" The .45 automatic glints in his hand.

So we squat down in the dust, leaden with regret. The morning is already turning hot, sweat trickles in my armpits, flies are stirring all around us. I hate flies. My stomach feels hollow as a drum, my mouth parched. No one has to tell us what's coming.

"Keep it simple," I say under my breath.

"Right, right on," Bones murmurs back, "keep it simple."

Within minutes, an olive jeep pickup pulls up in a quick stop, smothering us in roadside dust. They shove us into the back and cuff us to a metal bench. The ride back to the border station passes in a blur, jostling us to and fro on the hard seat like shackled dogs. Dread oozes through my body and mind, the opposite of everything I had been banking on.

Bones voice muffles in my ear. "Just stick to the story, we'll be all right. All they got us for is possession."

"Possession with intent to distribute, man. Get real."

"Maybe not, maybe not."

I glance at him sideways. We just got busted with five kilos of prime Mexican weed, not to mention the hundred some-odd tabs of high-grade acid I had stashed in those bolsas. Lsd is scheduled to become a major felony any day now, I'm just not sure when.

Leaning close, I say, "How'd you get back in the country last night? Why didn't you come across with me? They're gonna grill us."

Bones nods, leaning hard against my shoulder on a curve. "Yeah, I hear you. Let's tell 'em I hiked back across, just like I did. We got drunk, you bet me fifty bucks I wouldn't dare do it. So I did it. I took you up on the bet, just to see if we could get away with it."

We share a grin, a gallows snort. Why the fuck not? It's barely plausible, but just plausible enough.

We are thrown against the back of the cab. The jeep is braking hard, braking again, coming into the Tecate station with its hippie freak cargo. The pickup comes to a rude, quick stop. A big-bellied border guard steps out of the concrete hut, toting a short pump shotgun. He lets the rear gate down, smirking, "Been expecting you boys."

# Chapter 7

WE ARE UNSHACKLED and led into the rear of a cinder-block building, where we are identified. They take me into a pea-green room presided over by a wall photo of Lyndon Baines Johnson, and I wait at a metal table. After awhile, the stern border narc comes in and closes the door. He's taken off his gunbelt. He carries a clipboard that he taps with a ballpoint pen. For a minute he stands there, regarding me, then sits across from me like a patron with heavy news.

"I wish you had listened to me," he says in an sober tone, "and gone home. Now you and your buddy in there are in a world of shit."

This is not a revelation, but I give him his due. "So I gather. Yeah, you did warn me. So thanks."

Frowning, he takes a burl pipe out of his shirt pocket, tamps it, strikes a wooden match, sucks on the stem. His flint gray eyes study me, memorizing my face, trying to get inside my head. I am at his mercy now, but my head is off-limits to these assholes.

I say nothing more, just wait on him. He puffs out some repugnant cherry-scented smoke, then says, "We've got about ten pounds of marijuana in there, wrapped in Manzanillo newspapers, with your fingerprints all over it. Plus, one hundred and seven tablets of a substance we can't identify. Care to clue me in?"

I shake my head, saying, "I have no idea. We scored that stuff over at Crystal Pier yesterday around noon, from a Mexican. He was jabbering so fast I could barely understand him. But he offered us a good deal and we both smoke pot. Kind of meant we wouldn't have to buy grass for months. Then we stashed it in a drain pipe on our way over to Tecate."

Clamping down on his pipe, the man says, "Right, right. What, all for a hundred and eighty bucks?"

"I don't quite remember. Yeah, more or less, a hundred and eighty, maybe two hundred. Bones took care of the money part. It was a sweet deal. Only now I wished we had walked away from it."

My nemesis says, "Okay, son, enough of the BS." He lays his smoldering pipe on the gray table, staring at me hard. "And your scrawny pal hiked back across that border on a moonless night on a drunken lark. Is that really the best you can do? Because you're ass is on the line in this fiasco."

With an impassive face, I say, "So, Bones told you. Yeah, that's what happened. Why make up stories?"

Jotting on his clipboard, without looking up, he replies, "No one's going to believe that cock and bull story, least of all the court. You're in deep shit and your cooperation counts. You're facing serious jail time. You come clean with me, I might be able to help."

Swallowing, I meet his piercing gaze. "Look officer, I regret this stupid-ass mistake. Obviously, I regret it. But I won't incriminate myself or my friend. Your world is not my world. And that's my story."

Snorting with ridicule, he makes a notation, flips a page, then asks a few more terse questions. But the stalemate is on and he knows it. He lets me refill my paper cup from the water cooler. He reviews his notes and asks me to sign off on his accuracy. Since it's not a confession of smuggling, I oblige him.

Leaving his pipe on the table, he stands up, tapping the clipboard on his thigh, looking at me with curious disdain. He shakes his head, saying, "What in the hell did you think you were doing out there, trying to pull off this caper? Was that some kind of birthday present to yourself? Nice job, Acree."

With a mocking glance, he leaves the room. I breathe in and out, my pulse is calm. I am left alone to contemplate LBJ's color portrait on the wall, with mixed feelings. That sleazy bastard might have been involved in JFK's assassination. And even though he's pushing through the civil rights act, at the same time he's ramping up the hideous war in Vietnam. How can you trust any of these ruthless pricks? LBJ, just like the grim border narc, they are my mortal enemy.

The border narc's last barbed comment hit home. Next to LBJ's picture is an American flag calendar, and today's date is prominent, September

13$^{th}$, 1966. Today is my birthday, today I am twenty years old. Tonight I'm supposed to be at my parent's house in Santa Monica for a cozy birthday dinner. No, it hasn't slipped my mind, I just figured I'd be back in plenty of time. My blue-eyed Florida mother will be baking a lemon meringue pie, my childhood favorite. She's going to freak out over this unholy situation. My old man will crack his Canadian Club whiskey and brood himself into a morose drunk. My kid brother Evan will be stunned speechless. He's into all the Dylan records I've turned him on to, he's reading all the important books. I always keep him in a good lid of pot that our mom sometimes finds and hysterically flushes. And then there's Dawn, my dearest Dawn, who's going to flip out and lay her Injun grandma hoodoo all over me. Yeah, no matter how you slice it, this situation is a royal fuck-up. I sit at this metal table, in this ugly room, with only that grim-faced fuck on the wall, caught inside my own head. It's like staring into a whirlpool.

Later in the morning, a pair of Federal marshals show up. They're cordial and very efficient. They put us in the rear cage of a blue government sedan and transport us to the Federal Detention Center in San Diego. We ride in handcuffs all the way, mostly silent. But the crew-cut lawmen keep up an easy banter, like it's all in a day's work.

"I wouldn't worry too much," one cop says, "you'll have your day in court. And with a little luck things could go your way. Isn't that right, Frank?"

"Damn straight," Frank chips in. "And cooperation's the key. Keep that in mind."

I slide my eyes at Bones, who slumps in considerable discomfort, head hanging. Luck has deserted us like the fraying end of a bad bet. What these federal agents are really saying is rat-out your friends, rat out other dopers, rat them out and cop a plea. But I'm not copping out on anyone. I turn down their offer of a Baby Ruth bar, my stomach rumbling, on this, the worst morning of my life.


ONCE OVER IN San Diego, reality comes down hard. They take us through the rear entrance of a multi-story building that seems to occupy a whole city block. This massive jailhouse confines ordinary fuck-ups like drunk drivers, deadbeats, pick-pockets, whores and pimps, but also locks down much worst miscreants. One entire cellblock is stacked with armed robbers, violent psychopaths, rapists, murderers, and hapless smugglers like me and Bones. Some really bad actors call this joint their home, as we soon find out. We're booked, photographed, finger-printed, then traipsed through a series of electronic iron gates. The air stinks of stale cigarettes, rancid sweat, industrial disinfectant, and intensely negative vibes. Derisive hoots and catcalls about our long hair brings blood to my stoic face as we march past the bleak cells.

We get one lucky break by being shoved in the same cell together. A three-sided concrete box fronted by a steel bar door, a naked bulb in wire mesh, a lidless toilet and stained sink that reeks of harsh chemicals. One whiff makes you queasy. A double-deck bunk is bolted into the puke-green wall. Hunky-dory.

A loud siren goes off. Seems we've arrived just in time for the industrial lunch. We march into the giant mess hall with about a hundred other sullen inmates. The dubious crap they dump on the aluminum plates makes us gag—nauseating pork and lima bean stew, scoop of pineapple jello and a cornbread muffin, seasoned with the lustful smirks of our cutthroat table-mates. They figure were a couple of hippie fags. Bones tries to engage in conversation, but only gets grunts and mocking stares back. We sip the chlorinated water, make ourselves chew a few soggy beans. It's hard to stay clear, thoughts are muddled, anxiety prowls loud enough to be heard underfoot. High on the bleak gray walls, long wire-mesh windows let in a smudge of sunlight.

Bones moans under his breath and I understand. This is where the visionary hippie gets rubbed out. This is where your faith perishes and your heart torn apart. You're stripped of your freedoms and get buried alive. Even Vietnam, even that deadly hellhole, would be better than this catacomb where you're nothing, nothing at all.

We are allowed to meet with an erstwhile public defender. In a square beige room, he tells us to reconcile ourselves to doing some hard time. The border patrol has us dead to rights. Smuggling narcotics with intent to distribute carries twenty years or more inside the Federal penal system. With good behavior, it's possible, we might get paroled in ten.

"Jesus H. Christ!" I shout in his face. "Ten fucking years? It's only marijuana!"

But out legal servant only shrugs. He's sallow and weak, incapable of saving anyone, let alone himself. "Not according to the law, I'm afraid. Smuggling marijuana is considered a major narcotics felony, same as heroin. What can I tell you? Don't expect much if any slack. They're coming down hard on everybody."

"But they can't prove we smuggled anything," Bones insists, "no one caught us in the act of smuggling. They just caught us with possession of weed on the California side."

Blinking his myopic eyes, the man says, "Doesn't matter, doesn't matter at all. You were apprehended with several pounds inside the restricted zone, same as bringing it across. That fact is undeniable, and it's all they need. I'm sorry. I advise you to throw yourselves on the mercy of the court."

Choked with fear, we hunker down in our concrete cell box, demons rattling around in our heads. Ten to twenty years in this abyss? We stare at the floor, toss in our cots to fervently pray, O fluttering moth of prayer, praying like I've never prayed before. Or maybe just sink back in despair as the minutes seep past like water through a clogged drain. A white-haired negro trustee comes to our iron door with a not unkind face, he wants to know if we need anything. I sit up and regard him. The hint of an ironic smile plays across his lips.

"Are you serious?" I respond. "Such as?"

"Well, such as," the trustee drawls, "whatever you thinks you might need."

"Hey man, what we need, really need? is to get connected with a good lawyer. A real lawyer. Can you help us with that?"

Wrinkling his nose, he says, "Don't know 'bout that one. But I'll ask around for you an' let you know."

He limps off, leaving us with a shred of hope. But in here facing a possible twenty to life, the faintest upbeat sign makes you delirious. I look at Bones with a raised eyebrow, but he's stagnating under the pervasive grim vibes.

"Fuck man, at least it's a possibility."

Bones says nothing, doesn't even lift his head from the cot.

I stand at the iron bars, looking out the wretched multi-tiered cellblock. Dylan wails in my mind, *Man oh man, can this really be the awful end? To be trapped inside this hellhole . .* But no, this cannot be the awful end. There has to be a way out of here, I tell myself, and we've got to find it.

Our first day is a long and grueling day, the harbinger of all things dire. I get my one phone call, call my parents, get lucky, my kid brother picks up. I lay the bad news on Evan, glossing it over, telling him not to worry, give love to mom and dad, I'll be out of here soon. But I don't know whether a single thing of what I'm saying is true or not.

Bones escapes in his own way, sliding into oblivious naps. But my own restless mind gives me little respite. So I do Hatha yoga exercises, deep breathing exercises, visualizing light within and around me, make inner deals like a deranged monk, anything to not succumb to the fear gnawing my guts. Bones declines to even make a phone call, says he doesn't want anybody to know. He moans in the throes of a nightmare, his long hand pawing in the air. I watch him, reflecting on every detail of what went wrong on the border. In dreams you try to run but you can't run; your limbs are heavy as mud, the horror swarms all over you. Who will intercede for us? I've been in this hole less than twenty four hours and I'm already drowning.

Bones comes awake with feverish eyes, rasping at me, "Something good's got to happen, got to."

"Sure as fuck hope so, something better. Otherwise, fuck."

Then, out of the Stygian gloom, something comes our way. A tattooed cholo comes to our cell door and spits at his feet. "Hey chiquitas," he intones, "I got some messages for you."

I stand up and look him in the face. "We're not queer, man. That you need to know. Everybody needs to know that. We're in here on a Mexican drug bust."

He stares back with opaque eyes. "Oh no? Well, that's yet to be seen, in here, you never know. Anyway, it don't matter. Because El Jefe wants to see both of you right now."

"Who?"

"El Jefe, the Señor Rodriguez. The boss who runs this evil place, comprendo? He's got something to say and he don't like to be kept waiting. Vamanos."

Quicksilver intuition flickers on inside my head, Bones and I exchange a glance. "Okay," I say, "let's go meet him then, we're ready."

The cholo signals with his tattooed hand, the iron door slides back, and we follow him along the second-tier walkway to meet the Headman.

"Hey prison pussies," some creep hisses as we walk by, "panochas, come see me later."

# Chapter 8

Raul Rodriguez is a hairy-chested, barrio hard-case, with a boyish face and a craze of tattoos all over his torso. He lives by himself in the end cell on the upper tier, the undisputed potentate of our cellblock. He greets us wearing only flip-flops and red satin gym shorts, his black hair slicked back. His intelligent face take us in with curiosity, the face of a man who has come to terms with what is absent. But he is used to having others answer to his inquiring, dominant eyes.

Rodriguez dismisses the messenger, shakes our hands, gestures for us to sit on the bunk across from his padded chair. He offers a smile, the first smile we've gotten in this joint, his teeth strong and white. You can sense that he is completely at ease in his own skin.

"So," he begins, "you are not run-of-the-mill criminals, I gather this much. You are not like most of these losers. You are what's called new-age hippies, is this not so?"

"I suppose that's true," I answer. "But to be honest we're not into labels. We're just trying to live our lives the way we want, without being controlled."

"Ah, this I can relate to—the way you want." El Jefe rubs his chin, looking us over. "But that can be tricky, no? Society says to be the same joker."

"Aiyee, very tricky" exclaims Bones, "just doing your own thing gets booby-trapped. I'm a carpenter, he rides British motorcycles, we're so far out of the conformist trip we have to invent ways to survive."

Knowing it's time to be out front, I say, "And doing our own thing just got us busted down at Tecate, for smuggling primo jungle weed."

"Ah, siii, bonito jungle weed," Rodriguez nods, "so I heard." He lights up a Pall Mall straight with a cardboard match. "I like that phrase," he exhales, "doing your own thing. It covers a whole lot of sins, like smuggling, like fleecing the fat cat or fucking someone's naughty wife, free love—hah, all this free love I hear you hippies are into! All the psychedelic drugs and wild orgies, it is all for real?"

Venturing a smile, I say, "Yeah, mas o menos, more true than not true. But you know how those stories go. Things get exaggerated."

"Fuck, I do, do I ever," Rodriguez affirms, rubbing his hairy chest. "Those blown-up stories can make or break you. But I hear that you cats are a different breed, and you two are the first hippies I meet. This lsd, tell me, like your Timothy Leary claims, does it actually change the brain? This is of interest to me."

Flashing on his acute curiosity, I say, "Yeah, I would say so, in very unusual ways."

Furrowing his thick eyebrows, Rodriguez goes on, "I am locked away in this giant tomb, so I must entertain myself. If you had not shown up, I never have the chance for this conversation. Maybe you can show me something new, I crave different things. I was convicted of murdering a worthless cockroach, a traitor and his lying scum cousin to be exact. But killing one is all it takes. They throw away the key because they know I am an hombre who must be reckoned with. For five years already I call this ugly resort my home. And I might be here for I don't know how long, unless I cheat them and die first. And now, you are in my house, you are my guests. The word on the grapevine is that you need some help."

Rodriguez takes a drag on his Pall Mall, letting his words sink in. He scrutinizes us, making it known that he has the power to grant a request. His cell is luxurious compared to our own. He has an armchair, a folding card table, a rabbit-eared TV, a floor lamp and a blue rug, and a shelf of books. My eyes scan the used volumes on law, Zane Gray novels, Henry Miller, Webster's dictionary, Kerouac, Hemingway, Octavio Paz, James baldwin, and the King James Bible. If we have a prayer in this dismal pit, it is with this somber, cordial Latino.

Feeling the force of his black eyes, I say, "Nice collection of books. I love reading myself, we both do. It's always like taking a trip somewhere."

"That is true," Rodriguez replies. "I read many books. I enjoy reading, because to understand what you read, is an art, you must remember. These books are windows on a world lost to me, the world you are used to traveling in. But I don't blame you. I am where I am, you are where you are, and maybe now we have a new opportunity."

I simply nod. He seems to be one step ahead of us, and this is his domain.

Bones says, "I only wish we we're still playing out in that world today."

Rodriguez grunts, then smiles to himself, snubbing out his cigarette. "All right then, my hippie friends. Now tell me your personal story. They say you got popped for smuggling la mota down by Tecate? When your luck goes bad, it's always a fucking rotten day, no? I want you to tell me how it all happened. Tell me everything."

Taking turns, Bones and I piece together our vivid string of misadventures: the Oaxaca mushroom quest, the treacherous dealings in the barrios of Guadalajara, taking refuge on the beaches of the San Blas coast, only finally to be brought low at the border. El Jefe presses for details, how people looked, how things smelled, the colors and sounds, his bronze face absorbing every nuance. He commiserates, he laughs, turns down his mouth at the paradoxes, urging us to throw open the windows on his lost and once-magical world.

Spreading my palms, I say, "And now we are snagged in this desperate place. The pathetic public defender, he says they could bury us for years. More than anything we need a good lawyer."

"We'll pay whatever it takes, we are honest men," Bones emphasizes.

"Whatever it takes," I reiterate "We just need to get out of here to operate."

Rodriguez listens, taking us in with his solemn eyes. In his fingers, he keeps turning over and over a matchbook with a saucy pinup girl on the cover. Then he says, "I think you are hungry? You want to eat?"

Oh Jesus right, we are weak with hunger, our stomachs growl. But we will not eat the odious mess hall chow, we'd rather fast. But here, in his cell, we are almost overcome by the aroma of fresh fruit that seems to pervade the air. Bones explains that we are allergic to meat, the mere smell of a greasy bacon sickens us, we do not want to eat animals, we are devout vegetarians.

"Aha," Rodriguez laughs, rocking back, clasping one knee. "So that is why you refuse to eat downstairs. Some of the bad-asses thought it was because you are afraid of being poisoned."

"Hah, some truth to that," I admit.

"Si, we are leery," says Bones.

Squinting, Raul Rodriguez lights up another of his red pack Pall Mall cancer sticks. He seems satisfied with us, in his eyes we have some distinct value. I am almost drooling from the hallucinatory scent of ripe apples. What the fuck, am I having some kind of flashback?

"Raul," I ask, steadying myself, "is there some way you can help us?"

Rodriguez leans forward on his muscular thighs. "Maybe, maybe that is possible," he replies with a wolfish gleam. "You have your needs and I have mine, no? so perhaps there is a way. You both have conejos, I give you that. You are not afraid to take risks. You had some bad luck, and now, you are in this shithole with me. And in here, everything is negotiated. So I put it to you straight—what have you got to offer me?"

Glancing at me, Bones says, "Raul, they took everything from us when they booked us. Maybe a hundred bucks? They even took our beads and amulets."

Rodriguez scratches his neck, feigning puzzlement. "What I want to know," he says, "is what did you sneak in here to get stoned on. You are smugglers, no? What the fuck are you hiding?"

"Hiding, you mea, in here? Holy shit, man, nothing. How could we?"

"We had no chance, they searched us twice, frisked us down. It's im-possible."

El Jefe scowls, displeased. "You mean to tell me, you don't even try to do a keister stash? Remember, you only bullshit me once."

"A what? A keister stash? You mean, like up the asshole?"

"Si, up your asshole!" Rodriguez says, aping my startled face. "My spies tell me you have not taken a dump yet. What kind of dope do you have stuck up your asses?"

"Good God, Señor Rodriguez, nothing, no way. Why would we? Who planned on getting caught?"

"Aiyee," Bones blurts, "we never had time to stash dope up our butt. The bust, it happened too fast."

Rodriguez mutters in annoyed Spanish. But our logic is irrefutable and he knows it. Rubbing his hands together, he looks morosely at the floor.

"Look, Raul," I placate, "other than bundles of grass wrapped in newspaper, all we had on us was about a hundred tabs of acid. You shove a load of pure lsd up your butt, it dissolves, you're blown right out of your skull. Wigged so far out maybe you don't find your way back."

Rodriguez drags on his cigarette. "Not if it is wrapped tight in plastic," he points out.

"Fuck, we were lucky we didn't get shot. It was that weird."

He acknowledges this with a curt nod, saying, "It is unfortunate. I have been wanting to try this Lsd. I have heard the fabulous stories. In this joint what you get is mostly junkies. Their idea of a good time is shooting up heroin and a six pack."

Looking through the bars into that warehouse of human misery, I shake my head. "I don't think you'd want to drop acid in here, Raul. It'd be too grim."

"Yeah, dig," Bones says, "acid causes your brain to hallucinate in unimaginable ways. Every sensation and feeling, every thought gets wildly amplified and there's no way to control it, especially when you're peaking. And your scene can make or break your trip."

"And so? That does not frighten me," Rodriquez states, tapping his chest. "I live here inside myself and I like the places inside me. You see, I have no other choice. In this evil place, I am all I have."

"I dig that," I tell him. "Except a good dose of acid sends you on a sky-high trip that lasts ten, maybe twelve hours or more. You see and hear things right out of this world."

"Hah, what more could I wish for?" Rodriguez exclaims. "It would be the vacation that takes me far away. Maybe for good, who cares? Look for yourself. Who would want to come back to this zoo anyway."

We all nod together, it is true. If you can escape hell that way, why not drop a mega-dose of acid and go gloriously mad? Lose your mind, fly in your soul, fly far away. Rodriguez laughs again, stretching his thick arms, at ease. "Bueno," he says, "I hear you. You can't pull off a keister stash with a gun in your face. Esta bien, I appreciate you hombres. You are not like these other losers. So I think, trading favors here and there, we can make a good deal."

He studies his smoldering cig, as if mulling over his own words. Bones and I exchange a glance. What favors does he mean and who is to pay, and pay what? All this talk of assholes has made us nervous. Rodriguez's eyes are boring into mine with candid amusement.

"Here is the deal," he says calmly, "from now on you are both under my shelter. That means no spic, no nigger, no bad-ass honkie dares to mess with you. And for this cloak of protection, I propose a trade that will benefit all three of us."

Bones gulps, his sphincter tightening, I hold my breath. Rodriguez shifts onto one buttock, reaches down and flips back the blue chenille blanket covering his bunk. What he shows is mind-bending. A cornucopia, he hauls out a carton of ripe red apples, a box of Valencia oranges, and a bundle of luscious yellow bananas. We gape at the gorgeous fruit in disbelief, our mouths flooding. He shoves the boxes over our way with his flip-flop foot.

"This will ease your pain, no?" he grins. "Go on, dig in, my hippie amigos. You can have all the frutas you want and for me, in trade, you give me all the carnitas on your plates because I like my meat. Today is your lucky day and mine too."

Mumbling our profound thanks, we crunch into the juicy apples even as we reach for a banana. The fruit sugar hits us like an invigorating elixir, but I caution myself to take nothing for granted, nothing in here is free, Raul already said so. But for now I just gorge.

El Jefe watches us with moody eyes, smoking his eternal Pall Mall. Exhaling, he says, "Now, let us discuss your other fucked-up problem. You are going to need a real lawyer, and it so happens I know a good one. In fact, she is my very own attorney. Her name is Audrey Morgenson and if I ask her to come here to talk with you, she will come."

"Oh my God, that would be incredible, beautiful."

"But there are serious things to be honored," Rodriguez adds.

"What kinds of things?" Bones quips, all but drunk on his delicious orange.

"There is an agreement that must be made, and you both need to listen. Numero uno, I owe my life to this woman. She saved me from the gas chamber. Numero dos, I cherish her beyond words and although she senses how I feel about her, this is never to be spoken of. Comprendo?"

Bones and I nod our understanding, a pact between men, no problemo.

Stubbing out his cigarette, Rodriguez says, "Finally, I require that you treat her with complete respect at all times. If she decides to help you, consider yourselves lucky. Because this woman knows all the judges, she knows who to avoid and who to cultivate and how to cut the best deal. The fucking game is rigged, it's all a sham, and Audrey knows how to play it."

"Wow, she sounds like the answer to our prayers!"

"Maybe she is," Rodriguez says with somber eyes, "but I am not the one to say. However, know this. Whatever agreement you reach with her you must honor with your lives. Because if you fuck her over in any way, you will answer to me, and you would regret that day. Claro?"

"Raul, we would not do—."

"Tell me if we have our understanding," he interrupts, unyielding. "Because before to proceed we have to agree."

Bones sticks out his hand. "We will honor this agreement, on our word."

"Indeed we will," I say, "to the letter."

Rodriguez flashes his wolfish smile, and grips our hands. We might be striking a deal with one of Lucifer's sons, but it hardly matters. If the devil can get me out of this trap, then the devil is my friend. Raul fills a grocery sack with apples, oranges and bananas. "You are the only hippies I know," he muses, "I am glad we have this opportunity together. Here, take this back to your crib and ask for more whenever you need. And don't forget, send over to me all your sabrosa meats."

We stand up and shake hands. "Fate is strange," Rodriguez observes, "have you begun to notice? She can be a friend or she can be a bitch. Sometimes I think we are just play things."

THE WORD GOES out across the jail house. El Jefe has dropped his mantle over us. The smirks, the lewd hoots, the derisive taunts, it all stops overnight. Rodriguez is now the patron of the long-hairs, curb your tongue. We feast on the succulent fruit, replenishing our famished bodies. For the first time we relax a little, we feel hopeful. Gregarious by nature, Bones mingles with the other captives, swapping stories. But I stay mostly to myself, brooding over the absurd chain of events that led us into this hideous cul de sac.

If we had been more aware, only a little more alert, we would be home tripping on sunshine. Awareness seems to be the essential key, more than an ordinary awareness. I've been running the belief that I am in control of my life, I am the director of my own movie. Yet, obviously, this assumption is terribly flawed. This sudden accident at the border has sabotaged my world. And it seems stupid to write it off as bad karma, because what are we, just bleating goats tied to a stake? There has to be a way, a super-aware path, that takes a man clear of such pitfalls.

Then there is my partner Bones, and it's pointless to deny my anger. He fell apart in the clutch. He refused to listen, he refused to rebury the dope, he refused to play it smart. His ego trip got us both badly burned. But at the same time I know that I share some blame. Tired and acid-dazed, me making that fatal wrong turn put the border patrol on full alert.

Sprawled on my bunk, I play it all over in my head. We ignored the warning signs. We got spaced out on different wavelengths, and that could cost us dearly. It could cost us everything we cherish, even our lives. But why? The questions go begging in my head.

I wander back in memory to my early boyhood days in Texas, mid-1950's, when I roamed freely the post oak meadows and sandstone gullies outside of Fort Worth. One day I saw something that I'll never forget. I saw a miracle shimmering in the grass. This was before we ever had a black and white television in the house. We listened to the radio shows for entertainment, we looked at books, we played all day in the tangled woods in a seamless, waking dream. I was six, maybe seven. Those those eighty acres were my personal kingdom. I'd go out hunting each morning with my dog, MBF, carrying my Daisy lever-action bb rifle. MBF stood for Man's Best Friend, a smart, sandy mongrel with a doughnut tail who loved to roam with me through the fields, trees, and trickling arroyos. We hunted rabbits and robins, squirrels and mockingbirds, only the crows and hawks I left alone, they were different. Every day I drank deep of that freedom before I could even name it. Wandering at will, moving past the thickets to the fringe of a sunlit glade, we saw this most amazing sight.

That early morning was still cool, the air translucent, and there, a flock of tiny iridescent birds, hopping and fluttering in the grass tufts. We stalked creatures all day long but never had seen such birds. Their wings and feathers glistened in a fluttering, magical collage, I heard their voices. Restraining my dog, I got down on one knee and gazed in wonder.

People say that dogs are color blind but I don't believe this. At any other time, MBF would have lunged right into the midst of them, whooping and barking, trying to snatch one. But he cocked his head, crouched beside me, quivering, transfixed as I was by these feathered talismans ten yards away, dew still on the grass. I drew a bead with my lever-action rifle on a bustling clump of feathers. Because if I don't shoot one, no one will believe me. My older brothers would mock me, saying I made it up. Not only that, I know I may never see these unknown birds again. So, holding my breath. I draw a bead through the iron notch sight, thinking at the very least I will nail one up in my trophy oak tree.

But I cannot squeeze that trigger. Some instinct stops me, some reverence, some awe of beauty. MBF pushes against me, whining in frustration, he has never known me not to shoot.

"It's all right, boy," I sooth, hand in his ruff, "not this time, not those birds."

And in that instant the iridescent flock burst into the air, wings shimmering in the sunlight. They lifted into the air, a blaze of some long forgotten language and fled across the treetops. My dog bounded after them, barking madly, dashing into the meadow, sniffing, searching for some trace. I stayed on one knee, my heart beating, pondering what I had just seen, pondering the brushstroke of God.

And now, in the harsh confining cell, Bones finishes taking a jailhouse shit. There is no privacy in this concrete cage, no miracles, no magical birds, not even a window to gaze out upon a lost world. Nostalgia seems like a dangerous indulgence, one could break into pieces. Because in this bitter place, in the night, you hear the muffled cries of some pathetic dupe, you hear the pitiless laughter of his tormentors. Dylan wails again in my head, *"he not busy being born is busy dying."*

And I know beyond any doubt, that in this hellish place, my own soul is at stake.

# Chapter 9

OUR ONE DICEY chance with Rodriguez's attorney comes in the morning. The guards take us into a spare room where we meet her, Audrey Morgenson, dressed in a beige business suit, a short-haired brunette with intelligent eyes. Audrey comes from the straight world, she wears a wrist watch and a gold wedding band. But she has a calm and confident manner, just sitting with her makes us feel better. Now all we need to do is convince her that we're worthy of her time.

We shake hands and exchange names. Audrey opens her briefcase on the Formica table, saying, "I've reviewed the charges against you two guys, and I want you to know where I stand on these ludicrous marijuana laws. In my view, the current laws should be stricken from the books. But having stated that, you need to know that my opinion doesn't carry any special weight in the courtroom."

Impressed, I say, "Whoa. You actually believe that? You believe their basically wrong?"

Adjusting her tortoise rim glasses, she replies, "Yes, I definitely do. They're punishing all the wrong people. One look at you tells me that neither of you belong in this dungeon, yet here you are, thrown in with some very hard-core felons. It's morally wrong, plus it's a huge waste of tax-payer money."

Bones and I momentarily lock eyes, blinking. I have never paid a dollar of taxes in my life, although that hardly matters. Who is this angel of mercy and can she really spring us? Bones clears his throat, about to speak, but before he can I ask her, "How do you feel about the war in Viet Nam?"

"Don't get me started on that abomination," Audrey says, "it's reprehensible beyond words. Yes, I'm a liberal. But to stay on purpose her, you two are facing some charges that carry severe consequences if you're found guilty. You need to be fully cognizant of this. If you choose to make this a test case—and I wish someone would—I'll take it all the way to the Supreme Court. I'll do everything I can to win a dismissal."

She opens up to us like this, we can hardly believe our ears. "Ah, but money-wise," Bones says, "we're not in the best of shape. I've heard that legal fees in these situations can run sky-high."

Bones is only stating the truth—we're foot-loose, wing-it-as-we-go hippies, rich in dope and optimism but cash-poor, and not even rich in dope anymore since they confiscated our stash. Cops are devious bastards, they'll probably steal that primo weed for themselves and smoke it. I'm about to lay these thoughts out, when Audrey says, "If you don't mind, I'd prefer to get into financial details later. Simply know that money is not my prime motive for meeting with you. Think of me as a legal crusader, I believe in what I'm doing. So let's see where this conversation takes us."

"All right," I say slowly, "then as far as these charges go, how serious is serious?"

"Quite serious," Audrey replies, looking me in the eyes. "Smuggling pot in quantity is regarded in the same league as hard narcotics, absurd as that sounds. If convicted, you'll be facing at least ten to twenty years, with parole possible at some stage. Just be thankful you're not in Texas."

Bones groans, muttering under breath.

"So, so," I stammer, "the public defender wasn't lying to us?"

"No, they have to give it to you straight."

"But we're talking about a few pounds of grass? That's absolutely insane."

"Oh, I agree. Which is why I'm so adamantly opposed to these Draconian laws."

"Look," Bones says, "I need to ask, let me ask, just how good would our chances be if we took it to Supreme Court?"

Folding her hands, Audrey Morgenson compresses her lips. "To be frank, not very good. We'd have almost no chance of winning. In this country drugs and the counter-culture are being stigmatized. Most Americans are frightened—we live in the shadow of an atomic war. Vietnam is scary as hell, and conservatives think hippies are card-carrying communists. Anyone advocating drug legalization is immediately taken as a heretic. The name of the game is control, as you're finding out, right? Even the most liberal judge is reluctant to step too far out of line. Yes, I'm willing to take your case to the highest court in the land. But in this present political climate we would almost certainly lose, and it would be quite expensive."

Deflated, Bones goes a little pale. No one is adept at hearing shit he doesn't want to hear. "So you're saying," he swallows, "that we might be staying in prison for a long time."

"I did not say that," Audrey replies, lifting her eyebrows. "There are other solutions."

"Other solutions?" I ask, in a voice that sounds like jello must feel.

"Look, don't despair," she says confidently. "This is where I play my part. We can plea bargain these charges down to a lesser offense, one that automatically carries a reduced sentence. Yes, it's possible. Such as failure to pay import taxes on your undeclared contraband."

"Contraband? You mean like Cuban cigars, or exotic Costa Rican parrots?"

"Similar to that, yes, undeclared contraband is a kind of catch-all category. The contraband doesn't even have to be specified and a negotiated deal is not uncommon. But that's providing, and I do hope this is the case, that neither of you have any prior felonies. So I must ask you kindly, do you?"

For a few seconds Bones and I sit dumbstruck. Felonies? Prior records? Our minds race back, words tumble out, a few juvenile scuffles, speeding tickets, a drunken winter night's brawl back in Chicago where I busted a half-full Chianti bottle over one of the bastard's head who jumped us, waste of wine, flashing red lights, but nothing major, nothing bad, and likewise for Bones.

Audrey makes cryptic notes on her yellow pad. "Good," she remarks. "Now, if I take on your case, and assuming we can persuade the court to reduce the charge, you'll be facing more like two to ten years with a chance of supervised probation. And if I may be blunt, that's the best deal you're going to get. And I can't even guarantee it."

Swallowing hard, I ask, "Would we have to do any jail time, or no?"

"No. Probation is not parole. Probation is an on-your-honor release in leiu of jail time. You do have to report to a supervisor about once a month, but you're not behind bars. You're outside."

My heart does a somersault. It's like a fantastic gift and clearly this woman is all no nonsense. She means what she says. Looking into her brown compassionate eyes, I am ready to put twenty years of my life in her hands.

"Okay," I say, "just tell me how, how do we go about this?"

She gives an encouraging smile. "Well, first, I need to know if you're ready to appoint me your legal counsel. And I think it behooves both of you to keep this a single conjoined case, not separate."

With a glance at Bones, I nod, "Consider me all in."

But Bones hesitates, stroking his beard. He frowns, then says to Audrey, "To me, the main thing is we haven't really done anything wrong. We're just living our lives in our own way. We're not making a bad scene, we're not hurting anyone. So why should we have to cop out to being guilty of anything? You dig what I mean?"

"Bones," I interrupt, "we're not in a position to debate moral philosophy. We need to get out of jail. Our freedom's at stake here."

"But I hate pretending to an obvious lie. I don't want any part of that. That's bad karma."

With an impatient tone, I say, "Look man, the bottom line is we need to get out. You like the karma of being in jail better? You like the jailbird food and water, the groovy vibes, something I'm missing here?"

Wincing, Bones says, "Yeah, all right, first things first. We do need to get out of here. Got to get out. But I just want her to know where I'm coming from."

"All right, fine," I say, glancing at Audrey. "But are we ready to appoint her our legal counsel?'

Bones nods, replies, "Yes, I am. We are. Let's get the ball rolling."

Scribbling on her pad, Audrey says, "All right then. I'll get right to work on drafting the plea bargain. We'll need the federal prosecutor to agree to modify his case. But understand, this can get complicated and may take a few months. We'll probably need to move your trail date forward more than once—"

"Months? You mean months before this bullshit's worked out? But why?"

"Because it's imperative that we get you before the right judge, an empathetic judge. That's the most important thing."

"But Jesus God, months in here will do us in," Bones stammers. "We're vegetarians and the food is garbage. Rodriguez gave us some fruit but who knows for how long?"

"And everybody smokes, it's suffocating. Not to mention this joint is crawling with twisted psychotics"

Placating us, Audrey says, "No, not months in here. I mean that the trail itself may take months. Your arraignment takes place in the morning, in a courtroom right across the street. That's where your bond will be set, and with a little luck, I'll have you bailed out and on your way home. Then, down the road, we'll enter the crucial trail phase."

"You mean out of here, out of this hellhole, actually out, within a day or two?"

"That's right," she smiles. "I mean out of here within twenty-four hours from tomorrow morning's arraignment."

"Whew, far out, that's beautiful, Jake, man, can you dig it?"

"Oh yeah," I say, flooding of relief, "I'm digging it. But tell us, getting bailed out, how much is that gonna cost us? How much money do we need?"

"Well, we don't know yet," Audrey says matter-of-factly. "The judge that you'll be in front of tomorrow won't be easy. In his eyes you're a couple of renegade deviants caught red-handed smuggling drugs. He could set bail as high as fifty thousand dollars apiece or more. But whatever it is, don't even protest. Because I'll get it reduced."

"Fifty grand apiece?" I gape at the staggering sum of money. "Please realize we're not rich dealers, we're just ordinary hippies."

"We're not rich in the least," Bones wheezes. "We make it on a few dollars a day."

Blinking, Audrey asks, "Are you both completely without reserve funds?"

Reserve funds? The notion strikes me as incredibly bizarre. "Cash-wise, just about," I admit.

"But we do have resources, we have ways to make money."

"Yes, we have resources," Bones puts in. "We can generate whatever cash we need."

Studying our anxious faces, Audrey reassures us, "Then I am willing to work with your circumstances. You are both first-time offenders, that helps me get a reasonable bail set. It's all about timing. And we can discuss payment arrangements once you're out of here. I'm not looking to get rich on your case. So let's move ahead, shall we?"

We both nod our assent. Raul Rodriguez has vouched for this unusual woman. She places some papers on the table that we sign without really reading. There's no point in trying to interpret legalese mumbo-jumbo, you've just got to roll with your cards. Even if our asses end up in hock, at least we'll be in hock to her, not in the clutches of the cruel prison system. Freedom, the freedom of daylight is everything. We avoid any mention of Raul's threat to murder us if we cross her in any way.

She stands, we stand, we all shake hands. "I'll see you at ten in the morning," she tells us. "They'll bring you over in time for a briefing, and in the meanwhile, keep your chins up."

The implacable guards herd us back through the electronic gates to the rat hole. We munch an apple, we eat a banana, we talk things over, we send our thanks up to Rodriguez. But Bones and I avoid the thorn in our side, the rift, the subtle distrust that has grown between us.


THE GRAY MORNING comes with insipid oatmeal mush, which we eat, and stewed prunes, which we do not. At our arraignment, the disdainful judge slams us with the preposterous bail of fifty grand apiece. The scowling old bastard lets us know that if it were up to him we would not see daylight again. It's weird to be considered an anti-social deviant, it's a shaky moment. But they're all part of this evil, war-hawking system that sells its youth down the American river into devastating war or prison oblivion. I want to shout in his face, spit in his eyes, this puffed-up judge, but I keep my mouth shut and my face impassive. Afterwards, our female lawyer promises to come visit us later in the day. She tells us it's all standard procedure and not to worry. Like shackled captives, we are led away.

Late in the afternoon gloom, Audrey shows up. And just as she promised, in some miraculous way, she has gotten our bond reduced to fifteen thou apiece. Not that we have any hard cash, but it sounds like we can roll with this deal.

She explains, "Now, this is how this situation goes. I work with a bail bondsman who will put up your bond, which requires a ten percent cash deposit up front. Does that pose any problem for you?"

Bones clears his throat. "In other words, you're saying we need to come up with fifteen hundred each? Is that how it works?"

"Yes, that's how it works. Is that any problem?"

Grimacing, we lay out the naked truth, all the ridiculous facts. We have almost no cash on hand. Living down in Oaxaca's remote sierra, we'd been making it on a handful of pesos a day. Even back in California we really just wing it week to week, nonchalant mystic dopers, getting by on our ingenuity. Rent is cheap, we eat off the fig and lemon trees, a bag of brown rice and veggies is pocket-change, gas is twenty-five cents a gallon. The main motive for our smuggling gamble was to get together some real bread. But dear lady attorney, dearest Audrey, once we're out of here, once we're sprung from this trap, we'll hustle up the cash for your legal fees in no time flat! Once I'm back on my motorcycle I'll be wheeling and dealing, and Bones will do his part. We don't specify to her how we're going to do this, we just emphasize our ability to do so. We bare our souls, we lay it on thick. No one has to remind us that she is our only fucking hope.

She listens with a calm, thoughtful expression. She likes us, even admires us in some unspoken way. She listens as if reading some compelling and irresistible story.

Leaning forward, talking with my hands, I say, "I promise you, my most sacred word, we will not let you down. We are one hundred percent good for our word."

In a not unkind voice, she asks, "Do you have anything in the way of a good faith deposit?"

Bones pitches in, confiding, "Up in Big Bear, I own two lake view lots free and clear. Worth, I don't know for sure, maybe a few thousand dollars. As soon as I get home I'll sign the deeds over to you."

Hearing this, I do a double-take. I had no inkling that Bones owned anything more than his carpenter tools and the rust-bucket car we got busted in.

He looks at me and shrugs. "It's all I got out of a divorce a few years back."

News to me, but damned good news. Time to pony up, no time to hedge. Audrey scribbles on her cryptic notepad, or doodles, I can't really tell. I say to her, "And I've got six hundred bucks in an L.A. bank account, and that's all yours. I've also got two English motorcycles, a Matchless and a BSA. I can turn over the Matchless title as good faith. In fact, I'll just give you the bike, although I might have to borrow it if the other one breaks down."

Audrey smiles, and laughs softly. "No, Jake, that's not necessary. You guys might need those bikes, because you're never going to get that confiscated car back."

Out of words, Bones and I and I wait, all our chips on the table. Consulting her notes, Audrey taps her chin with her pen. It's weird to think that your fate can hang in the balance for a few lousy shekels, like Jesus, no blasphemy intended, but it might. You never know until the dice rattle out of the cup.

"All right," Audrey murmurs, "I do want to take on your case. So I am going to trust you fellows. I'm going to step out on a limb here and front you your bond money. And I'm going to be criticized for this, so don't make me regret it, please."

Jubilation leaps in our chests, into our faces! I could fall on my knees and kiss her hands. We pour forth our thanks. Almost blushing, she brushes our praise aside. "I'll have you out of here," she informs us, "by tomorrow morning. Here's my business card, one for each of you. Call me when you're out so we can schedule our next appointment. Now, let's talk about one other important detail."

"Okay, yes, okay, such as?"

"Such as your appearance."

"Our appearance?"

"Yes, your impression. In the eyes of the court you cannot afford to come across as counter-culture desperadoes. You'll be at the discretion of a judge who won't be partial to longhair and pirate clothes. Strike him the wrong way and you could end up doing hard time. He needs to see that you both have jobs or that you're enrolled in school, viable steps you are taking to become law-abiding citizens."

Come again? Real jobs? Our hair? Jesus had long hair, his disciples had long hair, most revolutionaries don't give a shit about haircuts. Our hair, our unique style of dress, we hasten to explain, these tribal ways are a personal code. It's not a matter of being against anyone, it's about us being for us. It's all about who we are.

"Not as far as the court is concerned," Audrey replies, unfazed. "You have appointed me your attorney, now you need to listen. You must seek the approval of the judge, because he will reckon your fate."

"But the jury," Bones protests, "why wouldn't they see it our way?"

"There won't be any jury. You'll be at the mercy of the court."

"Huh? But what about fair trial?"

"There is no jury in this scenario," Audrey says, shaking her head. "Realize, we're going to plea-bargain this down for a reduced sentence. In effect, you are pleading guilty to a lesser charge. You'll be at the determination of the judge alone. The impression you make on him will be critical. You need to come across as sincerely contrite, on your way to being reformed. Otherwise, he could drop the hammer on you. As I said, we have no guarantees. We need to do this right."

Bones is blown away by this info, but her words make diabolical sense to me. Our ideals aren't on trial here, only our right to personal liberty is. It's all a matter of pragmatic legal horse-trading, our philosophy has no horsepower in this deal. The judge can grant us conditional freedom or send us off to prison. We won't have a chance to debate moral issues. If we want to breath free air again, if we want to roam free again, we need to accept the game on its own unflinching terms.

Looking Audrey in the eye, I say, "Okay, I understand. It has to be played just so."

"Exactly right, Jake. We'll have very little wriggle room."

But Bones flusters. He argues again that his hair and the way he lives defines who he is, he doesn't want to go along with a pretense just to please the court. I feel like smacking him in the face. We're back on the border again. I'm dealing with a stubborn mule. He still thinks he can dictate what's fair and what's not, that his uniqueness has to be acknowledged.

"They don't care, Bones. Dig it. Time to get real."

"I am being real," he retorts. "I don't want to betray what I believe in. I mean, how do we know this is the only way out?"

Turning over my palm, I say, "Water in one hand, wishes in the other. What other choices do you see here? Or are you expecting the sky to open up just for you?"

His expression turns sullen, but I don't care. I am in no mood to indulge his pride. When the cards are stacked against you, you seize your best chance and you run with it. And if you can't see what your best chance is, then fuck you.

"Bones," Audrey says patiently, "Jake is dealing with the brass tacks. I urge you to reconsider. You can keep your hair long, you don't have to take my suggestions. But you're already behind the eight ball, so why work against yourself?"

Bones slumps back in his chair, saying nothing.

"She's laying it on the line for us, man. What other choices do you see?"

"It comes down to the hard realities," Audrey persists. "I may be sympathetic to your way of life, but it's moot to an over-worked judge. His job is to enforce the law. You won't be given a forum to make idealistic statements. If you're seen as defiant or arrogant, you can lose the whole game right there."

Dropping his chin, Bones says, "It's fucked up and I despise it. I feel like I'm copping out on myself. But I hear you, I understand what you're saying."

"Brother, we have to deal with what is, not what we wish would be. Isn't that what we always say?"

Drawing a circle on her yellow tablet, Audrey states, "I concur with that one hundred percent."

Bones vents a deep sigh. "Okay, if that's the best way and you say it is, I have to believe you. Count me in."

Audrey Morgenson and I share a complicit look, and that's it. We come to terms with our legal Bodhisattva. She leaves us with words of encouragement. There's a gritty tension between Bones and me, but to get free of this rap, I'm not getting hung up on anything.

The next morning, oh morning of our deliverance, they call our names. The metal doors slide back, they take us downstairs, we strip off the jailbird suits. They give us back our jeans and sandals and muslin shirts, my leather and turquoise wrist amulet, Bones' silver beads. We wait on a bench, then wait some more, impatient, starting to feel the mirth inside. We're going home, we're gonna eat whatever we want, swill cold beer, stoke up the hash pipe and turn the rock and roll up loud! I'm gonna jump on my 650 Lightning and jam up the Malibu coast with sarape flying and chrome pipes howling, drop some liquid mescaline and merge into the Pacific sunset. The all-out hustle is right in front of us, but first let's take a little holiday.

We sit on the bench, not talking. Bones nudges me, our eyes meet. He gives me a lopsided smile, I nod back. We are natural friends, we need to pull together, we clasp hands and shake. We need to get ourselves back on the high road again.

A burly, black guard with reddish eyes takes us through a couple of electronic gates. We sit against a wall as our release papers are processed. A raw-boned redneck takes charge, inspecting our documents, muttering into his desk phone. I wonder what's in those documents, and whether or not I'll be able to turn it too my advantage.

The redneck guard grunts, "All right Jake Acree, you're up." Scowling at Bones, he adds, "No, not you asshole, him first. You just sit there and wait."

Giving Bones a pat, I go over to the counter. Following the guard's instructions, ignoring his cynical eyes, I take the pen and scrawl my name several times. I calmly lay the pen down. He trips a switch and the last iron gate slides open. It opens onto a corridor leading to a double-door with a daylit window shining above it.

"Get going, Acree," the redneck drawls, "while you still can."

I step through the gate, then turn around and flash a smile at Bones. He's already on his feet, anxious, ready to sign his release, a lean horse ready to bolt.

"Stand where you are, Osgood," the mean redneck orders. "In fact, sit your hippy ass back down. You ain't going nowhere just yet. Nosiree, today's not your day don't look like."

Bones stares at him in bewilderment. "What are you saying?"

The guard shakes a teletype in the air. "Says here you are to be held until further notice. Just came down from the L.A. district attorney's office. Your scrawny ass still belongs to us."

Bones' long body jerks, his chest sags inward. His eyes register shock, he shakes his head in denial. Then he stammers, "There's gotta be some kinda mistake."

"No boy," the guard twangs, "ain't no mistake, says here you fucked up bad."

"Hey man," I say forcibly, "our attorney just bailed us out. We've been bailed out, what's the hang-up?"

"Shut up, Acree," the redneck sneers, "you long-haired fairy. What's the hangup? Your buddy here's going back inside to get his butt fucked. Ain't that right, Osgood? Cause this new warrant says he really screwed the pooch."

"Goddamn it, he has release papers! There's no fucking way!"

"Not anymore, he don't," the man says as he stiff-fingers Bones back through the electronic gate. "Step on back, Osgood, all the way through that door. You going back to your cubby-hole."

Bones shuffles backward, his eyes desperate, seeking mine, life draining from his face.

"What kind of fucking warrant?" I demand hoarsely. "For what?"

"For what? Well, seems your partner here sold drugs to an underage female a couple weeks back and fucked her. Then she got herself pinched and ratted him out."

My body twitches. I look past him into Bones poleaxed face, a gasping martyr that's just had an ice-pick jammed into his chest. Lurid images flash through my head. The stout black guard comes and takes Bones away.

The redneck chortles, "Well, Acree? Know anything about that dealio? Got anything you'd like to kick in?"

Stepping backwards into the hall, I say, "Nope, nothing about it. I know nothing at all."

He points his knobby finger at me. "Then get the fuck out of here. Unless you'd rather to keep your faggot buddy company in there."

I turn on my heel and it's all I can do to not run down that corridor.

Down the corridor away, pushing through the double-doors and stepping into sunlight and clear air that I suck into my lungs, almost sobbing. It's all I can do not to cry. I cannot answer anymore for my stricken friend. Sold a dime bag to some bare-bellied teenybopper, who got popped, then squealed on him. "Oh, he fucked me, he fucked me, he got me high and fucked me!" That's the way it goes down. And I know damned well Bones didn't do it for the cash, he did it for that fresh dewy cunt. And broke our rules and almost burned us to the ground again. Except I'm free.

I veer across the street and away from the jailhouse, afraid they might come out, shout my name, drag me back inside. Bones has hard dues to pay different than mine, and I know I have to cut my losses. I have to confront my mistakes and get my act together. I need to hop on my bike and start hustling up the cash for my female lawyer. I need to find shelter, become invisible, reinvent myself, because it looks like one hell of a hard road running out in front of me.

# Chapter 10

THE MORNING I first caught sight of Dawn Freitas something about her took my breath, something unnamed and untamed. I was standing out in the dirt alley behind my Venice Beach pad with my shirt off, cleaning my Matchless Typhoon. The 600cc single gleamed in the hazy sunshine. A dull blue '56 Ford comes snorting into the alley and lunges towards me, raising billows of dust. At first this pisses me off, but then I see it's my old running partner, Donny Kubiak. He's got a carload of people that I don't even know. He flashes me his handsome Pollock grin, then kills the rumbling 429 V8. But he leaves the ignition on, I hear the Byrds crooning 'Eight Miles High' on the radio.

"Well, what the hell, Kubiak," I laugh flipping the towel, "where you been?" He gives me the thumbs up.

It's been months since I've seen or even heard from this likable reprobate, and we share a twisted history together. Late last summer, we drove out from the Chicago in my green '55 Chevy all the way on route 66, towing a wooden trailer loaded with two British bikes. Both bikes had bent pushrods and wouldn't even run. Coming out of La Grange, we picked up a jive-talking, black hitchhiker that helped make for one wild, cross-country ride.

Donny gets out of the Ford, saunters over and shakes my hand. "What's going on, Jake, how's it hanging?" Wherever this guy goes, there's mischief nearby.

He casts an admiring eye on my black Matchless, fiddles with the compression lever. He unloaded his Norton 500 for quick cash when we got out here, then bought a plane ticket home. The Sunset Strip acid scene was not too his liking. I decide not to mention my new bike, the BSA 650 Lightning that's stashed in a neighborhood garage. He'll just want to ride it, then borrow it, and I don't loan out my bikes.

"How'd you find me, anyway?" I ask him, as three strangers pile out of his car and stretch. The girl catches my eye, a slender supple chick with long black hair that brings a sweet, wet taste to my mouth.

Donny seems slyly pleased with himself, as usual. "I went by your mom's house in Santa Monica. She told me you were living over here with degenerates, writing lsd-deranged poetry and wasting your precious youth."

"Hah ha, funny. That's because she wants me back in college but I have other ideas."

"You live in that place?" he asks, nodding at the shabby stucco fourplex.

"Yeah, it's sort of a crash pad for musicians jamming at those underground clubs on Sunset. But one of them's an old highschool pal of mine, plays in a band called Love. He gave me a room all to myself but there's not much privacy, so I'll be moving on."

Donny grunts, thumb-flicking a cardboard match to his Marlboro. He dresses like James Dean in those 50's movies, rebel without a cause look. "I don't know, man," he mumbles, the filtertip dangling from his mouth, "most of that psychedelic music is just too weird for me. It doesn't have that bluesy, soul feeling, know what I mean?"

"Uh huh. And you might just have to drop a little acid to dig it, man. It's a whole other kind of world out here, Donny. All the lights are on all the time and even the blues have a shine."

"Naw, not for me," he snorts, "I'm not dropping any of that mind-warping shit. Just gimme weed and a handful of dexies,—dexies and booze, a whole lotta booze."

We both cut our teeth on the Chicago blues scene and he's still locked into that vibe. The intellectual, avant garde, new art, visionary scene, Donny's not into it. He just basically wants to feel good. But we do share the love of wild young chicks and high times, plus he's old enough to buy liquor. Crinkling his baby-blue eyes, Donny shakes out another smoke for himself and one for me, then lights the match. Chances are he's right next door to being flat broke, I know this blond hustler like a book.

My eyes are drawn again to the raven-haired girl who's chatting it up with a beer-bellied, peg-legged dude, and a straight-laced kid who's probably paying for the beer and gas. That behemoth 429 sucks up gas like a vacuum and Donny like his ice-cold Hamms.

Laughing, she tosses her hair, and flashes me a smile that makes my pulse quicken. I smile back, yow, this nubile little babe. It's all I can do not to walk over and take a bite out of her.

Noticing, Donny says, "Like that, huh? Her name's Dawn. She's on the lam from a rotten marriage back in Joliet. Is she a little fox or what?"

"Yeah? Yeah, she's not bad," I say, feigning nonchalance. But this girl in her tight rolled jeans, high leather boots and belly-baring halter top definitely rings my bell. "How's she come to be with you and that peg-legged character?"

"It's a sordid story, I'll fill you in." Donny drops into his shyster voice. "But look, professor, you got anything stashed around here? I'm dying to get high. Haven't had any decent grass in weeks."

"Maybe," I say, playing my cards, "but no, not around here. But there is some primo dope around, don't worry. And that's what you get for going back to cold, windy Chi-Town."

"Yeah, I'm hip, look what I brought back with me."

"Hah, I'm digging it. And just so you know, I got a line on anything you want, Donny boy. Hashhish, grass, including some ultra-deluxe acid in case you're interested."

"Fuck no, none of that freak shit. That lsd will weird you out, man. Better watch it."

"Not really," I laugh, saying, "It's only weird for people who are afraid to have their perspective changed."

Donny flips his smoldering cig into the dirt. "Look, professor, I just wanna score a lid of good dope, not many seeds. Just a nice fat lid."

"There's no bogus shit on my radar, Donny. No pin rolls. So consider it done."

"Super, Jake, out of sight. I promised to get her and one-legged Keith high on some west coast bombers. And I wanna make good on that, know what I mean?"

"Oh yes, definitely. But what's the low-down on her scene? Is she with you or him?"

"I wish, heh," Donny mumbles. "No, she's sort of with him, at least for now. But Crash Keith's all right, man. I met him at that bike shop out by the quarries, where you bought your Matchless? He loves to have a good time."

"Crash Keith?"

"Yeah, it's his nickname."

Sensing that we're talking about her, Dawn's dark eyes flirt with mine. She wants to be sure I'm paying attention, whereas one-legged Keith throws me a sullen glance. The college kid doesn't count, he's not a player. Keeping my voice low, I ask, "What happened to his leg?"

"He lost it in a wicked bike wreck. Drunk as a coot, came roaring down the ramp on the Chicago expressway and broadsided one of those big semis."

"Ouch, holy fuck."

"No shit. But he got major insurance money out of the deal and that's what he's been rolling on. But he's just about blown through it."

"Messed up trip," I empathize, but flashing in on the scene. Pretty girl running away from home, the one-legged joker's got a bankroll, bankroll's almost kaput, and now she's getting restless. "And what about you, Donny? You got any bread yourself?"

"Not really, not at the moment. But I will have soon." He winks at me. "My mom's gonna come through any day now. She promised to wire me five or six hundred."

Same old Kubiak, doesn't work, always on the hustle, been bilking his doting mother for years. "Okay, let me guess," I muse, "you're hoping I'll front you some dope. Until your old lady comes through."

"Yeah, if you can, Jake. Please. You know I'm good for it."

"Probably can do. I can rustle you up a nice fat bag. But first Donny, tell me more about this chick. Don't play games with your old pardner."

Donny stubs the dust with his penny loafer. His blue eyes dart back and forth, figuring. He doesn't want me in the picture with Dawn, but how can he keep me out? He wants weed, I'm his connect. Give me the inside scoop, I'll front you the grass. Otherwise, nada.

"Okay, like I said," Donny says under his breath, "she's on the run from this wife-beating asshole who she hates. She's got a kid back in Joliet her mother's taking care of, a little boy. She's part Indian or at least that's what she claims. Says her grandmother was a full-blooded squaw. Keith met her in some Joliet bar flashing his wad and she split with him. She's hot, man, she seems ready for anything."

"Anything, really?" I say, growing more fascinated. "Indian? Like what tribe?"

Donny snorts. "What tribe? Fuck if I know, Jake. The tribe of fine young ass."

We share a low lustful laugh, then go over to his optimistic friends.

"Nice bike," Dawn says, putting her warm hand in mine. A sensual current passes between us, her brown eyes go ultra-feminine, even feral. My breath catches in my chest, suspended on a heartbeat.

"Yeah, I dig it," I tell her, "I like to ride. No, actually, I love to ride."

And just like that the scheme comes together in my head and she's the prize. I won't be fronting any weed to my old pal Donny, nope, not with this chick in the game. Oh, I'll score some righteous dope all right, me, the hip benefactor, and then turn them all on. I need to create a scene where she and I can get into a special groove, and I'm real good at improvising.

Standing together in the Venice Beach sunshine, we all share some friendly moments. I casually promise to give Dawn a ride. Donny tells me where I can find him, I reassure them I'll score us some weed. She lights a pair of cigarettes with her tempting lips and passes me one, while Crash Keith pretends not to be bothered.

THINGS HAVE A way of happening right out of the blue for me. I've been back in California about six months now, made the scene, met some far-out people, and one good chance leads to another. Your chances always comes through somebody, they just don't fall out of a cereal box, so you have to stay alert.

One improbable key to my recent lucky streak has been a strange cat named Jonathan Bender. Bender is a borderline schizo with a sunken chest, about twenty-five, with short Ivy League hair and a peculiar hunch as if he's anticipating some Freudian coup de gras. He's a twitchy egg-head who's been in and out of psycho-analysis for years. He blames all this shit on his emasculating mother, which strikes me as perverse. I don't see how you can blame your stupidity on other people, not even your parents. I mean, somehow we're always directly involved in what happens, we're always a participant.

Bender's a philosophy junkie too, but strangely paralyzed by what he studies. Camus, my existential mentor, throws him into intellectual confusion, despairs of T. S. Elliot and thinks Kenneth Rexroth is an imitator, of who, who knows, and, he doesn't dig acid rock or black jazz. How in the hell does anybody get like this? To him, life is an ongoing trick bag and he's always getting bagged. But one thing about Bender—he's got an incredible knack for meeting the people that matter, the people that make things happen.

Bender and I first met at the tea shop bookstore on Sunset where I sometimes hang out. I'm sitting on the bougainvillea patio sipping Oolong tea, smoking an Old Gold, and perusing an Alan Watts book on the cast iron table. Watts' Zen ramblings have captivated me since I was sixteen, this book is about his extraordinary LSD insights. Watts maintains that we don't have to do anything about all the revolting garbage piling up in the world, we can just leave it be, and if anything, change how we perceive it. The garbage is part of the 'is-ness' of our global civilization. To be honest, I don't quite know how to take this. Our civilization? What about the birds and the animals and the rivers and the forests, what about their existence? I wonder to myself if Watts has gone insane.

A couple of weeks ago I quit my job at a Culver City factory that fabricates electrical transformers for the aerospace industry, a job my father landed for me. Tedious slave-work that involved sticky toxic resins, hot ovens, and sickening fumes. This is the kind of work that gives people a lobotomy. But there was a lot overtime and before I flipped them off and walked out, I managed to buy my rare 650 BSA Lightning and save over fifteen hundred in cash.

Now, sitting on this umbrella patio reading Watts, smoking, sipping Korean tea, I notice this peculiar man edging closer to me and suspect he might be another Hollywood creep trying to hit on me. I'm not putting anybody down, live and let live is part of my creed, I just don't want to be bothered by slithering fags. When I look up with an accosting stare, Jonathan Bender stops dead in his tracks as if turned into a mannequin.

"Uh, excuse me," he stammers, "I'm not trying to butt in. It's just that I saw what you're reading, like Watts, man, Watts, and I wonder if we could talk? See, I'm trying to figure out how to meditate. Every time I try to do it my mind goes haywire, I mean, it skitters all over the place and I'm already hyper."

His eyes are probing, brown marbles, fixated on my green ones. A real weirdo. Shrugging, I say, "The Zen masters say the mind is like a wild horse that never stops running. Try getting stoned, it slows things down."

"Yeah, right, exactly," Bender titters, "getting stoned. I'm all for that!"

He drops down across from me, rattling the table, my ceramic teapot and teacup. I gaze at him for a few seconds. He asks me with a straight face if I consider myself to be an enlightened being. I tell him I've read about the Satori states, but the closest I've come was a fantastic experience I had on Panama Red back in a Chicago blizzard swooping in off Lake Superior.

Bender laughs, his Adam's apple bobs, almost speaks, doesn't, then just peers at me. I think now he's some kind of wounded freak, they're all over this jaded, faded town, many of them involved in sex therapy scams. Tapping the book, I say, "But dig. Alan Watts maintains there's another way to flash in—a cosmic flash-in on pure lysergic acid – and Timothy Leary openly says the same thing."

"Holy Moly," Bender sputters, twitching, "you're into Leary? You're into his stuff?"

"Yeah, somewhat. I'm reading his book on the Tibetan Bardos and different planes of consciousness. There seems to be a lot more than meets the eye, you know?. And Huxley wrote this amazing book, The Doors of Perception. He says that psychotropics like lsd and mescaline open us up to another exalted reality that exists right alongside this one, dig."

"Oh I follow, man, I dig" Bender laughs, in short staccato bursts, eyebrows jumping. But he catches himself and sits still for a moment.

Making a decision, I ask him, "So what are you into? What's your trip?"

He glances around like paranoid hipster, then confides, "Taking a trip is what I want to do."

"What kind of trip?"

"You know, man, a trip. I think I want to drop some pure acid, but I'm afraid to do it by myself. Can you score anything? It seem so hard to get for some reason."

Knowing why it would be hard for him to score anything, I say. "No, man, I don't have a connection either. But if I could get it, I mean get really pure lsd, I'd love to drop some. But none of this street shit going around, no thanks. Too many babbling basket cases. Leary says it's got to be super-pure and you need to set up your surroundings just so. Find a peaceful place, play beautiful music, unplug the phone, no boob-tube, no unwanted interruptions. If you want to really flash in you have to tune the world out."

Flaring his eyes, Bender whispers, "Wow, sounds like you've already been there. Have you, have you tripped?"

"No, not yet, but I'm definitely interested. But only when I can score the right stuff. I want my first trip to be something really magical, something like a revelation."

"Oh yeah, I do too, yes, me too," Bender enthuses, then says, "Okay, listen man, I was kind of checking you out. The truth is that I do have a connection and he's the real McCoy. He's a chemist out at UCLA who works in Sidney Cohen's research laboratory. And man, this cat is a total acid-head. He makes pure acid by the pound in their lab, then sneaks it out in his briefcase. He told me he's been dropping acid twice week for the past year and that now just taking a shower is like a holy sacrament."

Bender lays this rap on me, it hits me like a lightning bolt. All at once I realize why this oddball wandered into my space, he's the conduit for the psychedelic magic dust! I nail him down with precise questions, he answers like a nervous boy scout. He claims he can get us several doses with a single phone call, but only on one condition—he wants me to be his tripping partner. I don't have to think about this for more than a few seconds. This dude might be a closet nutcase but it's worth the gamble to get my hands on pure pharmaceutical acid. I've read about Dr. Sidney Cohen and his LSD research. Like Leary back east at Harvard, Cohen conducted psychological experiments at UCLA and published a thick, almost unreadable book called, 'The Beyond Within'. But the title is the only good thing about it. When Leary says turn on, tune in, drop out, Cohen warns that acid is too dangerous and should only be used under medical supervision. Hah ha ha, he's a square, an establishment bore, and I say fuck that, I loathe conformist naysayers like Cohen. They always want to seal the miraculous away in their private labs.

Leaning toward Bender, I urge him, "Call this guy, this renegade chemist. Get the goods, I'm good with it. How long will it take?"

"Not long, no, not long, and listen," Bender says, "I've got this garden cottage over in east Hollywood, it's real quiet, on a cul de sac with a backyard. No one ever comes there."

"Sounds like just the ticket. Let's do it this weekend."

"I'll call Charlie tonight. Charlie lives down in Laguna Beach. But listen, man, one thing. What I don't want to do is short circuit my brain. I've got enough identity problems already. I just wanna try maybe half a dose, know what I mean, just to see what happens."

"Whatever's right for you, man, that's what we'll do. We'll set it up so everything flows."

"Okay, okay. I'm trusting you." Bender cracks his bony knuckles. "You've got a strong, clear vibe and I'm trusting you. I don't wanna flip out."

"What? No, man, don't even think negative shit," I tell him, "that's number one. Don't indulge in bad thoughts, it'll all be cool."

Bender nods, taking frenetic mental notes. We exchange phone numbers, put the wheels in motion. On the way home on my spoke-wheeled BSA 650, I feel like the doors to a bright magical room are about to fly open. I've been dreaming and scheming for this trip for months. I'm honed, I'm ready to leap past the artificial barriers of this humdrum world. Let the meek suck life through a miser's straw if that's what they want, but not for me, I intend to soar!

# Chapter 11

TUCKED AWAY ON a side street near Griffith Park, I show up at Bender's bungalow sheltered by green bamboo hedges. The old garden court is engulfed in quietude. But his drab rooms are colorless, just a few pieces of modern furniture, no floor rugs, no tapestries, not even art posters on the wall. Is this the condition inside of Bender's head? But he does have a high-fidelity turntable and I've brought along some cool 33 rpm's. It's a November evening right after dusk, the drone of the sprawling, chaotic city pervades the atmosphere.

On a scarred coffee table, Bender lays out six gelatin capsules filled with a snow white powder. "Pure, all pure," he says nervously. "Charlie says each one is a mind-blowing, twelve-hour Nirvana trip."

"Far out," I say, picking one up, thanking my lucky stars.

Bender plucks my sleeve with his fingers. "Heraclitus says that everything is flux, that nothing is really solid, and that totally freaks me out. I don't want to dissolve into nothing, man, I don't wanna die."

"What the fuck you talking about?" I say, shaking him off. "Don't be ridiculous, Jonathan. All we're doing is delving into our own mystery, right? Putting the ego in the backseat. So just relax, let things happen. You're not gonna die."

"Don't call me Jonathon, call me Bender, just Bender. And God, I fucking hope so. My mother would kill me if I flipped out."

"But we're not going to tell her, now are we? Your mom's got nothing to do with this. Now tell me, exactly how much acid is in each of these caps?"

Bender chortles like an imp. "Charlie says each one is at least 500 micrograms, 99% pure. Says it's a guaranteed cosmic trip that'll take us into another world."

"Hmmm, okay, cool, so these are the real goods. Therefore, I'm going to drop a whole cap. But if you're worried, and I'm only saying if, just start out with a half-dose."

Bender sniffs, his eyes narrowing. "Why, don't you think I can handle it?"

"How would I know? You wanted to play it safe. Besides, there's plenty to go around."

Hearing this, Bender unknots his shoulders. But when I show him the records, he turns antsy again. Ravi Shankar's Three Ragas sucks him into limbo, he claims. Miles Davis is not his thing, too lugubrious. He doesn't care for Pachelbel's canon in d major, either, what the fuck? Finally, we settle on some austere koto music with a bamboo flute, then he starts fussing around in the kitchen.

"Look," I suggest, "let's just forget about that green tea ritual for now. A little pure water is all I want. Leary says we'll be rising to a phenomenal peak and we don't need all these distractions, okay? Maybe later."

Bender stops fiddling with the miniature tea cups, brings us a couple glasses of water. "Yeah, okay, I'm just anxious. I hope the fuck I don't slide face first into Hell."

"And why would you do that?" I reply, with a wary smile.

"I mean like Hell, dude, dig, like Dante says—"

Laughing it off, I say, "Fuck that nonsense, man. You want to take a trip into Hell with Dante, be my guest. But me, I'm heading into brighter realms."

I've never done this before but I feel pretty confident. I've studied all the relevant literature, I have a good idea of what to expect. Putting one of the gel caps in my mouth, I gulp it down with spring water. During the day I've basically fasted, like Leary suggests. I've eaten one ripe banana, along with a few dates and a few Armenian Ak-Mak crackers. If this stuff is what it's supposed to be, I'll be lifting off real soon.

"I'm going into that other room for a while," I tell Jonathan, "and go inside. I'm gonna meditate."

"Sure, do your thing. But how do you do that? Go inside, I mean."

"Well, I'm new at it, but you close your eyes, relax your jaws, relax your neck, then just flow with your breath. You just ride the ebb and flow of your breath inside, like a stream."

Bender swallows, "Okay, I'll try that. But listen, Jake. Leave the door cracked in case one of us needs some help, you know? Just in case."

"No problemo," I reply, making my move. "But please, let's just be quiet for awhile, tune in? No more talking until later. Let's see what happens."

"If there is a later," Bender quips, skittering off into a lunatic giggle. I go into the bedroom and dial him out. There is no bed in this room, just some cushions, a black metal desk, and an office chair. Bender must sleep on the couch.

Settling cross-legged on the cushions, I'm already feeling some unusual sensations. I let my breath subside, relax my shoulders, breathe through my solar plexus, yogic breathing. My pulse feels strong and steady. Closing my eyes, I focus into the electric shadows behind my eyelids. Within seconds these shadows start to undergo a remarkable metamorphosis.

From somehow within me, an intricate mosaic of brilliant symbols emerges—mythical hieroglyphs and images, an iridescent montage that seems to refresh itself like an inexhaustible fountain. The fibers of my nerves are resonate, rippling with a subtle bliss that I can taste at the root of my tongue. I remind myself not to analyze, to squelch any mentalizing static. Just go with the flow, just flow, but within minutes the notion of controlling anything becomes utterly absurd.

The super-pure Laguna acid kicks into flashing overdrive, kaleidoscopic patterns of energy burst through my cerebellum, clusters of light flooding and firing through my flesh and blood, surging floodlights of awareness. Glowing like a primordial Christmas tree, I hear my own amazed laughter—at least I think it is me laughing. If it's not me, then who is it? Things hidden are revealed at light-speed recognition and there is no pause switch. My brain reels from this bright storm of cascading images, I realize I have to roll with this cosmic surf or be scattered into smithereens. So I let go, I yield my persona, I go with it, I take the unknown ride, unbelievably awake. The very atoms of my body are incandescent, I gaze into the secrets of my ancient, ever-young being. At some point I don't even seem to need air, my breathing slows so far down, I am swept along in breathless awe.

Time evaporates, like dew on a sun-baked stone. From somewhere in the house, the house? across waves of scintillating energy, I hear Bender. "Oh God no, oh fuck no man no," he gasps, "oh fuck me, I'm made of sticks, I'm dissolving into sticks!"

"Just go with it," I manage to say, not quite remembering his name, "just flow with it, man, just merge."

His voice rises on a kite of hysteria. "Oh dude, dude, you don't know. I'm turning into sticks and straw! I'm gonna die, I'm gonna die!"

Incredibly, I seem to be able to enunciate without breathing, and I say, "No, you're not going to die because you can't die, you can't die, dig that." Then my voice translates into a pulsating river of amethyst laughter.

"Oh please don't laugh, no don't laugh," Bender pleads, scrabbling around on what sounds like chain-link mesh. Bender, or whoever it is, breaks into lunatic gibberish and hiccups and I tune him out.

I tune him out because I really have no choice. Swept up in tidal bursts of shimmering light and colors, it is all I can do to hang on. Fleetingly, I wonder if I took too much? But that thought is swept away in whooshing oceanic waves of incandescent energy and I hang on and ride, ride the lightning, ride the power, ride the roaring tide . . .

After an unknown time, I become aware of my body again. My diaphragm draws in an intoxicating breath of oxygen and my eyes open to a Persian wonderland of awesome beauty. Everything seems infused with its own exquisite illumination. I stare at the brass wind-up clock on the desk and try to make sense of it. The hands suggest that I've been sitting cross-legged for almost three hours, but my legs don't feel numb. That clock strikes me as unspeakably absurd—its time-parceling dial and ridiculous hands, the invention of frightened people who lost touch of the eternal moment. Hah ha ha, how absurd, I rebuke the clock! I feel incredibly joyful and impossibly alive, cleansed of the peculiar confusion that's been nagging me for awhile.

"Are you still there?" Bender's reedy voice pierces the glimmering Persian motifs. "I heard you moaning and laughing, sounded like you were going mad."

"Not going mad. Being reborn."

He's right behind the cracked door, Bender is, I can see his auric imprint. "You've been sitting in there like a stone Buddha laughing to yourself," Bender says through the panel. "I peeked in. I saw you. Your eyes were shut and your hands were fluttering like birds."

The sheer pleasure of being seems to rise and envelop me. Bender sidles into the doorway like a wraith, his eyes huge and demented, his narrow face aglow. He looks he's been skinned and glued back together. Leary's Bardo book forewarned me that I might see shit like this and for all I know, Bender could be a demon.

He hangs in the door frame like a bat, gawking at me "Tell me what's real," he blathers, "is any fucking thing real anymore? Are you real?"

I see now what I've seen before but chose to ignore. This erstwhile freak has no inner bearings, he's like a hamster paddling on and on in a spinning wheel. He doesn't know where to stop or where to begin, and I don't want to get hung up in his desperate trip. He's extremely agitated, desperate to identify with anything where he can say, *yes, yes, this is me, this I am!*

But I don't blame him at all, it's just who he is. I just smile at him.

Bender hangs in the door frame, then twitches into a cacophony of bestial, laughing snorts. "Oh don't look at me, man," he pleads. "Please don't look, don't look, your face is shining, I'm not ready!"

To my amazement, his slight hunched body begins melting right into the wallpaper, contorting like a pretzel as it melts, his desperate eyes beseeching me. Rising to my feet on a boundless surge of energy, I go over and place my hands on Bender's shoulders. He cringes, then slumps like wax and starts sobbing. I realize I have to do something quick or the wail of an ambulance could ruin this hallowed night. But Jesus fuck. What can I do?

"Don't be afraid, man," I soothe. "You're not going to die, you simply won't."

But my own voice sounds awfully strange to my ears. Bender might be about to croak and how can I prevent it? The lamp-lit air shimmers like a magic lantern illuminating our skin, our bodies, our eternal eyes in a torrent of unbelievable colors. It's almost too much too bear, these sensations. Bender hangs onto me, taking ragged, shallow breaths.

"Look Jonathan, let's put on some nice music, I mean Bender. Let's listen to some koto and flute, and I'll simmer some Jap green tea, how's that sound?"

Trembling with manic laughter, Bender gabbles, "Yeah, koto, koto music would be good. But dig man, dig, you gotta pull me outta this wall, this wall's sucking me in through my backbone—"

I tug him away from the wall and hold him up until he gains his balance. Shaking with hilarity myself, I take him over to the couch and plunk him down. Bender doubles over in laughter, laughing at his own crazed thoughts. Slipping the record out of its album sleeve, I ease the needle into the revolving groove, then stand back. The plangent resonance of plucked koto strings strike my amazed eardrums, swelling in the air, vibrating through our cells and atoms, some kind of auditory magic. Bender falls silent, transfixed by the jeweled cascade of micro-tones. The madness in his face subsides, his face opens in childlike awe. Going into the kitchen, I become engrossed in the hissing blue flames and boiling water, the rising calligraphy of steam and seeping green tea. I feel more totally present than ever before. I feel the present, I have escaped my mind. Things are transformed into their timeless, original, pristine state. Real is more real than I've ever imagined, and I am suffused in the awareness of it.

Bender pulls me out of my reverie. Squatting in front of the hi-fi, he keeps trying to regroove the stylus into a specific koto passage. Letting my annoyance go, I bring him a ceremonial cup of steaming, fragrant tea. He takes it from my hands like a gift.

"Dude," he whispers, his pupils huge and wounded, "I don't mean to freak you out."

"You're not, man. De nada. Everything's all right."

"No, I mean, it's just that you look just like one of those Hindu goddesses in the movie posters. I mean, Jake, you should see yourself."

Movie posters? What is he babbling about? "Naw, I don't think so, Jonathan, you're hallucinating, man. Don't take it too seriously."

"No, no," Bender whispers, "you're the most beautiful creature I've ever seen. Go look in the mirror, go see yourself."

I shake my head, not wanting to get involved in his twisted delusions. "Just flow with the koto sounds," I tell him, "just groove. Forget about me."

Bender blinks, tearing up. "Oh shit, you think this means I'm a faggot?

You think I'm a latent homo?"

"No, I'm not thinking that" I say, easing away from him, "nor do I care. Look man, don't let yourself get sidetracked. Don't sabotage your own trip."

"You think I'm just hallucinating?"

"You are hallucinating. You're tipping on cosmic acid."

"But what if I'm not? What if this is actually real?"

"You think you're not? Then that's what it is, you have to adapt."

"What if it never stops?"

"Then, fuck, then you're doomed, man. Hah ha ha, doomed! You'll be going to the wacky-hatch."

Cackling insanely, Bender collapses on the floor. He whisks his fingers through the candle flame. "That's what I keep doing, isn't it, sabotaging myself? Is that what I do?"

"Maybe. But right now just stay in the moment, try doing that. Just be aware. Don't think everything to death. Dig, I'm going outside for awhile, I want to go out on by myself. But I'll be back."

"Okay, I'm mellow," Bender says, creasing his waxen face. "Do what you want."

I slip through the side door, closing it behind me, I step into the green back yard, right into the forgotten wonderland. The misting night air feels like illumined rain. Crystalline dew hangs on the ferns, tiny lamps dripping off the tips with some serene, organic rhythm. In our mad scramble to acquire stuff in this world, to be somebody, we've lost touch with this moment to moment miracle. But why, why do we do this to ourselves? Why do we separate ourselves from this original Eden of our consciousness? Why do we try to define everything and then cling to those definitions as if they're reality? The question formulates itself like a dew drop on the fern tip, hanging there, but there is no answer. There is no answer to "why". Maybe the question itself is part of the hilarious joke we play on ourselves.

As I sit in this luminous secret garden, on the damp green earth, beloved earth, immersing myself in its presence, I remember one of William Blake's poems—

"To see a world in a grain of sand / And a heaven in a wildflower /

Hold infinity in the palm of you hand / And eternity in an hour."

Absolutely so. But even as I sit in this immaculate breathing space, I'm already bothered that I am going to lose this awareness, I won't be able to hold on to it. For the first time, I hear the chirping of a solitary bird that doesn't sleep. I hear its plaintive chirps in the deep Los Angeles night, a little bird, deranged by smog perhaps and the insomniac drone of the freeways. I communicate with it, in a hushed tone, murmuring about the immense mystery all around us, and it listens, the invisible bird chirps back.

I laugh into the misting night. All at once I realize that I haven't smoked a cigarette for hours. I don't feel the slightest desire to smoke. There is another, more subtle taste under my tongue, some yearning for the root of life itself. I crouch here on the damp earth, this breathing earth, in another skin, the primordial meanings breathing through me. If I have gone insane, I am okay with that.

But after awhile I feel curious and go back inside. The bombastic strains of Carmina Burana swell and boom through the little house, Bender is up to his tricks. The floor furnace has kicked on, creaking and rumbling, and he has crucified himself right over the iron grate. His hands are thrust out to each side clasping invisible rungs as if nailed to a crossbeam, his head sunk, staring into the hissing blue flames like a demented ascetic.

"Please, for the love of God," he croaks, "help me!"

Coming closer, I notice how truly strange he is. Bender's pasted a red skull cap on his head. He's changed into shiny black slacks, a starched white shirt, and a black clip-on tie. Sweat pours from his thin face, he squirms on the grate, apparently unable to budge from his diabolical rotisserie.

With an wry smile, I observe, "Having a little problem, Jonathan, are we?"

Panic glistens in his dark pupils, his fingers flex in the rising heat, his wiry body twists on the rack. Flicking his bulging eyes at me, then again into the hissing blue flames, he croaks, "Fuck you."

Reaching out, I yank him off the furnace grate and hold him upright. He clings to me, muttering incomprehensible nonsense against my chest. I shake him off, knock the thermostat down, then turn off the infernal choir of Carmina Burana. I resolve this will be my first and last trip with this madman. We are on totally different wavelengths.

Bender wobbles over and falls on the couch. "Do you realize," he gasps, "we've been high for almost ten hours—like, this entire endless night?"

The solitary bird chirps again in my ear, reminding me. I say to him, "But that's nonsense. Time has no meaning in this place. Time doesn't even exist."

Bender convulses, tittering with delirium. "What, what are you saying?" he hoots. "According to the clock, man, by looking at the fucking clock. Right over there!"

Casting my eyes around in mock confusion, I say, "There is no actual clock like that clock, Bender. That's just a device control freaks invented to persuade us that time exists. It's just a figment of our imagination, of our conditioning."

Bender throws his head back and yowls, bouncing on his ass. "No, that's mad, don't say that! How can you say that? The world has to make sense! We have to be able to measure time!"

"No we don't," I laugh, quaking with laughter, tears streaming from my eyes. "You can't measure the infinite with that silly clock over there. There's not even any over there, there, not really. There never really has been."

TWO WEEKS LATER down in Laguna Beach, Bender introduces me to the renegade chemist. Charlie lives back in one of the lush coastal canyons in a cottage enclosed by orange trees and flowering shrubs. He doesn't have an ocean view, but close enough to smell and feel the sea air. Charlie works for the staid Dr. Cohen at UCLA, but he's an apostle of the LSD Revolution. And like Leary, he believes that the sooner the whole world is turned on to acid the better the world will become.

"Pure acid can save this fucked-over planet," Charlie raves as we huff a potent bomber. "Never mind the non-believers, they're just afraid, they've always been afraid, and they probably always will be. They stare at their shoes, when they should be looking up into the sky. That's why they cling to the status quo like its some kind of old testament commandment. Our mission is to turn everybody onto lsd, everywhere, share it everyone from coast to coast. Turn everybody on, and turn the haters into lovers!"

"And stop this evil fucking war," I say, with an intensity of feeling. "Stop it now and forever, and hang every single motherfucker making money off it!"

Charlie puts his palms together Buddha-like, saying, "Yes, yes, stop this horrible war. Brave man, I am your friend and honest servant."

Charlie is a tall, stork-like man with a balding pate, maybe thirty or so, talks with his hands, paces the room as if drawing ideas from the air, gesticulating. He wears faded patched jeans, leather sandals, a loose collarless shirt and beads around his neck. We all love such threads, this hip and flamboyant style, all except for the oddballs like Bender, the messenger who balks at the message. But Charlie has no internal conflicts, he's an inspired evangelist. All he eats now, he confesses, are bananas and mangoes, almonds and almond butter, along fermented soybean curd and brown rice that he douses in Thai hot sauce. I don't even know what soybean curd is, it sounds disgusting, but I listen. I pay close attention, tuning into this hyper-intelligent ambassador of the psychedelic revolution.

"Over the past year," he says, appraising me through his coke-bottle, granny-glasses, "I've dropped pharmaceutical acid at least a hundred times. Sometimes three times a week, never less than once a week. I can work on it now, function beautifully, it makes everything so much more interesting. You might want to consider a method like that yourself, if you think your cerebral cortex can handle it. Not everyone's can."

Fidgeting, Bender says. "No, not me man. That first trip I took with Jake will do me for quite awhile. I was wigged out for like three days."

"We each have our own path," Charlie replies, affably.

Stepping in, I say, "You know, I'm hip to what you're saying. It's all about the transformation of awareness—mine, yours, his, in fact our whole society. Civil rights, war, peace, how we treat nature, that transformation is essential. Nothing really changes without it, it just goes on repeating itself. It's strange to me how a lot of intelligent people don't get this. They think the system will fix itself, which is ridiculous. We have to find a new way that works, that works better, that wakes us up and keeps us awake."

"Absolutely!" Charlie claps his hands. "So, I take it you both got off well on my special delivery package? A good trip?"

"Amazing, oh yeah, an amazing trip. Beyond belief. And that's why I'm here."

"Excellent, I'm delighted to hear that. Owsley Stanley isn't the only one doing good work."

He takes us into his inner sanctum, a solarium on the back side of his cottage. His housemate, a pretty girl who tempts me with her smile and sleek tanned legs, brings an iced pitcher of what she calls pomegranate-passion flower tea. "I'm Patricia," she smiles, then blows Charlie a kiss and leaves with an insouciant air.

Charlie's solarium is stacked with dozens of books, three-ring binders, jade spirit animals, an easel, and a large, imposing blackboard. The black surface is covered with a manic progression of symbols and mathematical formula, every square inch of space covered with haiku slashes of chalk. Pointing at the board with his finger, Charlie's myopic eyes gleam. "I dropped one thousand mikes of my own pure acid to work that out, it kept me up forty-eight straight hours. But it enabled me to solve the pointless enigma of reality through this cosmic equation!"

"Wow," I say, impressed, having never gotten past yawning high school algebra myself. "What the fuck does it say?"

Beaming, Charlie replies, "It says—Ah, it says, God is living among us, with us, even as us. Yes, even as us. Proves it beyond any doubt. And before I had this epiphany, I was a hard-core agnostic."

"Madness, madness," Bender titters. "Be careful, man. You might fry your noodle."

Charlie regards him with a bemused expression. "Well, if it's madness, then it's divine madness – madness as Dionysus himself was mad and I'll gladly dance to it."

"So will I," I say, cutting to the chase. "I can relate to what your equation. God is, whatever God is, whoever God is, whatever is breathing us, that's divine. I flashed into that or it flashed into me on that fabulous acid of yours. I mean like, talk about a cosmic lightshow, unbelievable. And Charlie, whatever you have, I'll take as much of that magic potion as you can spare."

Clapping his hands, Charlie exclaims, "Oh I have plenty, more than enough. And I'm so glad Jonathan brought you here to meet me. My cupboard is overflowing, it just depends on what your needs and purposes are."

Taking a sip of the pomegranate tea, my mind spinning, I say, "Okay, beautiful, could I see something? Can you show me what you have on hand?"

Charlie the mad chemist goes to an armoire and takes out a quart glass jar of crystalline powder. He brings it over to me with owlish eyes and puts it in my hands. Astonished, I turn the jar over and over, then look at him with a question in my face.

"Jake, my friend, there's enough pure lsd there for several hundred phenomenal trips. All you do is tamp it into double-ought gel caps, each one will give you about 500 mikes of magic dust."

"Holy fuck."

"Indeed, so true, so true," Charlie responds with glee.

Trying to keep my voice casual, I ask, "How much, Charlie? How much for this cornucopia?"

"Well, it's worth a king's ransom, but let's just call it fifty dollars. We're obviously in this together."

# Chapter 12

THAT'S HOW I became insanely rich, almost overnight, in the world's purest acid. And now, I'm going to use some of my magical stash to get close to this new chick on the scene, Dawn, and Donny is the key to my game. Kubiak is broke as usual, restless, hungry for good dope, and that makes him pliable. He'll play ball because he's impatient and wants what he wants, even though he might be screwing his own chances with Dawn. The mere thought of this flirtatious, nubile chick makes me hot, and I am choosy, with me it's either feast or famine.

My old pal Kubiak is lazy to the bone, and even though broke he won't work. Get a job, no way. His doting mom keeps sending him allowance checks in the hope that he'll clean up his act. But fat chance he's ever going to do that. At the moment he's crashing free of charge under dubious circumstances, sleeping on a couch in a 1920's Mission-style flat rented by a gay leather-boy. Donny swears it's all on the up and up, he's just waiting on his mom's cash, but I wouldn't put anything past him. Donny's only religion is the path of least resistance.

I ride over to the Wilshire District to meet him on my thumping black Matchless, still keeping the BSA Lightning under wraps. Donny's gun-shy of the big single's savage back kick and won't pester me to borrow it. When I ride up, he's standing with a cigarette in his mouth on the sidewalk, his hands jammed into his jean pockets.

I needle him about his suspicious sleeping arrangements. "Come on, man, 'fess up. You putting out some free rent?"

"Fuck you," Donny retorts, ducking his handsome, fleshy face. "Jesus fuck Jake, you know me better than that. You know I'm only into chicks. Shit, I won't even get drunk around these lewd fruitcakes. Besides, they think I'm taking VD medication, right? They think I fuck around with street sluts."

We share a sly leer, like the countless laughs we've had swilling Ballantine ale and peach brandy as we dialed in the Wolfman booming up from Juarez in those deep humid Chicago nights. Knowing he's in a tight spot, I lay a couple fat joints on him along with a crisp twenty dollar bill.

Feeling better, Donny takes me inside and introduces me to the owner of this pristine Mission duplex, an elegant swish named Paris. Paris runs an en-vogue beauty salon over on the Miracle Mile. He has russet Adonis curls and exudes movie-land verve. His pastel rooms are decorated with chic furniture, art nouveau lamps, lavish rugs and several marble heads of boyish Greek gods. But what catches my eye are his psychedelic paintings of unicorns, fairies, sorcerers, and erotic young revelers frolicking in come-hither landscapes.

Noticing my interest, Paris asks, "Oh, are you an artist yourself? Do you paint?"

"No, not really, but I do write short stories. And I'm working on a collection of vivid psychedelic poems."

"Wow, I would love to read some of those. I'm wild about anything psychedelic."

"I can see that. And since you're obviously into acid, let me offer you something extra-special." Taking a cloisonne box from my pocket, I tap out two gel caps of deluxe acid into his palm. "Primo lsd, Paris, as pure as moonlight, try just one when you have some time. I promise you a real magic carpet ride."

"Oh my word," he gushes, "an acid outlaw poet on a motorcycle! This must be my lucky day!"

Donny almost chokes, never at ease with this sort of repartee. But Paris is delighted. He jots down his home phone on his business card, asking me to check back in a few days.

"If it's as good as you say I'm going to want more. My friends are going to go wild for this!"

"Easy money," Donny acknowledges, taking me up the outside Satillo-tiled staircase to where he's crashing. His benefactor works days in an all-male nude leather bar and the apartment is empty, pervaded by the sour smell of beer cans, stale pizza, mashed cigarette butts and spewed jism. A miniature white poodle jumps all over Donny with a lapping pink tongue, then leaps onto the yellow naugahyde couch where he sleeps. The curly dog hops and wriggles in some kind of manic anticipation.

Shuffling his feet, Donny teases the pooch, then shifts his conniving eyes at me.

"What? What's with the poodle?"

"Okay, dig, professor." Donny's voice slides into his guttural Wolfman imitation. "I'm gonna show you something that'll bug your eyes out. Play with the dog. Be right back."

Snapping his fingers, Kubiak goes off down the hallway. Sometimes he calls me 'professor' because of my omnivorous reading of books, everything from Camus to Rilke, Miller to Watts, the Beats to James Baldwin and beyond. Donny himself never reads anything. He claims to have a medical condition called narcolepsy and that trying to read makes him nod out. Personally, I think this is bullshit, I know how lazy he is. But one thing for sure about Donny, he is a connoisseur of all things perverted.

The poodle prances back and forth on the naugahyde couch, whining and drooling. I have no desire to pet it. Donny comes sliding back into the room in his sock feet, lisping baby-talk to the dog, taunting it with a thick, flesh-colored dildo.

"Babykins, oooh Babykins, look what I got! Come look here what I got!"

The poodle flips out, bounding off the couch on pogo stick legs, whining and yapping as Donny waves the plastic dick over its head. Babykins goes into a frenzy of leaps, whimpering, nipping at the lewd phallus. Doubled over in laughter, Donny gives the dildo up and the poodle annoints it in a frenzied, whimpering tongue bath.

"Twisted fucking pooch, eh, Jake? Ever seen anything so degenerate, huh? Ever seen anything like that?"

"No, never have," I mutter, "you mean they actually trained this dog to—"

"Exactly," Kubiak snickers, "exactly. The butch fairy who lives here trained his poodle to lick cocks! You saw it with your own eyes!" He rips the dildo away from Babykins' nipping teeth. "They take the dog into the bedroom when they're popping amyl nitrates."

"That's fucking depraved, man. You can't live here. You've got to get out of this scene."

"Tell me about it," Donny says, luring the quivering poodle down the hall. "I told you, I'm afraid to fall asleep at night."

Going outside, we get on my rowdy Matchless and ride over to a beer bar on La Brea. Donny clues me in that one-legged Keith and Dawn are holed up in a flea-bag hotel over on Melrose, money running out. Keith is drunk, Dawn's sympathies are running thin.

"Thing is, she really digs it out here, she wants to stay. And she's itching to ditch Keith, because the fun's over. But she figures the only way she can do that is go back home to Illinois for awhile."

Quaffing my cold Olympia, I say, "But home to what? Why go back home? You said it was a terrible scene."

"No, not to her ex old man, she hates him. Fucker used to beat her up. But her mother's there in Joliet, taking care of her kid. The kid thinks mommy's on a little vacation to California, that's the story. But tell me, man, is she one bitching chick or what?"

"Yeah, she's outrageous, a real honey."

"Super-fine," Donny affirms, guzzling down his second mug of draft, burping. "But she's got enough money to take a Greyhound bus home, and she's about ready to split. If my mother would just come through, I'd like to help her. But fucking mumsy's holding out, hoping I'll come home and enroll in college classes. But fuck that noise."

"Yeah, later for that," I laugh. "But Donny, we don't want her to leave, no way. That would be a complete waste of a beautiful girl. If she want's too stay, we should help her. Although it looks like your pal Keith's gonna be singing the blues."

"Yep, looks like," Donny says, signaling the plump barmaid for another round. I'm paying, why not? He eyes me sideways, hunching his broad shoulders. "All right Jake, just what the fuck are you scheming up? You got to know I really dig this chick too."

Giving him a complicit nod, I say, "Relax, man. Let's just say I've got a good idea, a good plan. You interested in hearing the details?"

"Fuck yes. Lay it on me."

"Okay, dig. I'll get us a place where we can all stay together, all of us.

I've got some bread. I'll rent a cozy house where we can have some fun, smoke some grass, play the music, just groove. Then we'll see how it shakes out. We'll let her decide for herself. Chicks always decide anyway."

Donny narrows his baby-blues, figuring the odds. "Yeah, why not," he mutters, huffing on his Marlboro, reaching for the cold, foaming mug. He can't resist this easy-street offer, even though he knows I can be fast and ruthless. And I don't know how this girl might react, but I'm willing to take my chances.

"Think it over, pardner," I say. "Otherwise she goes home and we both gonna lose out."

Donny makes a pretense of being in quandary over one-legged Keith, but it's all nonsense. Donny has no morals He has no real loyalties except getting high and having as much fun as possible. Anything that doesn't serve those motives, he just laughs off.

Dropping into his Wolfman voice, Kubiak says, "Come on, professor, what's your hold card? You always got one, I know you."

"No hold card, nope" I say, draining my beer. "Whatever happens, that's what happens. We roll with it."

"All right, I'm digging it. You'll cover the rent? And we'll have plenty of booze, weed, decent eats? I mean, just until my old lady sends me my cash."

"Yeah, man, consider all that covered. And I'll lay some dope on you in the meantime. But I'm asking that you make it right with me later. You good with that?"

"Hell yeah, no problem man, you know I'm good for it!" Signaling for another round, Donny laughs, "Sheezzz, professor, this could be a whole lotta fucking fun!"


KNOWING DONNY WILL do his part, I throw myself into the hunt. Within a week, I find a gingerbread cottage shaded by a giant avocado tree in the Wilshire-La Brea District. But I have to fend off a barrage of questions from the crinkle-eyed, blue-haired landlady. She lives alone in the front house on this docile street of manicured hedges and rat-infested palm trees. Those palm rats come out at night, rustling around and biting each other, slithering up and down the telephone wires. But no place is perfect and I'm only looking for a temporary utopia.

The backyard honeymoon cottage is a charmer, yellow with white trim, the kind of place any chick will love. In my ardent and lustful appreciation of girls, I've learned a few things. You have to attune yourself to her feelings, really empathize, then get inside her head until you find the little girl. That little girl loves to come out and play, and have her most secret fantasies fulfilled. And thanks to drugs, booze and rock and roll, romance is on a fast-track these days. If she digs you, she'll open up like a wildflower. Almost overnight things have gone from Kleenex hand jobs at the drive-in to hot, wet blowjobs, and no one's looking back.

The blue-haired, widowed landlady would be scandalized if she could read my thoughts. She sees my BSA Lightning and at first doesn't want to rent to me. But I talk my way in by fabricating a job for myself at a Wilshire ad agency, complete with bogus references, knowing that Paris will cover. I offer her two months in advance, plus the deposit, show her a few hundred in cash, then watch as her bird-like face brighten with avarice. She takes the dough on the spot, primly reciting me the rules, and the next day I begin moving my few paltry belongings—some stick chairs, Formica table, dishes and cups, crates of books, Monet posters, a few towels, sheets, and clothes, along with a mattress that I flop on the floor. But when I come up the driveway with my loud Matchless scrambler, she panics. She rushes out from behind her peek-a-boo curtains and confronts me.

"Young man, I need to know if you intend to throw wild parties."

"No, not at all," I reassure her, "that's not part of my scene. I promise you."

"No, don't just promise me,'" she badgers, "you must swear to me you'll be good."

"Swear to you? Be good? Are you serious?"

"Yes, I must insist. The people on this street have been my neighbors for thirty years. I need to know that you are going to respect us."

"Well, okay then, you have my word. I mean, I'll invite friends over now and then, but they're polite people. There will be no wild parties."

"You swear to that? You mean it?"

"I mean it," I say, meaning it, giving her my best smile, and she goes away. She doesn't want to give those crisp, clean Ben Franklin's back to me. I just have to assuage her anxiety. This cozy honeymoon cottage is mine for awhile, enough time to work some special magic.

A FEW DAYS later Donny shows up in his bellicose 429 Ford with Crash Keith and Dawn, and their suitcases. The landlady corners me over by her rose bushes, demanding to know what I think I'm doing. I explain, these are my friends from Chicago looking for jobs in the movie industry, I'm going to put them up for a week or so. Clutching her garden trowel, she reminds me she is renting to only one person, two at the most. I counter that I believe in helping out friends, then ask her if she would like some extra money?

Shaking her head, she says, "No, no, just realize it has to be temporary," then retreats into the recesses of her own house. Every window seems to be well-curtained.

Gathering together in our canary yellow dollhouse, I let them know the low-down. The old landlady is hyper-sensitive. We have to keep things in check, no drag-racing on the street, no loud revving of pipes, no crazy parties, no freak-outs. Bottom-line, we need to respect the neighborhood.

Dawn tosses her copper-black hair. "Sounds good to me," she says. "I can use some quiet for a change. That sleazy hotel creeped me out."

Donny and Keith squint their eyes, both rolling joints out of the fat lid I toss on the bed. "Fuck that old prune," Donny mocks, "she needs to lighten up."

Big-belly Keith guffaws in derision. I exchange a look with Dawn, knowing there's bound to be tricky shit ahead. But it's not like there's any rules, we're making it up as we go. Something tells me it'll be worth it.

Our impromptu commune doesn't have much in the way of privacy. Their suitcases are propped here and there against the living room walls. We've got a small kitchen with a dwarf stove and regular fridge, and a cramped bathroom with a shower-bathtub. No curtains, white filigree shutters cover the windows that open onto the rosebush backyard. Behind swinging, saloon doors there's an alcove with built-in drawers and shelves, a space I lay claim to. This glorified closet has enough room for my air mattress and sleeping bag, with storage for a half-dozen lids, my lsd stash and trunk. No one complains, after all I'm the one paying the tab.

Breaking the ice, we pass around a couple of pungent joints. Looking at Dawn, then Keith, I say, "I know the sleeping situation is a little weird. But until Donny gets his bread together we have to make do. You're welcome to that mattress, I'm gonna crash in that alcove."

Donny shoots me an aggrieved look. "Three of us, on one double mattress? Come on."

"No, I'm not saying that. I've got extra blankets, extra pillows, you can make a nice pallet over on the floor."

"On the floor? With my gimpy back? What the fuck, Jake. My old lady's gonna be sending me Western Union any day now."

"I dig that. I'm not saying you have to sleep on the floor."

"Can't you just buy another mattress until she comes through?"

"No way, man. I already put out some serious cash to score this place. Sorry."

"You could always sleep in your car," Keith taunts him, double-toking. Donny mutters, hating to be the odd man out.

Rolling his fishy eyes, Keith hoots at his friend and jiggles his wooden leg on the bed. His fat gut pooches over his belt, cigarette smoke pours from his hairy nostrils. Dawn sits next to him, her slender back nudged against the wall. But she's looking at me, with a sly, flirtatious smile.

"Dig Donny," Keith snorts, rubbing it in, "you can always go back and sack out with the queers. They've got a wet spot for you."

"Ohhh low," I say, taking a healthy whiff.

Kubiak curses, and Dawn intercedes, "All right you guys, stop being mean. Donny shouldn't have to sleep in his car, besides, that would just piss off the old biddie." Her deft fingers are sifting seeds over a shoebox lid, sorting the zig-zag makings for another one.

"Fuck it all," Donny laughs, taking the smoldering roach that I pass off. He gives it a couple quick hits, then sucks the glowing ember into his mouth and swallows it. Butterfield and Bloomfield are ripping it up on the Hi-Fi, reefer smoke layers the room. We're all getting to know each other.

Giving me an intimate glance, Dawn says, "Listen, I've got the perfect solution and nobody has to suffer much."

"Donny sleeps in the bathtub?" quips Keith, chugging his beer, assuming certain prerogatives that may or may not exist.

"Nope, not even close," Dawn laughs, slapping at him. "No, until Donny can afford to buy his own bed, the three of us can share this one. It's big enough."

After a slack-jawed moment, Keith jerks his porcine body upright. "You can't be fucking serious, Dawn. The three of us, sharing our bed?"

"It's not our bed, it's hiss bed," Dawn replies, glancing at me under her lashes. "And since Jake's nice enough to give it up and since we're all friends, we gotta share."

My heart does a gleeful leap. Stoned or not, she and I are already conspiring! In one move she just stalemated Donny and Keith, no matter how they grumble. I'm pretty certain she doesn't have a thing for Donny, and she just poured ice water all over Keith. I flash her a knowing smile, her eyes linger on mine. Getting up, I go through the saloon doors into my private space. Jimmy Reed wails in the smoky air, Bright Lights, Big City. Unlocking my seaman's chest, I take out my jar of psychedelic elixir. I start filling some double-ought gel caps with primo Laguna acid, humming to myself, excited, feeling in control. Everything that happens, happens now.

On the other side of the swinging doors I hear Dawn laugh, say, "Uh uh, just remember both of you, I'll be sleeping with my clothes on. So forget about any hanky-panky."

# Chapter 13

MY NEXT MOVE is to get us all high as a cosmic kite. Somehow I have to turn this flirtatious mood into a passionate interlude, then steal her away from these jealous dogs. Just being around her, she turns my swollen balls to molten wax. She's obviously hip, super-sexy, and a few years older. It occurs to me that she could be playing me too, along with Keith and Donny, but I squash these doubts. I'm holding all the right cards, and all games become transparent under a full-bore hit of lsd. I just need to make sure that no one takes too much, nobody wigs out, no rescue sirens racing up this peaceful street. Besides, I don't want to be holding anybody's hands except her hands and feeling her lips on my feverish penis.

When I nonchalantly suggestion that we all drop acid together, Donny gets uptight. "No way man, not me," he says, ducking his blond head. "That shit's way too weird for me."

"How would you know, Donny? You've never even tried it."

"I heard all about it, I've read the bad reports."

"You read a bad report on acid? Where was that, in Hot Rod magazine?"

Keith guffaws at my gibe, Dawn giggles, even Donny laughs, then flips me the bird. Kubiak and I have done weed, whites, wine, dexies, and swilled booze together like soda pop. We've prowled through the blues clubs on Chicago's black south-southwest side, white boys taking our chances. He's a blast to run around with, but fears losing control, and I have no such fear.

"Dig, everyone," I say, "acid's not dangerous in light doses. I've dropped a couple dozen hits of acid and I can tell you, it's a beautiful trip."

"Is that true?" Dawn asks. "Because I've really wondered, you hear all these stories."

"Yeah, it's true, it's a really good trip. It's important who you trip with, but it's a real magic carpet ride."

"Hmmm," she says, her eyes lighting up, "sounds like my kind of thing."

"Bullshit, no way," Kubiak bitches, resenting my influence, helping himself to one of her Winstons. But she keeps her eyes on me, her foot keeping time to the radio, Marvin Gaye, the soulful music of love.

Hacking up a marijuana loogie, Keith grunts, "Uh, well dig, I'm sorta interested. How long does this magic carpet ride last, anyway? And how much is it gonna cost?"

"Let's say a light dose, maybe five or six hours? It's ultra-pure acid, no jangly speed, just wild technicolor hallucinations and you'll laugh and laugh until you're face aches. Coming down is smooth, it's no big deal."

"Then what the fuck, I want me some, I want a big fucking dose!" Keith thumps his stump on the floor, hoisting his Budweiser in the air. "Never mind the kiddie dose, give me the Popeye version!"

"Hmm," Dawn muses, "I think maybe me too."

"Don't do it," Donny argues, "you don't know, you could both end up in the loony-bin!"

"Naw, fuck that noise," Keith retorts, "I'm bored outta my mind. Whadaya think, babe?"

Dawn glances at him, then at me, meeting my half-smile with her own. "I think yes, I wanna go with what Jake's saying. Sounds like fun."

Donny grunts, knowing his luck is running low. Dawn reaches over and pats his hand. "Come on Donny, don't be so uptight," she teases. "You don't have to swallow anything you don't want to swallow, right? Let's all get high and have some fun."

Nailed by her clever double-entendre, Donny coughs, laughs, then says, "Yeah, okay, but just a light dose. I don't want to end up in a trick-bag."

"You won't," I tell him. "You're my friend and a light dose is mellow."

"Yeah, stop worrying," Dawn says with a playful laugh. "I think we should just trust Jake, he's the one who's taken the ride."

She looks me right in the eye, like she wants a special pact between us.

Then she says, "Just promise me this stuff isn't gonna mess me up in any way. Promise me that?"

Really feeling her vibes, I tell her, "Yeah, you got it. I promise that you're going to love it, and I promise I won't wander off anywhere."

Pissed, Crash Keith interrupts, "Hey, uh man, Mr. Jake, what about me? What am I all of a sudden, somebody's used rubber?"

Realizing that maybe I'm being too obvious, I reply, "No, man, not at all. What I'm saying is basically for everybody. What do you want to know?"

"Like, for instance," he glares, his doper shades down on his nose, "am I gonna flip out if I drop a heavy load of this magic dust? Any danger of that?"

"Fucking A, man," Donny says, "I'm telling you."

Ignoring Kubiak, I say, "Look, Keith, I can't give you any guarantees on 500 mikes of this acid, it's 99% pure. It's really high-octane. So start out with half a cap, then if you're liking it, do the rest. And to answer your other question, this trip is on me. Ain't no charge."

Throwing his blunt hand out, Keith snorts, "All right, man, that's righteous! And no, I'm not feeling any qualms, so hit me up with a full load of dat Hollywood Special!"

"You're all fucking loco," Donny grumbles. "But me too. Gimme half a ticket to ride."

We all nod and laugh, and shake on the deal. Dawn's fingers linger in mine, promising something more or so I'm hoping. Tapping out several capsules onto an oval mirror, I separate the clean white powder into little islands. We suck it up into our mouths with a straw, swish it down with a swallow of water. There's no going back now, we've punched our tickets. We lounge around expectantly, smoking, chatting, as the sensuous acid rises up our neural pathways. Keith unstraps his peg-leg, chortling, and flings it across the room. He asks that I hit him with some more, and I oblige. In no time, he's hopping around in a carnival conversation with people only he can see, jovial and red-faced. And my Dawn, as guileless as a brown-eyed nymph, her, slides closer to me on the bed. I don't remember getting on the bed, but here I am beside her. She plays with my hand, our fingers entwine. Donny ogles the surreal delight blooming all around him. He likes watching others get weird, he likes egging them on. But the potent acid sneaks up on him. He stops snapping his fingers, a confused expression crosses his flushed face. His chin slumps, his shoulders hunch into a shell. In all the time I've known Kubiak, I've never seen him go inward. He avoids introspection like a disease. Dawn notices too, we're both swallowing our giggles. She gently nudges Donny but he doesn't respond. Keith disappears noisily into the bathroom and doesn't come back out. She and I are alone, touching, almost panting, marooned on a island of racing desire. She pulls me up off the bed and dances into the kitchen, then pours herself into my arms.

"Unbelievable," she says breathlessly, "you weren't kidding It feels like there's honey pouring all through me."

"It is honey, baby, psychedelic honey," I whisper, tracing her lips, her eyebrows with my fingertips. With a little moan she lifts up on her toes and tastes my lips with her tongue, then gives me a soul-melting kiss. I feel her supple, yearning body mold into my atomic flesh.

"Let's do some more," she says, "should we? You and me, I don't want this to stop."

Shaping her waist and hips with my hands, the small of her back, I tell her, "Me either, I don't ever want it to stop. We can do whatever you want. But one we might want to do is get out of here for awhile."

Pushing her svelte belly against my ravishing hardon, finding herself in my eyes, she says, "Take me anywhere you want, Jake, anywhere. I'm ready. Just say the word."

We steal another delicious, body-trembling kiss, I whisper, "Okay then, let's get our act together. We're gonna split on my bike. But first let me get some more acid."

She skips into the bathroom to check on her one-time boyfriend, nothing stays the same. She's come awake in a magical wonderland with me. Going into my den, I pocket a couple of caps and lock my stash back into my steamer trunk. Glancing over the saloon doors, I notice Donny. He's standing in the middle of the room, a penny loafer in one hand, a table spoon in the other, mumbling to himself. He looks like a spooked, blond badger. Kubiak goes shuffling out the screen door carrying his shoe and spoon.

I can't find my oval mirror, so I tap a cap of acid into two neat halves on a queen of hearts card, a bit shaky, but I pull it off. Dawn comes in behind me, embracing my back, nuzzling me. Pure liquid soul pours from the radio. Smiling, I point at the card, offer her the straw, and one by one we suck the pristine powder under our tongues.

She kisses my neck, sucks my lips, finds my tongue, then pulls back and says, "I need to spend a tiny few minutes with Keith. He's acting really weird. But I'll be right back, I promise."

Not liking it, knowing that the fat boy would do anything to block this, I resist the urge to pull her down with me onto my air mattress. Instead, I say, "Do what you have to do, babe. I'm ready to go when you are What's he doing, anyway?"

"I'm not sure. He's just lying there in the bathtub in his underwear, babbling like a baby. He thinks he's playing in the water but there's no water in the tub." Dawn dissolves into giggles, then asks, "Should we be alarmed?"

"Fuck no, he's just hallucinating. I warned him about the dose. He'll come down sooner or later. You gonna be all right?"

"Yes, I'll be okay, don't worry." She squeezes my hands and anoints me with her eyes. I feel this chick like I've never felt a girl before. "I'll be right back."

"Okay, whatever. I'm going to go check on Donny, I think he's wigging out too."

She kisses me, then dances off, leaving me in a thrum of desire.

Going outside, I find Donny on the bench under the avocado tree. The limbs are hanging with the ripe, dark-green fruit. Donny glances at me, then scoops the pit out of an avocado with the spoon. He's in his white socks, both of his loafers are missing.

Intrigued, I ask him, "How did you slice that thing open?"

Giving me a what-the-fuck look, he replies, "With my pocket knife."

Laughing, I sit down beside him. "You know, I've never eaten one of those in my life. What's it taste like?"

"You've never eaten an avocado?"

"Nope, never have. For some reason it was never on my menu."

Donny spoons a glob of the green pulp into his mouth, thinking it over. Masticating slowly, he says, "Tastes sorta like mashed potato and butter, except needs some salt. Want a bite?"

"No, not now, maybe later." Mashed potatoes ain't what I'm craving, no. What I want is that delicious half-breed chick in there who's dripping with lust for me.

Keeping these images to myself, I say, "You doing all right, Donny my man? Everything cool?"

He frowns at me from under his furry, blond brows. "Tastes strange, you know? I mean, like everything does. Everything tastes strange on this psychedelic jazz, even beer."

I nod, in a way it's true. Pure acid does seem to release an electrified Soma via the salivary glands, altering the molecular taste of whatever you put in your mouth, even weed.

"Even cigarettes taste lousy," Donny scoffs. "This acid's not for me. It makes me think about stuff I don't want to think about. It traps me into thinking about shit that makes me feel guilty."

"Hah, that' strange. It doesn't affect me that way at all. It's the greatest high I've ever had, I love it. But dig man, help yourself to the grass in the shoebox and there's beer in the fridge."

"Yeah, gimme weed, dexies, and booze any day," Donny says, "that's my ticket. Fuck this hoodoo shit."

Feeling the fresh acid rush kick in, I laugh, a rich, loving laugh. The world is changing fast, but Donny has no affinity for a universe that shifts shape and sings in colors. Relying on boyish charm, he just wants to keep peeling panties off of schoolgirls and laying hotrod rubber on the streets. But each to his own, I have no problem with it.

I can't stop smiling, my face aches from smiling so much. "What's so funny?" Donny wants to know. His pupils are huge and dilated, trying to make sense of the Mystic.

"I'm sky high on lsd, man. And you Donny Kubiak, are my good friend."

"What are you up to with her? Jesus gawd, man, nothing like being so obvious."

"We're falling in love, what can I tell you? And all bets are off, anything goes."

"You low-down bastard, Acree. I shoulda known I couldn't trust you. You never play fair."

"Aw come on," I laugh, "never play fair? I'm just being me like you're being you. Coming into this scene, it was whatever happens, happens, remember?

"You telling me she feels the same way you feel?"

"Why don't you ask her?" I grin, standing up, reaching for the infinite sky, suffused with life-force. The fronds of the palm trees are haloed in light. "Three of us, one of her. It was anybody's game and somebody wins, somebody doesn't."

"Except you got the hot bike and all the dope, you prick."

"That's true, uh huh, and even some money too. Imagine that."

"Where there's dope, there's hope," Donny quips. "But what about Keith? Poor bastard, he'll fall apart. He's hardly glued together anymore as it is."

"Don't give me that bullshit, Donny. Their trip was already on it's last legs when she walked in here. Besides, it's up to her, not you or me. The chick always does the choosing."

"You're a low-down scam artist," Kubiak bitches, "you always have been."

Almost on cue, Dawn comes swinging out the door in a skimpy white halter top, tight jeans, her hair like a black cape across her bare shoulders, child-like and radiant, achingly delectable. Donny does a double-take and mutters under his breath.

She comes right over, puts her hands behind my neck, then kisses me on the lips, a kiss that says, Oh just in case anyone is wondering, I with this man! Swinging on my outstretched hands, she says, "Keith's turned into an infant. He's huddled in the bathtub and won't come out."

Dissolving in a rush of giggles, we hold onto each other. "Is he lucid?" I ask. "Is he hip to what's going on with us.?"

"Yeah, he sorta knows," she murmurs, gently biting me. "Says he saw it coming, says to do our thing." Her hand tugs at my Buffalo Nickel belt buckle. I kiss her sea-shell ear. Fuck, no doubt that we have to be going.

With a morose look, Donny complains, "You fucks are tripping your brains out. Nothing like rubbing his face in it."

Giving her hair a toss, Dawn retorts "Oh really, Donny? Are you sure you're not talking about yourself? And by the way, what we do or don't do, that's our business."

Surprised by her tone, I say, "Look man, we're gonna take a ride. Probably be gone awhile. So help yourself to the dope and guard the fort."

"Jesus fuck, you're going riding bombed on acid? Baby, you lost your mind?"

"Maybe I have," she laughs, squeezing my arm. "But you know how it is. We don't always get our way, but sometimes we get lucky."

Donny flushes, but says no more. I don't know what's gone between them, so I let it slide. Taking her by the hand, I go over to my BSA Lightning and kick it over. She gets on behind me, hugging my back. Beautiful Brit bike rumbling beneath us, acid flashing in.

Donny stands there, drooling with disgruntled envy. I've got the girl, he's got the avocado. He'll be figuring out how to get even with me down the road.

"Don't get lost, motherfucker," he smirks.

Winking, I drop the bike into gear and throttle us into the street. Whatever comes, I'll handle it. Dawn says in my ear, "He tried to warn me about you, you know, he says you're dangerous. But I don't care if we get lost, Jake, as long as I'm getting lost with you."

Falling in love plays by its own wild, spontaneous rules and takes you along for the ride. I've already realized that you have to claim what you want in this life, no one is going to give it to you. I have some money in my pocket, I'm thinking of a loose bar and motel up near Malibu.

We make sweet, ravishing love together, the scent of gladiolus filling the room, devastating love. Nothing stays the same. You fall into the looking glass, into the holy fountain, you rewrite the script and you know it, ahh God, you know it.

# Chapter 14

T HINGS SORT THEMSELVES out at our little commune, Dawn makes the situation clear. No big deal is made of our sudden romance, but no doubts are left in the air. At night, she sleeps with me in my alcove behind the swinging doors. Our connection is playful, wanton, and intense. But in some ways we're quite unalike. She's fascinated by my ideas philosophical speculations, like looking into another world, but she's not in the least intellectual. Dawn reads movie-land fan magazines, she entertains herself by tripping on the dreck in the National Enquirer. Instinctively, she sidesteps existential questions about existence, why feel bad about life? To me this is hilarious, and no matter, we click. She glances up, catches my eye, the most delicious passion takes over. I am possessed with the torrid desire to devour her, yes, I confess, I want to eat her, to make love with her anywhere, to go crazy with her, and she wildly reciprocates.

Our sullen housemates are not happy with this turn of events, reduced as they are to stoned eunuchs in her eyes. They are bored and quarrelsome, needing money, brooding on revenge. Dawn and I realize we're gonna have to ditch these bozos soon. She wants a real bed with real privacy in our own place, and so do I. I want to give Donny the time I promised him, but he and Keith are burning through my weed like smokestacks, swilling beers and scarfing food, incorrigible lazy fucks. Something's got to give.

This tension comes boiling over one late wasted night, after midnight, as we sit in front of a black and white TV picked up in a garage sale, toking another joint, mesmerized by Cal Worthington's zoo animal commercials. Crash Keith comes barging through the door, wired, boozed to the gills, a fat aggressive blur of chaotic energy.

"Candy man is back," Keith bellows, turning his pockets inside out and tossing wads of cash into the air.

"Holy fuck," Donny yelps, snatching at the loose bills, "where'd you get all the loot?"

Flashing me an alarmed look, Dawn says, "Yeah, Keith, what?"

Triumphant and red-faced, Keith leers like a pirate. "Six hundred and some-odd skins, baby! I'm loaded again! And Donny you hear, I need me some help! I busted through the backdoor of that corner grocery and rifled the place. Plus, there's boxes of beer and vino and cigs just sitting there. We gotta go back and get the goods, ya hear me Kubiak?"

"Ah fuck, fuck no," I swear, getting off the bed. "You ripped off that old couple? Those are our neighbors, man, those are good people."

"Tough shit," Keith retorts, hopping around in peg-legged machismo. "Ain't no skin off my balls, just a couple of old kikes. And now we got moola and can boggie the hell outta here!"

"Dammit to hell, Keith," Dawn shouts, "You shouldn't have done that! Those old people have been nice to us!"

"Fuck 'em, too late, it's my turn. Like all that cash, huh Donny? Huh? Cash to flash, cash to flash!"

Donny dances on his nimble feet, clutching fistfuls of bills, eyes darting. "Anybody see you? Didn't the fucking alarm go off?"

"That's the best part," Keith gloats, "there wasn't no alarm. I just busted the pad lock on the alley door. All that shit's laying there for the taking, let's go get it!"

Donny chortles, popping his fingers. "Fuck yeah!. It's party time, people! Let's go scoop that shit up!"

"Count me out, motherfuckers," I say, furious. "And if you get your asses busted, don't bring the heat back here. You dig?"

"Me too," snaps Dawn, "count me out. That was low-down and mean, Keith. I don't want any part of it."

"What the hell," Keith blurts, almost tipping over, waving his hands for balance. "This was for us, baby, I did this for you and me!"

"For me? I didn't ask you for any of this stuff, go fuck yourself!"

"Hey, Dawn, come on—"

"No! You robbing an old Armenian couple doesn't blow my skirt up. Get lost!"

Keith gapes at her, his fishy eyes goggling on speed. Dawn goes into the bathroom and slams the door. I say nothing, relishing how her stiletto sinks deep into his fat, sweating torso. He bulges his eyes at me, leaning toward me. I stare back at him with a ruthless calm, quite ready to knock him down and beat him bloody with his own wooden stump.

Donny jumps in, saying, "Hey, forget this bullshit! I mean, who gives a rat's ass? What's done is done, let's get with the program! Let's go score the booze and cigs, hey Jake?"

"Yeah, you do that, Donny. But just remember what I told you. No heat. You bring heat, it's on you, on both of you."

"All right, all right," Keith vents, like an amped-up maniac. "I hear what you're saying! But goddamnit, stop hassling me! Nothing's gonna go wrong!"

"Nothing's gonna go wrong? Cool, I'm gonna hold you to that."

"Yeah, okay hotshot," Keith mutters, thumping for the door with a vengeance.

Donny jives after him, snapping his fingers "Don't be so uptight, professor," he jeers. "This neighborhood's like a grave yard, nobody's hip to anything. You can't always have everything your way."

"Don't bring the heat down on us, Kubiak. Don't bring the cops."

But they're already gone. I hear the monster Ford pipes fire, as they back into the midnight street. There's a knot in my stomach and my mind has gone into overdrive. Dawn comes out of the bathroom and throws herself across the bed.

Hair partially covering her face, she says, "Those stupid fucking dopes."

I sit down on the bed, she slumps against me, I put my arm around her. "It's a bad scene," she murmurs. "We're the odd-balls in this neighborhood, somebody could come around checking."

"Yeah, I know it," I reply, surveying the guilty room—an open lid of reefer, empty beer cans, suitcases, illicit cash strewn on the floor, not to mention my precious acid stash. "Baby, we're gonna have to vacate this place post-haste. It's not safe for us."

"But what about them?"

"Them too. They can't hang around here. The cops will be all over this area by morning and guess what? We've all got to be long gone. I don't know where, but somewhere."

"Out of sight, out of mind, right?"

"Yeah, something like that."

"Okay yes, I've got a newsflash, Jake! An idea, I know what to do!"

"You know what to do? Okay, tell me, I'm all ears."

"All right, dig. Keith keeps talking about going down to Mexico to hang out, right?. And now, suddenly, he's got all this bread burning a hole in his pocket . . ."

Taking in her sly smile, I laugh. "Yeah, that's right, he does. And he needs to spend it far away from here, like down in Ensenada, the perfect getaway. Think he'll go for it?"

"Oh, don't worry," she says in pragmatic confidence. "He'll do just about anything I ask, believe me."

Not really liking that, but still, I know it's our best course of action. Incognito holiday south of the border, gringos on a spree. "Okay then, get him on board. But Dawn, remember, we need to be out of here by daylight. Because morning's gonna bring some bad news to this scene."

She and I start straightening up – cleaning up the seeds and stems, dumping the empties, counting the bills—almost seven hundred dollars in stolen loot! I organize my acid stash and makings for a quick getaway. We're in the dead of the night, hours to kill, but not really.

The reckless assholes come back with three cases of Hamms, case of Blue Nun, case of odious Cold Duck, and several cartons of Marlboros and Winstons. Sweating like a pig, Keith flops down on the mattress and fans himself with his Cub's baseball cap.

"Hey, Jake," he wheezes, "I don't mean to be a problem child, but I'm crawling out of my skin." He thrusts a wad of cash at me. "Here, here, take this."

"I don't want that, no thanks. I've got my own money."

"Naw, listen man, a couple hundred bucks, take it. I wanna pay my fair share around here. Plus I wanna buy thirty or forty hits of that good-time acid of yours, I dig that shit." He flips his cap at the cases of booze. "Check it out, I do good or what?"

Thinking fast, I say, "Okay, I get your drift. For the rent, and for the magic dust. But all that booze has got to go back in the car because we're clearing out of here. All of us. Come daylight, we need to be gone. Everybody dig this?"

Donny nods, toking on a fat roach. "Yeah, yeah, I'm hip, sounds good to me."

Giving me a cockeyed look, Keith replies "Yeah, Dawn clued me in. I'm not stupid. We're heading on down to the Baja, so no sweat. It's where I want anyway."

My girl is in our alcove, stuffing my army surplus pack with essential gear. I'm thinking I might as well take his cash. Looking at Keith, I say, "Okay, man. How about four bucks a cap? That sound fair?"

"Done," he rasps, peeling me off six more twenties. Really, easy money.

To Donny I say, "Listen, Kubiak, we gotta get both bikes outta here to my friend's garage in Venice. Can you follow me on the Matchless?"

"Yeah, damn straight, if you kick it over. Does that headlight work?"

"Yeah, pretty much. I'll take it easy and we'll stay off the freeways."

Keith brightens, "So, then me and Dawn follow you two in the car? I'm liking it."

"Right, we do it all in one swoop. No coming back here for at least a week. Don't leave anything lying around, pack it up, we can stash it with my bikes. We're all going to Ensenada in Donny's Ford."

"Outta sight," Keith enthuses, hopping to his feet. "Mexico, here we come! Acid, booze, weed, and speed, baby, speed! Fucking A, we gonna get crazy!"

Whooee, I'm thinking to myself, this is going to be one madhouse circus. My intimate groove with Dawn is all messed up by this fiasco but we've got to get-gone. I have an instinct about cops, I know they'll be knocking on the doors. They'll be looking for anything out of the ordinary. And that's us. So we scramble around and gather our stuff, then vacate the yellow doll house. We make a bit of a racket. As we pull out of the driveway, both bikes, the bellicose 429, all motors running, most of the lights in the landlady's house go blinking on.

ABOUT TWENTY RAUCOUS hours later, the seedy bars of Tijuana in our wake, I stop the car on the dim Baja coast two-lane highway. The waxing moon is up, haloed by a misty penumbra. A few bright stars are visible in the sky. Fog has crept in off the sonorous, opaque ocean, the air is cool, moist. We need to stretch our legs and maybe take a leak. Dawn slides out the passenger door without a word, engrossed in some private mood. Keith is conked out beside Donny in the backseat, both snoring and oblivious. They drift in and out of drunken consciousness, their agitated nerves buzzing on Tijuana dexedrine. Slitting one eye, Donny mutters, "I need to get into a bed, Jake. My back's killing me. We ever gonna find a fucking motel?"

I tell him not to sweat it, I'll find one soon, he fades back into his infamous swoon. Typical Donny, an incorrigible reprobate, always ducking shared responsibilities. Basically he doesn't want to drive, he wants to stay stoned and dream. But I don't really care as long as this trip plays out my way. I watch as Donny's head lolls to one side, drool glistening from his mouth. All too reminiscent of our last bug-eyed crazy road trip together.

We came out to the west coast on route 66 from Chicago last summer, fleeing a city wracked with racial tensions and burning riots. We drove all the way in my green and cream '55 Chevy coupe, hauling a swaying wooden trailer loaded with his 500 Norton and my 600 Matchless. Both bikes had bent pushrods and weren't running. Chicago's great south and southwest side had turned into a combat zone, smoke poured into the humid air, the blues joints shut down, black people getting shot in the streets. If there was ever a time to roll the dice and head for fabled California, this was it. We made our break.

Coming over a wooded rise on the outskirts of La Grange, we spot a lone hitchhiker—a thin black kid with his head wrapped in a red dew rag, toting a big army surplus duffel. He's trying to wave us down.

Donny's snapping his fingers to the Isley Brothers on the tubes. When he realizes that I'm slowing down, he swivels his head at me. He recently had a close-up with an Afro switchblade on one of our southside capers and he's still feeling the jitters.

"No, Jake, fuck no. Don't pick up that spade."

I just smile and ignore him. He thinks my ardent passion for civil rights is misguided, nothing can be changed, big money calls all the shots.

He doesn't trust Martin Luther King, he mocks Robert Kennedy. He loves the negro blues, but is extremely leery of segregation. For me, that's just a lazy man's cop-out.

"Too late," I tell him, "besides, we're gonna need extra gas money for this cross-country run. So don't get uptight, just be cool."

"Motherfuck," Donny grumbles, his comfort zone suddenly zapped out of shape.

Going slowly past the dew-rag kid, I pull onto the shoulder and stop with the engine on. The kid comes running with his olive duffel bag to catch us. He thrusts his lean, hopeful face into the open side window. "Oh brothers," he says to us, "can you give me a ride? I gotta get outta this fucked-up city, they shooting black people down where I live. I'm axing you, can you pleeze?"

"Yeah, man, maybe we can," I reply, affably. "Where you heading anyway?"

Donny glares at me, then says to the kid, "Hey look man, we know it's a bad scene down there but we're loaded to the hilt. I mean, see for yourself."

Donny's actually not exaggerating. The back seat is crammed with boxes of my beat and existential books, jazz, blues and Dylan records, clothes, sleeping bags, blankets, my army surplus pack. Even the trunk is stuffed with our suitcases and tools. More boxes wrapped in a tarp are tied down beside our bikes in the trailer. And you can't carry a man cross-country in an open trailer anyway, the highway patrol will bust your ass. So the only available space is in the front seat between Donny and myself, right over the four-on-the-floor Hearst shifter.

"Where you heading?" I ask him again. "Saint Louis? Can you chip in for some of the gas money?"

In that instant the dew rag kid snaps to the fact that I am his best and only chance. His desperate eyes fasten on me. "No I don't, no I don't, truth is, I need to make it clear out to L.A. to my sistah's and I only got ten dollars on me. But I can drive, man, hell, I'm a helluva good driver. Just give me a chance."

Frowning slightly, cause I was hoping for more, I feel Kubiak groan. But what the fuck, here I am face to face with my own heartfelt convictions, and I know it. I've never ridden with the southern Freedom Riders, but I consider myself a freedom rider in spirit.

Leaning across Donny, I say to the brother, "Dig man, we're going all the way to L. A., but we're really short on bread. I'm worrying about having enough gas to even make it."

"Well okay then, you can have my cash, I give it all to you." His earnest brown eyes pluck at me. "Plus, dig brothers, I got some reefer, I got me some fine reefer. You guys like to smoke?"

Donny jerks out of his sullen slouch. "Hey, no shit man? You carrying weed? Fucking-A we like to get high, weed's as good as gas any day, right Jake, wouldn't you say?"

The dew-rag kid cocks his head in mock affront. "Hey, what's mine is yours, I already said it. The signifying monkey do not lie. Just make a little wriggle room for me."

Nodding my head, I say, "All right man, looks like we all just had a stroke of luck. Climb on in. We're gonna do this thing together."

Rearranging our gear, we mash his fat duffel into the backseat, all but cutting off my rearview. At first it's a little tense, this black kid in his greasy head rag skinning in between two eccentric white boys, wondering what he's getting himself into. But we share Old Golds, exchange names, soul-shake, and take off on the mother road into the mythical west.

From the get-go it's a crazy and madcap ride. The dew rag kid, Malcolm, hasn't bathed in days. He's been hiding out, laying low, sleeping under houses, ducking the mayhem. Malcolm is so nervous that he chatters every waking minute, jive-talks non-stop, until he passes out. Maybe he's afraid we're going to dump him out in the KKK boondocks, who knows? He jabbers on, often in rhymes, mainly about a signifying monkey and the monkey's nemesis, a cruel and hungry lion that stalks him. But the monkey stays up in the treetops, taunting the lion, and won't descend where the lion can eat him. The monkey is too smart, he knows how to outwit the beast. Malcolm's repertoire of jive-ass shit is astonishing, the wiggy rhymes, the savant variations fly out of his mouth. And at first I really dig it, man, I laugh and follow along, shrugging off the racial undertones. But the dew rag kid has no stop button. Eaten up with anxiety, traveling through the wilderness with white motorcycle motherfuckers, he keeps up his relentless jabber and mooches our cigarettes. He smells so bad that I have to drive with the windows down, breathing through the left side of my face. But the real downer is when his reefer turns out to be the worst shit in the history of mankind.

The kid is generous with his dope, it's his only currency. Squirming around and rooting in his bag, he brings out a red Prince Alpert can that holds maybe two dozen or so stingy pin-rolls. After indulging in a couple of these delicacies, I have such a God-awful headache that I turn it down. I mean, I've never turned down a joint before, pot is too hard to come by in Chicago. But this shit is beyond hideous.

Perplexed and sweating, Malcolm asks, "What, you don't want no more, Jake? You don't want no more of this righteous reefer?"

"No, man, uh uh," I grunt. "I got hay fever, you know? It's just too much for me."

But Donny does not share my allergic hesitation. Filled with loathing and desperate to escape the insane monkey stories, he sucks up pin-roll after pin-roll, nursing a six pack of short-can malt liquor. Donny croaks with delirious revulsion under the kid's linguistic assault. Finally, he starts nodding off and Malcolm soon nods out with him, right on his shoulder. Kubiak shrugs the kid's dew-rag head off; his head rolls away, then rolls right back, drooling on his shoulder.

It's all unscripted madness and laughing to myself I drive like a banshee, on fire to make it into the far west, sensing we have no time to waste. I drive thorough the green afternoon and into the blazing sunset and across the wide Mississippi on a two-lane lamp-lit bridge, stopping at a gravel-lot beer joint on the other side. The sign says we are in Oklahoma. We spring for a carton of fried catfish and a couple six packs of cold Hamms. Donny is old enough to buy liquor, his ace in the hole with the schoolgirls. Wolfing down the delicious catfish, draining a beer, I push us back onto 66 and flee into the gathering night. To stop for long might mean we meet arrest, defeat or oblivion, so I drive. A hundred miles farther along I pull over for gas at a Flying Red Horse sign, ethyl twenty-one cents a gallon. We get out and stretch our legs, fill the tank. Malcolm goes bouncing off across the neon-lit gravel to the men's restroom, his head up.

"Let's ditch that jive ass," Donny proposes. "He never fucking shuts up, his grass stinks and so does he. Come on man, let's just toss his bag right here on the ground, leave him a five-spot, and split. Let him catch a bus or something."

Shaking my head, I say, "Nope, no can do, Donny. Not gonna happen. I'm not about to leave him out here in redneck country. Just smoke his dope and deal with it."

"You and your asinine ideals. Fuck, he is that spooky monkey he keeps raving about."

"Maybe so, but he's coming with us," I say, watching the kid come bopping back, his red dew rag drawing some hostile stares from other motorists. I fire up my 265 V8 quad Chev, yeah, it's a bit of a hassle. I've got four on the floor and have to shift through Malcolm's skinny legs, but so what? Like Martin Luther King says, we are all the family of man. When they killed JFK, I realized the score. I stood on the sidewalk of downtown State Street with grown people crying all around me, the news spread like wildfire. They killed the president, they shot JFK through the head. They could kill any one of us standing up against their despicable system. Nobody needs to explain a goddamn thing to me. You're either on this freedom ride or your soul belongs to them.

"Think of it as the real-life blues, Donny, because that's what it is."

All through the night I race the gloaming prairie wind, the bike trailer swaying behind us, the signifying monkey moaning in the hollow of my ear. Kubiak polishes off most of the beer, inhales the vile reefer and passes out, snoring like a mule. Malcolm falls out again too, his head rolling onto my shoulder now like a coconut wrapped in a red bandanna. Shaking with rueful glee, I race on into the tunnel of the enveloping night. My right headlight is cocked off at a right angle due to an accident, like an eyeball probing the darkness. Refugees, we are refugees way out here on this starlit prairie, refugees from the Land of Normalcy. Things are never going to be the same again.

I keep pushing the dew-rag kid's head off my driving shoulder, with little shrugs. I nudge him toward Donny, but his head comes rolling right back, moaning to himself. It is a strange dash-lit comedy. And somewhere out on the rushing plains of the Panhandle, I start hallucinating. Maybe it's the two bennies I dropped a while back, I don't know. Things flicker in the stinging corners of my eyes. Roads appear out of nowhere veering into nowhere, mirages glimmer in the windy darkness, postcard lakes, high country fir, a roadside carnival all eerie and abandoned. Ignoring this shit as best I can, I twist the radio dial searching for anything other than the awful country-western twang, hoping for the Wolfman booming up from Juarez, but they must be jamming him out here in this redneck desolation. Finally, I settle on a deranged preacher coming out of Tulsa, shrilly predicting the End of the World as we know it, Russian Armageddon, God's wrath coming down on the plague of moral turpitude and dope-fiend youth about to be sucked into Perdition in order to cleanse the slate for the new Kingdom of Jesus. He's insane and ridiculous, I snap him off. Fuck all these conniving religious bastards. The road is a black ribbon unfurling in my single good headlight, wind whistles in my ears, I am alight, I know that I am glory-bound.

My companions stir awake every now and then, mumble some shit, spark a pin-roll, guzzle a beer. They're sharing beers now, tossing the cans out, then nodding back out. Donny pleads with me to pull over so he can stretch out on some roadside grass, unroll his sleeping bag, sleep, ease his back. He is without shame, lazy and delusional.

"There is no grass out there, man," I tell him. "Only snakes and rocks and scorpions. You wanna lie down in that?" He gives me a morose, pathetic look and swoons away. Fuck him too.

All night, in love with the infinite darkness, I drive into the mesmerizing country of night. The only pit stops are for gas, cardboard cups of scalding coffee, and cigs. We stumble to the urinal, stretch our numb bodies, then I push us back onto 66 into a stiff and rising wind. I've become obsessed with the idea of getting to Los Angeles non-stop. Because dig, we're running low on cash and if anything goes wrong out here we're royally screwed. We've got tools in the trunk but no extra money for parts. It's now or never, so I push the small block Chevy for all it's worth, the hotrod pipes rapping behind me, the trailer rocking in the buffeting cross-winds. Except for the random car or truck going the other way, we are alone on this two-lane starlit highway, road to the promised land, jackrabbits darting off in my cocked headlight, the fleeting gore of roadkill, or a hell-bound semi almost bowling us off the pavement.

Crossing into New Mexico, the yellow and red sign, I find myself boring into a strong windblown rain, right into the most fierce lightning storm I've ever known. The black sky crackles and rips with blue-white slashes, exploding over the terrain. The radio mutters in static, rain beats on my windshield—glimpses of barren hills and flash-flood arroyos being drowned in the kind of rain that almost drowned Noah. Horizontal sheets of rain that slows me down to fifty miles per hour, then to forty, windshield wipers batting on the fogging glass. Zonked out, Donny and Malcolm don't wake up. I am alone inn this immense, flash-lit, rain-pounding night, alone, aquatic headlights, the only moving creature in conscious migration. I can barely make out the real road from the phantom roads veering off into the rain-swept darkness, beckoning me. The dew rag kid talks in his sleep, Donny mumbles back, lost in the their dreams. Zen quicksilver, I am the one that Nietzsche spoke of.

Somewhere out on the high and lonesome, in the mountains east of Albuquerque, knuckling the wheel, blinking myself awake, rain hammering the car, praying that my trailer doesn't flip, the fierce apparition rises up before me. A gaunt old man rises up on the right shoulder of the road, glaring at me, a long stout staff raised above his head, the night-wind tearing at his white-robed body, at his long white beard and madman's hair.

Gaping in astonishment, dabbing the brakes, trying to not skid, I croak, "Donny, fuck Donny, get a load of this! Wake up, man, hey wake up!"

The tall old prophet steps forward into my cock-eyed headlight, menacing his staff, his raving eyes boring into mine. "You crazy old fuck!" I scream, mashing the brakes in a desperate attempt to not run him over.

"No fool, go back, go back fool!" the prophet bellows as I skid past. His staff comes crashing down on my hood like a sledge hammer. The violent blow jolts Kubiak out of his stupor, yelping, "Hey what the fuck man, hey, hey, what? What?"

The Chevy coupe hydroplanes sideways across the slick pavement, the trailer starting to jackknife behind me and I'm thinking we're shit out of luck, we're done for. But somehow, dabbing the brakes and reversing the wheel, me frantic, the rig straightens out and slides down the road. We come to a stop way over on the wrong-side shoulder, trailer angled into the oncoming lane. But even in this blinding rain I see that nothing's coming, no headlights, nothing's out here, except us and the insane old man.

"Damn, goddamn," Donny mumbles, his eyes swollen, "what was it?" He's braced against the dash and the door, trying to push a conked-out Malcolm off his shoulder.

"Fuck if I know, Donny," I pant, "but some really weird shit just came down. Some crazy old coot leaped out in the road beating on the hood with a big stick."

"What? What, are you serious? Beating on the car? Out in this rain?"

"Yeah, dig it. Some crazy bastard slamming the car, with wild white hair and crazy eyes."

"Jesus H Christ, is that what I saw? I thought I saw something too!"

With a low moan the dew-rag kid collapses into Donny's lap, done in by his own evil weed. Donny jerks back, pushing on Malcolm. "Aggh, get the motherfucker off me, get him off!"

"Listen to me," I blurt, words tumbling out, "some bizarre old man in a white robe and wild hair jumped out in the rain and smashed down on the hood of the car. He was bellowing at me, telling me to go back, 'go back, fool, go back!'"

Donny pushes Malcolm into a heap between us, saying, "You flipped your gourd, Jake? An old man out in this storm? Man, you gotta be seeing things."

"No, you heard the blow yourself, it woke you up. Some crazy hermit leaped out and almost put us into the ditch."

"Fuck man, show me."

We scramble from the car with the engine running, lights on, wipers still flapping. We stand in the pelting rain and peer back down the ink-stained highway. But the lunatic prophet has vanished. But when I point to the serious dent in the hood, Kubiak's eyes go wide. I point at the steep ditchbank where we almost skidded off to our doom.

"Holy fuck," Donny mutters, drenched and shivering. "If a big truck comes barreling through here, we'll be dogmeat. We gotta get back in the other lane."

"Yeah, you're right," I say, trembling. "But I can really use some relief driving now, man. It's getting too weird. I need some shut-eye."

Kubiak ducks his square blond head, a gesture I know too well. He always ducks like that when he wants to escape something. He goes to the center stripe and helps me get the car back on the right side. But then he cops out on me. He's too bombed, he complains, too exhausted to drive. Chug-a-lugging another can of beer, he nods out again, the dew rag kid contorted between us. Through all this shit, Malcolm has either stayed asleep or pretended to be asleep, not wanting to deal with out-of-their minds white cats.

I drive on into the howling night with sand-blasted nerves, through the wind-torn canyons at forty miles an hour, grim and determined. My cock-eyed headlight illuminates a rainy sequence of red rectangular signs—*The Man / Who Passes / On Hills / And Curves / Is Not A Man / Of Iron Nerves / He's Crazy / Burma Shave.* Oh yeah, fuck yeah, I think, laughing, the ragged laughter of a man who has cheated death or whatever it was out there, cheated the mad old prophet of his pound of mangled flesh.

Finally, rain letting up, we come down out of the windy, desert mountains. On the outskirts of Albuquerque, I pull into an all-night filling station, get out and stretch, fill the tank. Donny rouses himself, climbs out, hands me a few bucks toward the gas.

"Listen man," I tell him, "I'm burned to the quick. I've gotta catch some zees. You need to drive for awhile."

Donny stuffs his hands in his pockets, slouching in the neon light. "Shit, professor, I'm bushed too. Those wicked pin-rolls are a knock-out pill. Why can't we just rest and sleep till daylight?"

"You're bushed? Bullshit. You been passed out half the fucking night! We've still got a long ways to go and we're running low on money. What's wrong with you?"

"But I'm wasted, I don't feel right. My stomach's all messed up."

"Fuck you, Donny. You're gonna drive."

Malcolm thrusts his puffy face out the window, saying, "Hey Jake, my man, I'll drive. I'm a real good driver, lemme drive."

I consider that idea for a brief second or two, but no. I'm not going to trust my car, my trailer and motorcycle to a hitch-hiking stranger. As insufferably lazy as Kubiak is, at least I know he can drive.

"Thanks anyway, Malcolm. I appreciate it, but this rig is tricky." Fixing Donny with a hard look, I say, "Get behind the wheel, man. It's your turn."

He bitches, but complies, and soon we're back on the road. To the rumble of the pipes I plunge into a river of sleep, vaguely aware of their voices, then zone out. I float like a cork, then slumber deep. But in that river bottom of flickering images, I know intuitively that something isn't right, something keeps harping at me.

COMING AWAKE, NOT sure when or where at first, I realize the motor has stopped. Opening my eyes to early daylight, I notice that we've pulled off onto a flat gravel patch. As far as you can see, there's red clay desert studded with stunted shrubs, rocks, cactus, sagebrush, and table-top buttes in the distance. It reminds me of a technicolor John Wayne western. Someone lives out in that formidable landscape, or something, amazing as it seems.

I reach for a cigarette. The dew-rag kid says in my ear, "I think we started blowing smoke out the back tailpipe."

For a second his words don't register. Donny's hunched over the steering wheel, his red, sodden eyes peering at me. "Professor," he mumbles, "I'm done in. My back's killing me."

It's almost hilarious, almost, and I ask, "How long have I been out?"

"I dunno. Hours probably. I think we burned a valve. And I gotta crash, sorry."

"Yeah, you look like a stomped frog, Donny," I say, lighting up. "Come on, let's switch."

Feeling refreshed, actually pretty good, I take off due west across that stark desert painted in the colors of a mythical sunrise. Trailing behind us is a long plume of dark oily smoke, for sure, we've blown a valve. My wounded Chevy's down to only seven cylinders now, really straining. I wonder if Donny was floor-boarding the gas pedal to show off. He's already caved back into his narcoleptic swoon, or faking it. The dew rag kid fidgets beside me.

Without looking my way, Malcolm says, "You think we gonna make it,

Jake?"

I give him a sideways look. I this brave black kid with his pocked face from Chicago's underbelly. "I don't know, man," I reply, "but I'll tell you what. We're sure the fuck gonna make a run for it."

Nodding, we share a rueful laugh. "Yeah, that's it," Malcolm grins, "we rolling the dice. We gonna make it. We gonna make it."

Truth is, I do feel optimistic. We've crossed into Arizona, traversing the barren plateau toward Flagstaff, mesas and buttes breaking up the far skyline. There are more mountains up ahead, the roadmap says so. I hope like hell my dilapidated Belair V-7 can make it all the way to the California coast. Because in Los Angeles we'll find some refuge, if we can just get there. The dew-rag kid rides beside me, rubbing shoulders, at ease now, no longer rapping his jivester rhymes. Kubiak's face mashes against the smeared side window, he snoring. I've never known anyone who can sleep like Donny.

Keeping the car at a steady fifty, I drive across the rolling prairie and stop in Flagstaff for gas. Then, as we drop down through the hoodoo rock formations around Williamsburg, an Arizona state patrol car flashes me over. Fuck, we're pouring black smoke out the tailpipe, empty beer cans on the floorboards, ugly little roaches litter the ashtray. Fuck, how bad can this day get?

"I'm going back and talk to the cop," I tell them. "Play it cool. Kick those cans out of sight and gobble those roaches."

I walk back with a weary, bloodshot smile, ignoring the hoots from a passing pickup. Studying my driver's license, the highway cop observes, "Chicago. All three of you coming from there?"

"Yes sir," I reply, looking into his mirrored aviator shades. "All of us. We're heading on out to L.A."

Frowning at the wooden trailer, he says, "L. A., huh, riff-raff central. Well, the brake lights on that contraption aren't working, in case you don't know. And you have been polluting Arizona highways with that damned car since at least the New Mexico border. That's illegal here."

"Yes sir, I'm sorry about that. We blew a cylinder a ways back. The brake lights must've gone out when I went through a really bad thunder storm last night."

"I see. Well, tell me, do you suppose that jalopy will make it into California without breaking down?"

His tone is caustic and I can't read his eyes behind the shades. Why do cops have to be such robot assholes? I say, "Yeah, I'm pretty sure it will. At least that's my honest plan."

"All right, then, I'm not going to write you up. I'm going to let you slide on those taillights. But I want you the hell out of my state asap, don't stop, just keep on going. And that refugee you got in the middle? The one with the red rag on his head? Make damned sure you don't leave him anywhere in Arizona. And that's all I've got to say to you."

Stunned, almost tripping over my tongue, I say, "But gas, we're gonna have to stop for gas, use the bathrooms. I mean, man, we've got to do the basic things."

"You do that. You do the basic things. Then you keep right on rolling."

CHEWING ON A voiceless rage, I drop into the blistering heat of the Colorado River basin, making for a town called Needles. I tell dew-rag Malcolm and Donny what the cop said and we ride in a heavy silence for several miles.

"It's my black ass they hate," Malcolm speaks up. "They'd shoot me if they got the chance. They would."

"I hear you, yeah," I say, "but it's not just you, it's all of us, together. Because change is happening so fast in their straight-laced world and they're scared shitless of it. They don't want change to happen, but there's nothing they can do to stop it."

"You a righteous man, Jake," Malcolm replies.

"He says it like it is, he always does," Donny kicks in, staring through the bug-spattered windshield. "Yeah, they hate the fact that you're a cocky arrogant Negro, yeah, they hate that. But the truth is the bastards hate anything they can't control."

Donny hawks a lugie out his window, then adds, "They want everybody to act alike, think alike, dress alike, and if you don't go along you're on their shit-list."

"Oh I hear what you saying, oh believe me, I do. I know it first-hand."

"They're filthy fucking pigs to the core, almost all of them. And I hope they drown in their own shit. I can't stand cops."

Flabbergasted to hear such words come from my apathetic partner, for a few seconds I'm speechless. Then we all burst out laughing. The laughter breaks up the heavy mood, we feel a little better, we push on.

Nursing my oil-belching Chevy into the sweltering Colorado River canyon, I wonder if I'll make it back up the other side. But at Needles we pass through the state checkpoint, add two quarts of recycled oil, and take a free breath of California desert air. Maybe, just maybe we've got a decent chance.

Late in the afternoon, we limp into the Los Angeles basin on a freeway choked with cars smothered in a dense and drifting smog. A long rope of black smoke trails out behind me and up ahead huge plumes of smoke tower above southwest Los Angeles. The radio reports that Watts is going up in flames, Watts is burning. We stare at the lurid sky in awe, the three of us, on this August day, 1965. It seems like the whole world is being torn apart by fire and hatred.

"Where you want me to take you, Malcolm?"

"You can drop me anywhere, don't matter. You done your share, man. You got me here like you said you would."

"No, tell me where, man. We've come all the way across 66 together, tell me where you need to go."

"Oh, okay, if you put it that way," Malcolm laughs. "Drive over toward all that smoke, only don't drive too close."

"All right, you got it. Donny, what the hell's that weird noise?"

"Sounds like the tires," Donny says, hunkered down. "Sounds like those retreads are flapping. We're falling apart."

Getting off the freeway, we navigate the cross streets for several miles, until we hit Compton Boulevard. And people of all colors are standing around on the corners, shielding their eyes, talking, pointing at the blazing inferno in the near distance. The drifting, acrid haze stings our nostrils and burns our eyes.

"Jake, say Jake, stop here," the dew rag kid says, pulling my arm. "You don't need to be going any closer, I know where I am."

"He's right, man," Donny mutters, "this is a bad fucking scene."

"You sure, Malcolm?" I ask, my face taut as leather.

"I'm sure. Drop me here, it's cool. I can make it to my sister's from here."

I pull over to the curb, with sirens wailing near and far, I pull over and let the clacking engine run. We all clasp hands in a passionate affirmation, without words, knowing we have done something off the charts. Donny tugs Malcolm's duffel out of the backseat, wishes him good luck. The skinny black kid moseys around to my window, his red dew rag askew. We have been on the road together for two and a half days, we have crossed enemy territory.

Grinning, Malcolm takes my hand. "You a righteous man," he tells me in a hoarse voice. "Jake, if I never see you again, Jake, I'll always remember. Thank you, man, thank you."

"Thank you too, my brother," I say, meaning it, "just for being who you are. Take good care, and don't let 'em run you down."

"I hear that, yes I do! And maybe we be seeing you in the congregation one of these days? Maybe we be seeing each other on that other bus." Grinning, he shoulders his duffle bag and strides across Compton towards a destiny unknown to me.

DRIVING ON TOWARD the ocean, into fresher air, Donny and I made it into Santa Monica that day, the sun smoldering in a sky of burned-out cinders. We felt drained, excited, and grateful. I knew that my parents would put us up for a week or so in their Santa Monica house, and Donny was already itching to fly back home and finagle extra cash. On Olympic Boulevard, gasoline was only nineteen cents a gallon, I filled up the tank for a measly few dollars. We had covered two thousand hallucinatory miles on route 66 and landed in L. A. with two dollars and thirty nine cents left in our pockets. I never doubted for a single minute that we couldn't do it.

A few days later, our bikes unloaded and the trailer hustled off for fifty bucks, I brought my '55 Chevy Belair to an abrupt stop at an intersection and the right front end collapsed. Kubiak looked under the car and told me the A-frame had snapped. So we made it by the skin of our teeth, and all I could do was laugh. I sold my battered hotrod for a hundred dollars cash for parts and salvage. That gave me just enough bread to get my 600cc English Matchless up and running, running free in the California sunshine.

# **Chapter 15**

T HINKING BACK ON that wild cross-country ride, I grin at my reflection in the mirror. But out here in this foggy night, on this pot-holed Baja highway, all that seems like another life. And it was another life—a life before psychedelics. Except that once again Donny is conked out in a stupor, and I'm doing the driving. Crash Keith slumps beside him in the backseat, his fleshy, unshaven face bristling with sweat. The moon has risen above the fog, an amorphous glow drifting in the sea clouds. We've come a good distance from the honeymoon cottage crime-scene.

I slide out the door and stretch, looking to see where Dawn has wandered off. She's standing about a hundred feet up the deserted road, in a nimbus of strange light. She seems be faintly illumined, dressed all in black and talking to someone, except nobody else is there.

I walk up to within a few feet of her, then ask, "You all right, baby?"

Looking at me, she hugs herself. "Yeah, I'm okay. I'm fine."

"Who were you talking to?"

"My grandmother. She was just here."

Far out, I nod slowly, once or twice. "Your grandmother? But she's already gone, she died, right?"

"Yeah. She passed away on the Black River Reservation last summer. But that doesn't mean she can't come and visit. She always comes and talks, especially when I'm feeling blue."

"Okay, I understand." I'm really into this chick, so I groove with it.

Dawn comes closer to me, hugging herself. She studies my eyes, looks toward the sound of surf off in the misting darkness. "Your eyes, Jake Acree" she murmurs, "you've got such green eyes. Got a smoke for me?"

I fish one out for her, light it by thumbing a cardboard book match. Smiling, I ask, "So what does your grandma say about this trip?"

"I told her about you, about how you make me feel. And that sometimes it frightens me."

Lighting an Old Gold for myself, I inhale. "And what did she tell you?"

"She says that you're wild, but you have a good heart, and you need my help."

A little surprised, I laugh, "Oh, is that so? She said all of that?"

Dawn gives me a mischievous smile, then leans against me. Looking back at the car, she says, "Are those two flakes still asleep?"

"Oh yeah, they are. Stoned out of their skulls."

"They hate it how we took up together."

"Hmmm, too fucking bad."

"Keith wants to make a big show down here. You know that, right?"

"Whatever. It's his stolen money we're traveling on. But he's got to know what's what."

She kisses me, cradled in my arms. "I'm feeling really sort of tired, Jake. Can we just go hideout in a hotel somewhere?"

"Yeah, we're gonna do that." Taking her hand in mine, we walk back. "Let's just follow this road until we find a good spot."

At Rosarita Beach, we come across an older motel for about ten dollars a day, eight bungalows lined up in a row towards the long sandy beach. A low reef of fog sits off-shore, the summer gloom. Morning breaks with overcast skies, only the weakest sunlight filters through the haze. It's not what we had been envisioning—even the beach has a dull sheen. But we hang out on the sand shingle drinking Carte Blancas boosted with amber shots of tequila. Inside our bungalow, we smoke fat joints and eat soft spicy tacos from a cart vendor, listening to the loud Mariachi and poignant Norteno musica on the plastic radio. This cabin has only one large room and a bath, the other seven bungalows were already reserved. So it was take it or leave it, and we needed to get off the road. We have two double beds and two folding cots, and things feel decidedly awkward. We're all ripped on Tijuana Dexedrine caps and at least half-drunk. There's half a lid of grass tucked in my boot, and fat Keith brought along the acid I sold him. Not that anyone's raising their hand for psychedelics at the moment. Tension pervades the air like a spark.

Keith hops around in a buzzed, desperado mode. "Hey," he announces to no one in particular, "just for the record, I never go down without a hard fight. I'm ready for a fucking fight anytime."

Dawn gives me an edgy look, but I already know anything could happen here. I need to keep on toes and my wits about me.

Taking a slug from the tequila bottle, Keith croaks, "Where can I buy a pistola around here? I want to get me a Mexican Saturday Night Special."

"You can't," I tell him. "Pistols are illegal to own in Mexico, unless you're the law."

"Well, fuck these spics," he snorts, "I don't have to play by their rules."

He's an asshole, there's no other way to call it. Even Donny seems subdued, careful with his hipster pranks. Licking at the bad vibes, he keeps up a running banter, blue eyes darting around, cracking atrocious jokes, racial slurs Benzedrine hotrods, Triumph Bonnie versus BSA Lightning, why everything is backwards but we just don't know it yet. We give him a few yucks, but for the most part shine him on. Keith and I bore into each other's head without words. The real prize here is the dark-eyed, sultry, half-breed chick and he figures he's still got a shot. One of us might end up face-down in the Mexican dirt.

Dawn tries to break the tension by leading us down to the beach, to the placid surf, to the distant pewter horizon. Agitated and buzzed, Keith yammers for attention like a hirsute ape. He goes with Dawn on a hobbling walk down the beach, pleading his case, gesturing in the air. She gives me a signal to let it happen, so I don't interfere. They walk a ways off. Keith makes his desperate pitch. She keeps her head down, every now and then stooping to pick up a seashell, a polished stone. My guts feel like they're being twisted inside out, knowing something's got to give. She hasn't so much as kissed me since we arrived in this forlorn place.

But later, with night falling, on the porch steps, she comes and cozies beside me. Keith and Donny are inside whooping it up on cheap mescal and raucous Mariachis. Mist veils the palms, the warmth of her body steals into me.

"I hate this speed, baby" I tell her "It makes my skin crawl. I'm not taking anymore."

"Me too, it makes me feel like I'm not me, like I'm somebody else."

"Yeah, dig it, speed is bad, speed is for losers, speed kills."

She's quiet, then says, "Jake, tell me something. Tell me what you really want?"

"What I really want? I already told you. You. I want you."

"But what does that really mean? You want all of me, my whole life? Or just the part of me you like?"

Whoa. Knowing that Keith was yammering in her ear, I take a swallow of my beer. She nudges me, wanting an answer. "I just want you, Dawn. It's simple for me."

"But just me on your terms? Is that question too hard for you?"

"No, it means just what it means. I'm in love with you. I'm here, right now, with you in Mexico. I'm here for us. Because of the way we are together—if we ever get that chance again."

Leaning away, she clasps her knees. "I hear what you're saying and I feel that too. You know I do. But I'm also thinking about other things."

I don't really want to hear about the other things. I just want to get her into bed, nubile, wanton, and naked, and eat her alive, with no blustering idiots around.

"You and me," I murmur in her ear, lifting her hair and licking her nape, feeling her shiver. She yields with a soft moan, then slips away from me and stands up.

One arm akimbo, Dawn gives me a moody look. "You really get under my skin, Jake, it's true. But you're not really offering all that much, you know?"

Taken aback, I stammer, "What the fuck does that mean? I'm offering you me."

She crosses her arms, looking off toward the muted boom of the surf. The rising moon is a lambent glow in the misting night. The Mariachis wail through the window blinds.

"Dawn?"

"Never mind," she sighs. "It's just me being stupid and dumb. Wishing for stuff that probably can't even ever happen."

"Ah, okay, mind telling me like what?"

"Nope, not now, Jake. I just need to go take a walk and get my head together."

And with those words, she turns and heads down toward the beach on the dim path, doesn't even glance back. Going off to do what, converse with her ethereal grandmother? It hits me hard that I could be losing her, chewing my lip, nothing has been promised. I could be left sitting in an empty room, holding the loser's bag and I hate to lose. I don't really hate anyone, I'm into peaceful vibes, I fight only when pushed. But I hate to lose. And my feelings for her are far too possessive to hide.

Inside, above the raucous music, Keith's deranged laughter splits the air. This Rosarita Beach trip is going off the tracks. The Tijuana speed, all the cheap booze, no sleep at all, we're already singed to the marrow. This could turn into a very bad scene, seems to me. But I notice that the cabin next door is empty now, the Mexican love-birds have left. Most likely the wild-eyed, gringo borrachitos drove them away.

The door is unlocked. I go inside and sit in the dark room, smoking Mexican cigarettes, trying to get my head straight. I pride myself on knowing what I'm doing, and on doing things that I intend. When you do that, you've got your act together. But I don't like uncertainties hammering inside my head that don't have a definite answer. And the answer, whatever the fuck the answer is, has her eyes and lips, her voice and midnight hair, her intoxicating scent and essence, that much I know.

When morning comes to the fog-bound coast, I make it clear to the maid that I'm staying in the new cabin and to let the proprietor know. "Si, si senor, entiendo," she murmurs, scurrying away. I know I probably look like hell warmed over. During the hollow spaces of the night I managed to catch a few hours of fitful sleep, then awoke to the damp gray light, took a long piss, grateful that the amphetamine is working out of my system. I feel loneliness as keen as a knife blade between my ribs.

Going outside, half-naked and shivering, I sit on the porch steps and smoke. The faint sun hardly penetrates the pewter-gray haze. This weather has apparently driven the other beach goers away. The courtyard feels empty and abandoned. Donny's dull blue Ford is the only car in sight. Fuchsia bougainvillea runs up the cracked walls like an errant paint stoke. I have lost track of the others, no one seems to be at home next door. I trudge up to the manager's cabin and trade a few American filter tips for a cup of strong Mexican coffee. The innkeeper is a thin, stooped man, with a Chaplin mustache and moist eyes. He lights up one of the smokes, I count out some cash for the extra cabin, he smiles at me with stained teeth.

"Senor, it is all okay," he says, shrugging. "You scare the maid but I know you are simpático. You keep your head about you. But por favor, no let the other two hombres wreck mi motel."

I assure him that I won't let the pendejos bust anything up, shake his slight hand, then take my java mug back to my cabin. Hunkering down, I sip the delicious black coffee and smoke, gathering my thoughts. I'm smoking again, but on acid I don't have the slightest desire to smoke. I lose all interest in the coffin nails and in liquor and that says something interesting about psychedelics. Feeling somewhat better, I go outside and gaze at the gradually clearing sky. This old beach motel has begun to feel like a movie-set, or maybe just a set-up period.

Dawn comes up the path from the ocean, alone. She sees me, she gives me a smiling wave and skips like a girl. My heart gives a skip too, a sudden bird of hope.

She comes up and hugs me, pressing her body close to mine. She smells impossibly good and fresh. Gazing into my bloodshot eyes, she says, "I need to be alone with you, mister. Can we go inside?"

"Sure, why not? This is my new private cabin."

"I kinda figured."

I glance past her down the path, to see if peg-leg Keith is lurking anywhere around.

"Don't worry," she laughs softly, "he won't bother us. Trust me."

We go inside, lock the door, and draw the slatted blinds. Dawn lies down, folding some pillows beneath her head. She tries to coax me down beside her, but I'm not quite ready. The doubt still hammers in my skull. I pull a wicker chair over and lean in close, caressing her hip, kissing her forehead, her eyelids, her delicious lips. Her breath catches, she regards me with such unabashed desire that I feel almost undone. I've never felt desire like this before, not even close. But I make myself form the nagging question.

Taking her hands, I say, "So what's the story, little girl? Please tell me."

"Little girl?" she smiles. "You see me that way?"

"Sometimes, yes, I see you as an adorable young girl. Ready to lose herself in a wild new dream."

"Are you sure you're not just being wishful?" she teases, but slides beneath me, looking up into my eyes. She moves my hand to her warm breast. "Keith says that I'm a manipulator."

"Fuck Keith. I'll beat him over the head with his own wooden stump." Lowering my voice, I say, "You're beautiful and holy in my eyes, and I find you irresistibly desirable."

I am aware that I've never spoken such words to anyone before in my life.

Her lithe body stirs under me, she blushes. "In your eyes," she murmurs, her voice hushed.

"Si, en mis ojos," I whisper, dropping like a falcon to her yearning lips. My body trembles with racing lust and she is the only cure. But I draw back and say, "I feel like I'm hanging out in the air, Dawn. What's going on?"

Holding me with her dark, angel eyes, she says in a rush, "Nothing's in our way. This is about you and me. I told Keith no, I'm not going back to Joliet and play house with him. I'm in love with you, I told him so."

A rush of pure joy floods my chest. I pull her to me, a jaguar with his quivering prey, my heart snared in her eyes, intent on consuming her, in one fervent motion she meets me, devouring my mouth with lips, undoing my belt with her deft hands. "Now make love with me, Jake Acree," she says. "I need you. I want you to fuck me."

In a rush we shed our clothes, her tiny panties and bra, my jeans and shorts, her luscious breasts, my feverish cock springing free and urgent. She takes me deep into her magical mouth, naked, her black hair falling, then she is on me whimpering and passionate, we move, plunging into that primordial wellspring that washes away all worry and doubt.


THERE'S NO NEED to spell anything out, because the deal is done, no apologies needed. We gather ourselves together to leave Rosarita Beach under a benign sun that finally burns off the morbid haze. I take half a case of the revolting Cold Duck up to the innkeeper's office and ring his brass hand-bell. The slight, elfish man comes through the bead curtain, his mustache gleaming with wax. "Ah, what is this?" he asks me, with a quizzical smile.

"My gift to you, señor, mine and hers, for putting up with us. We did not break anything. And my apologies for all the noise and the mess."

"De nada, mi joven amigo," he says, hefting one bottle, studying the label. "Quack, quack? It is good? Esta bien?"

Shrugging, I say, "Depends on what you like, I guess."

"Si, that is always the way, no?. We like what we like, sometimes even if it kills us."

"Hah, I hope that is not the outcome for any of us," I laugh, shaking his hand.

"Me too," he agrees, arching his eyebrow. "But tell me – which one of you muchachos won the dark-haired muchacha? She is really something special."

"Looks like I did, at least I think so. That's why we came down here, to figure that."

"Claro, my money was always on you, I saw how she looked at you when you first checked in. And I hope you will come back to see us. Mexico will always treat you well, I think."

Pausing at the door, I say, "Con muchas gracias, señor. I'm sure that I'll be back."


BEFORE CROSSING OVER the border into California we make a stop at a Tijuana farmacia for hangover medicine. Keith hobbles inside and returns clutching a vial of seconals. He and Donny gulp a couple of reds without a moment's hesitation, eager to knock themselves out for the trip home. They're both burned to a crisp, and have no desire to deal with their rueful hand of cards.

Looking at Kubiak in the rearview, I say, "Man, I don't want to drive that through the checkpoint with those reds. Not worth the gamble."

Donny frowns, "Hell, you carried across some weed in your boot coming down here."

"They never check coming down here. It's when you're going back where you have the problems."

Donny flicks his baby-blue eyes at Dawn, then shrugs the hassle off to

Keith. Keith gives me a very sullen stare. I start to turn around but she intercedes, cajoling him, "Come on cowboy, just hand your dope over to me. You know I'm always your best bet."

Reluctantly, Keith hands her the vial. She presses Donny for his last few dexies. Turning the key in the ignition, hoping that she and I are on the same page, I give the boisterous 429 a couple of foot-taps.

Donny says, with a lewd twist, "Where you gonna stash that dope, Dawn baby?"

"Right here," she laughs, flashing her eyes at me, tossing the dummy's stash out the window into the gutter. I gun the gas-sucking Ford hotrod into the border-town traffic before anyone can so much as blink.

# Chapter 16

 ACK IN THE city of fallen angels, we move into our own pad over in East Hollywood. The garden-court apartment is friendly and private, there are no landladies We have a sheltered backyard that blooms with hibiscus, morning glory and passion flower climbs the brick wall. The alley gate lets me wheel my bikes in and out of the yard. We buy a stereophonic radio to go along with my hi-fidelity turntable and stacks of records. The Loving Spoonful croons about being lost and found in a daydream, and yeah, we roll and toke our daily manna, we're right where we want to be.

Crash Keith takes the train back to Chicago with one hundred hits of Laguna Beach acid and vanishes from our world. Donny receives money from his mom, makes good with me, then flies back to Chicago to try to persuade her to buy him a Triumph Bonneville. He leaves his 429 Ford in my keeping, telling me he'll be back soon with a new bike and a girl named Mindy. I know Mindy, in fact I introduced her to Donny about a year ago. She's a pretty young chick with curly brown hair and trusting eyes, who always dresses in short black skirts, beatnik stockings and berets. Donny began drooling for her at first sight, and to my surprise she went for him too. Somehow or other, she confused him with someone out of a Kerouac novel.

"Two or three weeks at the most, professor, then I'm back," he says. "She's of legal age now. We're all going riding together, Topanga, up in the canyons, be ready to have a blast!"

Donny's far too devoted to rock and roll and getting high to bother holding any grudges, I dig that about him. But I'm so immersed in the moment with Dawn, I'm not making any promises. Every thing that happens, happens now, and now is always happening. We Gotta Get Out of This Place, the Animals ry, and she and I are so wildly in love with being in love that everything else fades. We're riding a swift, acid-blown, motorcycle romance through the Santa Paula orange groves, the secret byways of Griffith Park, the windy sunsets of the Malibu coast with our hair and Mexican ponchos flying, smitten to the core with unfettered happiness. There's no separating us, and we're making it up as we go. All that happens, happens now.

Dawn has lots of bright, restless energy. Reminding me of how her grandmother said she's supposed to help me, she lands a job as a barmaid four day-shifts a week at a beer joint over on La Brea. It's an inconspicuous little joint, the poseur studs hanging around want to fuck her, she makes tips by the handful and brings the money home to me. Not digging the bar scene, I stay away except to pick her up on my bike in the late afternoons. For my own part, I sell my deluxe acid to an expanding group of connoisseurs, along with the occasional half-pound of Michoacán pot. My Laguna Beach connection is solid, there's always more. Lsd has refined my senses to such an extent that I've stopped smoking cigarettes altogether and seem to be losing my taste for certain foods. It's not a bummer, it's just inexplicable.

The only demon dogging my days is the ruthless escalation of the Vietnam War. Kubiak can laugh it off, his one bad kidney has bailed him out, but I'm prime fodder. I've followed the steps in the blue Conscientious Objector's handbook for over a year now. I'm doing everything I can to thwart the intentions of those murderous bastards. I've written a series of appeals to the Selective Service System requesting that the draft board reclassify me on ethical and spiritual grounds. Yeah, I know I can bail-out with a student deferment or get married and sidestep it that way. But I'm not trying to run a scam on the draft board, I'm dead serious about my moral convictions. Vietnam is a ruthless, military scheme of aggression that only benefit's the military-industrial complex and its political hucksters, fuck, I know that, anybody with half a brain does. To gain their imperialistic ends, the power-brokers will slaughter tens of thousands of young soldiers and civilians without remorse. They'll bomb southeast Asia into oblivion. Masters of War, Dylan called them, the most traitorous bastards on earth.

In my letters to the Department of Justice, I've included several pages of my shimmering, hallucinogenic poems. Life is sacred, life is miraculous, life must be revered. War is the greatest crime afflicted on humanity. I know these poems are mostly incomprehensible to the squares and suits, but it's better they think me mad. No one wants a whacked-out acid-freak passing out psychedelics in the barracks. Their dreary universe of Mr. Jones phobias has nothing to do with me. I take an impassioned vow to do everything in my power to bring war to an end on our beloved planet. Fuck your wars, fuck your theories of war, fuck your rationalizations, fuck your criminal draft, and fuck your bogus authority over my life. You are the worn-out anachronism, not me. My ongoing conflict with the United States Government is my personal guerrilla war.

AND WHEN YOU get right down to what doesn't get said, there's always a bummer lurking around. Dawn's private heartache is another kind of bugaboo altogether. She misses her three year old son big-time, she's feeling real guilty about staying away. I don't indulge in guilt myself, so anything I say about the situation is moot. Her once-a-week pay phone call back to Illinois isn't cutting it. She keeps it to herself but I can hear the conversation in my head. When is mommy coming home? When is your vacation gonna end, runaway mother? Dawn might consider what she's doing as a kind of wild lark, but for me it's a way of life. She knows I have zero interest in mundane, domestic lifestyles, or in raising kids, I have been completely honest and up-front. No babies. I'm not into having any babies. Okay, all right, she laughs, I'm good with that, no more for me either! But she's so nonchalant about taking her birth control pills it worries me, and neither one of us like to use rubbers.

"Don't worry," she tells me, "I can't even have another kid. The doctor said it's not possible, that I'll miscarry every time. Something about my the shape of uterus."

This is a total mystery to me, I admit. I'm thinking it sounds too good to be true. "Are you positive, Dawn?"

"Yes," she murmurs, caressing my swollen cock. "Hmm, just trust me."

"Ahhh," I gasp, "what about an IUD?"

"No, I tried that, it hurts. Just hush, I won't get knocked up. Besides, you know how much I love going down on you."

So I take her on her word, this captivating, delectable woman-child. I fill her with my ardent sperm, her delicious pussy and avid mouth, and she brings home to me all her money except for the portion she sends back to Joliet. I never even ask, she just hands it to me with a girlish flirt. Afternoon sunlight pours through the French Door window panes, the bees hum in ecstasy at the passion flower vines, we are so much in love that we almost feel like thieves. We sidestep most of the downers with ease, but no, not always, not always.

Because there are down days that shadow us, those fatiguing days, when that other world creeps in. She doesn't like to talk about it but an acid-head can't lie to another acid-head, acid is the ultimate truth serum. She feels that gnawing guilt about her boy, even though he's safe with her mom. And her morose mood seeps into me through a kind of psychic osmosis, trying to steal our happiness. The only way to escape is to stay laughingly high and Dawn is always game, she's insouciant by nature. We drop acid, take one of the bikes out, and blow away the prosaic shit. Let people point fingers, who cares, who really cares anyway? Stay in the here and now, be here with me, I'll be here with you, and they can never own us.

On Saturdays I ride out to Santa Monica and bring back my younger brother. Evan is still living with our parents and recently dropped out of high school, bored with the conformist crap, at loose ends. But he's a beautiful, intelligent young man, another misfit trying to find his way out of the soul-withering American limbo. I've turned him on to all of Dylan's protest records, Highway 61, Blonde on Blonde, plugged him into Jefferson Airplane, Ravi Shankar, Buffalo Springfield, this radical new music that is our bridge to a new language and a new world, never mind the school books riddled with bullshit because you can't bring forth a new world out based on old lies. I've turned Evan on to good grass, make sure he has his own fat lid and zig-zags, which he hides in his bedroom. Snooping around, sometimes mom finds his dope, flips out and flushes it, hah ha ha. I've told him about the magical mystery trip that lsd confers, shown him my poems, given him books by Watts, Leary, and Huxley, those signposts on the super-conscious, cosmic quest. And Evan gets it, now he has a certain look in his eye. I'm proud of the way we are, I'm in love with the unknown path ahead. Let those who live in fearful ways live in those limitations, we consciously choose another way.

Back at our garden court apartment, Dawn, Evan and I sit around the kitchen table with a flour sifter, deseeding a fresh half pound, drinking beer and rolling wheat-straw bombers. Donny comes over with his girlfriend Mindy, we all get ripped to the eyeballs and laugh the night away with the Stones, Lightning Hopkins or the Animals rocking on the hi-fi. Seized by munchies, Dawn whips together spicy Chorizo and refried beans wrapped in tortillas warmed on the gas stove burner. Life is wild and free, the primordial energy is meant to be spent.

Later, Evan dives into slumber on our used ratty sofa. She and I snuggle together, naked on the Murphy bed in the other room, tantalizing each other. TV doesn't exist for us. We don't waste our time with the boob-tube, we sleep with the windows open to the ageless mystery, to the solitary little bird that never sleeps. The greatest theater in the world plays freely inside our heads. Dawn covers me in kisses, we find ourselves in tender, enthralling pleasure. She slips into dreams with ease, sometimes sleep eludes me. I lie awake, with her cuddled against my chest. I listen to the vast, humming city outside in the night, to the solitary cheeping bird who is my friend and knows me. The arc of my intense obsessions seek their own unknown geographies.

THINGS GET A little strange. I hang multi-colored lawn floodlights on the walls, to conjure moods at night. We don't have a house phone, I won't answer the door because I suspect it might be my former girlfriends, trying to cause us trouble. I find myself growing fanatical about what I eat and drink. Convinced that the tap water has been poisoned with chlorine and fluoride, I insist on using spring water in heavy glass bottles for drinking and cooking, for brewing the strong delicious Turkish coffee that I'm fond of, for brewing green tea or boiling brown rice. Almost overnight, reading certain Zen books, I become obsessed with purifying my blood stream. I forsake the eating of red meat of any kind, banish white bread from my diet, cast out white sugar and candy, and put myself on a regimen of macrobiotic brown rice and steamed root vegetables. For breakfast I resort to whole wheat toast, natural peanut butter, bananas, apples and raisins with a large mug of black coffee. My darling Dawn is miffed that I'm turning down her redolent, spicy chorizo omelets. She thinks I've gone off the psychedelic deep-end, she chides me for dropping too much acid. I have been taking a lot of pure acid, that's true, but the smell of frying meat in hot grease turns my stomach. So I begin to make my own pure food, hoping she'll pick up on the new vibe.

Donny notices this strange rift between us and hoots in derision. He wolfs down dripping cheese burgers right in my face, fried onion rings, or scarfing up one of Dawn's shredded beef-jalapeno burritos that I have declined. My girlfriend and old running partner make mock of me. But something unusual is happening to me and I heed my awakening instincts.

One sunny afternoon up in Griffith Park I'm out riding with Dawn, free-wheeling my thumping Matchless single down a winding hillside road with her tucked on behind me. We glide through the curves and sun-dappled shade, the engine idling in neutral as we descend toward the golf course. I knick the 600cc scrambler into second and ease the clutch out, but the big rear sprocket freezes. The rear knobby goes into a wild slide down the narrow lane, whipping the bike back and forth in mad, skidding sequence—as I trip the compression release, finger the clutch, tap on the shifter—all in vain! The black Brit bike careens down the road like a gyroscope, whipping from side to side with Dawn clinging to me, holy fuck, lunging so far over we almost touch pavement, and she cries in my ear! The bike flips back over as we go into a psychotic slide into the tee intersection, stop sign blurring past, chain link fence dead ahead, totally out of control, out of room, out of time, neon thought flashing in my head, "we're fucked, we're fucked, we're fucked!"

But somehow, in that final instant, the big single cylinder fires to life and throws us into a ninety degree pivot that sends me lurching down the center-stripe of the parallel road to the fence. A green Austin Healey convertible comes racing toward me, horn blaring, the glamorous blond at the wheel screams obscenities as she whizzes past. Dawn clinging to me, hugging me tight, we break into frantic laughter, knowing we barely escaped. Death was in that intersection, waiting for us, but we dodged it.

Then she says in my ear, "Jake, my knee got mashed on the road back there when we went over. It really hurts like hell."

Within the hour her knee swells up to the size of a grapefruit, she can't even walk. I ride over and borrow Donny's car, come back to our place, carry her out, then drive her to County General Hospital. They keep her in bed for a day and a night until the swelling subsides, then put her knee and lower leg in a plaster cast. They give her codeine, a pair of crutches, and tell her to stay off her feet. One more quarter of an inch on the bike lean, the doctor says, and her knee cap would have shattered. I make a silent vow to never free-wheel a single cylinder motorcycle downhill again.

I do all I can to make her comfortable. She stays stoned on weed and codeine, I feed her whatever she wants—machaca burritos, cold beer, guacamole, pizza, chicharrones, Lebanese blonde hash dissolved in sweet Turkish coffee. I help her into the bathroom, help her to shower, take her into the backyard sunshine. I offer to rent a black and white TV, she watches the inane soaps moody and pissed that we don't have a house phone. There's a pay phone down on the corner, but not an easy hobble in her cast.

Frowning, she complains again that I'm dropping too much acid, it's making me weird.

"Hmm, now that's funny. Since when do you have a problem with lsd?"

"I don't, you know I don't. I still dig it. But there's such a thing as too much of a good thing. You ever think we might want to get our heads straight?"

"Get our heads straight? You mean, like in some version of normal? Please, spare me the agony."

We dissolve into giggles, she shakes her head no, no not that. But something keeps hanging in the air, unsaid.

We avoid it, not interested in any strung-out hassles. She flips through her movie star mags or sits in the backyard smoking pot and studying tiny insects in the grass. That's her thing. She still plays with me, she still adores spontaneous sex, she's nubile and flirtatious even in a plaster cast. We almost always have that certain something going on.

That heavy cast comes off and she gimps around on crutches, anxious and restless. She worries and frets about her barmaid job. She wonders if I really love her or do I just keep her around for uninhibited sex? Her tone is sarcastic, I think she's getting hooked on the codeine. These erratic mood shifts are driving me crazy and we end up shouting at each about nothing. Oddly enough, she seems gratified by these skirmishes. She tunes me out, loses herself in her pulp magazines, or scrawling letters to her mother, or doing Ouija board trips with her dead grandma. But I shrug it off and take long, meandering rides on my motorcycles, chasing away the weird vibes.

By the time she can walk again, her easy dayshift job is gone. She bitches that the fat lazy owner give it to a blond who sucked his cock. Within days, she scores another gig over at a biker hang-out on Western and this one runs till past midnight. Suddenly our private groove is gone. This chick is a biker's wet dream, and I'm not feeling good about any of it.

In the midst of all this emotional quicksand, Jonathan Bender shows up. Dawn is fond of Bender. She takes pity on his anxiety-ridden persona and gets him to laugh. But this time Bender comes around with a tall, quirky hippie named Bones Osgood who has a Jesus beard and smiling, gray-blue eyes. Dawn is lounging on the couch in her short Lolita shorts, painting her toenails a vermilion red and smoking her Winstons. Bender introduces us, I go in the kitchen and put a brass pot of water on to boil for Turkish coffee. It's unusual to have a stranger over. But this cat seems quite friendly, and at ease with himself.

Standing in the middle of the room, Bones wrinkles his nose against the Winston fumes. Looking at Dawn, he says, "You know, that cigarette smoke is murder on your lungs. It's not herbal like pot. They treat those C-sticks with the most lethal chemicals imaginable. You need to drink lots of fresh fruit juice to cleanse your mucus membranes, and deep diaphragmatic breathing helps too."

Dawn stares up at him with instant loathing, then stubs her cigarette out. She won't tolerate the slightest hint of being patronized. Mumbling, "Thanks for the tip," she gathers her stuff and goes into the bedroom. Leaving the door ajar, curious as always, she turns on a soul station.

Bones gives me an apologetic look. I shrug and set the viscous, thrice-boiled coffee on the kitchen table. "Don't sweat it," I tell him, "she's had a rough time lately."

"She almost broke her leg when Jake crashed his Matchless," Bender says, a peculiar gleam in his eye.

Nodding, vaguely annoyed at Bender, I add, "Yeah, she just got out of the cast about a week ago. She's still feeling some pain."

"Aiyee," murmurs Bones, "that'd bum me out too, ouch, no problemo." He gazes at the Zen Calligraphy scroll on my kitchen wall, a smile crinkling in the corners of his eyes.

"So what brings you dude over?" I want to know, taking a sip of the thick, honeyed coffee. "Jonathan tell you about the Laguna Beach acid?"

Bones Osgood gives me a prescient look, brings the demitasse to his lips, sips, dries his mustache with his fingertips, glances at Bender.

Leaning in, Bender confides, "He knows where the sacred mushrooms grow down in Oaxaca. He went all the way down there by himself last summer."

Stunned by this news, I set my cup down. "No fucking shit," I say, appraising Bones with new eyes as my mind does some cartwheels. You never know when revelation's gonna hit. It just happens right out of the blue.

Only a few weeks ago Bender and I had been talking about Oaxaca. I found this old Life Magazine article describing the sacred mushroom cults of ancient Mexico. The anthropologist told of a remote mountain region where a Mazatec Indian cult still flourished. The wild mushrooms imparted visions so strong and vivid that this cult had its own high priestess along with pagan Catholic saints, and ceremonies shrouded in secrecy. The reporter didn't give the exact location of this mysterious village, only that it was up in the cloud forest at a place called "The Land of One Thousand Waitings."

That article blew my mind and set me off on a passionate search for more information. But try as I might, I couldn't find any more traces of the Oaxacan magic mushroom cult. Nothing at the Bodhi Tree bookstore, nor in the anthro-metaphysical section of the fabulous downtown library. Reality is, no one knows much about magic mushrooms, mainly just rumors and speculation. The peyote cactus is pretty well-known, but the psilocybin mushroom is the holy grail of the psychedelic adventurer. Bender went looking too, ferreting through the L.A. headshops and underground coffee houses, asking around. And with his peculiar knack, just as he found me, he found this lanky hippie with the serene, mystical eyes. Bones not only knows where that cloud forest village is, he traveled there last summer only to be turned back by the Mexican Federales. Sometimes the confluence of luck and day-dreaming is incredible!

Now we all sit here at my kitchen table, Bender, me and Bones, toking my custom marijuana blend and going over my National Geographic map of southwest Mexico. Anything is possible, always. You just have to be alert enough and brave enough to dare.

"So the village is right about here," I surmise, tapping the map, "in these mountains above Teotitlan? And you say there's a road leading up?"

Bones nods like a Cheshire cat, his eyes shining. "Yeah, right there. A little pueblo called Huautla de Jimenez, a place with no electricity, no telephones, nothing like that. It's high up a river canyon and tricky to reach. Like sometimes, during the rainy season, the dirt road going up the mountain washes out. By our standards, it's completely primitive."

"So why go when it's raining?" Bender wheezes, hacking out a fog of ganga smoke that puffs from his nostrils.

Bones' long hands draw in the air. "Because the mushrooms only grow when the monsoons come. In late July and in August, torrential tropical rains. If you go too early there's no mushrooms, and if you go too late, there's nothing left. For some reason, or at least so I've been told, the mushrooms are only good when they're fresh. When they dry out they lose their potency."

Pausing, he tokes on the joint, then says, "It's like the mountain spirits have ordained a certain time, you know, otherwise you're out of luck."

"Far out," I reply. "So happens that I really love rain, except when I'm out riding."

"Far out grass," Bones murmurs, beaming with appreciation.

"Yeah, righteous stuff. It's a blend of the best Michocán and Acapulco I've gotten over the past few months. It really brightens things up."

"I'll say. Can you lay your hands on maybe a pound of this stuff?"

"No, not like that. That's my own custom blend. But there's some good weed around, no doubt."

We share a complicit smile, a sense of camaraderie that all wily dopers share. We shake hands over the map, digging the vibes. Dawn is back on the couch in the front room, taking it all in. After a moment, she retreats into the sunshine and shade of the backyard. We have marijuana plants growing out there in redwood tubs, about two feet high, sprouted from select seeds, but spindly and impotent. I realize there's some kind of secret to cultivating marijuana, but I don't know it yet.

"You got a line on anything decent?" Bones asks, with the most ingratiating smile. "My own connections haven't exactly panned out lately."

"Yeah, actually, I do," I drawl, "some primo green-gold Michoacán."

He opens his embroidered kit bag and takes out a few hand-tooled bronze and mahogany pipes. He offers to trade me one for a sample lid, saying, "I've pretty much gotten my trip down to a simple barter system, if you're into that. Money can be a real drag."

"Yeah, why not," I say, intrigued by this character. "Excuse me a minute."

Going into the bedroom, I rummage in the closet, then come back with a nice plump lid. I lay it on Bones, then press him for more details. What actually happened down in Oaxaca? Why did the Mexican cops turn him away?

Osgood strokes his goatee, saying. "Aiyee, the fucking Federales are bad news, man. They threw up a barricade at Teotitlan, where the gravel road starts to climb the mountain. They're afraid that hippies will make a mecca out of Huautla, move in and take over. And since they tote submachine guns, you can't really argue with them. They make their own rules."

"Damn, you mean the word is already out? That little Shangri-la is already flooded with hippie nomads?"

"No, not really, not yet. Only a few Americanos live up there now, but people like us are wandering in. A couple friends of mine have been living up there for over a year, anthropology students from UCLA. They're writing a thesis on the pagan mushroom cult. Richard sent me a letter, telling me to try again this summer while there's still a chance. He thinks they'll close off the road for good soon, and send all the foreigners home."

"Down there," Bender wonders, his eyes fox-like, "how far is it down there?"

"I'm not exactly sure, I didn't keep track. But maybe two thousand miles, more or less straight south. Most of the roads are in pretty bad condition, and some are terrible."

"That wouldn't bother me," I say, shivering with excitement, "I like primitive country. But only in the rainy season, you say, and so that means when?"

"That means pronto," Bones Osgood grins. "Anyone who's going has to be ready to travel in five or six weeks. And I'd love having somebody to go with this time. It's a long trip down there all by yourself, speaking only pig-latin Mexicano."

It takes me no more than a mental flash to mull this over. The only question is whether I can persuade Dawn to come with me. "Count me in, man. This is exactly the kind of adventure I've been wishing for. You walked right in today with the answer."

We soul-shake on it, partnering up, then look at Bender. Hunching his shoulders, Jonathan says, "I don't know. Those Mexican Federales sound like bad news to me. If we try to sneak past, they could throw us into some shithole prison."

"No, that won't happen, man," I laugh, "don't even think like that. We'll find a way through before they throw up their roadblocks."

Bones' face brightens. "Confidence is good for traveling overland in strange lands. That's what the I-Ching says."

"Right on, worries are like a leaking bucket. So how about it, Bender. You in or not?"

Bender gets up from the table with a stoned chuckle. "Yeah, I think maybe I am. I just gotta figure out some particular arrangements, like for my cat. Let me work on it." He wanders out the French doors into the backyard where Dawn lies on the grass with her knees up, sunning her svelte legs. He loves talking to Dawn when he's high, he secretly lusts for her, and she gives him sisterly advice.

Bones and I share a knowing glance, already realizing that he probably won't be going with us. We sit head to head at the Formica table, working out detailed plans on the map, sharing our lucid thoughts. Bones tells me that astrology is his thing, and that he'd like to cast my horoscope.

"You know, I've never had that done for me before, far out. And tell you what, Bones, for that horoscope, in the spirit of barter, I'm gonna lay some of the best acid in the cosmos on you free of charge—my gift."

"Righteous," murmurs Bones, sealing our friendship with a strong soul-shake. "Looks like this is meant to be. And no matter what I'm going back down there for those sacred mushrooms. This might be the last chance. I don't want to miss out."

"I'm in all the way, brother," I say, meeting his gaze. "We're going, no matter what."

# Chapter 17

A FEW DAYS later, I tie a knapsack to the rear seat of my BSA Lightning and head down to Laguna Beach. Charlie, the renegade chemist, greets me like a mystical comrade in his canyon lair. His long-legged girlfriend has split on him but he doesn't seem to mind. He is in his own realm.

"You cannot allow yourself to be blackmailed by sex," he observes, serving me Oolong tea and raw honey with a beatific half-smile.

"You know, it's funny you should say that. Lately, I understand what you mean."

Taking his granny specs off, Charlie hands me an amber jar full of countless tiny white tablets. I examine a few tabs close up. They are perfectly uniform. Each minuscule tab is divided into precise quarters by a thin cross. "Very interesting," I say. "And what exactly am I holding here? No speed, right?"

"No, no infernal speed, never. That, my brother Jake, is the purest lsd on the face of the earth, maybe even better than what I've been making. It's from the Sandoz labs over in Switzerland—incomparably cosmic, inter-galactic acid. One eensy-weensy quarter of one of those little pills will send you into psychedelic ecstasy, you have my word on it."

"Holy Moses, Charlie. You serious?"

"You know that I am. Albert Hoffman's own brand. Only problem is they aren't making anymore of these babies. Sandoz shut down production because of some bizarre suicide that happened at their headquarters. And just so you know, I'm no longer in the production end of things either. I've retired from the Cohen research lab. Too many restraints, too much bullshit, too many timid squares. But for you, my friend, I have some special gifts. You are one of us."

Charlie hands me another vial of what he claims to be one hundred and fifty purple tabs of fabled Owsley acid. "Whooo," I exclaim softly. "This has gotta be a figment of my imagination."

"Nope, I'm absolutely sure of the source," Charlie replies, beaming. He hoists his long feet onto the copper coffee table with the grace of a stork. The window curtains billow inward, a canyon breeze smelling of orange blossom and honeysuckle. In his backyard, through the sliding glass doors, a red carp windsock catches the breeze. A Beethoven sonata revolves on his turntable, barely audible. Paradise exists in the moments.

"I despise the street shit just as you do," he says, crumbling some Nepalese temple hash into his Nargila pipe. "It's a travesty that destroys the sacred human frequencies."

"Yeah, they're lacing it with pcp now, angel dust. Bonafide psychotic shit."

"Not our worries, Jake," Charlie confides, "All of this Sandoz and Owsley lsd comes through the Brotherhood of Eternal Love. It's one hundred percent pure and certified and all I'm looking for is a buck a tab. Just tell me how many you can handle." He puts a wooden match to the long-stemmed, silver nargila. Seconds later, I smell the dark, delicious, opiated hash. Exhaling, he beckons me to take a hit and we tap fingers.

Doing business with Charlie is always good. I lay five hundred and fifty skins on him, replenishing my stash. The Brotherhood of Eternal Love is an outlaw alliance of acid producers said to be committed to a world-wide psychedelic revolution. They're rumored to live on hidden ranches, in teepees and Tibetan meditation huts all up and down the California coast. Few people know the details, and no one gets close without an invitation.

"Many thanks, man. You're a brother, Charlie. I can't say how much I appreciate it."

"De nada," he says, with an airy gesture, and we smoke the dreamy Nepalese hash. Beethoven is replaced by the slow, magical strains of a sarod raga by Ali Akbar Khan. The curtains billow, I smell again honeysuckle and oranges on the breeze. We are at peace with the beloved earth. How absurd to think that what we are doing is regarded as illegal by the militant slaves of this hoodwinked society.

"Jake," Charlie tells me, "you need to know, I'm disengaging. I'm going over to France to live for at least a year, to study the mathematical intricacies of Gothic architecture. Those cathedrals are quite amazing, imbued with esoteric secrets that rival the pyramids. And you say that you're heading into the lost lands of Mexico in search of the miraculous— equally amazing!" Charlie claps his hands. "So who knows when we will see each other again? But you'll be in my thoughts, and I'm going to leave you in good shape."

Taken aback, I reply, "Well fuck, Charlie, I hope we do see each other again. You've opened some incredible doors for me. But I can dig what you're into, I can definitely relate. When are you splitting?"

"In about two weeks, and here's the other thing. Whenever you wish to be resupplied, this is the card of a trusted friend of mine in Newport Beach. Just give her a call and say your name, mention me. She already knows who you are, you're in like Flynn."

Swallowing my surprise, I accept the hand-printed card he offers, grateful, but also leery. I don't want the whole world to know that I'm dealing several hundred hits of acid a month, I'm a freak for my own privacy. And whereas possessing and selling lsd isn't a crime yet, there's talk that it soon will be. But I trust Charlie, and I'm going to need another good connection.

As I make ready to leave, roping my knapsack onto the BSA bench seat, he says, "If the draft board tries to come after you, and the evil motherfuckers might, just come over to France. You can hide out with me. They'll never find us."

"Right on man, hah," I say. "Right, if it comes down to that, I'm going to disappear into Mexico or India, or I'll come over there and look you up. There's no way I'll sign on to fight that criminal fucking war, they can all go to hell. I'd rather make war on them first."

Charlie watches the sky-blue clouds scudding off the sea, then says, "We are on a higher path, Jake, my brother. We have to make this world more real than it's ever been. We have to prepare it for love."

"Yeah," I say, embracing him, "I totally dig that. Make it more real than it's ever been."

I kick the red and chrome Beaser over, the mojo hand prominent, and drift on down the canyon road, then swing onto the coast highway all the way to Redondo, with sunshine freedom singing in my ears.

MY DARLING DAWN'S new barmaid job is at night. She goes on at six and doesn't get off till one, jazzed, frazzled, and often half-drunk. Scroungy, horny bikers flock around her like mongrels. She wants me to pick her up and naturally I do. But this is no hippie joint and I've come to shun uppers and downers like death, the cocktail of choice for most of these chopper braggarts. In this bar, I am the interloper, and plainly resented. Resented, because I'm the acid head riding the limey bike and sleeping with the mouth-watering, alluring babe in black leather boots. Not that I give a shit what they think, and they pick up on this too. Dawn always greets me with a warm smile, squeezes my hand, let's them know *this is my boyfriend,* and never makes me wait.

But I'm not happy that she's usually tipsy when she gets off. "Look, baby," I say, "my old man was a heavy-duty drinker when I was growing up, and still is. So I don't really care for it, you know? Once in a while, getting drunk can be fun. But since you started working there, seems like it's getting to be a habit and that's a sleazy clientele. So I'm wondering if maybe something's rubbing off?"

"Oh, don't be silly," Dawn chides me, "you're exaggerating things. They're a decent bunch of guys, Jake, and they tip me damn good."

"Baby, they're dealing speed in there, and speed is for losers. I've got eyes and I'm just telling you what I see. And I don't like that blond asshole putting his hands on you."

"Dale? Nonsense, Dale's like a kid brother to me! He's not trying to feel me up. Jesus, you're being paranoid."

"I know what I'm seeing, Dawn. I read people real good. They'd do anything under the sun to break us up. They're not into our scene at all and they don't respect our trip. All that asshole wants to do is get into your hot, little pants."

"That's not true, that's an exaggeration."

"Yeah it is. Why are you playing the naive chick all of a sudden?"

"Believe it or not, Mr. Know-It-All, some of those guys are getting to be my good friends. I like making new friends. You oughta try it sometime."

"They're a bunch of pill-popping dimwits who have no respect for us. Dawn, I was born at night but not last night. They'll say or do anything to split us up."

"You don't even know them," she retorts, her dark eyes flashing. "Why are you putting them down?"

"Don't really want to know them, either, they're not my kind of people."

"Oh fuck this!" She leaps off the couch, seething and half-drunk. "You're such a goddamn snob sometimes it makes me sick!"

She rushes into our bedroom and slams the door. Twisting my lips, I sit there stoned, feeling righteous but not necessarily right, wondering what just happened. It feels like we're slipping into a murky pool of misguided words and resentment, and I'm not sure how to stop it.

Emerald hummingbirds flit at our red brick wall of blossoms, hovering in the vines. Mexican doves call from the nearby trees. I hear them calling in the morning, at midday, and in the evening. Their haunting cries speak of a hidden path, one that I have sought all my days and I long to share this secret with her. But she seems to be holding something against me now, we seldom agree. We bicker and toss sarcasms at each other, ridiculous nonsense about nothing.

Well, no, not exactly about nothing. On the surface we argue over Oaxaca, about how my plan is coming between us. She dislikes the idea of the long rough trip just to get high on a Mexican fungi, harps against living in a place without running water or electricity. Have I lost my mind? Why do we even need a magic mushroom, anyway? Why isn't pure California acid good enough anymore? Her mocking little laugh annoys me, it's getting under my skin. It's like Pandora's box has sprung it's lid in our house and all these discordant imps are running loose. I do my best to tune it out and keep things mellow. Bones tells me she is a double Pisces and that we are astrological dynamite together, both good and bad. Essentially meaningless but rather disturbing information.

The good thing is we still make love, we love making up making love. We drop amorous acid together on a sun-struck morning and ride up around Griffith Park Observatory, with almost no one around. Dawn takes delight in the little natural things—the anatomy of flowers, meandering insects, unusual stones, dragon flies, the texture and taste of pollen. I notice the arc of a hawk, the track of a deer, cloud language, the coyote's scat. These alchemical hours are the sanctuary where we still play and breath together. But what if happiness is just an accident and can never be guaranteed? Happiness seems to be shadowed by something that wants to rebuke it, but why? Why do we always fall out of the eternal moment? Lsd gives us this special energy for a few hours, but then we lose it.

Dawn has the ability to pull me out of my daydreams. One afternoon, she slumps down across from me, regarding me with a drawn face. Her shoulders are pulled in. I close the Karl Jung book on archetypes. When I offer her a bowl of some glorious new Acapulco bud, she shakes her head. She goes over and turns off the Hi-Fi without lifting the needle. Brian McClain, Arthur Lee and Love go dead with a black-board squelch.

"Sorry," she says, standing in the slanted light coming in the French Door panes. She looks outside, not seeing, wrapped in thought.

Swiveling toward her, I ask, "What's the matter, Dawn? Tell me, please.'

Compressing her lips, she goes over and sits on the couch. She looks at me with brown solemn eyes, then drops her gaze to the worn Oriental rug. My heart thickens. I go over, kneeling in front of her, holding her eyes. "Tell me, baby. I need to know."

Giving her mouth a little half-twist, she says, "A surprise you're probably not going to like, Jake . . . I'm pregnant."

At first I think she's playing a joke on me, or no? Because she can't get pregnant, it's not possible, at least that's what she's always said. But her face betrays not the slightest mischief.

Settling into a cross-legged position on the rug, I ask, "How can that be?"

"Ahh, because you shot a load of hot cum up inside of me?"

"Don't be a wise-ass, Dawn. What I'm asking, is how? Didn't your doctor say something about your Fallopian tubes that made that impossible? Getting pregnant?"

"Yes, he did. He said there was no way I could develop a fetus again, that I'd always miscarry. But it looks like he was wrong. Because I am. I am pregnant."

"You sound so sure. How can you be so sure? Have you missed your period?"

"I'm not a fool, Jake. I've missed more than one period and I'm feeling queasy in the morning. I've been here before, you know. There's no way around it."

I almost don't breathe, my thoughts coagulate. How, all of a sudden. I hate it when people say there's no way around something. I don't relate to that attitude. Is it written somewhere on the side of a mountain in stone? Did Moses reincarnate?

Dawn sighs, sniffs, and mumbles, "Kinda figured you'd feel this way."

"Look, to be honest, I don't even know what to say."

"It doesn't really blow my skirt up either, believe me. So what do you wanna do?"

Do? For a second my mind is a blank page, then self-interest kicks in. "First of all, honey, I don't want to be a father and you know that. How can we have a kid living the way we do? But I like the way we live, and I don't want to sacrifice it. You're at the most, what, maybe two months pregnant, right? Let's just do the smart thing."

Her face takes on a stubborn cast, I feel a churning in my guts. Giving me a feral look, she says, "I want to have this baby, Jake, it's our love child. This baby is very special."

"What? Oh no way, that's crazy. You know I'm not into that kind of a life. I'm an acid freak on a motorcycle, for Christ's sake. I'm here for a completely different purpose."

"What's that supposed to mean?" she retorts. "Anybody can change. I can, and so can you. Mindy told me she wants to have Donny's baby too. These things are part of a natural life!"

"Oh well, so fuck me, what are we in family week or something? Have you flipped out?"

"Please don't be an asshole?"

"No babies, Dawn, remember, I said that in the beginning. No squalling babies, no stacks of shitty diapers, no thanks. Babies mean that your world stops, you no longer own your own life, they own your life.

Nope, that's not for me, and we do have other choices."

"I'm not gonna have an abortion, mister, if that's what you mean. So just forget about that idea. I'm not going that way. Fuck, you don't even care about how I feel."

Feeling as though I've been ambushed, I say, "Feel? It feels to me like you've already made your mind up and mine with it. What are you trying to do?"

"God decides these things, Jake, it's not just about you and me. You wouldn't be here if you're mom had thrown you away. And my grandmother says this is a very special child."

Getting to my feet, I retort, "Bullshit, that's unbelievable bullshit. What am I, some kind of no-say man-slave? You're grandmother's dead. And my parents wanted to have kids, that's the difference. I want to do things on purpose, not by accident."

Suddenly I'm looking at her in an unfamiliar way. I can taste the subterfuge, I've been tricked, I know it. She's almost sneering up at me, her arms crossed over her breasts.

"Why do you have to be so fucking weak?" she taunts. "Try being a man for once, just once."

My jaw drops open, I'm speechless. We have never had such words. This has got to be the insidious influence of her new friends, I'm thinking, as I slip into a clear, calm rage. I move to a chair and light a cigarette. Then I say, "I'm not going to have this baby with you, Dawn. You're not deciding my life for me, I am. I've always been up-front with you and you've known my deal all along."

Jumping to her feet, she screams, "Oh fuck you, just fuck you! You think you can always have your way? You're weak, weak, weak, you motherfucker! Weak!"

Flabbergasted by the hostility crawling out of her face, wondering who this bitch is, I reign in my emotions. I've never hit a woman in my life and I'm not gonna hit her. But the weird thing is, I think that's what she's trying to provoke.

"No, I'm not weak," I say in a hoarse voice, "but I do know what I don't want and what I don't want, Dawn. And I'm fucking done with this conversation."

Hissing at me, she grabs her purse, gives me the finger, then goes pell-mell out the door. My head is abuzz, my mouth is dry, my heart is a precarious blur taking my stomach with it. Even worse, I suspect that I might not even be the father, another dissonant pang. For the past several weeks she's been getting rides home after work, telling me I don't have to pick her up. Her chopper buddies have been giving her rides, I mean what the hell, it's all so convenient. Except she's rolling in around three in the morning and a couple of times closer to daylight, making for unpleasant moments. I've never had a chick cheat on me, and I can't quite believe she's really cheating on me. But I'd be a fool to ignore the implications and something's definitely come between us.

When I confront her, she denies it. "There's no way I'd lie to you, Jake," she cries. "I know I've been a little off but it's just been innocent fun, believe me. This baby can only be yours, you're the only guy I've been in bed with."

I don't know whether to believe her or not. A part of me wants to believe her, but another discerning part does not. How do we really know when we're fooling ourselves?

Spread out on the coffee table in front of me is the National Geographic map of Oaxaca, my fervent inspiration. "All right, Dawn. But it's still just you and your mom planning all this, along with your long-gone grandma, right? never mind what I might want. Sort of an imbalanced situation, wouldn't you say?"

She sniffs, glancing at the map, then out the window panes at the blue morning glories climbing the back wall. "That place you're talking about," she murmurs, "isn't even on the map. I checked."

"It doesn't matter, it's up there," I reply, tracing the Sierra Occidental with my fingertip. "And it's good it's not on the map. That way dilettante, day-tripping dope fiends can't find it."

Throwing me a peevish glance, she says, "You mean people like yourself? You go off into an unknown wilderness to get high on a fucking mushroom, where nobody even speaks your language? Who's crazy here?"

"I'm going, so save your breath. Or come with me."

"I'm pregnant, you bastard, with your baby. You could get shot down there."

"No Dawn, no one's going to shoot me, what? And the sky could fall in, too. Do I seem like an idiot to you?"

She's begging off the trip, I can dig it. But wandering into the uncharted mystery is part of my reason for going. But if you're afraid, you should stay home. If you're afraid, don't go.

Her dark eyes implore me. "If you're not careful you'll get in trouble down there. They don't play by your rules. And I'm not promising I'll even be here when you get back."

I glance down at the holy map. I intensely dislike being coerced. There's an abused quality coming out of her that I haven't sensed before, that has nothing to do with me.

After a moment, I say, "I'm sorry, Dawn, I do love you. But I never said I'd be anyone or anything other than who I am."

"Yeah, you're sorry," she replies with wounded eyes. "Just think about how I feel."

# Chapter 18

I N HIGH SKY blue summer, Bones and I take the vagabond road south into Mexico. We pitch our first camp on the northern tip of the Sea of Cortez after a long drive in his '52 Mercury Coupe. The gulf is placid, and fringed by desert, the beach is more a gravel shingle than sand. We're feeling good, knowing that we've left the USA behind us and now beyond the border zone. Plunking my army surplus pack on the hard ground, I roll out my canvas tarp and worn sleeping bag as a cushion. In this heat, I intend to smear on mosquito repellent and sprawl on top of the bag. The olive U-frame pack holds a ton of gear and I've stuffed it for the long haul—enamel camp cook-wear, clothes and towels, a sack of brown rice, a folding Buck knife, Turkish coffee, Japanese green tea, dried dates, figs and apricots, along with some books, sandals, and two canteens of spring water. Wrapped in a hand towel, at the bottom of the pack, I've stashed a baggie of my custom weed blend and an amber vial holding about 150 tabs of pure acid. I figure on the road to Shangri-La acid this good might be as good as gold.

Five select books are tucked in my nomad's pack. A red leather-bound volume of Patangali's Yoga Aphorisms, commentary by Vivekananda; a black leather pocket edition of the King James New Testament; a blue hardcover of Paul Brunton's Wisdom of the Overself; a photo book of the Hatha Yoga Asanas; and Paramahansa Yogananda's chapbook, Metaphysical Meditations. These will be my field manuals in "The Land of One thousand Waitings".

The sun falls into the Sea of Cortez like a burning coal sinking into a vat of molten oil. We gather some driftwood and make a fire, pouring water from a canteen into a small pot and simmering it for tea. Bones eats a handful of sunflower seeds with a banana and rambles on about the volatile moods of women. He tends to talk out most of his thoughts, as I am learning, whereas I tend to keep my own counsel.

The air is warm and heavy along this arid seashore, sundown on the water stirring only the faintest breeze. Watching the random birds, I fan the driftwood flames while Bones speculates, talking to me, to himself, to whoever else might be listening.

"Chicks can be so strange," he says. "No matter what you do somehow it's not enough, or it's not what they really wanted. And then in their minds, you owe them. You and me, we owe them."

"You think so? I'm not convinced of that."

"Because you're supposed to make up for their other disappointments."

Considering that, I say, "Well, one thing's for sure. Things can go to hell in a hurry."

"Mind-blowing," Bones agrees, tossing away the banana peel. "For the ants and bugs."

I pour the steeping tea into a couple of mottled enamel cups, then dig out my weed vial and roll a couple of tapered zig-zags. Something on the wing swoops low along the twilight strand like a fleeting gesture, maybe an owl.

"Aiyee," Bones laughs, "you carried that grass across? Kinda risky, don't you think?"

"Naw, not really. How can it be smuggling when you bring weed back into Mexico?"

Bones takes a lusty hit, then another, holding the smoke in until he grunts, "Caramba."

"Not only that," I confide, taking the pass from his adroit fingers, "I also brought along some primo lsd in case anyone's interested. Who knows who we'll meet? But let's just remember our key promise—no smuggling shit on the back way home into California."

We nod in agreement, this journey is a spiritual quest, not mercenary. The excellent marijuana suffuses us, the driftwood crackles and smokes, we ease into the dying embers of a vast Baja sunset. The shoreline is deserted and treeless, although birds are winging their way home to somewhere.

"The female psyche is animistic and possessive," Bones maunders on, "once you fuck them, I mean really fuck them, then they think they own you, specially if they're sucking your dick."

"Are you saying that ownership has its carnal privileges?" I parry with a thin smile, trying to duck the swirling wood smoke. You're mine and I'm yours and don't forget it, that possessive discord seems to worm its way into every romantic passion-play. But right now, out here on the road, it's just Bones and me, mystical nomads. Dawn flaked out on me. She abruptly moved out into her own apartment, and I moved in with Bones and his chick VeeGee for about a month. Then VeeGee blew up, convinced that Bones was two-timing her. She told him not to come looking for for her when he got back from the Mexican boondocks, hurling a shoe his way.

Bones took this in a pale stoic way, neither admitting nor denying guilt. But for me, the newcomer on their scene, it was déjà vu. Chicks not getting their way blowing up a relationship.

But now, sitting on this remote horn of the Sea of Cortez, all that confusion is fading. The flickering campfire gathers the night around us like a cocoon. We munch black Mission figs and dry roasted almonds, sipping the cooling dregs of gunpowder green tea. Bones keeps his beatnik rap going, I drift in and out of his monologue. The immense sky is clear as dark glass, stars one billion strong, the regalia of some celestial civilization, glimmering above us, an ancient message, almost readable.

"They wig out when things don't go their way," Bones is saying, "they don't like not being in control. And once they get their resentment going, watch out, dude."

"Hah," I say, rekindling the sacramental roach, "that does ring a certain bell."

"Dig, as soon as VeeGee and your girl realized they weren't calling the tune, they backed out on us. All of a sudden we were selfish men, we only think of ourselves."

"Yeah, well, fuck that. I've heard enough of that riff."

"Yeah, fuck it," Bones laughs.

I pass him the hot roach, not wanting to talk about it anymore. Sometimes it's hard to say who's actually right and who's wrong. The train goes off the tracks, you're working overtime to not to get swallowed up in some hideous negative trip. But some people seem to thrive on negative energy.

Bones whistles low into the night air. "Man, sometimes I think they aren't sane in the way we are, you know? They only pretend to be sane so we'll like them. Then they start dishing out all kinds of chaos to gain an advantage, and I hate that shit. I'm not into control trips at all."

Nodding to myself, I toss a few dry sticks onto the glowing coals, watching them flare. Bones words strike a chord, although I'm hoping that's not always true. Because I still love Dawn, I do love her. She and I have shared each other's very essence.

In the firelight, Bones' lean, bearded face looks medieval. We reach across and clasp hands.

"Tomorrow, brother," I say, "let's find a cantina and drink a few beers to all we intend to do, and fuck the static."

"Right on, for sure let's do that, amigo."

Lying back on my sleeping bag, I gaze up into the shimmering core of the Milky Way. Does God live out there or inside of us? Surely, I think, it has to be inside and outside and all around us, even in the stones under my back. God has to be everything, without exception. A slight breeze washes in off the moonless gulf, I hear a night bird calling down the strand.

"But I admit," Bones murmurs, "I love to get naked with them. Women love to fuck and I love fucking them. I hope we meet some saucy chicks down on the road."

Turning my face, I say, "Well, I wish you luck with that. Just don't get your cojones hacked off. But for me, I'm going to do without sex for awhile. I want to see where this trip takes me on my own."

For a minute neither of us speak. Only the rustle of the dying fire, the lapping of shore waves, the invocation of an owl somewhere in the mystical darkness.

Then Bones chides, "Jake, man, we're liable to run into some sweet hippie babes down here. They'll be in the mood to get it on. I wish you'd get off that celibacy vibe."

"Dig, if we happen across any, you're welcome to my share. I'm on a pilgrimage, Bones, that's why I came."

We leave it at that, not liking to argue We drift into shifting dreams on that beach of pebbles and sand, under the oceans of starlight, in a place without clocks, and suffused with gratitude.

THE MORNING SUN rises like a furnace over the Sea of Cortez desert coast. We push south through Hermosillo and Guaymas down the blue-sky gulf, knowing we have to stay ahead of the monsoons, we drive the old Merc flathead all day long and into the night. Tropical rains in the Oaxacan highlands will bring forth the mythical mushrooms, and we want to be present. But the deeper we go into Mexico, the more sapping the heat becomes, heat like a heavy, steaming blanket. The occasional toke on my special blend tends to cool us down, we guzzle mineral water in green glass bottles with poetic labels. We refuse the sugary canned fruit juices that are sold at every road stop. Once in a while we get lucky and score some fresh squeezed orange juice from a cart vendor, jugo de naranja, but fresh fruit only becomes plentiful when we reach the coastal region around Mazatlan. The arid desert gives way to palms and lush green foliage that curtains the blue seascape, the humid heat alleviated by the off-shore breezes.

And in Mazatlan, I begin to feel like we're getting somewhere. The pot-holed Mexican highways are taking a ruthless toll on our ramshackle car. We make frequent stops at the ubiquitous tire repair shops along the road, getting our rubber retreads patched and plugged for pennies. Talking and gesturing with the people over the loud Norteno music, we come face to face with another, harsh reality. But these swarthy workmen are friendly and smiling, they dig our long hair and converse freely in a mixture of Spanish and English words. On the flipside, out on the highway, the militant Federale checkpoints make for some grim moments. We show our visas and endure the scowling faces of soldiers barely old enough to shave. Norte Americanos are supposed to be rich and drive flashy cars, whereas we manifest a flagrant lack of gringo ambition. They stare at us with an attitude of puzzled contempt.

Somewhere I read that Mexico is a paradox within a dream, and now I see it. The deeper we go, the more vivid the contrasts. The common folk are shyly amazed to meet us, two long-haired Americanos who dress much like they dress, eating pinto beans and rice in their fly-swarming cafes as we plead with them to not spray the hideous Ddt over the tables. We arrive in a battered brown jalopy that could be one of their own, wanderers with far-seeing eyes. I find myself falling deeply in love with these simple people.

But we don't linger anywhere for long, obsessed by our mission. My pardner Bones likes to drive as much as I do, except that he drives like a turtle. He seems to have limited stamina, although fresh fruit and fruit juices easily revives him. But when he starts angling for an early rest stop, I take over behind the wheel and push the rattling coupe over the devastated roads, shrugging off his admonitions about stress, plunging ever deeper into something unknown. Night falls swiftly in the tropics and we are hit by lashing rain squalls. Belatedly, we discover that our windshield wipers don't even work. But we rig some cord to the blades that allows whoever's riding shotgun to tug them back and forth, through his window wing. Manipulating this jury-rig in the downpours, stoned and laughing, we follow our aqueous headlights into the labyrinth of dreaming Mexico.

In Mazatlan, Bones has a bohemian friend named Arturo. Bones sent him a postcard a few weeks ago to foretell of our coming. Arturo lives on the old waterfront in a faded, green shack, with an outer lean-to latrine shaded by a rusting tin roof. He welcomes us with open-hearted enthusiasm, inviting us to stay as long as we wish. He feeds us tortillas and beans stewed with onions, jalapenos and garlic, washed down with bottles of Pacifico cerveza plucked from an ice chest. We smoke my custom la mota, sharing our stories, then sleep the sleep of satisfied dogs.

The rooster wakes us before the sun has risen, to shuffle around and make strong coffee in the faint, humid light. Then, sitting on his concrete steps, watching the butterfly net shrimp boats going out to sea, Arturo tells how he used to live in California and plans to go back.

"For the easy money," he grins, "and the friendly mujercitas, L.A. can't be beat."

We all agree, L.A.'s laissez-faire appeal can't be denied. The fishing boats move in and out of the harbor, rusting steamers sway at anchor in the oil-sheen water. We drink black coffee in the sunshine and eat watermelon and bananas. Arturo wants us to stay for a few days, but we've already rolled our gear and feel anxious to get on the road.

"For the mushroom rains," Bones explains. "We need to get up there before the road washes out."

"Ah, comprendo," says Arturo. "I hope you have better luck this time getting past those fucking Federales. Eat some mushrooms for me, please think of me, I could use some magic."

"Come with us, man," I encourage him, "we can make room."

"I would love to, but no, I cannot," he says, scratching the stubble on his chin. "I need to work on those smelly boats for awhile longer, clear up some old debts."

We all embrace, promising to meet again either in Mazatlan or Los Angeles. Into Arturo's curious palm, I tap out six tabs from my amber vial of pharmaceutical Sandoz. "My friend," I promise him, "you will have a beautiful and magical trip with this ultra-puro acid. Just don't drop more than half a tab at once unless you want to fly off into the solar system."

Ogling the treasure in his hand, Arrturo says "Ah, Lsd supremo, huh? Gracias, Jake mi hernano, muchas gracias. This is worth more than dinero down here."

"Try not to die from laughing," Bones grins. "That stuff is way out, really incredible."

"Seal it away from the humidity," I advise, "and stash it in a cool, dark place. But don't let it sit around too long."

"Oh, don't worry," Arturo quips, "with this gift, I am already planning an orgy."

We load our gear into the beige coupe, fire up the 90 horse power tractor engine, and wave good-bye. In the dense heat of the old harbor, Arturo watches us go with wistful eyes.

WE FOLLOW THE winding, dipping coast road south at about fifty miles an hour, Bones' favorite speed, dodging potholes, dodging the giant trucks that hog the Mexican highways, roaring past within inches, spewing their lethal fog of diesel fumes. Our windows are open in the rising heat, we hold our breaths until the stench blows clear. We slow to a crawl to let wandering cattle and burros cross the road, then the road climbs and curves, glimpses of the turquoise sea below the jungle cliffs. Everything conspires to slow you down, it's pointless to resist. Now and then our radio catches blasts of mariachi or ranchero music, or voices too staccato to grasp. We listen, we frown, we laugh and take a toke of weed, we twirl the dial. The impenetrable jungle, the infinite Pacific, the flying clouds of red and green parrots captivate our thoughts.

Around noon, we swing away from the coast, making for Guadalajara and its famous giant mercado where for a handful of pesos you can buy anything made or grown under the sun. Rain showers come and go, drumming on the car roof, precursors of the monsoons that will drench the coastal jungles, the inland plains, and the lost mountain hideaways. We have to make good time, but we can't really go any faster than we're going. We grind over the disastrous roads on our dubious tires, consoled by the fact that we're carrying two spares in the trunk. The heat is insufferable, marauding flies dart in and out of our windows, sweat trickles from our armpits, we smoke my hand-rolled, medicinal joints to pacify our tormented minds.

In the huge Guadalajara mercado we stock up on raisins oranges and bananas, score a kilo of peanuts roasted and salted in the shell, delicious black, thin-skinned avocados that you can eat like an apple, and more bottled mineral water. In the shade of a cool concrete wall, we gorge on fresh guacamole and thick maize chips seasoned with lime and salt, taking in the astonishing carnival of people. Then we grind our way out of the chaotic city, through insane heat and honking traffic and suffocating exhaust. Beggars seem to be everywhere, piteous women with feeble infants, beseeching waifs, frail old men beaten down to next to nothing, almost unbelievable, this mind-blowing poverty.

At last, the crumbling suburbs behind us, we escape on a narrow highway that leads into the foothills and climbs into the Sierra Occidental. The air is much cooler on this alpine road, even though our flathead six sputters on the low-octane gas and chugs up the grades. The tall pines bring relief from the lowland miasma and the Federale checkpoints vanish. Ah, for the first time in days we stop sweating. At ease, I roll us a fat number and we get blasted in the rarefied air as little farms and hamlets and open-range cattle glide past, goats chewing the roadside grass. We breath in the clean sweet freedom, California far, far behind us now.

# Chapter 19

Further up the mountain road, we spot a hand-painted billboard, then pull off the worn asphalt and bounce down a rutted track into a valley. Brown cattle graze in the field along with some goats, we descend into a village of perhaps a dozen scattered buildings. Wood smoke rises from the roof of a dilapidated adobe, Coca-Cola and Carta Blanca signs hammered to it's walls. Aiyee, it's a cafe by God and we are famished. The strong weed and high altitude has instilled the munchies, and we need something more substantial than bananas and peanuts.

Parking the car in the dirt lot, alongside a 1940's Willy's Jeep, we stroll onto a plank porch with a long, overhanging roof. A hitching rail runs in front of the porch, for horses and donkeys and mules. We stand for a moment, taking in this rustic scene. Chickens peck and squawk in the dirt, flies buzz around, a mottled cow ambles past in the field with a bird riding on its back. Dogs are barking back and forth a ways off, insanely, the way country dogs do. It's only a few hundred yards off the highway but it feels like we've stepped into a time-warp.

"Whooee, far out," Bones muses. "Wonder where everybody is?"

"Maybe in the cafe," I reply, "hmmm, dig it, smell the rico comida?"

We go inside. The low-ceiling room has some wooden tables and chairs, dried red chiles and garlic hang from the rafters, smoke drifts, rising from an adobe fire pit towards a hole in the roof. A plump woman in a smudged apron stares at us, transfixed, even as a teenage girl pauses in mid-motion when we appear—we might be the first gringos to ever set foot in here, outlanders from another world, but we smile, fumbling in our pitiful Spanish, gesturing that we want something to eat. Yes, si, comida por favor, si, we are mucho hungry. The girl hangs on our words, our strange accents, panic gleaming in her black eyes. She keeps wiping her hands on her white apron, glancing over at the petrified cook. Aiyee, the long-haired gringos, what are they saying? Whether we are a visitation infernal or benign they are uncertain, and except for us the place is empty.

"Outta sight," Bones murmurs, "outta sight."

Laughingly high, trying not to laugh, we make ourselves understood. We want hot frijoles and rice, tortillas, salsa caliente, and si, quiero cerveza fria, por favor. The young waitress asks short confused questions that we cannot grasp, so we just nod, amiable and bright-eyed, trying to put her at ease.

"But no carne, no carnitas," Bones insists, his gray-blue eyes like lamps. "Our lips cannot eat the flesh of animales, no greasy cerdo por favor."

"Porque no?" the waitress pleads. "Señor, no carne? Señor, ayudarme, no entiendo!"

"Fuck it, man, let's sit down at this table," I laugh, delirious from the spicy aromas. "Give them a chance to sort it out."

"She doesn't dig that we don't eat meat," Bones says, stroking his goatee. Beaming over at the cook, he says, "Por favor senora, no carne for us, no carne, no fat, no greaso."

The waitress stops wringing her hands and looks at me with imploring eyes. I pat my chest, point at Bones, then say, "Vegetarainos, we are vegetarainos. You have tomates frescos?"

"Ah, no, si," she giggles, "tenemos tomates verdes!" Turning to her co-worker, she rattles off some words. Shaking her head, the plump Mestizo cook goes into slow-motion around the firepit, stirring an iron pot, immune to the eye-watering smoke.

Gesturing to Bones, I pull a chair out and take my seat. He shrugs and sits down across from me. "Caramba," he mutters softly, "I hope they don't bring us chicharones."

The young waitress hovers near, smiling hopefully. She makes a drinking gesture and utters a timid question.

"Oh si," we respond, "si, we'd' love some, dos cervezas! Nice and cold, cerveza mucho fria!"

She rushes off and returns with two tepid cans of Tecate, an insipid beer rumored to be cured with Formaldehyde, a concoction that shrivels people up like living cadavers. The cans are barely cool, we shake our heads. She explains that Tecate is their only beer and they are out of ice today. "No hielo, lo siento, lo siento," she says, certain she will be chastised.

"No problemo, es okay," we reply, magnanimous dopers I take a swig of the potentially lethal brew to prove it. She hurries off to give a hand to the curious, sweating cook.

"Far out," Bones says, grinning, "it's like some old western movie set."

"Yeah, for real, hah ha ha. But we're just passing through this one horse town."

The women bustle and whisper around the firepit, casting furtive glances. The girl watches us out of the corner of her eye. As soon as she sees that we have drained our cans, she brings over two more. She has been mistreated by someone, I sense this and don't like it, but what can you do? Within minutes she brings over clay plates heaped with steaming pintos and white rice garnished with slivers of green chiles, slices of cucumber, and tortillas wrapped in a warm, moist cloth. Placing this aromatic feast before us, she scurries off and returns with a bowl of chile verde. Aiyee, we praise her, praise the cook, thank you, muchas gracias, then fall on the mouth-watering chow like starving wolves. Finding it a tad bland, I slather my plate with the spicy chile verde.

Two swarthy, hard-bitten men come through the door, stare at us in wonderment, then take a table. They give their orders in low, gruff voices to the fidgety waitress.

Waving the noxious flies away, Bones says, "You know, they had chickens outside. I bet we could have gotten scrambled eggs, fresh brown farm eggs, if we wanted."

"Maybe, si, bueno protein, but scrambled in what? Lard? Maybe pig fat?"

"Aiyee, good point, yeah, no thanks. Hey Jake, go easy on that green chile—that'll burn your asshole out!"

But I do not go easy on the chile verde, it is delicious and stimulating. Going easy is not in my nature—I go all the way, full-throttle. Hmmm, this hot green chilie is muy sabrosa, I gobble it up with the juicy pintos, adding a few thin slices of fresh jalapeno for emphasis. In seconds I burst into a profuse sweat on my forehead and under my eyes. Tilting my chair back, I take a gulping pull from my beer can. A high-pitched ringing sound spaces through my head, a hollow drum opens and all the sounds in the room go oddly dissonant. A sharp metallic pop goes off in my ear, a sudden plume of fire shoots right up my backbone and into the base of my skull, electrifying my synapses, turning my eyeballs to light sockets. Bolting upright and staggering sideways, I knock over my chair and my beer at the same instant. My head flips back and I gasp out something in a language I've never known but somehow vaguely remember. Everybody in the room freezes—Santa Madre de Dios, the long-hair is loco, aiyee, the gringo is mad! Spoons pause in mid gesture, glasses half-lifted, curses muttered, their dark eyes piercing me with violent superstitions. Then, pierced by this primordial energy, I whirl in the light stream in my head and start shouting to the rafters.

"Jesus fuck Jake," Bones cries out, "what's happening, dude, what's wrong?!"

His urgent plea barely registers through the roaring inside my skull, pulsing with electrons, my hair afire, my mortal body humming like a Luciferian blues harp. Gasping, lurching, I make for the brilliant daylight flooding the open doorway and stagger toward it. For a moment, I cling to the door jam, trying to steady myself, then stumble down the porch to the burning post and just hang on. My whole body seems to be dissolving in a race of primal energy, thoughts of me, them, him, this, it, they, images spun and snatched away as I spin on the brink like a firefly, swaying against the post, an open field in front of me, the sere beaten grass, flowering weeds, a brown ambling cow, an Indian women in a red shawl squatting on the ground pounding into a stone mortar, her pestle hovers, her stoic eyes flick my way in disapproval, ahh, she thinks I am borracho, a foolish drunk, a foolish borrachito stranger.

Focusing on her, hanging to the rough post, fighting nausea, I try to vocalize. No Senora, de nada, no borracho, no soy tonto, it's all okay. But another swoosh of flame bursts up my spinal chord and the woman, the field, the world, the images fly into a thousand pieces as a swift black bird passes across my vision and my sense of gravity vanishes. Somehow my body makes a spontaneous leap into the fleeing lightstream, I turn a long somersault in the glittering air, hanging there like a feather.

*Jesus Cristo, Jesus, God, where am I, who am I, am I dying or born?*

EVER SO GRADUALLY I regain my senses, the sensations of my being, a trembling leaf as my eyes focus again. I have landed in the field many yards from the porch, only a short ways from the Mestizo woman. I've landed cross-legged in the dry, beaten grass. The squatting woman stares at me, her eyes two shining pits of fear. She mutters under her breath, I see her stained teeth.

Gesturing, I say, "De nada. It's okay, de nada, senora, lo siento."

At the sound of my voice she shrinks back, dropping the pestle, mumbling some kind of invocation. The gringo diablo speaks, it blows her mind. Even worse, I'm aware that my ass is all wet, there's a vaporous stench. I move my hips, squishing around in something odious.

"Ah fuck me," I mutter, glancing back at the porch. Somehow I've catapulted thirty or so feet in the air and landed out here cross-legged, crapping my pants in mid-flight. But wait. Peeling my sticky ass off the ground, getting to my knees, I realize the truth. I've landed in an oozing plop of fresh cow shit. The poor woman moans and covers her head in her red shawl. Concentrating my strength, I stagger to my feet. The seat of my pants and back of my thighs are rank with sticky cow shit.

Bones' urgent voice turns me around. He's on the porch, signaling me. "Jake," he hisses, "we've got to get out of here pronto! These people are freaked out! I almost got into a fight, I think those dudes went after machetes!"

Machetes? My mind grapples with this lurid image, machetes are dangerous. Moving toward Bones, I feel strength returning to my legs. One sandal is flopping, dangling by its strap. I hobble over to the porch and stare up into his lean and harried face.

"What are you saying? What's going on?"

"I think they think you're possessed by an evil spirit."

"No way," I laugh, panting, still weak. "That's fucking crazy, man, really, crazy."

"Not to them it isn't. The fear of devils runs in their blood. Aiyee, you're white as a ghost. What happened out here?"

"What happened? Bones, man, this intense jag of fire shot up my backbone and pushed me out here, then somehow I somersaulted off this porch and landed clear over there by her."

"Damn, look at her run," Bones whistles through his teeth. "She's totally spooked. If you leaped out there like you say, she thinks you're a gringo demon for sure."

Indeed, the terrified woman has gathered her dried corn into her shawl and fled. Beyond her, out in the barren field, there's a knot of men coming with tools, axes, long glinting blades, pointing at us, what the fuck? Bones jumps down off the porch and we make a beeline for the old car.

Throwing open the door, I say, "Hey, just a second, I'm all covered in shit. I landed in a pile of fresh cow shit."

Bewildered, Bones looks over the roof at me. "Come again?"

"The big leap, I came down out of the air into a stinking heap of cow shit. I need a towel."

"Oh fuck, well, hurry it up, hurry, they're coming, they're coming for us!"

Rummaging in my pack, I drag out a blue towel and spread it on the front seat, then squish myself in. I make a horrible face, the stench nauseating, but we're laughing. Bones coaxes the cranky engine to life, jams it in reverse, then pulls onto the rutted track leading uphill. Glancing across the field, I see the dark knot of men pause, watching us. One of them raises his arms as if shooing us away. Begone, you gringo devils, begone. In the high noon glare, they seem like shadows etched in the space just above the ground.

We rumble up the slope and careen onto the pitted highway, then start climbing the mountain through the tall pines. Feeling more solid, I tell what happened in detail, the shooting spinal fire, the odd sounds, the leap into the shimmering void, the physical disintegration.

"Holy Moses," Bones laughs, "that strong grass of yours, and the high altitude, those fiery chili peppers, I tried to warn you!"

"Yeah, you did, you did, but the Kundalini came roaring awake!"

"You must have been hallucinating out of your gourd."

"No, not hallucinating, Bones. I literally flew off that porch into the air. There was a strange fleeting bird. I could never have jumped that far. Don't ask my how but I flew, I flew off that porch."

"Man," Bones mutters, "you are turning into some kind of a brujo. You freaked that whole village out."

"Sorry about that. But at least we got away without our balls getting hacked off."

The straight-six Merc groans up the mountain side, sucking the thin air, spewing gas fumes as we pass through dappled sunlight and shade, cooling pine trees, rock outcroppings. The terrain is rugged and beautiful, but I cannot stand myself another minute.

"Pull over, pardner. I've gotta get out of these shit-stained britches, I gotta change."

He eases over onto the shoulder of gravel and pine needles. I slide out, the towel sticking to my buttocks. I peel it off and toss it away, dig out another pair of jeans, then slip-slide down the slope to a level spot under the pines. A raven caws at me from the high limbs. Removing my sandals, I tug the odious jeans off, then wipe myself and fling the soiled rags into the underbrush. I button up the fly of the clean Levis, then fasten my sandals. A hot zinging sound whips through the overhead limbs, chased by the violent crack of a rifle. In alarming suddenness three or four more shots ring out, the bullets whistling through the tree tops. I hear Bones frantically calling my name, I go scrambling back up the hill like a banshee.

Reaching the top, Bones sees me, his head just above the dash, motioning me to stay low. Crouching, I scuttle over to the passenger window "What the fuck's happening?"

"Bandidos," Bones wheezes, "bandidos, aiyee, they're coming down the mountain!"

Casting my eyes up the grassy slope on the other side of the road, goddamn, maybe eighty yards off, several men are angling their way down toward us. These are not the village farmers, no. These hombres wave rifles in the air, almost comically, and call out to us.

"Hola amigos, gringo amigos," one cries out in accented English, "wait for us! We want to talk to you! We are friends! We have some favor to ask!"

Studying him from beneath my eye-shading hand, I yell back, "What kind of favor?"

"Oh, just a little one!" the man laughs. "We are friends! Wait for us!"

But they are not friends, one of them sights his rifle toward us, an intimidating gesture.

"No, fuck you!" I howl back, "go away! Leave us alone! Fuck off!"

They all halt together, clustered on the slope, talking among themselves. Within seconds, a bullet clangs off the rear bumper, the rifle shot echoing through the tree tops.

"Aw fuck," I mutter, ducking down low, "the rotten motherfuckers."

Bones thumps on the steering wheel. "Get in, Jake, get in, we gotta run for it!"

I tumble into the front seat as Bones floorboards the gas pedal and the Merc sprints up the road like a lumbering hippo, more shots ring out, whistling past, but missing us. These bandidos must be all borracho or they're just piss-poor riflemen. We climb out of their range and around a pine-sheltered curve, then exchange a wild-eyed handshake, giggling like madmen.

"Bandits, Bones, hah ha ha, you said nothing about banditos. All we were trying to do is get something to eat."

"Yeah, hah ha, I guess I forgot to mention them. But they're infamous down here. On these lonely roads they hide in the rocks and rip off travelers, especially touristas. We got lucky, whew. They must've figured we were ripe for the picking."

"Then they must have really bad eyesight. I mean, dig what we're driving?. We're just a couple of poor, wandering hippies shitting in the woods."

Bones laughs, maneuvering through the steep bends. "But you're standing there flipping them off, and they have guns? That's pretty ballsy, man."

"Yeah, well, it's not the first time I've been shot at. And we didn't come all this way to be robbed by a bunch of drunken pendejos."

"You kidding me? Like where? Back in Chicago?"

"No, not Chicago. Way up in Montana when I was a kid," I reply, looking out on the steep rocky terrain, remembering. "Up in the Swan Mountains, when I was about thirteen. Me and a friend named Lockwood rode horseback up the mountain into the forest, making our own trail, riding, hoping we wouldn't run into a grizzly."

"Far out, man. So what went down? Who took the shots at you?"

"Something really weird happened that day. Right out of nowhere this crazy old coot started shooting at us, from up on the ridge. He was up in the trees looking down at us, shooting into our campfire knocking shit around. He knocks the coffee pot over, scatters the burning wood, hollering at us like some kind of demented maniac."

"Whoa man, saying what, hollering what?"

"Like he's yelling at us to get off his land, that we we're trespassing on his property. Get off my goddamned land, then blam blam blam, bullets whizzing all around. But that was bullshit, we both knew that. Because all that country around there is National Forest Land with grazing rights, it doesn't belong to anybody except maybe the bears. So we duck behind this log with our single-shot .22 rifles, shouting for him to leave us alone."

"Aiyee, far fucking out. He must have been some insane hermit. What happened?"

"He kept shooting, man. I mean, we're just kids, right? He puts a shot zinging right over our heads and the horses are starting to spook. He puts a couple of shots right into log we're hiding behind. Get off my land, he's screaming Get out of here, you pissants!"

"You make a run for it?"

"Hell no. We didn't want to risk the horses and besides, by then we were good and mad, so we shot it out with the crazy old fuck. We couldn't see him but we knew more or less where he was up in the trees. He was hunkered down and we started peppering that area. Not really trying to hit him, you know, trying just to scare the shit out of him."

"Aiyee, you grew up a gunslinger?" Bones says, his eyes watering with mirth.

"Sort of, yeah, ha ha. But dig, it worked. The crazy bastard comes scrambling out of that thicket and hightails it over the ridge. He had wild bushy hair and was wearing some kind of a blanket. Later that day we found his lean-to and destroyed it."

"Hah ha ha, that's an outrageous story! That actually happened?"

"Fuck yeah, it happened, we were just wild kids. Hey, man, watch out for that cow!"

Bones swerves to avoid a scrawny Mexican steer planted in the road, staring at us. He grins over at me, saying, "Bandidos, can you believe it, Jake? Fucking banditos."

"Si, bandidos, fucking cabrones. But no way, hombre, no way they get us today."

# Chapter 20

I N THE LONG shadows of afternoon, we arrive in the old silver mining town of Guanajuato. Pastel houses are stacked on the precarious hillsides like decks of cards. The streets are narrow, really no more than alleyways. At a roadside produce stand, we munch slices of watermelon and dip into our kilo of raw peanuts in the shell. The canyon-built city basks in the long rays of the sun, the beguiling pastels, then succumbs to a violet twilight.

Bones claims to know a man who lives in Guanajuato, someone he met last summer. But when we try to find him we have no luck. A woman who lives next door on the street where he used to live tells us that he moved to Durango, she thinks. So, no free crash pad for the night. Instead, we find a rundown motel, a place with screens, sleeping cots, and a shower where we can rinse off, keeping our lips sealed to the teeming microbes in the rusty water. During the night, I dream of a woman the colors of daybreak who speaks to me in a voice of a bird. She shows me the unusual movements of her lithe body, then gets frightened away by a rifle shot. I hear the shot like it went off right outside the door. What was she trying to reveal? A faint pearlescent light seeps through the curtainless windows.

The morning comes on as translucent as glass. Our road leads south across the great central plateau at an elevation of over seven thousand feet, aiming toward Mexico City. To the map in my head, Bones seems to be taking us on a round-about route, but at least we're making good time. The relentless sun bakes the car, we're sweating like pigs, our bodies plastered to the vinyl seats. The closer we get to Mexico City, the more clogged and monotonous the highway becomes. Cars, trucks, jeeps and buses, mule carts, a mudslide of belching traffic converging on the capital.

Smoking the cooling reefer, I consider our meandering crawl across the immense terrain. How long have we been out on this road? Days, it seems like days, our skinny vegetarian asses are road-sore. The sprawling slums of the city suck us in, a vortex of restless, unwashed humanity pulsating with desperate need. They scramble along side the cars and trucks in the choking fumes, pathetic beggars pleading for a scrap of life, hands outstretched. There is nowhere you can turn that you do not see, and in seeing confront the wretched failure of our civilization.

"California, hola, hola!" they cry out, tapping on the glass, patting their chests, trying to clean the bug-spattered windshield with filthy rags. They have no tomorrow, no way out, only the thinnest chance of life seasoned with the bitter hope. I would burn our so-called civilization to the ground to help these people.

"Can you believe it?" Bones mutters. "This is the underbelly of our greedy soulless political system, the peons who never get the slightest chance and no one in power gives a fuck! Most of them don't even have a place to sleep, or if they do, no bread, no food, no nothing, nothing, because they are nothing to their insane governments!"

And he speaks the truth, Bones, my brother, and the truth takes no prisoners. The truth reveals brazen reality. These people are the cast-aways, the human wasteland, the appalling poverty, while rich nations squanders tens of millions on their criminal wars rather than nurture and lift them. It lays waste to the heart and destroys one's faith. You have to be a brain-washed moron to acquiesce in the face of such violent human suffering, shrugging it off to God's will or whatever. Back in California, Bones and I make it in easy style on a few dollars a day, with good food and pure water, friendly dope to smoke, but here, in this bleak, blasted scar where birds drop off the wires from smog-poisoning, a few gringo dollars are a soul's ransom.

Out of this honking chaos, a shriveled unkempt woman in a sack dress appears at my window, scratching at the glass with filthy nails. "Senor," she rasps through devastated teeth, "senor, mira, la nina, mira!"

Leering at me, she lifts a writhing infant swaddled in dirty rags up to my sweat-stung eyes. The child has a shock of black hair, gummed-over eyes, two gaped teeth in its mouth, with a fly crawling over its bulging forehead. The weird woman hisses at me, insisting that I ogle the child, snared in this maelstrom of honking traffic and brutal heat.

"Brujacita," the crone hisses, "si, si, brujacita!"

Unable to peel my eyes away, I mutter to Bones, "Is she saying what I think she's saying?"

"Aiyee, fuck, I think she's telling us the child is a witch. Those two can put a curse on us, fuck our car up, mess up all our plans."

"Aha, then, let's fix it," I say, digging into my pocket, rolling my window down a few more inches. I wag an American five-spot in the leathery hag's face, she snatches it from my fingers, breaking into an incredulous and toothless smile even as she turns away.

Cranking the window back up for protection, I roll my eyes at Bones. "Man, we need to get out of this trap. It's madness. Turn anywhere, any road with a sign, it doesn't matter."

"I'm trying," Bones grunts, eyes twinkling, lurching the car forward like a tortoise. "Aiyee, you might have just saved our asses from that bruja's curse!"

"Hah! But I think we cursed ourselves when we took this route. Let's make tracks."

It takes us hours to get clear of the hellish labyrinth of Mexico City, tormented by lethal exhaust fumes, confusing road signs, and snarling motorists. But at last we break free and start making good time to the southeast. The rains come in the late afternoon, sudden fat showers, harbingers of the oncoming monsoons. We aim for Tehaucan, and beyond, crossing the high plains already tingeing green from the billowing cloud showers. Soon, quite soon, up in the Oaxaca highlands the rare mushrooms will sprout in the fields and meadows and we still have many miles to go.

At the crossroads town of Teotitlan we take a deep, road-burned breath, needing to eat and rest. From here one can follow the valley roads southwest to La Ciudad de Oaxaca, or climb the perilous dirt roads that run for hundreds of kilometers deep into the remote sierra. For us, there is only one choice. We arrive in Teotitlan a little past noon, a huge reef of cloud banking against the immense mountain range immediately to the east. Up there, in the fabled cloud forest, high above the wild river canyon, lies the old village of Huautla de Jimenez.

The relentless push down from the border has frazzled our nerves. One look around at the open-air fruit and vegetable market persuades us to lay over for the night. Luscious mounds of vine-ripe tomatoes, piles of avocados, fat oranges, nuts, green onions, yellow squash, ripe papayas, mangoes and gorgeous bananas stoke our gustatory lust. Fuck yes, we are ravenous, drooling with hunger, the mythical mountain will still be there in the morning. For now, let's kick back and relax in this peaceful colonial town. We rent a room with real beds in the quaint hotel on the plaza, hoping for no cucarachas. We'll eat and rest, and make ourselves ready for the last leg of this marvelous journey.

We settle in dark wooden chairs under the hotel ceiling fans, making ourselves at ease in the cantina. The amiable proprietor speaks an engaging style of English, making us smile. He takes our starved vegetarian request for guacamole and chips, frijoles, rice and salsa, shrugging off our disinterest in his house special carne asada. He is a man of the world, he has traveled beyond his country, nothing much surprises him. He tells us that we are the first long-haired Americanos he has seen, this year and he is glad we have come. We ask him about the condition of the road leading up to Huautla in the sky.

"To my knowledge there are no washouts, no problemas," he replies, his eyes bright with interest. "So, you come for the sacred mushrooms? You will be glad to know that there are no Federales around. The bastards have not shown up yet."

His candor takes us aback, we glance around to see who might be listening. But it is siesta time and we are the only customers.

"Si, senor, that is why we are here. We are psychedelic adventurers."

"Esta bien," the suave innkeeper nods, "and don't worry, I won't tell a soul. To be honest, I have thought that one of these days I'm going up there myself to see what happens. Life becomes so hum-drum, you know? If you don't find the nerve to do something different, it always remains the same."

Bones flashes his ingratiating smile. "Well, senor, you can always close this place down for a week or two and come with us."

"Hah, don't tempt me," our new friend laughs, and starts bringing us the delicious comida, with cold perspiring bottles of beer, manna for the road-burned traveler.

But noo sooner do we begin eating then a burly American stomps into the cantina, rubbing his hairy chest. He is shirtless, wearing only a black leather vest with silver buttons, black jeans and cowboy boots. Spying us, he hoots, "Hey, that old Mercury with California plates belong to you cats?"

Mouths full, chewing, we take him in with wary eyes. This dude is brash and brawny, but going to fat. He sports lizard skin boots and stove-pipe jeans, and a silver concho belt. His face has that fleshy meat-eater's look, with narrow-set eyes, unkempt black hair and a three days stubble. Standing there, he grins down at us like he has just lucked out.

Taking a swallow of beer, I say, "Yeah, that's our wheels, man. And yeah, we're from California. What's happening with you?"

He yanks out a chair, reverses it, and straddles it like we're all instant comrades. Running his fingers through his oily hair, he gives us an insider's grin. "Well shit, check this out. I just got here by bus a few hours ago from may-hee-co city, and I've been hoping I'd run into some real Americans down here, somebody I can talk to. Seems like these greasers don't get a single word of what I say."

Aiyee, I think, what do we have here? I take an instant dislike to this swaggering buffoon. "My name's Hightower," he goes on, "from Buffalo, up in New York. And you heads gotta be from either L.A. or Frisco, am I right?"

"Right on," Bones affirms, wanting some common ground. "L.A., actually."

"All-fucking-right," the Hightower declares, thumping the table like he's won some kind of bet with himself. In my head I nickname him the Buffalo Cowboy, already wishing that we'd gone on up the mountain and not even stopped for lunch.

Hightower takes Bones affable face as an invitation He calls out for "three beers fria", waving some crumpled dollars in the air. The proprietor comes over with three bottles, giving me a sidelong, skeptical look. I know what he means. The revolting American from Graham Greene's novel has just walked in the room.

"Here's to getting higher than high," the Buffalo Cowboy snorts, tilting his head back and chugging half the bottle down, belches, then guzzles the rest. His thick, stubbled neck is greasy with sweat.

He helps himself to our chips and guacamole, then begins telling how he got to Teotitlan. Three weeks ago, on a drunkard's spree in Greenwich Village, he dropped a few hits of street acid that almost blew his mind. Coming down hard on reds, he got into a bitter fight with his "slut girlfriend" who turned around and ran off with a "nigger trumpet player." Getting revenge, Hightower emptied their joint bank account, scored a bag of black mollies, and took a train south that took him clear to El Paso. Across the border, in a Juarez bar on his amphetamine binge, he runs into a wandering hippie who told him about hallucinogenic mushrooms that grew up in the mountains of Oaxaca. The hippie even drew him a map on a bar napkin. Hightower bought a ticket on a slow train to Mexico City, then figured out how to get here to Teotilan by an even slower bus.

I listen to this tale with an inward sense of dismay. If people like this boastful jackass start flocking to Huautla de Jimenez to get high, they'll ruin the scene in no time.

Gobbling his pork carnitas, the Buffalo cowboy says, "I'm willing to bet you guys are heading up there, right? Why else would freaks like you be down here in the middle of nowhere? Am I right?"

His obstinate eyes probe us, he chews his loathsome tacos with an open mouth. We admit those are indeed our intentions, yes, verdad, that is why we're here. Out past the cool shadows of the veranda, the afternoon clouds open up and huge drops are splashing on the cobble stones. Staring into the sudden rain, I wish him gone.

"Well hell, I don't mean to butt in," Hightower grunts, "but I've been having a lousy time in this fucked-up country. I'll fill your gas tank if you'll let me hitch a ride up there with you. What do you say? All I'm asking is for a ride up the hill."

I almost laugh out loud. Bones and I exchange a wry glance, facing our fate. It would be just plain mean to tell him, "No", and besides, what goes around comes around. Bones reads my face until I assent with a little nod.

"We can probably work that out," Bones says, "one good thing for another."

"Fucking A righteous," the Buffalo Cowboy crows, ordering another round of cervezas.

All through the mosaic afternoon the rain falls on the cobblestones, obscuring the mountains in scrolls of mist. We sit in the open veranda windows, beneath the slowly whirling fans, sweating, drinking the amber bottles of Carta Blanca, swapping stories, but mainly listening to Hightower brag. I tune him out, letting my garrulous partner carry the conversation. The proprietor comes and sits with us on the porch, sipping a coffee, talking about the Indians, the ancient Mazatecs, the mushroom cult that has existed since before Cortez came.

"They are an unusual and isolated people," he relates, looking toward the vast mountain curtained in rain. "They come down and trade with us every so often on the supply truck or the mountain bus, sometimes even by foot and burro although that's a long walk. They have their own language, and their mystical cult has it's own high priestess named Maria Sabina."

"High priestess?" Hightower says in a lewd chuckle. "Well damn, I hope she's a fox. I ain't had a piece of ass since I left New York."

The conversation freezes with a wince, I give our host an apologetic glance. Bones says something to Hightower that only makes him snort. He is a world-class asshole and I make a promise to ditch this sorry fool as soon as we reach the top. But for now, my eyes look right through him. I listen to the rain falling on the veranda roof like a musket barrage, shrugging him off, as Mexico always shrugs off its crass intruders.

"You need not concern yourself," the proprietor remarks, his eyes inscrutable. "I doubt you will have the chance to meet her, let alone see her."

"And why the fuck not," the Buffalo cowboy blusters, "why wouldn't I get the chance?"

Getting to his feet, the innkeeper says just loud enough to hear over the drumming rain, "Because she was here before the priests ever came, priests that wanted to burn her but never could. Like certain elusive birds that only come out in the silver of night, she will not give you even a glimpse of herself."

Looking at me with prescient eyes, he says, "Now I must return to work, amigos. Que tengas buen dia."

# Chapter 21

A<sup></sup>S EVENING COMES on there is a lull in the falling sheets of rain. We walk out into the humid twilight, onto the wet cobblestones of the town square. Someone approaches us from across the plaza, another Norte-Americano who recognizes us as fellow countrymen. A thin teenage boy with longish blond hair and a hesitant mustache, wearing faded jeans and ragged black sneakers. Over one shoulder, in perhaps a dramatic gesture, he has slung a hand-woven black and white sarape. The kid tells us that he came over the border at Nogales, then hitch-hiked across Mexico without speaking a word of lingo. He has been hanging out here in Teotitlan for almost a week, camping outside of town, living on tinned sardines and canned pineapple juice.

"I got the shits real bad," the kid confesses, "so I'm afraid to drink the water anymore."

Bones befriends him with a benign expression, another needy refugee. But I'm struck by the odd coincidences that are piling up. Shaking the kid's hand, I ask him, "Tell me, how is it, of all the places in Mexico, that you came here?"

Rubbing his blond-whiskered chin, he says, "I heard about these cosmic mushrooms that grow up in those yon mountains. This psychic teacher living out on the Tucson desert told me about it, said if you eat them they show you your soul."

Hightower guffaws in his face, smirking. "Shows you your what? Get real, boy."

"No, it's what I said," the kid counters. "He told me to follow the roads to Teotitlan and ask around. So here I am."

Ignoring the idiot Hightower, I say, "A psychic, you mean like a clairvoyant, told you that?"

"Yeah, kinda. He's more like this hippie guru that goes off into peyote trances. Lives up there in a commune they call the God's Eye People. I lived with them for awhile, but it was a weird scene. The leader wanted to fuck everybody, men and women alike."

Hooting in derision, Hightower stomps off. "Gotta go piss, har har har. Need a beer."

"Is that why you left?" Bones asks the kid, sensing he's had a rough time.

"No, that wasn't it. They made me leave cause I wouldn't hoe in their damn gardens. I don't do that kind of work, it ain't my style. Except," he says with a sly glint, "I stole that self-appointed guru's map to this place, I know where the secret village is. Only problem is I'm down to my last twelve bucks. I've been living on sardines and crackers. Ever eat Mexican sardines?"

Bones and I flick our eyes at each other. I don't like what we're getting into here, and Bones knows it. We're not down here to save aimless and penniless vagabonds. People on the road either carry their own load or they mess things up, and I don't like getting sidetracked.

The leering Buffalo Cowboy comes back with three fresh beers, and starts right in mocking the kid. The kid turns red-faced and starts to stammer. I hand my beer to him and tell Hightower point-blank to lighten the fuck up. He stands there, a menacing oaf, glaring at me. But there's something in me when I get mad that makes people stop, and I know this asshole is mostly braggadocio. I'd as soon beat the fuck out of him right now with anything I can lay my hands on and be done with it.

"Hey cool out," Bones intercedes, "let's everybody lighten up! We don't need these hassles, come on. We all met for a reason way down here in Oaxaca, just think about that."

"Yeah, maybe so," I reply, watching Hightower with deadly calm eyes. He puffs out his thick chest, challenging me, but then starts fishing for his Lucky Strikes.

"I'm from Saint George, Utah," the kid says in a placating voice. "I ran away from this Mormon family."

"You mean, you actually ran away?"

"Yeah. They were all sexually twisted. And believed that black people were the sons of Ham and belonged to the devil. That they were wicked sons of the devil."

"Fuck that nonsense," I tell him, still watching Hightower, "Only racists fools believe such shit. I would've run off myself."

Hightower grunts, flicks a match to his Lucky, and looks away.

"Aiyee, dig," Bones says, appealing to us all. "Why don't we all go out to that field where you're camped and smoke some good dope? Let's lose these bad vibes."

"Hell yeah," the kid enthuses, "I'll show you my camp, it's a good camp! And I ain't smoked any grass since I left that stupid commune."

Giving Bones an affable nod, I say, "Yeah, that sounds like a real good idea. Let's all go get high and mellow out. What say you, Hightower?"

"Yeah, I'm all for it," Hightower throws in, offering me his hand. "I'm gonna go buy us a cold six pack, just gimme a minute."

Bones and the kid start joshing each other, he has that gift of putting people at ease, Bones does. I go over to the car and dig into my olive pack for the makings. I'm not really smiling, but I'm all for making peace. Make love, not war, I believe in that. The lampposts on the square twinkle on one by one. The low sky hangs with heavy dense clouds the color of a gunbarrel, with a slash of crimson on the far horizon.

OUT IN THE empty fields, in the gathering dusk, we build a sputtering fire against an outcrop of rocks. The air feels pregnant with moisture, the earth is damp, although the kid has some dry sticks wrapped in a plastic tarp. He doesn't have any real camp gear, not even a pot. Other than his hand-made sarape all he's got is an army surplus blanket. When the rains come, he wraps himself in the blanket and burrows inside the tarp with his kindling, living more like a rodent than a man, no wonder he seems so pensive.

"They stole my backpack, the Mexicans did," he tells us. "I got drunk in Zacatecas and passed out. They took my pack and my clothes, and about one hundred dollars."

"Yer lucky they didn't steal your shoes," the Buffalo cowboy mocks.

"These shoes?" the kid retorts. "Hell, no ones would want these raggedy black sneakers. They smell something awful."

Our damp fire gives off a wavering, smoky flame in the circle of stones. Hightower pops the caps off the beer bottles with his pocket knife and I roll a fat number from my stash. Lighting it, I pass the joint to the kid who takes a huge hit, hands it to the buffalo cowboy, who doubles down, then thumbs it over to Bones. Bones treats it with Buddha-like aplomb, and in no time flat we are all laughing like old friends. But the Buffalo cowboy is ego-tripping, one-upping whatever he hears and lying through his teeth. He has the social grace of an aggressive doberman pincer. A ragged flash of lightning bursts across the somber sky, long rolling thunder, and we all whoop together.

Hightower bogarts the fat roach, his lips working it. "Fantastic good shit," he rasps, sucking the ember into his mouth. "You score it down here?"

"No, no way," I smile "that's a special Mexican blend gathered by hand from different jungle plantations, mixed by my own hand, and destined for us at this very campfire."

"Aiyee," Bones laughs, "it's true, there are no coincidences!"

"Man," the kid chimes in, "if I had me some dinero I'd pay five dollars for another doobie like that."

"I'll goddamned second that idea," Hightower says, "and I got the five bucks!"

Another zig-zag bolt of lightning slashes across the foothills like a neon brushstroke, followed by an ear-splitting cannonade of thunder. There's no doubt rain's coming our way and coming fast. Fat heavy drops are already hissing into our smoking, reluctant fire.

"Gonna rain some more," the kid mutters, looking a tad forlorn.

"Makes the sacred mushrooms grow," Bones points out.

"Uh, man, I got that five dollars," the Buffalo cowboy says again.

Reaching into my shirt pocket, I flourish another tapered bomber. "Let's fire it up, boys, it's on the house. Let's enjoy that cosmic light show coming yonder!"

"Aiyee, the cosmic light show," cries my partner Bones, "riders on the storm!"

Lightning cracks above the long mountain range again, a flickering eerie sheet, and rain comes sweeping across the dark plains in an audible rush. Cupping the joint, beer bottles in hand, we cluster around the hissing fire sharing lusty tokes. The monsoon skies erupt in savage lightning, smelling of ozone, the wind rises like an invisible curtain being torn back. We run into the electric night laughing and calling like Dionysian spirits, wild figures spun in the arc-light turning the dark landscape into flickering snapshots as our eardrums are walloped by thunder. We cavort like mad men, a stoner's glee club set free. But when lightning strikes a mere hundred yards away, shaking the earth and deafening us, I realize that someone could die out here in this Mexican field!

In the surreal light I grab the dervish Bones by his long arm. "Hey, bro', we gotta find some cover or somebody might get hit! Fried alive, Bones, fried like bugs!"

Bones turns his strobe-lit face to me, but at once serious. "Holy fuck, you're right! How close was that last one?"

"Too close, the other side of the field! We need to get under shelter pronto!"

Another shuddering blast detonates right above us, lighting the field up in a bluish-white, neon frenzy, Hightower and the kid are cavorting like lunatics, Bones runs out to them, waving his arms. Against the ink-blot canvas of night the mountains are lit up with protean sheets of lightning, my whole being is primed to run for it. Death is dancing in this field with us, death is present in mad delight. The kid comes running past me laughing his wits out, never even breaking stride as he heads for town.

Bones trots over, hair plastered to his skull, water running off his beard. "Let's go," he wheezes, "we're all too young for a funeral."

Hightower stomps out of the ozone darkness, bitching at me, "What the fuck, man? Why's everybody running away?"

"Stay if you want, get your dumb ass electrified. We're outta here."

Bones and I turn and jog for the aqueous lights of Teotitlan, running as best we can in our soggy hauraches. The buffalo cowboy comes thumping past us in his snakeskin boots, snickering like a maniac. The black sky splits in another huge deafening flash as we all hightail it.

IN THE MORNING, the plaza cobblestones glisten in the early sunshine. The immense mountains directly to the east are clear again, wreathed in horsetails of mist against a blue sky. My partner sidles over to me as I jam my pack into the backseat. I already know what's on his mind.

"About Hightower," Bones says, "we still cool about taking him up with us?"

"He's a braggart and braggarts are bad luck. You tell me."

Stroking his beard, Bones grins, "Yeah, but we sorta gave our word. He's only got one suitcase and dig, we can always ditch him up in Huautla"

Impassive, I take his shoulder bag and wedge it on the floor. "Yeah, that we did. And there's enough room in the backseat. And who knows, he might come in handy. I'm sure sick of changing flat tires.'

"Yeah, me too," says Bones. "So we're good to go?"

"Yeah, I'm good with it, just so long as we shoo him off later."

"Right on. Plus maybe a little good deed comes back to us, know what I mean?"

I take a look at the blue mountains capped in mist and sunlight. Bones makes me smile, I like his easy-going hippie philosophy. "We're solid, man," I tell him, "you and I got no problems."

Nodding, Bones points out, "That poor lost kid wants a ride up there, too. But that's another story."

"Sure as hell is. He's flat broke and doesn't ever have a change of clothes. We can't be a rescue service for everyone we meet on the road."

"Yeah, I hear you," Bones concedes. "He shouldn't really even be here. Because now someone just has to take care of him."

Bones is admitting what I already know. He wants to rescue that kid too, he wants to save everyone, even if it's to our own detriment. "Look, Bones," I say, "the smartest thing for him would be to hitch back to the border, before he gets busted and thrown into jail. He'd be dogfood in a Mexican jail."

We glance over to where the Arizona kid slouches against a white-washed wall, alone and brooding. Last night, he crashed on our hotel room floor on my sleeping bag, Hightower grabbed the couch, Bones and I slept on the twin beds. This morning anybody who wanted a shower got a shower, we all ate some breakfast, but there's only so much you can do.

We study the kid, putting our heads together. "How about we just pitch in and get him a bus ticket home, you and me? That's probably the best thing."

"You took the words right out of my head. At least it'll give him a decent chance."

"How much you think it'll cost us?"

"Shoot, I'll bet you $25.00 American will just about cover a ticket to Nogales."

"Right on, then," Bones says. "Which is about all we can afford anyway."

We open our wallets and put our bread together, Bones walks off to find the bus station. We're going to actually hand him a ticket home, not just fork over the cash. I amble over to where the kid sulks with downcast eyes. Hightower comes barging onto the hotel veranda, shoots me a thumb's up, flips his cig into the street, then makes for the car toting his valise.

"Shotgun," he crows.

"Wrong," I throw back, walking past him. "You ride in the back or on the roof."

The Arizona kid stands in his mud-caked black and white sarape, trying to brash it out. I hand him a folded ten dollar bill, saying, "That's so you have something to travel on. Buy yourself some food and water."

"Thanks, uhh, what's that supposed to mean? You guys taking that asshole up above?"

"Yeah, we are. We're giving the Buffalo cowboy a ride to the top, like we promised. And we're buying you a bus ride back to the Estados Unidos."

"But I don't want to go back. I wanna go up there with you and your pardner. I wanna get high on those magic Injun mushrooms."

"Man, that's not going to happen this time. Maybe next year, those mountains aren't going anywhere. But first you need to get your act together. No one's going to take care of you up in Huautla, we've all got our own trips."

"But why that bragging jerkoff, why not me?"

"I just told you why. Because for one thing he's got his own bread. And he gets to go because we gave our word before you even showed up. But mostly, dig, we don't want to be responsible for you on top of that mountain. Sorry."

"My act would be together," the kid grumbles, "if they hadn't stole all my shit." He scuffs the ground with his toe. Shoving the ten-spot in his pocket, he pleads, "You and Bones gonna get some kind of place, right? Why can't I just crash in the corner? I'll clean up for you, fetch the water, whatever you need. I'll more 'n do my part."

"Like digging in that guru's garden?"

"Huh?"

"Never mind, just no, not gonna happen this time. You're cool, but we're on a spiritual quest and we're going it alone."

"Shit, so you leave me and take that ignorant asshole up there?"

"Yeah, well, I can appreciate that you detest his guts. Anyway, see Bones coming there? He's got your bus ticket to Nogales. Just shake the dust of Mexico, go on home, and regroup."

Bones saunters up with his benign smile. I shake the kid's hand and walk over to the car. I'm not into long goodbyes and there's nothing else to say. The morning sky is a robin's egg blue and the sun is on the rise. There's a dirt road leading up that vast, green mountain, through the mists of time, the final miles of a journey promised to me in a prophet's tongue. Time to go.

# Chapter 22

THE PRIMITIVE ROAD to Huautla de Jimenez snakes and climbs up the long mountain into the cloud forest. Gravel and clay all the way, carved out of rock, traversing canyon cliffs that yawn so deep that your mouth dries up. The rough track is usually wide enough for only one vehicle, winding up and upward to the old village in the sky. You get a shallow turn-out every five miles or so, carved into the mountain's stone face. But if your engine dies or your brakes fail, you're fucked. If you have a blowout between the random turnouts you have a serious problem. Once you start up that relentless grade you hope like hell you don't meet anybody coming down.

Even the boastful Hightower shuts up and holds his breath. When he fishes out his Lucky Strikes, we don't let him light up. Bones behind the wheel, going less than twenty miles an hour, and for once I don't mind. We crawl up the canyon road around blind curves on canyon edges that make you goggle. Aiyee, below, far below, a thousand feet or more, a silver ribbon of river sluices its way down from the highlands. That prehistoric river tells the time, but if you drive over the edge you'll never be missed. We clinch our jaws to endure whatever this road brings, not even sure the rattling old Mercury can handle it.

The first blowout comes about twenty or so miles up the gorge. The rocks punch a hole right through the rubber retread on a blind man's curve. We switch into one of our two spares, using Hightower's adrenaline-shot brawn for leverage. Lipping his Lucky Strike, he works fast. I stand watch on the hairpin turn, to see what's coming down. The flathead six groans on up the arduous trek like a wheezing yak, clinging to the cliff face, the canyon drifted with mist and sunshine, the yawning chasm. We have not encountered another driver nor even seen another human being.

We see birds of prey, giant eagles, hawks, vultures, gliding on the thermals. We see furry animals scurrying among the rocks. We see a dun-colored cougar that moves like a shadow in the transparent sunlight. Or did we see it? Yes, I saw it, I did see it. We converse in short sentences, monosyllables, in gestures, in awe of even being here. But you dare not daydream on such a road.

The second blowout comes with a ragged hiss a mere fifty yards past one of the cliff-cut turnouts. Bones backs us down and nudges the car into the tight space. Hightower goes at it again, sweating out last night's booze, grunting how bad he needs a nip, the hair of the dog, fuck, a beer, anything. He yanks the flat tire off and muscles on our last spare. We stack both flats in the trunk, grim accusations that we are down to our last four rubber retreads. The immense mountain still looms above us.

"Shit," grumbles Bones, who hardly ever grumbles, "I wonder if they have a tire repair stall up where we're going?"

"Don't know," I grimace, "but we're up shit creek if another one goes."

"Damn it, I'm gonna go real easy. Gonna keep it down to fifteen miles an hour."

"Fifteen miles an hour?" Hightower protests. "Fuck man, it'll be to-morrow till we find a bar! I'm hurting, I need a drink bad."

"Yeah? Well dig this – if we lose another tire and we could be walking all day. We won't get very far on those rims."

"Aiyee, if it comes to that we might be forced to push this crate over the edge to clear the road."

Hightower shakes his head, cursing. But Bones observation is correct. Junkers get pushed over the canyon edge. We've seen the rusting carcasses of abandoned wrecks on the rocks below. There's no mercy on these roads, no tow-trucks, the doomed are doomed.

Letting Hightower take a smoke break, we hear a harsh roar coming downhill. Around the bend a dirty red truck comes shambling towards us at breakneck speed. Two Mexicans in baseball caps are in the cab, grinning like lunatics, hoisting beer bottles. They rumble past in the red flatbed sending a shower of gravel all over the place.

"Motherfuck," I mutter. "God help us if we run into another one of those."

Bones throws me a pale glance, wondering how much further. High-tower's jaw hangs open in somber imagination.

We plod on up the steep grade in the old coupe, bouncing, rocking on creaking springs, hoping against hope that our luck holds out. The road moves away from the precipitous chasm and into a narrow, ascending valley. Our destination is somewhere up ahead, two hours, five hours, quien sabe?. Huautla is about a hundred or so road kilometers from Teotitlan, but our odometer doesn't work and we are traveling at a snail's pace.

Around noon we come on a roadside hamlet, no more than a handful of stone and adobe huts strung along the road for about a hundred yards. There are no signs, no stores, no electricity, no gas pump, not a single car or truck visible anywhere. But on the high side of the road, on a low bluff, we see a bustling throng of people. They are dressed in bright birdsong colors, singing and dancing. It's obviously a celebration of some kind, we hear musica, a guitar, a flute, bursts of laughter, people tripping in and out of an adobe hut with a tin roof.

Intensely curious, we slow to a crawl, then pause with the motor run-ning waving up at them.

Some people peer down at us, an excited clamor arises as these Indians realize they have a visitation from another world. Two hombres in white shirts and striking hats come to the bluff and hail us. Grinning like madmen, making theatrical bows, they stand above us calling out in some kind of dialect. Who are we? From where do we come? Why are we here? One of them wears a silver-clad black sombrero and possesses an air of authority. His stout friend sports a straw bowler with red and yellow feathers stuck in the hat band. He spreads his arms wide, points at us, then laughs up into the sky.

"They gotta be drunk," Hightower mutters hopefully, smacking his lips.

"Sure looks that way," I agree, "drunk as loons."

Bones puts his amiable face out the window. "Hola amigos, donde esta Huautla? Quiero go to Huautla de Jimenez, entiendos? Amigos, tiene any cerveza?"

The two men explode in gut-splitting mirth, then come clamoring down the knoll to the strum of a guitar, the peal of a wooden flute. They slide down the rain-sodden bluff and come rushing over to us. Pushing their swarthy faces right into our side windows, they examine us with unabashed curiosity, They flash silver-toothed smiles that reek of raw liquor, clasping our hands with rough, gentle hands, beckoning us to step out. So we do, we all stand together in the road, smiling up at the excited congregation on the bluff. Through a jumble of Spanish, local dialect and gestures, we communicate. Huautla de Jimenez? No, Huautla is still another three hours up ahead, maybe more, way up in the clouds. Magic mushrooms aqui, los pajaritos? No, no senores, both men frown and laugh and shake their heads, no pajaritos magico, those pajaritos are for the malo loco! But mescal, ah, amigos, they make avid drinking gestures, mescal y licores de maiz muchos! The headman in his black sombrero pours from an imaginary bottle and downs an eye-rolling shot. He cradles his heart, someone he loves, perhaps his daughter, has just taken her marriage vows. In all improbable timing, we have just happened on a wedding celebration in this tiny mountain town! And what is the name of your village, we ask. La Aurora, they proudly tell us, this pueblo es called La Aurora.

We nod cordially, piecing the news together. These exuberant men pound on the hood, insisting that we join in their nuptial debauch. Come, come drink with us! Fate has brought you here from your distant land, Fate has decided it! Laughing with them, for indeed, surely the hand of God has written it, we follow them up the bluff on some muddy stone steps.

The headman takes us into the milling group with a grandiose air. These Mestizos greet us with wondering and impassive faces, while the shy women hang back. They're wiry and tough men, few of them over five foot five, wearing canvas pants and white or blue wedding shirts, some with machetes affixed to braided rope belts. We shake their hands with an honest respect, at least Bones and I do. They stare into my green eyes and admire my sun-streaked hair, murmuring salutations. I have never felt like a specimen before and it's a peculiar feeling. For them we are strangers from an unknown world of legend and myth.

"Hot damn," mutters Hightower, "these boys are as drunk as skunks and their women are cute. This is our lucky fucking day, I'm thinking."

"Use your head," I tell him, realizing the moment is lost on him. "We are total strangers here, outlanders. Show respect."

"Aiyee, no hassles, and remember," Bones says, "be careful not to insult anybody. Do not mess with their chicks."

The headman takes me by the arm and makes a proclamation in their incomprehensible dialect, lifting his black sombrero and encompassing us all in a gesture. The people laugh in agreement, the women clap their hands, the men pat our shoulders and backs. We are ushered into the adobe shed with the tin roof that serves as their cantina. One wall harbors an eight foot plank bar, a row of green-glazed clay cups, and a few simple stools. The little chief pours a clear liquor out of an umber clay jug, showing his strong friendly teeth. We are amigos, are we not? We shall drink today our satisfaction, we shall drink today like hombres! He fills a dozen or so of these clay cups to the brim, signaling for all present to partake. Men and women, young and old, step forward and take a cup or wait as more cups are filled.

Someone places a clay cup in my hand, I take a whiff of the primeval booze. The fumes surge up my nostrils, making my eyes water. "Senor," I ask the headman. "Que es esto? Tequila?"

"No, no agave," he says, his black eyes gleaming with pride. "Maize, licores de maize, muy fuerte, siete anos de aqui!"

"Aiyee," Bones says, nudging me. "Seven years old, the local firewater. We're in for it."

"Fucking A," the Buffalo cowboy crows, "down the hatch!" But before he can toss his whiskey, el jefe, the chief, holds a chiding finger in his face. Holding the finger up for a moment, he expounds about some ritual that needs to be honored, nodding toward the shy bride and groom holding hands at one of the tables on the packed dirt floor. Hightower turns red, but has enough sense to curb his tongue.

The headman turns and smiles at Bones, then at me, knowing we have understood. He reaches out and taps me on the chest, right above my heart. Lifting his cup, he cries out a salute to the newlyweds and everyone joins in, Maria, Juan, Juan, Maria, wishing them health and good luck! Buena suerte! Then we all throw the burning firewater down our throats.

Ah Madre de Dios! It's like gulping nectar from Hell, a stream of lava fumes down my gullet, setting my lungs on fire! We gasp and choke, our eyes tear, our ears ring as the liquor shoots into our bloodstream, much to the delight of our new comrades. Several toasts follow in rapid succession, they clap us on our backs. We are hombres like them, we are hermanos ahora! Aiyee, we are gut-shot gringos who are wildly drunk in a matter of minutes.

A raucous party explodes all around us, a vortex of homespun music and sudden friendship and brilliant inspiration. We all crowd together, doing our best to communicate. We pour in and out of the bar in the luminous falling drizzle, laughing, trying to find common words and phrases like optimistic lunatics. Ah, but do not flirt with their pretty women, I remind myself, do not be so reckless. Touch their young females, they might split you open and feed your innards to their dogs. No, instead, we join in their songs, the battered guitar played by an elfin man in a felt fedora with buckteeth who smiles and smiles. Everyone sings, the jug of corn mash goes round and round, a well-spring of jubilant thanksgiving. The day swirls away like a bright race of mountain hummingbirds.

At some point, I notice Bones down on the road kneeling beside the car with a couple of curious natives. Standing up, he gives me a enigmatic gesture. "Another damn flat," he calls up. "Looks like we're stranded."

"No, damn it to hell, hah ha ha, no. We'll drown in this moonshine if we stay here. Can they not fix it?"

"No one even has a car around here. They say maybe up in Huautla."

Resigned, Bones comes trudging back up the knoll. I watch him come, looking out over the steep green landscape, smiling to myself. The roof of the sky seems only a few hundred feet above our heads, air damp with mist and intermittent drizzle, more flat fucking tires, but so what? We are in another world now, wee have escaped, beyond ordinary time.

"How bad is it?" I ask him. "Fixable?"

"Not totally screwed," Bones says. "They're basically inner tube flats, the tires aren't torn. They say a truck or bus might come by later today, going up or down."

"Might? We're in another world, my brother. Do they even know?"

"They say today or manana," Bones grins, "but they think today. Going up, I hope. I don't want to go all the way back down to Teotitlan"

"Me neither. Fuck that, they have clocks there. Hah, things could be worse."

"Where's that idiot Hightower? I need to pull that flat off while we have time."

"Around here somewhere and royally fucked up. He has a knack of pestering everybody."

"Not good, you were right about him. I'm gonna go ahead and take that tire off. If somebody comes along, I'll take a couple of flats up to Huautla. If we get lucky I'll make it back today."

Ever optimistic, I love that about Bones. "That sounds like the ticket," I reply. "This shindig could go on all day and night and it's getting out of hand. The headman already had to break up a scuffle in the bar. Everyone's drunk. You hip to those long knives they're carrying?"

"Dig, whoa, I noticed" Bones says in a low voice, squinting his eyes. "I hope they're just for skinning the rabbits that raid their gardens."

We laugh, because it's funny and we're borrachito on the moonshine. And in that very instant a furious commotion erupts from inside the tin-roofed cantina. Hightower comes boiling out of the doorway in a drunken knot of pushing, enraged men. One of them shouts into his face, stabbing his chest with an angry finger.

"Fuck off, you dirty greaser," Hightower bellows, shoving the smaller man so hard he falls to the muddy ground. A woman screams. The insulted Indian leaps to his feet with blood in his eye, a knife flashes in his hand. The Buffalo cowboy is about to get hacked into dog meat. El Jefe leaps into the melee waving his black sombrero, shouting, "No, no ya, no para nada! No mas, peleas!"

Hightower staggers like a drunken oaf, knocking the headman's ornate sombrero into the mud. Bones lifts his hands, imploring, "Por favor! Por favor!" And I rush forward and pick the sombrero up and start brushing it off. The wiry chief spins and glares at me, a welt of furious energy. But I offer him his splendid hat, saying, "Lo siento, senor, lo siento. Perdon us, por favor."

His black implacable eyes bore into mine, for any sign of deceit. I hold his hat with respect as he decides our fate. We are hemmed in on all sides, ignorant gringos, completely at their mercy.

Bones pulls the glowering Hightower from the crowd, shouting into his face, "You can't mess with their women, stupid! You can't even touch them!"

"Silencio!" roars the headman, abruptly lifting his arm and almost everybody shuts up. Then, with a formal bow, he accepts his sombrero from my hands. Nodding, he says to me, in a not unkind voice, "Esta bien, Oro, esta bien todo."

Turning on his heels he again commands, "Silencio!", with a slashing gesture. Everyone shuts up, even the angry young man who was wronged. El Jefe gives an order in rapid, terse dialect, the blade is put away. But the young man still bristles with indignation, his pride wounded by that brutish gringo. And I understand his feelings, for we are the intruders here. We are the cause of these unruly troubles.

I try to apologize in my broken Spanish, but the headman lifts a placating hand. He points down to the road where Bones already has the Buffalo cowboy pulling off the flat tire. He wags his solemn finger at Hightower, as though erasing him from their world. Then he moves close to me and grasps my forearms in his callused hands.

"Oro, tu eres mi amigo, somos amigos," he says, tapping my chest, then tapping his own. Turning his fierce eyes on his people, he says, "Esto es Oro, si, Oro, nuestro amigo!"

Several of the men come forward and shake my hand in their respectful way, saying, "Oro, esta bien, estamos amigos, todos amigos."

Bewildered, amazed, I murmur back, "Gracias mi amigos, gracias, senores, gracias."

The black-hatted chief jabs his strong finger down at Hightower, declaring, "Es un hombre malo, no respeta. Bastardo. Se destierra!"

He makes a sweeping gesture over the green hills, laughing, uttering confidential words that I do not understand. He nods at me, makes a wing-like gesture with his hand, closes his eyes, then blinks them open like a hawk. For a flickering instant I am looking into the topaz eyes of a hawk.

Then the little chief gives me a stained smile. "Ah, Oro," he says, "bienvenidos. Puedes quedarte con nosotros. Si, puedes."

"Entiendo," I murmur, my intuition ablaze, "si, senor, I understand."

I turn around smiling, letting them all know that I get it. I am among friends here, I can stay, Bones too. But Hightower the pariah, he is banished from this place and this moment forever.

The young man who was insulted comes to me and shakes my hand. His face impassive, but his eyes clear of resentment. "Bien, Oro," he says firmly, "esta todo bien."

A murmur of accord goes through the people, someone pats me on the back, cool bottles of beer are passed around. Where this cerveza comes from I don't know, but it tastes delicious. Gathering together, we raise the botellas and guzzle the beer down, laughing and burping. The singing starts again, plaintive and beguiling. Some couples start dancing in a way I have never seen, the wizened guitarist wails into the silver sky of cloud and rain. The clay jug reappears, aiyee, we pour shots right into our thirsty mouths.

Someone points down the road where a straining motor can be heard, climbing the grade. The headman and a few others scramble down the muddy bluff. Delighted and confused, I go to the edge of the knoll and call down to Bones. "What's happening, bro? What is it?"

Bones stares down the road, making sure, then flashes me the V-sign. "It's a truck, a truck is coming! This could be our rescue!"

A dirty white truck grinds into view even as ninos dash out into the road, a flatbed truck with wood-slat sides, hauling staples up to the sierra villages. It's loaded with cases of coca-cola, beer, sacks of flour and rice wrapped in plastic, boxes of canned goods, two cages of squawking chickens. Bones and I spread our arms and laugh at this improbable happening, even as the rain begins falling on our faces. But Hightower does not laugh. He slumps against the car in the muddy dirt, hating the deal he has dealt himself, sullen and inebriated.

A few boxes are passed down to the people in the road, some money is exchanged. Bones and I huddle together, working out our new plan. Everyone seems to haggling in a spirited way, divvying up the supplies. The headman helps us haggle a transportation fee with the driver, who will do us the favor but only for some dinero. Ah, la modida! He rubs his thumb and forefingers together, pursing his lips. Bones will take two flats up to Huautla for repair, then come back down with the driver, except the return time is uncertain. I'll stay with the wedding fiesta, keeping an eye on our car and our gear, although I already know these people would not take a single thing from us.

Taking Bones aside, I say, "You have to take the asshole with you and make sure he doesn't return. El Jefe has banished him. They'd as soon skin him alive."

We glance at the surly outcast, scrapping mud off his boots. "Yeah, I dig it," says Bones. "Don't worry, he and his suitcase are going up the mountain with me."

"And dig, my brother. I don't know how much longer I can hold out. These hombres have hollow legs and I'm trying to keep pace with them. So try your best."

"I'll be back today, Jake. I promise. I'll bribe that driver if I have to."

Standing together, we gaze out into the drizzling silver rain, into the mountain light. The hills, the trees, the fields are illuminated with a wild, green light. A profound thrill runs through us, right to our very core. We are here, we are free, the other world has been left behind.

The muddy white truck is ready to get underway. The three of them climb into the cab and the engine cranks over. But some kind of disagreement ensues, the driver curtly shaking his head. Hightower gets back out, cursing, then climbs into the back, trying to get a foothold among the coke-bottle crates. Grabbing ahold of the weathered side-slats, he glares down at me.

"That spic won't let me ride up front," he gripes. "What a shithole this country is!"

I shake my head in feigned sympathy, suppressing my mirth. The Buffalo cowboy carries a bad vibe and the word has gone out on him. The truck lurches into low gear, slamming Hightower into the weathered slats, bitterly cursing.

"Pendejo," sneers the headman, flipping him off as the truck lurches on up the rough road.

"Si, si," we laugh together, "que un gran pendejo!" Then he tugs on my arm to come, come mi hermano, vengas, let's go up and get out of this weather. His eyes twinkle, his black sombrero drips with rainwater.

I put my arm around his wiry shoulders, we slip-slide our way back up the muddy bluff. The fiesta is happening again, la musica spills from the tin-roofed bar. And my friend the weathered headman sings a song in my ear, in a voice of rawhide and corn whiskey, singing of a place not tainted by greed. He rasps his whimsical song and we laugh and stagger like long-lost brothers.

The rain falls all afternoon long, swallowing the hillsides in luminous mist, we drink like lords, laughing and sweating, men who have no past or future. And in my lucid inebriation I grow wise. I start drinking clay bowls of fresh water to replenish my feverish blood. With every searing shot of moonshine, I drink a bowl of delicious well water and piss in the lean-to latrine. The guitarist strums and bangs his his old box guitar, the wooden flute trills, we sing like drunken wolves, free men and women, me riding along on the edge of a frontier, will I be found again, will they come to get me hah ha ha, does it even matter? We share our histories in scrambled words, in garbled phrases, in gestures with sound effects. I show them how you ride an English motorcycle, they show me how you communicate with the whistling birds. We wander in and out of the falling rain, spun together in this happy, improbable event. The shy friendly women bring in platters of roasted goat meat and hot chili-spiced frijoles. Wrapping the beans in a tortilla, wolfing it down, I explain that I never eat meat, nada, no goats, no sheep, no cows, no pigs, no rabbits, no chickens, not even fish, although I will occasionally eat an egg. They don't care, they embrace me with amusement in this immeasurable afternoon of eternal rain and cloud light. I am welcomed, they make it known I can stay with them from now on. They show me a stone house with a dry roof where I can live. And in my heart I know that I could do this, I can merge into their world, take on another skin, another life, another name, indeed, who is there to stop me other than myself?

The proud little chief thwacks me on the shoulder with his palm. "Hermano," he laughs. "Tu eres nuestro hermano, para siempre!"

This is his day and these are his people and he speaks the truth, we are brothers and sisters, all of us. Bright with gratitude, I know that I am at a crossroads. My way does not lead back the way I came. My way is being made up by me and for me and though me with each rising day. And in this endless rain we drink some more, aiyee we do, mis nuevo hermanos y yo! We drink to the wild beauty of life on this ancient green mountain and to the love that never, ever dies, and I hold on. I do not falter in front of these brave and honest people. If called upon, I will fight for them and stay on my feet with them until the end of the world comes and goes.

But before the world does end, my brother Bones comes back. He climbs down out of the mud-splashed white truck, flashes me the peace sign, and pulls two inflated tires out of the back. Skidding down the hill, I help him remount the tire on the precarious jack. Our amigos cheer us on, laughing like children, making incomprehensible suggestions. Bones tells me that in Huautla it's all done by hand, there's no electrical power, our tires were inflated by men using an old foot pump. I pass a thick joint around, some of the men partake, clustered together in the holy, falling rain. Rain falling out of the vast pewter quilt of clouds, rain that is the only measure of time, rain that anoints our bodies, dripping down our faces, vitalizing the air in our lungs, rain that is the living spirit of these primeval mountains.

Finally, Bones and I leave with manly embraces and drunken vows. The headman's somber eyes are lit in a boyish smile. Oro, he whispers, my brother, ah mi amigo, spreading his arms, hugging me, come back to visit us, regresa a nosotros. Yes, my hermano, I promise you, te prometo, I will return. We are family now, always, until the end, and these words of ours are as true as daylight.

WE GRIND ON up the muddy road through the silver rain light and green corn and effulgent mist. And under my breath I whisper, *'These people are not lost at all. Maybe forgotten to an outside world that whores and sells itself every day, but what does that matter? In this place, their own place, they are complete in their knowing of life.'* We rock and jounce up the mountainside, ignoring the wet windshield and flappers that do not work. The rain falls and glistens, then dissipates, then comes again. The forested slopes are ethereal green, drifted with sheets of mist, infused with a phenomenal light.

Bones looks at me, asks softly, "Aiyee, what happened to you back there?"

And I smile, feeling a great love for my friend, for this earth and sky and for everything. "Something wondrous, Bones. I'm not sure I can even discribe it. They kept calling me Oro."

"Maybe the sun-streaks in your hair, the gold flecks in your eyes?"

"Maybe. He kept calling me his hermano, his brother, the headman did. I think they invited me into their village. They invited me to stay there and live with them."

"Jake, that is far out, man, just imagine. They'd find you a chick to have ninos with."

"Hah, yes, very far out and far in," I laugh, laughing with my friend, an almost soundless laugh, two visionary nomads ascending a mountain where few gringos have ever been. And gradually, sipping mineral water, I sober up.

We climb the rutted road up into the cloud-forest highlands. I doze a little, but mainly stay alert. This upper section of the road is not so treacherous and our patched tires hold. On the steep green slopes we see how the Indians have terraced the hillsides, hanging plots of green corn and and melons and squash. The terrain is so steep and tillable land so scarce that rope ladders are used for the men to climb up and down with baskets slung on their backs. We slow the car to a crawl to observe them, a dreamscape opening before our eyes, the threshold of a world unknown.

On the high rocky outskirts of Huautla de Jimenez, a blue rift opens in the clouds, the sun shines through, and all things glisten with a protean light. The old one and two story buildings are constructed of moss-covered stones caulked with mud cement, or made of adobe and weathered wood. Some scruffy kids run out into the road, signaling us, jabbering loudly. They come to our windows, dangling sacks of moist, muddy mushrooms in our faces, bargaining in shrill excited voices.

"What the hell, man," I exclaim, "what is all this about?"

"No gracias, no gracias," Bones keeps saying, until the disappointed urchins fall away. With a twist of his lips, he tells me, "My friend Richard told me about this scene in his letters. When you first get here the ninos swarm around, hustling mushrooms to the turistas. They go out after it rains and pick them. But he says don't ever buy from them. They could be peddling toxic toadstools and not even know it."

"Wow, man, that is truly bizarre—poisoned by street-hustling ninos?

Welcome to Shangri-La!"

Bones laughs, then says, "Richard's an anthropologist. He'll turn us onto a real guide. We won't have to mess with the street economy at all."

Huautla de Jimenez is a remote sierra outpost, perched on a high mountain ledge, fringed by cloud forest and rugged terrain. It's hard to even imagine a local street economy for psychedelic mushrooms. I glance over at the jiggling gas gauge, there's less than half a tank left, In Huautla there is no gas station, no electricity, no telephones, no television, only a single strand of telegraph wire that snakes up and down the vast mountain from Teotitlan. Not that this causes me the slightest dismay, no. This is what I came for. But when we go back down, if we go back down, we'll have to scrounge up some petrol somewhere.

Bones and I share a prescient glance, reading each other's thoughts. We have come to the edge of the mapped world to find something hidden, for revelation. We have no plans beyond this moment, and I have never felt more enthralled.

# Chapter 23

Eating the freshly plucked mushroom is much more visceral than swallowing a tab of Lsd. You consume the living flesh of a spirit plant and the sensations are notably different. Once the door flies open there is no turning back, you go wherever the power takes you. If your skin morphs into the sleek hide of a jaguar or your eyes become the gaze of a thermal-gliding hawk, you absorb what that teaches, you ride it out. This is where attitude comes in, as to whether you fear or trust yourself. Because without that essential self-trust you are no more than a burning reed. There are no emergency clinics in the far-away pueblos of the Sierra Occidental.

The laconic Mazatec guide who takes me into the high fields after the nightly rains points out the sacred mushrooms with an air of quiet respect. He shows me what is right to consume, and what I should never consume. Esta bien, esta nunca, he murmurs, making sure I understand. We go out on a few morning field trips together and soon I can identify the slender umbrella mushrooms called *pajaritos,* "little birds", as well as a more muscular variety. Bones seems less than eager to venture forth, claiming that he needs to recuperate from the long trip. I shrug, tell him to rest up, then go roaming on my own like I always do.

In Huautla de Jimenez the mountain road comes to an end. Foot and donkey paths fan into the hillside barrios, but the town square seems to be dead end for cars and trucks. We park and leave the battered Mercury near the post office, then go looking for Bone's friends, Sarah and Richard. The congenial Mexican who operates the town's only mercantile tells us where to find them. His friendly smile puts us at ease and his loquacious teenage daughter glows as she practices her basic English on us. She's drinking a green bottle of coca-cola, her teeth are already dark with cavities. The chemical erosion of this remote culture has set in, many of the Indian traders on the square have bad teeth. Modern soda pop seems to be the favorite refreshment, making you want to shout, "Don't drink that shit!" But the Empire of Coca-Cola has already staked its claim.

Richard and Sarah live on the down slope of Huautla, in a cluster of small, well-built haciendas that stand out. Richard tells us they lived here for almost a year before they got fortunate enough to rent such a house. The white-washed adobe with the clay tile roof has a tiled interior patio, potted plants, hanging orchids, and a spacious kitchen off the main living room. Running spring water flows through a pipe in the kitchen wall, into a stone basin, then back outside through a channel in the floor. The floors are laid with ocher tile, the windows have wavy glass panes. For many years this casa had been the home of a government official.

We sit among the plants in wicker and wooden furniture and converse. Sarah says their rent is the monthly equivalent of forty dollars Americano. They resemble brother and sister, these two young anthropologists. Richard has reddish blonde hair that wreathes his head, Sara has long reddish brown hair straight down her back. Both are devout vegetarians who have gone native. He wears canvas peon pants and a plain white shirt, she wears a long skirt and embroidered chemise, with no make-up. Sara shows us their five laying hens and a strutting rooster, explaining that rice, beans, fresh eggs and local goat queso supply all their protein. I have not eaten an egg in awhile and have almost forgotten what cheese tastes like. Would I be sabotaging my purist vegetariano path if I ate a fertilized egg?

These two beautiful people have been living on this mountain for almost two years. They arrived before most of the hippie seekers, living on anthropology grant money from UCLA. But that money is all but gone now and Richard's thesis still not finished. But they are the wise ones. He tells us where there might be a house for rent, and the landlady's name who lives behind it.

"It's not much," he says in owlish sympathy, "but casas are hard to find up here and you can get it dirt cheap. You might even get it just by trading for repairs."

"Aiyee," says Bones, "that's right up my alley. What about tools?"

"I don't know," Richard replies, "you'll have to ask her about that.

She's a widow who lives by herself and if something needs fixing, she has to hire someone."

Sarah brings in mugs of honey-sweetened Chiapas coffee. "To be honest," she shrugs, "there's not much that ever goes wrong in these places. Just a roof leak now and then. No electrical wiring or much plumbing in Huautla to worry about."

Bones and I share a complicit glance. "We'll go and talk to her," Bones says, his eyes bright, imagining that this widow might be responsive to his erotic wiles.

"Yeah," I affirm, "a roof over our heads is our numero uno priority. By the way, coming in, we got accosted by some kids trying to peddle mushrooms. Naturally, we said no. But how do we go about it? How do we get the real deal?"

Richard fingers the fat tapered joint I hand him, saying, "You know, oddly enough, grass is hard to come by up here. Muchas gracias."

Laughing, Sarah says, "We'll introduce you to an Indian guide in a day or so. He'll stop by to trade for some of our eggs. His name is Ezequiel, he'll take you out. Only eat what he shows you to eat. The other kinds have too much arsenic and strychnine in them."

"Yes, you've got to be careful," Richard adds, "and remember, most Americans that come here act like fools. And they usually leave like fools, too."

We're grateful for these insights, Bones and me. Still, I feel a bit envious of these two amiable explorers. They arrived here ahead of us, before the psychedelic influx, it almost feels like we're coming on the scene late. Their charming hacienda with wind chimes and tranquil rooms and ocher tile floors seems dream-like. Somehow I doubt that we'll be living in such a place.

Savoring my own excellent weed, I ask, "What's back in these mountains? I mean deeper, beyond the roads? How far can you go?"

"Tiny villages, remote outposts," Richard says, his eyes aglow, eager to share. "Little bands of Mazatec Indians who probably have never even seen long-haired wanderers before. But there are old trails. They say you can travel by burro and on foot clear to the Caribbean coast."

THE SQUAT MESTIZO woman in her shapeless dress does not want any money for her stone hovel. Instead, she wants someone to lay down a plank floor on top of the packed dirt floor that already exists. I can tell at a glance it's an arduous job, and I am here for mystical trances, not splinter-handed labor. But Bones is taken by the romance of the offer, the senora appeals to his carpenter instincts. They engage in a halting conversation. Turning aside, I cross the barren yard that separates the two houses to check things out. The stone hut for rent sits atop a rock wall that rises above a foot path leading up from the village square. Cold spring water gushes from an old pipe in the rock wall right below the primitive hut. The hovel consists of a two undivided rooms, with a make-shift kitchen against the back wall. You go in and out through a plank door that hangs on weathered leather hinges. The interior smells musty, as if animals have been sleeping inside. There's a low stack of rough-hewn lumber, waiting to be planed and fitted on the uneven dirt floor. Slightly above the lower room is another room, like a bedroom mezzanine. There's a stone fireplace in one corner, but no chimney pipe. Any fire will have to vent through a hole in the sloping roof or out the two narrow, shuttered windows. The walls have open chinks between the stones where the old cement has fallen out.

I go back outside to inspect the mossy walls and crack-tiled roof. It seems solid, at least the hut is not sliding downhill. Two unglassed windows are wedged into the rock walls, one can only hope that insects are not too bad at this elevation. There's a crude outhouse set to one side between the two dwellings, and an outside shower stall with a gravity-feed cistern stands beside the widow's house. This will do, I tell myself, half-listening to Bones barter with the haggling woman. I go down the stone steps to the trail to where water gushes directly from the rock, green and translucent. Using the tin cup that dangles from a spike, I drink. Never have I tasted water this pure, this delicious and cold, arising from some deep, unquenchable source in the heart of mountain.

I leap back up the steps two at a time in the clean, blue air and go over to the widow's house. "She doesn't want any money," Bones mutters, "she's stubborn. She wants someone to put down the floor and if we do it, we can live rent-free for six months. She says we can share her squash and corn, and use the gravity-feed shower anytime we want."

I glance back at the hut and consider the idea. Bones waits, smiling at the wrinkled crone. She peers up at him, then at me. "Mira, aqui," she says, reaching behind her front door to lay her arthritic hands on something.

"Bones," I say, squinting, "that job would be a real ordeal. None of that lumber is close to being finished, it's rough as hell. The floor is lumpy. It could literally take us months."

"Hmm, I hear what you're saying. And we didn't come all this way to play Jesus the Carpenter."

"Right on. And I don't want to work on that floor while I'm high on sacred mushrooms. Tell her we'll pay her good dinero, that way she can hire a local workman later."

But the old woman has seen the Nazarene gleam in Bones' eyes. She stands there, clutching a rusting saw, iron chisel, heavy mallet, and antique plane in her gnarled hands. Bones takes these implements with an air of reverence, saying, "Dig, I think I'd like to give it a try."

"Okay, whatever," I laugh, "but it's on you. This is your project, not mine. I'm going to be wandering those green hills out yonder."

"No problemo," Bones replies. "If it doesn't work out, we can always pay her later."


WE HOOF OUR gear up the steep path from our plaza-parked car and into the stone hut. We go about making the place home, and I take a closer look at the widow's hand tools. They are from another era, maybe from another century. Back in California, they would be in an antique shop or a museum. Bones has signed on for a lot of blisters, that much is clear to me. But I like this archaic hut, it suits my mood. The cold clean water rushes out of the old pipe hammered into the rock wall beneath us, a well-spring from the frontiers of time, the people on the trail say that it never goes dry. The trail leads away up the mountainside beyond the village of Huautla, into the backcountry. Over the foot passes into the haze of a myth, a primordial source, of a world existing before the world ever was.

Here, if I wish, I can drop all my history like an obsolete sack and walk away. There is nothing to stop me except my own doubt. I have never felt freer.

On the village square there is a small rundown hotel, a cafe with its plume of wood smoke, the merchant store where we buy sacks of rice and pinto beans, coffee Mexicano and wax candles. A post office where you can mail letters that go out on the rambling mountain buses. You can send a telegram that clicks back down the mountain on a strand of wire. You can't use a telephone because they don't exist here. The local policia operate a ham radio for emergencies, the Mexican merchant has a strong radio for receiving outside news. In Huautla de Jimenez, you are a long ways from nowhere and you know it.

On some mornings I sit on the brick patio of the little restaurant, drinking coffee negro infused with a sticky brown sugar, as the stone fountain in the square gurgles with the inexhaustible Sierra water. Once in awhile there's a Mexico City newspaper laying around that has made its way up here by bus. The headlines blare the gruesome news about the bloodbath in Vietnam. They talk of another world, an ominous alter-reality light years away. But here in this Oaxacan Brigadoon, in these lost mountains, I am not touched by any of it. The predatory bastards don't know where I am and I'm not about to send them a patriotic telegram.

On Monday, Wednesday and Saturday mornings, there is an open-air mercado on the gravel square. When the rain lets up the little bronze women put out their wares on hand-woven blankets that they spread on the ground. Colorful garden vegetables, squash, turnips, ears of corn, onions and wild garlic, chili pods and fresh green herbs, and hand-made clay bowls and cups in a green-brown glaze. But fresh fruit is scarce in Huautla. We can dicker for the tart green apples about the size of tennis balls. But other than the costly bananas the merchant hauls up from the lowlands, sweet fresh fruit is hard to come by. No juicy oranges, papayas or mangoes, even melons are rare. The little women speak in a sing-song dialect that has no echo in Spanish. They sit on their woven blankets, studying us, using their fingers and hands to communicate. We communicate using simple phrases and signs, smiles, nods and shakes of the head, kneeling in front of them. Their faces have an Asiatic cast, their eyes shine with an unfamiliar light. They have no idea who we are, they are cautious, but curious. They barter only for Mexican peso coins, refusing to take any kind of paper money. They seldom smile, when they do their teeth are stained. They are old, they are young, they are ancient yet seem to have no age. Their hand-grown vegetables are good and fresh, so much better than the canned junk in the mercantile. But famished for natural fruit sugar, we buy clay pots of wild mountain honey and smear it on tortillas warmed over the hot stones back in our fire pit.

Bones seems to be in no hurry to do anything. He goes over the rough-hewn lumber with a languid air, measuring things with a worn metric ruler, trying to get a handle on the medieval tools. He seems content to putter around the edges for days, approaching the challenge at an oblique angle. Whereas if I can't side-step an unwanted problem altogether, I deal with it head on. I've got to feel convinced that what I'm doing is really worthwhile, or fuck it.

Richard advises me in the secrets of the mushroom, how to prepare it, how to use it.

"Go easy with it, find your own rhythm," he says, folding himself like a cat into his wicker chair. "Here in this place, we are a long ways from anywhere. Hippies have gone insane and wander off to God knows where. But Bones says you've had a lot of experience with psychedelics, so you've probably got nothing to worry about."

"That's true. I've taken a quite a few trips, mainly in an esoteric way. I learned Leary's approach, where you make the experience sacramental. You consecrate yourself."

"Hmmm, I can relate. And you seem really together after all that cosmic voltage. For me, acid tends to blow me off-balance and peyote makes me deathly sick. But the psilocybin mushroom gives me a uniquely different, organic kind of trip, profoundly spiritual. I recommend you steep them in very hot water, brew a dark tea, and be sure to sip it with a little food, not on an empty stomach."

"Hah, interesting, why do you say that? Because with other psychedelics food absorbs the psychoactive elements, slows the whole trip down."

"But this isn't like acid, believe me," Richard says, tossing squash seeds into a green and yellow parrot's hungry beak. The bird makes guttering sounds, swinging in its wicker cage. "The spirit of the mushroom is a living presence. Los pajaritos give you a biological kind of high, much more organic than acid and not nearly so cerebral. But the alkaloids can be hard on the stomach, they can overload your sympathetic nervous system. And I'm just telling you what I've learned first-hand. So go slow, sip the tea, find out what your limits are."

"Thanks, man I appreciate it," I tell him, flashing back on my out-of-the-body leap on hot chili peppers. "In case you're interested, I brought down with me some pharmaceutical Sandoz acid. Unbelievably pure stuff. I'd be happy to share a few tabs with you and Sarah."

"Hah, that is really far out," Richard laughs, stroking his curly, copper beard. "Sandoz acid in the wild of Oaxaca? There really is a revolution going on, isn't there? But I think we'll pass, Jake, thanks just the same. We've been up here for awhile and it changes you. The mushrooms put you on a different frequency. It changes your organic rhythms, even the way you think, and naturally that scares the shit out of some people. But it's a sacrament, as you say, and we don't even use it more than a few times a year."

The parrot lets loose a raucous squawk, shaking it's cage, crying, "Agua, aguacita!" Sara brings the audacious bird a white porcelain bowl of fresh, pure water.

BONES SIPS HIS morning coffee, tokes on a roach, and cogitates on his plank floor, while I take to the misting green hills in my quest for revelation. At first I make these jaunts with Ezequiel, the soft-spoken guide, who uses a mixture of dialect, Spanish phrases and hand gestures to instruct me. We kneel in the sunlit grass on the edge of the sky, on the earth damp from the rains. We walk the slopes, green and luminous in the morning light. He shows me what to see, his words are almost tender, the sky above us a sheltering presence. We amble from here and there, searching in the meadow grasses, behind moldering logs, in concealed places. From these high fields, we can look down at the rooftops of Huautla and across the deep river canyons.

"Aqui, alli," Ezequiel murmurs, pointing to a particular tawny mushroom that has sprouted overnight. "Numero uno, los mejores." Kneeling, with his pocket knife, he shows me the proper way to harvest the sacred plant.

Meanwhile, Bones stays preoccupied in his old-testament chore, putting these field trips off. He seems to be putting the purpose of our journey off, I'm not sure why. We have settled into the primitive stone hut. In the afternoons the monsoon rain falls, the rain falls all night from the black well of sky. Rain that beats on the old roof tiles, becoming a torrential roar. Everything smells damp, but for the most part we stay dry. There are a few trickling leaks that soak into the earthen floor. Bones has hand-planed a dozen or so planks and laid into place, at his sidereal but steady pace. These high-elevation nights are much cooler than down below, a breeze chuffs through the porous stone walls. I find an old sweater stowed in my army surplus pack, which warms my lean and shivering body. But Bones is not so fortunate. He dons all three of his cotton shirts and huddles close to our smoking firepit.

We eat like peasants, simmering staple rice with a handful of pinto beans, chunks of jade green squash and dashes of sea salt and cayenne into the pot. I slice the psychedelic mushrooms I have gathered and brew a murky tea as we eat.

"Let's only take some of that," Bones proposes, "until we know what's what."

"Do as you want, but dig. We're already diluting the effects with food. Ezequiel says that's about right for two grown men, to drink slowly, poco a poco."

"Yeah, but I want to go easy. We're a long ways from rescue up here."

The notion of rescue strikes me as very peculiar, why dwell on potential negatives? Isn't that why we're here, to be a long ways from home and stepping into the mystic? I've never freaked out on psychedelics, and I know I can handle this trip. Still, to appease Bones, I brew the tea on the mild side. We sip the acrid liquid together, blowing into our clay cups. We listen to the downpour of rain, rain that turns our stone house into a hollow drum, humming in the rising glow.

It's good to be here with Bones, my companero of the road. Our back and forth talk subsides as the unusual phenomena comes on. We draw into ourselves, going to our sleeping bags on opposite sides of the room. Cross-legged, closing my eyelids, I breath in rhythm with the monsoon rain beating on the roof, breathing as an infant breathes, taking breaths through my navel. An exquisite shudder runs down my back. The damp chill seems to lessen, the worn rafters glow, the stone walls seem to have their own inward illumination. Above me, on the roof, an umbrella opens up and expands like a luminous fan. The room is enveloped in a vibrating and clarifying energy. A motile awareness suffuses me, of rain shooshing off the roof, converging with the translucent cadence of my breath. My thoughts slow way down, become singular, as the sensation of rain is absorbed into my skin. The sphere of luminosity hangs all around me, but the intensity wavers. Some potential seems to be lacking. The luminous energy hovers in the eves of my awareness, in the rafters, in the wind-moaning walls. I focus deeply on my breath, I concentrate. Bones is moving around but I keep my attention inward, wanting more. But nothing happens, only the promise of more. With a twinge of regret, I realize I should have heeded my own instincts. The tea wasn't strong enough, and the rice in my belly diluted the mushroom's psychedelic potency. It seems like a misstep, a wasted opportunity.

I'm not sure how long I've been sitting here, cross-legged, waiting for a supernatural moment that didn't occur. But I decide not to define anything as good or bad, instead just a beginning. My legs feel only slightly numb. When I open my eyes and stretch, Bones gazes at me from across the room, tending the fire with a stick. His long face is bathed in shadow light, the smoke being pulled toward the narrow rock windows and sucked into the pitch-black night.

"Aiyee, I was wondering when you were gonna come around." Bones says, tossing some twigs into the flames. He looks like a bearded, medieval shepherd.

"Well, no, I never really got there. It started to happen, then just stopped. Tea was too weak."

Bones shakes his head. "Whew, well, for me, pretty weird trip. Not really all that pleasant."

"How do you mean? I think we just brewed that tea too weak. We never got a decent lift-off." My voice echoes off the rock walls, the wind moans through the chinks, pushing the smoke around in the damp air. I breathe through my mouth, tasting the smoke.

But Bones doesn't answer. Did he even hear me? The rain drums on the old roof tiles above us, drumming in an unwritten language, some message beyond our ken. But I feel it, feel it deep inside my physical being.

"Well, I mean the weird noises," Bones finally says. "I kept hearing these scuttling noises, over there, in that hay by the corner. Started flashing on rats, you know? But when I got up to look around, there's nothing there, nada. Then I started hearing wing beats, like pigeon sounds, only this was a trapped pigeon and something was scuttling after it . . ."

"Whooee, man. I heard you moving around. That does sound a bit freaky."

Bones nods, his face pensive. "Yeah, pretty weird. I think my system must be a little stressed. All that hard traveling. I just need to relax and replenish."

"Yeah, I hear that," I say, respecting my friend's fear of stress. After all, my first taste of the mushroom high didn't pan out either. Drowsing in the folds of my sleeping bag, I resolve to wait three days and then take the sacrament again. My dreams are the sounds of the night wind, an auditory montage of thunder and eternal downpour. My prayers commingle with the prayers that Noah once uttered as he was being washed away. But down deep I feel an immense gratitude for the simple reality of being here in this cloud-hung world of sky and rain.

Around daybreak, the nocturnal rains let up, everything everywhere drips and glistens. I start my morning with boiled black coffee, a handful of dried figs and salted in the shell peanuts. Infused with the most intimate passion, I turn my steps to the green hills. The forested slopes and slanting meadows glisten with a nameless light. Most of these strange flowering plants are unfamiliar to me, although I have become adept at identifying the sacred mushrooms. I am prepared now to hunt alone, just as I did in my childhood. The canyons are hung in sun-struck mist, lit by windows of transparent indigo, conveying an ancient message not forgotten by my blood.

I wander where I will, kneeling on the moist earth, in the high grasses, under the measureless sky, depositing a few choice mushrooms into my satchel, nibbling pieces of their flesh for energy. Yes, I eat the fresh wild plant as I roam, for it imparts an incredible physical endurance. I roam the foot and donkey paths into the roadless hills, ever deeper, striding for hours on an empty stomach. I see birds that I have never seen, birds unknown to me, and insects unlike any bugs I have ever laid eyes on. I come across one black and orange wasp about three inches long that hunts its prey on the ground along tiny trails. Its veined wings flutter and flit on its striped back, but seem incapable of lifting the broad body into the air. This wasp is indifferent to my close-up scrutiny. It is a magical creature and I do not disturb it.

In these forays, I see the small strong men in canvas pants climb rope ladders into their steep garden terraces, tending and harvesting the precious maize. Sometimes, when I come across a row of corn, I strip off an ear and eat it raw. The kernels are white, sweet and tender. If I happen across the farmer herding his burro or carrying his implements, we share respectful greetings. Not once am I made to feel unwelcome; for them, I am a friend until proven stranger.

One hot day, a few miles back into the lost range, I walk into a hamlet of six or eight adobe huts clustered around a stone well. A man in a worn straw hat beckons to me, inviting me to come and drink from the well. He speaks a little Spanish, as do I, so we are able to converse. He hands me a gourd dipper of sweet pure water, with a smile, and watches as I drink. We squat in the dirt beside the well, piecing together our story. He wonders why I am here, what am I doing back in these montanas? I show him my satchel of sacred mushrooms, he nods with empathy. His wary, prescient eyes confirm my reason for being here. He rolls a cigarro from crude tobacco in his leather pouch, lights it with a wooden match, and offers it to me. We sit smoking in the shade of the well, with few words. The sun is already past noon and high above us, thunderheads are massing into dark, formidable towers. Soon, I'll have to head back down the slope to avoid getting caught out in the afternoon downpour.

Gesturing up at the distant green cleft that cuts through the peaks, I ask him "Amigo, arriba en el paso, hay un camino?"

He nods his head, exhaling a stream of blue smoke, murmuring yes, there is a road, an old trail that leads clear to the sea, a road that existed even before the Spanish came, muy viejo camino. He himself has never made that journey but they say a healthy man and a burro can reach Vera Cruz in seven to ten days and along the way you will find many splendid things. Squatting, watching as he draws his knowledge in the red dirt with a twig, sharing his water, his tobacco, I know that I am being changed. I will never be the same. A portal has opened within me, and I am going through.

IN THE IMMENSE silver afternoons, when the air cools and the billowing clouds open up, I retreat to our stone hut and delve into my holy books. I read The Wisdom Of The Over-Self by Paul Brunton from cover to cover, delving into meanings, seeking esoteric correlations. I study Vivekananda's commentaries on Patanjali's Yoga Sutras, the royal road of self-mastery. Vivekananda was the first Hindu swami to come over to America from the crucible of India. In the 1890's, as a teenager, he addressed the World Conference of Religions in Chicago. He spoke of the crucial need for modern man to awaken to his moral responsibilities. When asked if he had one wish, what would it be, Vivekananda said he would like to burn this misbegotten civilization down and start over.

Such pure anarchy from a man of God strikes me like a clarion bell. How direct and clean it would be to erase this global hierarchical aberration that we call modern society, this cunning manipulation that seeks to control every person, every animal, every resource and thing, smothering personal freedom. What sacrifice would it take to accomplish such a goal, to wipe the slate clean, and would God actually permit it, if God truly exists?

In these twilight afternoons of endless rain, I read and scribble in my journal, while Bones struggles with the floor. Once in awhile I lend him a hand, but to me that floor is a thankless task. I search through the revolutionary teachings of Jesus the Christ, my body and being infused with the organic elixir of a pre-Colombian world, holy water, holy sky, holy earth, holy fuck, holy wonder.

Looking at my frustrated friend, I say, "Drop that shit Bones, leave it alone, dig this."

I hold aloft the slim red leather volume of Patanjali's Yoga Aphorisms in one hand, the black leather edition of the King James New Testament in my other, keys to understanding. The meanings are clear to me, uncertainty has been erased from my mind. Eat of my flesh. The understanding is in the action itself, the doing brings forth the quintessential knowing.

"Damn it," Bones blurts, "I can't do this job with these fucking stone-age tools. It's too much, it's insane, look at my hands."

He throws me a look of dejection, extending his blistered hands like one crucified, and indeed, Bones would make a good crucified Jesus. The dull primitive plane dangles in his fingers, mocking his early gringo enthusiasm. Keeping a straight face, I nod in sympathy. Bones stares at me, Look, see how I tried, have I not tried with all my strength?

"Let that trip go," I console him, "we came here for bigger purposes. Let's just give the old widow some moolah. Then will make her happy."

"She told me the last hombre she hired walked off, didn't even come back to be paid."

"Hah, and now you know why. Those ancient tools were even too much for him. He probably went off to grow more corn for white lightning."

Bones face lights up. "Aiyee," he laughs, "I hate to give up but I've had it. I'm ready to do some more mushroom tea. You're so tripped out, look at you, man, you look like the wind is blowing right through you."

"Ah it is, my friend, it is." I beckon him to come closer, holding the New Testament. "Dig this. Listen to what Jesus said to his people. *These things I do ye also shall do and even greater things shall you do, because I go unto the Father.*"

"Whew," Bones murmurs, kneeling beside me on the earthen floor, "that's gotta be one of the most far-out statements in the whole Bible. But what did he actually mean?"

"Well, he also said, *ye are gods*, that those of us who know are the sons of God, sons of the most high. He's laying out the same trip the yogi saints talk about, that we are super-conscious beings in a mortal body. But somehow we've forgotten who we really are."

Bones rocks his thin torso back and forth, cogitating, as rain patters on the roof. "You pick some good mushrooms this morning?" he asks. "Do we have any fresh ones?'

"Oh yeah, we do. I picked some real beauties, newly sprouted, super potent."

"Okay then, let's trip, Jake. And let's make a strong batch this time. Let's do it right."

Although I ate a large raw mushroom out in the field this morning, I agree. I want my partner Bones to get mystically involved. In the crepuscular rain light we eat nothing at all, and brew a much stronger tea. I take a washed and tender umbrella shroom and slice it into thin strips that we can also chew on. We eat a few of these acrid pieces as the tea brews over the wood fire. The mountain absorbs the cloudy light of sunset like a lantern being doused, as we blow into our clay cups and sip the bitter brew. Then we wait, unconcerned with any sense of time. I never wear a watch and neither does Bones, the artificial notion of time makes us shake with laughter.

The phenomenal sensations come on much quicker and stronger than before, a sudden chute opens up. If pure acid is a magic carpet show, the sacred mushroom is an effulgent metamorphosis of your physical self. It radically changes your physical sense of being, a startling change. This must be why some dabblers lose their minds. They don't want to lose their familiar shape, their usual reference points of straight reality. They don't want to become an animal or a bird or a snake, they fight against the transformation and their wits fly to pieces.

To pieces, or into profound awareness. An profound stillness envelopes me, filling my body with a rippling light, a luminosity that spreads across the ceiling and hovers like a hummingbird, oscillating. This effulgent glow floods my chest and my bloodstream, sentient, calming my mind, bringing me to immaculate attention. Its nature is undefinable. Its nature is silence, pure elegant silence, a breathless silence. Semi-anticipating the kaleidoscopic trip that Lsd brings, I wait for another dramatic phase to kick in. But the subtle glow only deepens, ringing in my ears, suffusing my body, illuminating every fiber of my body and whatever I gaze at with palpable, rippling illumination. I feel an infinite, vibrant space inside me. My thoughts slow way down, merging into a stream of non-thought, of fluid non-verbal attention. Even though my eyes are closed, I can see every feature of the stone hut in perfect detail.

This transcendent moment goes continues, an inner glow breathing me, although I have lost all sensation of breathing. There's a bright expanding strength at the core of my being, amazing me. I cannot relate this to anything I know. If I try to conjure a matching thought to this perception, the idea dissolves into nothing. This trance cannot be captured, it's indifferent to my wants. I shake with a divine sense of mirth. I want to ask certain questions but the words seem meaningless. Words relate only on some lower strata of consciousness, not here, not now, in this miraculous state, words are useless embellishments.

It occurs to me, with a stab of pure glee, that I might be going insane. Yes, that is possible. I am present, I am the glory that breathes itself, that breathes my own being. One is pulled in, hah, you never come back the same, if you come back at all. In the eternal falling rain, I hear the pure gleam of silence, silence that is the matrix of everything, an unwavering essence within me.

But above me, there is another brighter room that exists above the room that I sit in. I intensely want to go there. But there is no doorway, no stairs, no passage for me. Before this upward motion is allowed, I must study myself in the most ruthless and unsentimental manner. I cannot lie, I cannot deceive, I cannot pretend. This realization comes with a shivering jolt. This is a sacred space, not a place of pretense. My personality, whoever I imagine that I am, cannot go there on an impulse. Some profound surrender is involved.

A shuddering breath moves through me. With slow and determined effort, I move my body. I overcome my sense of being rooted to the earth, taking conscious breath all through my body. This causes a shift in the hovering light, the light coalesces into form. I see the flames in our fire pit, burning. There are tiny faces in those flickering flames, intimate faces, but I can't make out what they're saying. Bones doesn't seem to be inside the hut and Bones could be anywhere. He could be sitting on the roof, he could be dancing naked in the rain, and wherever he is, he is. But I know we have arrived at that deep and unchanging place the Mazatecs call, *The Land of One Thousand Waitings.*

I sit in complete stillness, staring into the flickering fire, unperturbed by the swirling smoke. This circle of stones is not our common firepit, I'm not sure where it came from. The inner ring of stones glow hot, but their outer surfaces are covered with a green living moss. As I stare at this paradox, a tiny devic creature detaches herself from the firelight and twirls up before my eyes. She is exquisite, rippling with luminosity, no bigger than my little finger. This creature hovers at the fire's fringe, looking intently into my face as the fluttering of wings echoes off the walls. Astonished, I realize that my lungs have stopped working as a natural bellows. They are simply at rest, although I don't feel at all deprived of oxygen. The deva comes a few inches closer, and I perceive an expression of joy on its little face. But when I formulate words, when I make myself say—"Who are you?"—the ravishing creature vanishes back into the embers. She cannot be possessed, the wing-beats subside, I cannot summon her back. I grow aware again of the drumming rain, pouring into the moment of my always-existing awareness.

The presence stays in the room, it persists, like a luminous caress. My focus shifts. I slip into a vivid dream where I find myself in the hills, striding with an impeccable energy, shed of all fear, and as I come closer to myself, I see my hands. My hands and forearms are covered with sleek, primordial fur, the fur of a jaguar or a leopard. The markings of my fur possess a savage vitality, fully conscious of its own nature.

The shock of this other-worldly perception jolts me back into my physical body, the damp stone hut, slumped forward at the waist with my forehead all but touching the ground. The fire is burning out. A feminine voice from somewhere above me states, "You will not be exalted for the sake of a whim. You must become that which speaks with the voice of all things."

A rift of light open in my cerebellum, then wanes. Have I been found somehow lacking? I can not bear to even speculate on this, that would lead to anguish. But I repeat to myself what the voice said, so I will not lose it. I lie back and let a profound relaxation overtake me. I whisper to myself those words, her words, and the rain bears me away into the palaces of morning.

When I come awake, Bones stands in the room drenched in rain. Daylight shivers in through the narrow stone windows. His face is drawn and tired, his eyes engrossed in some inward conflict. I sit up and take him in, then ask gently "What has happened to you?"

He makes a weary gesture, like a man who has been tricked. "What happened to me? I cannot even begin to tell. But when things talk to you, but you can't make out their words, although you know it's super-important, it kind of wigs you out, you know?"

Sighing, he lowers himself onto his pallet, turns on his side, facing me, then closes his eyes. His skin has the color of old parchment. I sit without moving for several minutes, without the slightest impulse or need to speak. Something inconceivable has happened to us, and how does one know what it signifies? In how many ways are we real, or are we unreal? My awareness seems like a translucent vessel of air without boundaries, of some unknown geography. I need to walk I put on my leather huaraches with the rubber tire soles, take my pencil and notebook, and make my way down the path to the square for a mug of hot Mexican coffee.

# Chapter 24

THE LONG NIGHTS of rain and shining mornings converge in a timeless seamless flow, an inhalation and exhalation that has nothing to do with anything except Now. If I move away from this transparent moment, I am only confusing myself. Moments that I feel suffused with joy, other times with a haunting loneliness, and this loneliness is an adversary that eats at me. I can leave it behind like a shadow that flits in my wake, but it can pull me into a quicksand of feeling and memory. I write Dawn long intense letters, describing where I am and what I see, the endless rains and monastic diet, the laconic Mazatecos and their holy plant. "I only wish you were here with me," I write, "in this incredible place, in these rainbow mountains where time has been suspended."

Down at the telegraph/post office I mail the letter, buying a floral Mexican stamp and plain envelope. How long it will take to get to Los Angeles, I ask in poor Spanish. The taciturn clerk looks at me, as if I am a imbecile. "How am I to know that?" he replies. "But I would not be holding my breath. At least three or four weeks, mas o menos."

I explore, I wander, I roam. I wander onto a grassy bluff overlooking a communal well, in Huautla, but off the beaten path. I sit on the knoll in the clean blue air, watching the moments take place. A man comes along with a donkey loaded with firewood; he stops to drink from the hanging bucket. Laughing children chase an excited dog down the path, glancing up at me with shy curiosity. I smile and waggle my hand, they giggle and run wildly after the dog. Their mothers admonish them to leave the stranger alone. Crows have gathered in the tree branches, cawing, cawing. The women come to draw water, to fill the red clay jugs they carry on their shoulders and heads. I watch their work with rapt attention. I hear the water sluice from the wooden bucket into their jugs, hear them talk. But few of these mujeres make eye contact with me, other than the most glancing manner. They are about the arduous business of living, I am a stranger who is out of place. I am not put off by their aloofness, though it does increase my sense of isolation. If I am to live in these mountains, I need to learn their ways. I must become fluent at Spanish and their dialect, otherwise I'll be the eternal outsider.

One slender, brown-haired girl catches my eye. In her mid-teens, she comes back and forth to the adobe well many times. She carries a pole across her thin shoulders, a clay water jug hangs from each end. She fills each jug, then, stooping and balancing, she lifts them and walks off into the warren of casas that terrace the hillside. Sometimes she goes down one path, other times she goes up another. If she speaks at all it is but a murmur to the others, her stoic acceptance remains unbroken. This sinewy girl in her drab calico dress makes at least a dozen trips to the well, in the same measured intent. Most of the other water-fetchers tend to ignore her. She seems to be aware of me being aware of her up on the bluff, but does not look up. I wish that she would look at me, but she never does. To look up might be devastating, to look upon my inconceivable freedom.

I realize that this grueling labor is her task, she does this all day long in order to survive. She is a servant or an orphan or a slave, and I am devastated by this knowledge. This is her harsh reality, the world we will never know. Where mere the act of gathering enough food to live can break your back. Such brutal work would kill the typical norte-Americano in a matter of days, no, we wouldn't last even a single day. We would whine and whimper, and rail against our fate. But this implacable fate is all she knows, she has no chips to bargain with as she nurses her pointless daydreams. Explain karma to her, that she is working off past bad actions and that someday, sometime, maybe somewhere, she too will be free, go, explain that to her, it is meaningless. She fills my spirit with awe. I do not understand why in this world so many are enslaved while others live a life of indifferent luxury. *For am I not she, am I not this girl, and is she not my very self?*

I wander away from the bluff in a confused rage. Why should this remorseless set-up be allowed to continue? If it does not truly serve the family of man, what purpose does it serve? Who does it serve and why do we allow it to go on? I know in every pulse of my being that this slave conditioning must be shattered. We must first shatter it within us, then shatter it in the world. And until we do so, we will ever be in bondage to our own fear.

The monsoons come across the mountains in a great tide. I have stopped keeping track of the days and dates. We are somewhere deep in the Sierras, that is all I know. The endless rains fall from the sky in a biblical deluge. I write to my brother Evan, another report from the frontier, describing the incident of the girl at the well. I tell him we must try with all of our strength, all our intelligence, all our conscious intent, to change this flawed and ruthless world. I propose that every American student should live in a third-world nation for at least one month, live and study with the people of these places, and that this visit be mandatory for high school graduation. In that way they can see for themselves, they can come to realize a sense of justice, they can participate, all the petulant whining and complaining might stop, in order to give those who have been cast away a real chance at life.

A strange self-fulfilling prophecy is at work down here, I tell Evan, a struggle to even imagine another kind of life because so little evidence of it exists. They throw their hard-scrabble despair at the gilded slippers of pompous Catholic fantasy, and in so doing play right into the hands of their cynical rulers. Such poverty is a crucifixion, there is no reprieve. And hardly anyone cares, everything is negotiated. Their governments are enormous scams, their religious cults reinforce it. My loathing for all governments of man deepens every passing day, becomes an anthem in my blood, and these moods are hard to shake.

But when I roam into the hills in the high mornings of mist and sunshine, I am born again. Because being right here and now, the bleak paradox loosens its grip. Throw back your head, spread wide your arms and laugh into the sky. I let the moods wash right out of my consciousness. I space into the wind and sunlight of my infinite mind, realizing I don't have to be bothered by thoughts anymore. I am the effulgence, the hummingbird on the bright wing of daybreak. I don't have to think about anything I don't wish for myself, there is no need to get strung out. The wind of Spirit floods through me in awesome and translucent synchronicity. Whatever story I have told myself about myself, I can rewrite it. I am not bound by any belief. And the primordial face behind that story-teller—that is the face I seek.

COMING OUT OF the post office after mailing Evan's letter, standing in the cloudy sunlight, the desecration of paradise makes itself known. One of the ramshackle mountain buses comes grinding into the square, belching exhaust fumes. Crates of chickens flap on the roof, suitcases, boxes, stuffed burlap bolsas. The ninos who hustle their muddy mushrooms to newcomers dash out, primed for action. A contingent of gaudy freaks are on the bus, decked in flamboyant attire, taking the scene in through tinted granny glasses. One of them dangles his arm out the window, waggling cash at the ninos. These Hollywood interlopers are the harbinger of the end, and don't even know it. One gawking freak spots me, that high-as-kite-on-acid grin, and flashes me the peace-sign. I flash it back, peace bro, then turn and trudge up the stony trail chewing on my restless misgivings.

Back home, I relate to Bones what I have just seen. He keeps scratching both his lower legs in a distracted manner.

"Aiyee," Bones speculates, "if the Whisky Ago-Go crowd has discovered this place we're in for some weird days."

"Yeah, Huautla's days are numbered. These clowns will ruin the local scene and stand out like sore thumbs. They'll bring in the Federales, man. Watch it happen."

"I think you're right," Bones mumbles, scratching madly at his shins. "The Federales could run us all off this mountain. They seem to have some kind of vendetta against hippies."

"Bones, why are you scratching like that? Did you get the crabs from the old widow?"

"No, no, ha ha," he laughs, "just some kind of allergy from that straw I've been sleeping on. I'm gonna walk down to the pharmacia and get some ointment."

"Medicine? Aiyee, man, don't let them smear you down with any strange chemicals."

"No, I won't, don't worry. Something natural. I'm gonna take care of it."

"Bones, dig this idea. We can move deeper into these mountains. We can get away from those day-trippers. There are burro trails that go way back through passes, that lead over the Sierra and into Mayan country. We could live back in there for months, maybe even years. One of the Indians drew me a map."

"Far out. You have a map?"

"Well, yeah, I have the map in my head. He drew it in the dirt."

"Jesus, that would be fantastic. But what about money? We're running kind of low."

"We don't need that much bread. Dig, we could sell the car to a Mexican, it would be more than enough. It would be the most incredible journey imaginable. Then, later on, we can take a train out of Vera Cruz back into the states. Bones, we would be like hippie gods."

"Fucking far out," Bones murmurs, his eyes aglow, nodding, scratching, trying not to scratch. "Right on, hippie gods, hah ha, I can dig it. Let me talk to Richard about what he knows, let me think. But first I gotta deal with this mind-blowing rash."

"Yeah, do that," I encourage, hoping it's not contagious. "But don't let them spray you down, man, don't let them spray you with ddt!"

"No, no," Bones laughs, "Jesus God, don't even think that!"


A DAY OR so later I come back into Huautla from one of my rambles, approaching the village from down the mountain. In my canvas satchel, I have some prized mushrooms and a few ears of sweet white corn, a gift from a hillside farmer. Now, I'm hurrying along the foot paths, trying to stay ahead of the thunderheads forming like giant anvils in the sky. I've already been drenched more than once out on these hikes and it's not easy to dry your clothes in this mountain air in the rainy season.

On the low-lying outskirts of Huautla, I come across a dirt lane of poor hovels below the main square. I ask a tiny white-haired woman for some agua; she gives me a brimming gourd and watches as I slack my thirst.

"Where are you from?" she asks me, with crinkled, curious eyes. When I tell her from the Estados Unidos, in California, "Ahh," she intones, as if I am talking about another planet.

THANKING HER FOR the delicious water, I hear a commotion break out on the next lane over, some shouted English words, and I walk along a hedge to see what's what. An angry crowd of boys are on the hilly street, throwing rocks at someone out of my sight. I can't see who, but these ninos are really pissed, casting insults along with their whistling stones.

Then, to my astonished ear, I hear him bellow, cursing in profane American slang. I step beyond the hedge to see for myself and there he is, the Buffalo Cowboy himself, cursing and stomping in the rutted street, trying to fend off the vicious stones. Hightower is obviously borracho, sporting the grimy stubble that only a drunk will endure, his fancy clothes smeared with mud. This is the first time I've laid eyes on the dude since the melee at the wedding fiesta.

He spots me, roaring, "Goddamn, it's you! You and your skinny compadre are sure as fuck incognito!" He dodges a whizzing stone, crying out, "Can you believe these greaser bastards? Ouch! Ouch!" Ducking, he staggers up the dirt track. The vengeful ninos pursue, shrilling curses, hurling their rocks at him as though at a rabid skunk.

"I hate all you Mexican cocksuckers," Hightower bellows, "I hate your worthless country!"

Noticing me, the ninos pause, gauging me with their bright, feral eyes, hefting their stones. I lift one respectful palm while scowling up toward the wasted malefactor. Laughing, the ninos start throwing at Hightower with renewed ferocity. A cluster of women standing nearby also fling imprecations his way, one half-naked mamacita jabbing her finger at him, yelling, "Malo hombre! Malo horrible gringo!"

The Buffalo Cowboy yowls at me, "So now you're siding with the spics?! Well fuck you too, you faggot freak! I hope you all go to spic hell together!"

"You better clear out," I shout back. "Whatever you did, they'll hold it against you! They'll come in the night with their knives and cut your balls off, maybe your hands, your feet too! They'll cut off your balls, asshole! If I were you I'd hightail it off this mountain!"

Glowering, Hightower flips me the bird and plunges into the bushes, the ninos mocking him with their shrill taunts. I make a placating gesture to the enraged women. "Lo siento, senoras," I say, "lo siento," then walk away with a jubilant and thudding heart.

Another night of momentous rain, in my sleeping or waking, the beguiling girl at the well comes to me. I hear the water slosh in her clay pots, I feel the strain of the yoke across her taut shoulders. I hear the birdsong, and smell the wood smoke of the morning fires. She turns, she looks at me with an ineluctable knowing in her brown eyes, that look of recognition that eclipses all other considerations. I draw closer and she speaks to me, her eyes ancient, her face young, her voice like the earth, in a language like water flowing over stones, she tells me, *"The sounds that are unmade is the doorway within you."*

I awaken with a start, opening my eyelids to the cloudy skylight. Her voice is still in my inner ear. *The sounds that are unmade is the doorway within you.* I understand this is an omen, the young girl who carries water has given me a message. She is the servant, the priestess, she is the daughter of the mountain rain. I lie on my back on the dirt floor pondering this enigma, wondering what I need to do to be worthy, repeating her words.

The stone hut seems to fill with morning light. I have slept a long time, longer than normal, the shuttered windows have been flung open. I sit up on my pallet, rubbing the sleep from my eyes. Bones stands in the weathered door, saying my name. I haven't seen him in two or maybe three days. His long bearded face looks blotchy, pallid, his slate-blue eyes are feverish.

"Jake," he says again, "Jake, I am in dire straits. I've been infested by vampire fleas, fleas that are eating me alive."

"What?" For a moment I think that he's lost his mind. "Fleas? Bones, how can that be? Have there been any dogs in this place?"

"No, no dogs." Bones blinks, licking his lips. "But maybe before. Remember I told you something was biting me? From that straw over in the corner, I think. Look!"

He hauls up each pant leg and exposes his shins and calves, a mess of bloody, oozing welts. Tiny black insects swarm in his leg hairs. "Fuck, man," I mutter, "you are being devoured! But the pharmacist? Didn't he give you something?"

"Yes, I did, yes, but the ointment didn't help. He gave me some horrible smelling stuff but it seems to make it worse. These fleas are feasting on me. They're working their way up to my crotch, I can't stand it."

"Holy fuck, Bones, you weren't high on shrooms when they attacked?" The bad thing is that I've been scratching at my own legs, almost unconsciously. Bones babbles on inconsolably that yes, yes he was high, the fleas first struck when he was peaking. Dropping my pants, I realize that I'm covered with at least a dozen itchy red welts and tiny fleas hop on my almost hairless shins. Cursing, I brush them off.

"Goddamn it, Bones. I forgot to tell you. I saw Hightower. You won't believe this. He was being stoned by some ninos and he looked like he's gone insane. He looked bad."

"Fuck him, who cares," Bones retorts. "I have to get off this mountain, away from this place. These fleas are infecting my blood. Richard says there's a clinic in Teotitlan that can make me well. He says the fleas bring a fever that can cause lasting nerve damage."

Nerve damage? At once I understand the gravity of the situation. My friend might waste away in these remote mountains, a gibbering, demented gringo. Everything else has to be put on hold. We have to find a real doctor. Besides, the tiny blood-suckers are trying to make a run at me, although I know my immune system is strong and pure.

"Yes, Bones, you're right. We need to get down off this hill. What shape is the car in?"

"Bad shape, I just checked for the first time in weeks. Two total flats. The Mexicans say they're too far gone to be fixed."

Fuck. We scramble around the village looking for another way. The mountain bus is not due in until late tomorrow, there are no taxis in Huautla. Bones shows me our ruined tires. Those threadbare, torn retreads have been patched, plugged, and repatched. They will not hold up to another bandaid. We cannot ignore the reality of our situation.

"We need to buy two good used tires in Teotitlan," Bones mumbles, feverish with anxiety. "We can get some decent ones for a few bucks, I'm sure we can."

What he says is probably true, but it's not the only solution. In reality, the battered Mercury has little value left. It got us here, that was its main purpose. But now it can sit here and rust away for all I care. I'd rather sell the jalopy to a Mexican for a couple hundred bucks, money that would enable us to live indefinitely in the uncharted backcountry. Fuck retreating, we can strike out on the mountain and jungle trails that lead into the ancient Olmec and Mayan country. But Bones does not seem ready for such an adventure. He's been infested by carnivorous fleas that are driving him insane. So I put my wishes aside, I help him wrestle two grimy tires into the plaza.

Around noontime, we bargain with two Mexicanos going back down the long mountain in a supply truck. The driver frowns at us, emaciated long-hair gringos with luminous eyes, at first shaking his head. Senor, por favor, we plead, es un emergencia, we cannot wait for the bus, por favor, necesito el doctor pronto! The two men make sympathetic sounds, knowing we are at their mercy. They are not our local Mazatecs, these are hustling lowlanders. The driver turns his mouth down, rubbing his thumb and forefinger together, ahh, la mordida, the bite! There is no way around it, they hold the aces. While Bones haggles with them, I check out their rig. The red flatbed has wood slats on the sides and behind the cab, and a chain-link barricade that serves as a tailgate. The bed is loaded with cartons of empty coke bottles stacked two deep, nothing else. Somehow, we have to get our footing on top of those treacherous bottle necks. Bones offers 200 pesos to the scheming driver, about seven bucks American. He takes it, jerks his thumb toward the back, saying, "Okay, vamos, vamos." We haul the two heavy rims into the bed and wedge them in, then slip-slide over the clinking green bottles to the cab. No sooner do we lay hands on the front slats than the truck lurches into first gear and we begin our rumbling descent.

"Egad, they smell like tequila," Bones says to me, "and they've got a case of cerveza on the floor."

"Aw shit, I wish you had told me. Borrochitos? This can't be good."

The ride down quickly turns into a full-blown nightmare. The Mexicans are mad with drunken glee. The red truck starts at a breakneck pace and never really lets up. We hang for dear life to the weathered boards, gritting our teeth, banging our ankles and shins on the coke bottles, scrambling for purchase. The guy riding shotgun glances back through the smeared window, leering at us aha, aha, look at the pitiful gringos, hah ha ha! The show-off driver is either too drunk or too stupid to be afraid. He careens down the washboard road as if in a race against the devil. We blow through the wedding hamlet with the horn blaring, a few prople are visible, they wave in semi-recognition. The clanking bottles rattle under us, our ankles roll, grit flies in our eyes. Our deranged tormentors refuse to slow down no matter how we shout or bang on the roof. Soon we will be on the perilous track descending the river canyon, where we all might die like fools. I should not have listened to desperate Bones, we should have waited for the slow mountain bus. Bones clings to the rocking sideboards like a man being flayed alive. It's pointless to curse the sadistic Mexicans, we are all trapped in this skidding deathtrap, and I miserably beg God for mercy and strength.

The chasm descent almost makes us shit our britches. The manic driver slows only a little on the tight narrow curves, sliding toward the precipice, the gravel flying. Drunken hyena laughter reaches our ears as we absorb the relentless bruising from the wooden crates and bottles. In an instant we can be turned into bug-spatter and no one back in L.A. will ever know. I keep my own eyes wide open, confronting the awful moment, if it's gonna happen, I want to see it coming. I have no doubt these two borrachos are going to die one day soon, this suicide road will kill them. The Empire of Coca-Cola will take another human sacrifice. But I pray O God, don't take us with them, don't let this day be that awful day!

# Chapter 25

FINALLY, BEATEN LIKE mongrels, we reach the foothills and the road straightens out. Our benefactors make a skidding stop at an intersection in Teotitlan and let us out, our ankles bruised and bleeding. Bones passes down the tire rims, then sags to the road like a potato sack. I glance into the driver's side mirror and see his swollen face staring at me from under his baseball cap. With grudging respect he gives me a thumbs-up, as if we had passed some kind of gauntlet. Then he grinds the truck back into gear and rumbles off.

Bones limps over beside me. "Unbelievable assholes," he says, visibly shaken. "I almost thought we were goners."

"You can say that again. Their days are surely numbered, but hey Bones, we made it. We made it. Let's go find some water and shade."

"Right on," says Bones with a wan smile, "water and oranges. Aiyee, I'm dying for fresh squeezed orange juice."

Fact is we haven't had any citrus fruit in weeks now, and the appeal of fresh orange juice is overwhelming. Lugging our heavy tires, we hobble off toward the open-air Mercado, famished and optimistic.

Every purist vegetarian reaches that tremulous stage where he is fanatically hungry. The smell of a ripe tomato at fifty feet will set your mouth to watering. After enduring the sparse highland diet, we find ourselves drooling in a paradise of tropical fruit. The wooden stalls of the mercado spill over with luscious fruits and vegetables that would put a Gauguin painting to shame. Nostrils aquiver, trembling, we roam this cornucopia like men awaking from a hundred year's starvation. The ripe yellow bananas, blushing mangoes, round green aguacates, gorgeous pineapples, tender papayas and fat juicy oranges throw our senses into shock. We buy big red-yellow-green jute bolsas and stuff them with fresh fruit along with ripe tomatoes and a kilo of raw unshelled peanuts. We score a six pack of chilled agua mineral in green bottles, then find some shade away from the swarming flies on the bloody animal carcasses, and gorge ourselves like starving refugees.

Teotitlan drifts through its noontime siesta, Bones and I fight off drowsiness with strong Mexican coffee, sitting in the shade of some banana palms. Geckos dart up and down the green trunks and into the crevasses of an adobe wall.

"Whew," Bones grunts, "I cannot eat another bite and I've got to find that clinic—these fleas are still killing me."

"Let's' do it. Let's go find that doctor and get you well. All this fresh fruit is a blessing, but it's weird, on the mushrooms I don't really miss it that much. There seems to be something in the psychedelic compounds that takes away hunger."

The reality is, we have both lost at least twenty pounds on the meager Huautla diet. We were already thin, now we're starting to resemble beggar-bowl ascetics. Gazing back up at the long blue mountain, I say, "Somehow, Bones, we need to get better food up there to Huautla, to stay in good condition. Maybe we can strike a deal with one of those trucks that go back and forth."

Bones follows my eyes into the cloud forests. "Dig," he says, "those mountains up there, those mountains can swallow us whole. I mean, to the extent we don't even exist to the outside world anymore."

Draining my coffee, I smile. "And so what, why should that bother us? If you want to realize something different, you have to realize do different. Me, I want to go deeper into those mountains as far as we can go, beyond the map, to where we have to draw our own maps."

"You'd need some money to make it, and we're running low," Bones points out. "Then there's the language hassles. It's risky to take off back there on just a wing and a prayer. Shit, what about the bandidos? We'd be easy targets on foot."

Fuck the bandidos, I laugh, but have to admit the money part is rele-vant. We're almost down to our emergency bail-out funds. I happen to have a few hundred dollars back in a Los Angeles bank, but no way to access it. The bank book is stashed in my rented Silverlake garage.

"All right, I'm hip about the money. but what about the car? Bones, we can get two or three hundred for that beat-up Mercury down here. The Mexicans love junkers like that. And dig, we can live indefinitely back in those hills on that kind of bread."

Bones tugs at his scraggly beard, a forlorn cast to his face. "I need to get down out of those mountains for awhile, Jake. The fleas, the skimpy food, the Spartan scene, it's too much. Even the mushroom trip leaves me feeling drained, you know? It's arduous."

"Not if you go with the flow, man. Just go with the flow."

"I am going with the flow. Plus, there are no chicks up there at all, nada."

"So then what are you saying?"

"I just need to detach for awhile, I need some relief."

"You talking about going back to California?" I ask, never having expected anything so abrupt.

"No, not right away," Bones replies, scratching his thighs. "But we cruise on over to the Pacific coast, laze around on the beaches, maybe figure a way to make some down-low money. Aiyee, bro, I've got to find that clinic, these things are driving me mad!"

Bones twitches, his eyes moist with fever, lit by the awful knowledge that his flesh is being devoured. I feel for him, but what the fuck is he rambling on about?

"Right on, let's go find that doctor," I say, getting up, "But I'm not ready to just abandon Huautla, Bones, I'm not done there. And even if we leave, I'm coming back. I'm coming back even if I have to sell one of my motorcycles. In fact, I can ride that Matchless scrambler all the way down here and up that mountain. I can sell my Beaser and live for a year or more on the bread. Dig it, I'm coming back soon."

"Jake, no problemo," Bones replies, as we lug our bolsas down the street, "I'll come with you, we're partners now. But don't sell your beautiful bikes, you don't have to. I've got an idea how we can make some good quick loot. We just have to sort out some details."

"What the fuck. Are you talking about what I think?"

"Man, I'm telling ya, we can make this thing happen together. We have the brains and the nerve."

"What thing? Bones, what the hell are you trying to say?"

"Aiyee," Bones raves, "first the fleas, first these goddamn fleas, I've got to kill these fleas! I've got to get rid of them so I can think!"

I'm not sure whether Bones is babbling to me or to Buddha or whoever, but we hustle into a concrete medical clinic painted an antiseptic green. He shows his ravaged calves to a clucking nurse. There are some sick people hanging out in here with woeful vibes, so I go back outside. I don't want to pick anything up through psychic osmosis. Across the street, I prop my back in the banana palm shade of an adobe wall, innervated by the withering heat. I peel a fat, juicy orange, talking to myself. Bones seems deranged by fever. Whatever happens inside that clinic he isn't going to like it. I know my own blood is strong and pure, I've already shaken off the blood-thirsty mites. Bones' refusal to sell the rust-bucket coupe annoys me, and his cryptic comments are perplexing. I don't want to put myself in any kind of trick bag.

The lowland heat pours down like a wet blanket and I snooze in the cicada buzz. Finally, Bones emerges from the green clinic with an ashen face. Coming over to me, he slumps down. "Fuck," he mumbles, "they made me strip off all my clothes. Then they sprayed me down with some kind of odious chemical. My clothes, too. We had to wear these little masks. I think it was a pesticide . . ."

"Jesus, man, ddt, don't tell me that! Fuck, no! They doused you down with ddt?"

"Aiyee, it's true. They ignored my protests. But at least the fleas are dead."

I commiserate with his misfortune, trying not to laugh. We almost die in the back of a hurtling suicide truck, now he gets hosed down with a lethal pesticide. It almost seems like our luck has started to run against us.

We trudge on over to the bus station, sweating like pigs in the humid air. On the way we stop at the tire shop to pick up our refurbished tires. The costs are more than we expected and the grimy dealers are in no mood to haggle. Hideous gnats buzz around our heads, trying to drink the sweat from our eyes. We fork over the cash, then carry off a fruit-laden bolsa in one hand and a heavy tire in the other. Old Mexico is showing its ass to us now, take it or leave it, gringo long-hairs. We stagger up the sun-baked street.

At the bus station we guzzle mineral water and find out that the bus up to Huautla has been delayed, mechanical problems. It will not leave until manana around noon. Do we want to buy a ticket or no? Exasperated, we hand over more dinero to secure a seat. The idea of flagging down another bone-crushing truck is too daunting. We lug our gear across the street and relax under a moss-hanging tree. The thunder clouds are building in the shining afternoon sky.

"Fuck," Bones gripes, "these nickel and dime expenses are killing us. Where are we gonna sleep tonight?

"Not here, that's for sure. We'll get drenched like borrachitos."

But I get his drift. We can't afford to keep squandering our precious dinero. We can't sleep in the wet dirt and we don't want to spring for a hotel room. But we notice the Indians, the Mazatecs, waiting to go back up the mountain like us. They're camping out in the bus depot, clustered together, sprawled out on the hard wooden benches taking naps. Capricious ninos race about chasing each other, chickens squawk in bamboo cages. The solution is obvious. We stake out a bench over in one corner, stacking our rubber tires and jute bolsas as a sign of claim. The long, dull wait looms ahead, it is too hot to really even think.

Feeling better, Bones bats the greasy flies away. He regards me with questioning eyes.

"Shoot," I say. "What is it?"

"I've been thinking over possibilities," he replies, "about how we can accumulate some fresh cash."

"Fresh cash, hah," I say, feeling a tad leery. "I'm all ears."

"Well, dig. We head back across country to Guadalajara, that's going toward the coast anyway. Remember that big central Mercado? In that giant, multi-leveled maze you can buy anything under the sun. And I mean anything, literally."

"Anything? That covers a multitude of sins. Anything like what?"

"Anything like fresh peyote buttons and rare jungle herbs that get you high. And weed, man, good Mexican weed. That mercado is an open-air beehive, anything's possible. There are hundreds of little stalls and everybody is peddling something."

"Far out. You mean, really good Mexican grass? We can score kilos in that place?"

But no sooner do I utter these words than I feel a twinge of remorse. We took a vow about not doing any drug-dealing on this expedition. Erasing the words with a gesture I say, "Forget I said that. That goes against the promise we made."

"No, no," Bones enthuses, "that's not a hang-up because things change. We need to replenish our wallets, right? And yeah, they probably have loads of weed stashed in there, and if not right there then somewhere close by. Tons of good dope goes through Guadalajara and it's way cheaper than up north."

"Hmm, you know someone who has actually done this, Bones?" I ask, not wanting to become another tourista rip-off.

"No, not exactly, but listen. When I passed through there last summer I bought a few ounces right at a bar near that mercado. And those dudes offered me bricks, Jake, at an incredible price. I'm telling you, we could score really big."

"Man," I reply in a somber voice. "You realize what we're talking about doing? We're talking about scoring some keys and hustling it back into California. Dangerous, Bones, and not only that, it's exactly what we swore we would not do."

Bones strokes his beard "Yeah, but we promised that mainly for the chicks. We promised them we wouldn't get involved in any smuggling so they'd lighten up. But they shined us on, man, they're not even here."

"Not only for them. We decided not to mix spiritual and mercenary energies. Who in the fuck knows where this could lead? I don't want to step off into no-man's land."

"I hear you, but we're not really mixing things up – because our mushroom quest is over for awhile, now we're moving on. Look, we're gonna be heading back home and what do we have to show for it? Fucking nada. I'm talking about scoring some really primo dope and turning it into a nice, fat bankroll."

"I've still got a half pound of pretty decent pot stashed in my garage, plus all that excellent acid in amber jars. I've got at least five hundreds hits left. It's not like we're destitute."

"Right on, but dig. You still gotta hustle all those dime bags to broke-ass hippies. I'm thinking we score some super-primo weed that'll make the Topanga Canyon freaks flip out. If we can score even a couple of keys, along with your acid, we can make a nifty profit. Then we come back and get some more, do it again, and then presto! We're rolling in dough! Now we've got the money to live in Huautla for a year easy, we can do that Mayan trip. We can do whatever we want."

Intrigued, and undeniably thrilled, I say, "But what about our funds now, Bones? Do we even have enough bread to pull it off? What can we actually buy and still get home?"

"Realistically," Bones muses, "if we do the deal right, I think maybe two or three kilos. And we'll have enough spare cash to make it home to Silverlake."

"Aiyee, man, that would be wild. That would be a super cool deal to pull off."

His musing doper logic is seductive. Even though I promised myself and Dawn I would steer clear of such shenanigans, we are perilously low on funds. And the idea of setting up a conduit for high-octane weed has big-time appeal. We could be literally rolling in high cotton within months. But smuggling is a risky enterprise and the grapevine is lurid with hard-luck stories of reckless hippies who gambled and went bust.

Hung up on this daunting image, I say to Bones, "Let me think it over. I like the possibilities, but I need to check my inner vibes."

"No problemo," says Bones, regaining his nonchalant confidence. "And I'm cool with whatever you decide. I'm just saying it's a fast way for us to get flush real fast. I've got contacts up in Laurel and Topanga that'll really fatten our wallets."

Cogitating, I dedicate the rest of the afternoon to eating like a famished wolf. I stuff myself with yellow finger bananas and ripe papayas, I gorge on handfuls of raw protein-packed peanuts and raisins. Disgruntled about leaving the mountains, yet intrigued by the idea of turning smuggler. But why the fuck does life have to be always about money? Who set up this bizarre, mercenary system and why? Up in the cloud-forests of Huautla few decisions are required, only the pursuit of mystery matters. Through the humid, lowland afternoon Bones naps, recovering from the fleas, and I gorge like a feral young beast.

By sundown, I have a belly-ache of enormous proportions. I rock on the depot bench wracked with pangs. My body breaks out in torpid perspiration, I shake with chills. Bones urges me to drink more water to flush out the toxins, but in my dizzy nausea such advice isn't worth much. What I desperately need to do is take a shit. I stuffed myself all afternoon with mucho raw peanuts, fat avocados and not-quite-ripe bananas, now I'm paying the fool's price. Intense waves of peristalsis rumble in my swollen bowels, presaging an odious blast of hot feces.

Afraid that I am about to humiliate myself in public I lurch to my feet, my head swimming. Waving Bones off, sphincter clinched, I duck-walk to the banos de hombres. But inside the bathroom the stench of putrid turds and sour piss fill the toilet bowels, every one of them. Over in the corner, some poor borracho squatted down and released a hideous mess of drunkard's shit, leaving soiled scraps of newspaper to mark his crime. Fighting back my gorge, I waddle into the fresh evening air, my whole body shivering in revolt. I look around in frantic urgency, see a dark-green, flowering hedge. Crawling inside the dusty bushes, I swat empty beer bottles and dried garbage aside. Trembling like a dog, I squat and expel the most prolonged and hideous crap of my life. A torrent of odious fecal goo slithers from my intestines in a slime-green mound, leaving me gasping and grateful. I wipe off with a crumpled paper bag.

I crawl back out of the hedge, sweat cooling on my forehead, and stand on very shaky legs. Moths and bugs swarm in the flickering buzz of the street lamps. When I went into the bushes it was still twilight, now night has swept over Teotitlan. Some borrachitos smoke on a bench across the way, observing me, clearly amused. The gringo took a shit in the weeds, he is one of us, hah ha ha. I give them the thumbs up and they clap as I walk back into the bus station. I relate my hideous moment to Bones, who dissolves into a fit of laughter.

"At least you didn't defecate all over the bus station floor," he teases me.

"I know, thank God huh? But as it came exploding out I had this insight, Bones."

"Insight? What kind of insight?"

"I flashed on us doing this smuggling thing. I flashed on us going for la mota, scoring big, and smuggling it over. Then coming back to live in that lost Shangri-La."

"All right, man, paint that picture for me. I know we can do this!"

We put our heads together, talking in conspiratorial tones about the road ahead, how we can make it happen. Then I stretch out on the hard wooden bench and sleep a restless sleep. I dream of a ruby-throated hummingbird that hovers in my palm, taking sips of amber honey. When I murmur my wishes to the tiny pajarito, it zooms off in a blur of iridescent plumage.

During the night it rains some more, but the monsoons seem more sporadic here on the plains. After a breakfast of thick toasted bread, strong coffee negro, and watermelon slices, we board the old school bus and are lucky to find seats. The bus is jammed with laconic Mazatecos and a few morose Mexicanos. One Indian cradles a small pinto goat in his lap. Lashed to the roof are crates of chickens, our two tires, various baskets, sacks of rice and stales, other cargo. The shambling bus grinds up the implacable mountain at ten to fifteen miles an hour, the passengers tittering, fingering their rosaries, or maintaining grim silence on the treacherous hairpins that hang in the air. The silver band of river winds far beneath us. Aiyee, it's a long ways down. I don't really want to look, but I can't not look. Death waits in the canyon, leering at these old buses, biding its time. If we go over we are all dead men. The mountain roads of Mexico are infamous for ramshackle buses pitching into deep chasms, the driver drunk or nodding off, brakes failing or tires blowing out, wiping out all aboard. It's common knowledge but none of us want to think about it The morning is beautiful, the sky a transparent blue window, no one wants to think of that awful slide into nothingness. So we laugh, we grimace, we clench our jaws, we murmur together. Some of us turn inward, taking refuge in the invisible friend. A common bond unites us all as we skirt the edge of oblivion.

# Chapter 26

W E LINGER IN Huautla de Jimenez for a few more days, repairing the car, saying our good-byes. Richard concurs that the monsoons are tapering off, which makes leaving these mystic highlands less regretful. The vagrant curiosity-seekers are already abandoning the scene, Huautla is too primitive and boring. But I wish that I could stay on, stay in these lost ancient lands beyond the paradoxes of modern life. I take my holy vow to the holy earth, to the sacred sky, to these beloved mountains that I will return, I will come back and claim my place.

We leave right after daybreak. We make the harrowing drive back down the mountain without a single blowout. We stop in the wedding village to see if anyone is around. But the men are out tending their hanging gardens or hunting small game or gathering wood, and only a few women are around. I give my folding knife in its leather scabbard to one of the grandmothers, telling her softly, "Esta es for el jefe, mi amigo. Este regalo es de Oro, from Oro, y dice por favor, voy a volver."

She nods her understanding, with a wrinkled smile, squeezing my hand. I leave with tears in my eyes and a lump in my throat. I leave because it is time.

WE HEAD OUT across the vast green plains, fresh from the rains. Our intention this time is to avoid the withering vortex of Mexico City, to stay well to the south, taking minor roads across the sprawling countryside, heading westward toward Guadalajara, eager for new discoveries.

In a range of lambent hills, in a village called Valle de Bravo, of cobblestone lanes and flowering trees and stone fountains, we pause and rest. In a patio bar a gringo ex-pat tells us that Valle de Bravo is the friendliest place he has ever lived. "The rat race doesn't exist here," he confides. "The poor slobs back in the states can't imagine what life can be like if you just get out. They're slaves to their mortgages and taxes and alimonies, just like Henry Miller said. Here you can rent a ten room hacienda with maids for only a hundred dollars a month. No lie, it's paradise. Just ask around."

Bones and I listen with wistful eyes, taking mental notes. Living in the avocado peace of Valle de Bravo for awhile would be sheer bliss. Bring whatever you want or bring nothing at all, make it up as you go. I have to admit this is strong motivation.

We bend into the long drive overland toward fabled Guadalajara, staying mildly stoned. And way out on that rolling shrub desert in the middle of nowhere, under a furnace blue sky, the strangest thing happens. Two blonde hippie chicks with backpacks jump out into the road, madly flagging us down.

"Whoa man, what the hell? Are they for real?"

"Aiyeee, dig it," Bones beams. "Can you believe our luck?"

Both girls are thin and streaked with road-grime, brown from the sun, wearing skimpy cotton fuck-me dresses. Bones has been without nookie since we left Los Angeles, Bones slams on the brakes. The rust-bucket Mercury skids to a stop. One chick is tall and horsey, the other petite and waif-like. But a crazy eagerness lights their faces, they ogle us like we're manna from heaven. The horsey blond puts her face in Bones' window, saying "Wow, imagine meeting you guys way out here! Where you heading?"

These girls reek of patchouli and armpits, it hits us right away. But Bones, with a swelling hardon, grins boyishly. "Over to Guadalajara," he says, "then maybe out to the Pacific coast."

"Well, hey," the little blue-eyed one pipes up, "we'll gladly fuck you both for a ride. We've been trying to get to Guadalajara. This pig of a Mexican dumped us out here after she'd already put out, you know? He wanted me to suck him off but I didn't want to, he was too fat."

This brazen confession freezes further inquiry on our lips. All at once I identify their cloying smell and want no part of it—rank, fermenting, unwashed sex. But Bones has no such qualms. He's grinning like a lewd Cheshire Cat, making eyes with the tall one.

"Well, as you can see," I say, gesturing toward the back, "we're kinda crowded in here." Most of our gear is jammed in the backseat, including a box of Oaxacan clay pottery that we acquired back in Huautla. The trunk is stuffed with our spares tires.

The antsy little blonde, who has come around to my window, blows me a kiss. "Oh come on," she giggles, "I can easily squeeze back in there. And Tammy can sit up front between you two. You wanna get your dick sucked, don't you?"

Trying not to laugh, I think no, not with you, but she's right. There's enough room for her lithe body and their knapsacks. Bones leans over and whispers in my ear, "Hey bro, we lucked into two hot, horny babes. What more can we ask? Let's get it on."

My thoughts peel away like an onion, up against my celibacy vows again, feeling embarrassed. We get out of the car and banter with them by the road, listening to their outrageous story. They left San Fernando Valley about a month ago on a stoned lark, with little more than what they were wearing. They've been hitch-hiking back and forth across Mexico ever since. They claim to have almost no money, their flagrant young cunts have been their traveler's checks. They want to see how far they could go trading sex for food, rides, and a place to crash, just for the sheer fun of it. They figure an emergency phone call back home will bail them out of any really bad jams.

To be honest, although I don't show it, these are the kind of frivolous chicks I can't stand. I do some rapid calculations as to how many grunting, unwashed fucks with god knows who this fantasy trip has involved? I'm all for uninhibited, Bohemian free-love, but this is twisted. These girls are lucky their throats haven't been slit. At a loss for words, I light up a joint and pass it around. My companero Bones is already feeling up the horsey one's ass. The brazen little blonde rubs her tits on my arm as she breathes ganga smoke into my face. "I give unbelievable head," she mews in my ear, "I'm gonna make you really happy."

Bones and the tall broad traipse off into the desert shrubs. They unfurl one of the olive surplus blankets, chattering and smiling, then sink out of sight. I back away from the stoned minx purring against me, telling her, "Listen, I need to explain something to you."

She reaches out and squeezes my tumescent cock, which instantly turns super-hard. "Tell me later," she coos. "Let's get in the front seat and I'll blow you, then I'll sit on it, baby. I have a tight wet pussy and I'm not wearing any panties."

Blushing, I push her away. "No, wait, you need to listen to me. I'm following a special yoga discipline, I'm practicing celibacy. Yeah, for real. I don't want to fuck you."

"You've got to be kidding," she yelps, "that's total nonsense! Sex is good for us, what's the matter with you?!"

"Nothing's the matter with me," I retort, stepping away, taking a breath. "I'm just doing what I'm doing. I'm doing what's right for me."

"Is something wrong with me?" she whines. "Or wait, wait. Are you some kind of fag?"

"I'm not a fag, no. I'm following an esoteric yoga practice. And it's not about you, you're cool. I'm just not into having sex right now."

"That's fucked up. I give the best blowjob going, you don't even know. Come on, let me just show you. You can come in my mouth, I like it, I swallow. Forget all about that nonsense."

"No, dig, no, sorry, I'm not interested. We'll give you girls a ride somewhere, whatever. But I want you to stop pestering me."

"Oh, you are a queer, aren't you," she says, squinching her face up. "You can't hide it, you know. Why don't you just be up front about the way you are?"

"Fuck off. Why can't you just accept that I'm not into you?"

Taking the roach with me, I walk off and stand in the chaparral, listening to the doves call. I see the little blond get into the front seat, where she sits sulking and chain-smoking, flicking ashes out the window. She probably figures I'm some kind of sadistic homo, not that I give a fuck. She doesn't appeal to me in the least. I'm not going to interrupt myself for some silly nympho who's fucked her way all across Mexico.

Lucidly high, feeling calmly detached, I let the calling of the doves pull me deeper. I reflect on what it means to be clean and free out on the road. You have to respect your body. Wash your underarms at least, wash your crotch, wash your ass crack. You have to take the grunge off or it accumulates until you become the grunge, and all grunge goes down the drain. It's the same way with the mind, even more so. Don't get involved in weird trips that aren't yours, bypass them, the entangling hassles just aren't worth it.

I hear Bones whistling long and low, one of his signals. I see them moving back through the mesquite toward the car. He's letting me know he's coming back in case I' m in flagrant delicto. At least now we can get back on the road.

Bones is mellow and spent and the rank horsey blonde rides between us. She tries to maintain some pleasant chit-chat but her friend bristles with resentment. As we come into a crossroads town, I catch Bones' eye, saying, "Look, everybody, I'm don't mean to be a killjoy but this scene is nowhere. I don't want to ride all the way to Guadalajara with these kind of vibes"

"Yeah, Tammy," the little blonde chirps, "this is a total fucking dud for me. Let's get out and take our chances. Prince Charming here doesn't get a hard-on for girls."

Tammy rolls her eyes, glances at Bones, Bones sighs, then laughs. "My pardner is really dedicated to his metaphysical trip, and yeah, that's the way it is."

He pulls over under some shade trees directly across from a truck stop cantina. He and the chicks scramble out with their few belongings, the horsey blond gives Bones her phone number. The little one, whose name I don't even know, flips me off. "Yogi faggot," she taunts.

I slit my eyes and shake my head, glad to be able to breathe through my nose again. She saunters toward the cantina where some burly Mexicans are already ogling her. After kissing Bones, the tall blond trots after her.

Bones slides back in with a debauched grin "Come easy, go easy, right? Actually, I'm glad you said something. Both those babes need a bath really, really bad."

"No problemo, amigo. Glad you scored. Now let's go find our fame and fortune."

WE PUT IN another day of hot, hard driving and make Guadalajara's famous mercado around noon. The summer heat is blistering, sapping our vitality, but we're in good spirits. We seek the deep shade of the concrete monolith, wandering the corridors and tiers, peering into the stalls, rejuvenating on cool watermelon slices, confirming with our own eyes that everything imaginable is for sale in this giant bazaar. We skirt the blood-soaked carne section in horror, shallow mouth-breathing to ward off the stench. Slabs of skinned carcasses hang on hooks, cattle, pigs, goats, rabbits, sheep, chickens, maybe even dogs too, all swarming with a mantle of black flies, being hacked apart by the blood-spattered butchers. But up on the fourth level, we find the stall of a dealer in arcane plants and herbs, an old man who has lively eyes but the face of a shriveled wineskin. We talk with him about native medicine plants, in furtive voices ask to see his clandestine goods. He takes from beneath the plank counter a brown sack full of plump peyote buds. Aiyee, si senor, muchas gracias, this is what we seek! We pass him a few Americano dollars for the paper sack. But when we ask about marijuana he shakes his head, saying he must close for lunch. But I am delighted by our stroke of luck. I've taken synthesized powder and liquid mescaline and loved the effects, but never sampled raw shaman peyote. We decide to save the scarlet-green until we reach the Pacific beaches, where we can relax. First things first, first La Mota said to be stashed somewhere here in Guadalajara.

At a maze of converging streets not far from the Mercado Centro, we take a room in a hotel that was built in another century. Once elegant, now falling into dilapidation, the hotel has a parking lot where we can move the car off the streets. We take a large upstairs room with peeling wallpaper and two sagging, iron beds, a creaking overhead fan that stirs the humid air. Cracked hand-painted tiles cover the floor, the large bathroom has a stained marble basin and a shower big enough for three people. The tepid, tea-colored water flows from the old copper pipes, soaking the sweat from our bodies, refreshing us, as we keep our lips and nostrils pinched against the teeming microbes We laze around under the fourteen foot ceiling, under the whirring fan, munching on delicious sliced papaya and smoking a number.

"Dig, brother Bones," I drawl. "if that peyote is an omen then the dice might be rolling our way again."

"I know it," Bones nods with a slow grin. "I want to go outside and mingle and ask around. Nothing's taboo in Guadalajara. We just need to find someone who's hip."

In the languid shadows of the afternoon, Bones ventures out to find what he can find. I stay in the room doing my Hatha exercises and practicing breath meditation in the torpid heat. The cacophonous street noises seep through the tall windows and make it hard to concentrate. So I stoke up the fat pungent roach and kick back, scheming and daydreaming.

Bones comes back, turned on by all the fantastic street energy that he's run into. "Dig, there's a hustler on every corner, everybody's hawking something, radios, watches, chicks, jewelry, yeah, it's wild. I've got a feeling, this might be our night."

We stay pleasantly stoned on my dwindling stash as the Guadalajara twilight comes on, the blue smoke being sucked up into the whirring fan blades. After awhile, we venture outside to explore the crowded streets, people are everywhere, jamming with a purpose, maybe just grooving after work. The people laugh and joke in the cooling air, they flirt, boom boxes blaring Mariachis and heart-breaking Norteno ballads. Street vendors cook over iron grills at every corner, a drunken melange of aromas—garlic frijoles, fish tacos, fresh fruit juice, thick juicy burritos, carnitas, rainbow snow cones, roasted corn on the cob, scoops of fresh guacamole, peeled cucumbers rubbed with limon and red chili pepper, strawberry ice cream. In no time at all we are drooling.

At the curbstone, a stout mestizo roasts ears of corn over a charcoal grill. He beckons us, smiling, missing a couple of his tobacco-stained teeth as he turns the fragrant corn with metal tongs. He rubs them with slices of fresh lime and sprinkles on coarse sea salt. "Ahhh," he says, "muy sabroso, tomen una mordida!"

The well-roasted ears smell delicioso and we gladly give him a few coins. We sit on the curb, munching through two ears apiece, munching as only stoned dopers can munch. The street lamps come on, traffic blares on past, the Guadalajara dusk radiates an animated revelry.

"These people, Bones, they're all in a festive mood. Like the whole world is out on the sidewalks. Is this some kind of holiday?"

"You're asking me?" Bones replies, cleaning his mustaches. "I have no clue, I lost track of days up in the mountains. Maybe it's Friday night."

"Say what? So then, they're drinking for the joy of drinking."

"Aiyee, what were you asking me?

We laugh together, flashing on the whimsical absurdity of our conversation. We are lucky to be here in this marvelous place, alive and aware in this marvelous moment, and we know it.

"Bones," I say, "check out that cat over there slouching against the lamppost, dig his outfit. He's Marlon Brando, man, he's Brando, right out of The Wild Ones."

Bones sees what I'm saying, laughing low. For sure, the young Mexican across the street is a spitting image of Brando's character in the movie—black leather jacket, engineer boots, jeans rolled up into bucket cuffs, even the black leather cap on his duck-tailed head. This dude is some kind of solo artist, leaning against the lamp post smoking, taking in the street with worldly eyes.

"Interesting," says Bones, "these hip, happening Mexicans seem to be caught in the 1950's film culture. Even their mannerisms. They must pick it up from old American movies."

The Mexican Brando notices that we're watching him. He gives us wry acknowledgment by touching the brim of his cap. He smiles, perhaps flattered by the attention from two wandering Americanos. I stretch my arms out and pretend to be riding a motorcycle, crying out, "Dónde está el Triumph?"

The leather-clad hipster shrugs, calls back in halting English, "No, I wish, I only wish, maybe some day."

Another man walks up and speaks to him, pointing down the milling boulevard. They share a few words. Marlon Brando waves at us, then turns and walks off with his friend.

"Hmm, looks like some kind of street action, Bones. Wonder if he could connect us?"

"Maybe," Bones muses, "maybe we'll see him again later. But there's a lot of action to check out. These are the Guadalajara streets, man, anything is possible."

"Sounds good to me," I laugh, getting to my feet, "Let's go find what we can find. But first let's go back to the room and fire up that number."

Awhile later, doubly stoned on the religious roach, we amble down the neon boulevard that is ablaze with life and chaotic energy. All shops are open, the trivial trinkets of civilization on full display in the windows, radios, watches, eight-tracks, miniature TVs, provocative dresses, leather boots and ranchero hats, candy and liquor, treats galore, loud speakers blaring out musica as the smarmy pitchmen work the excitable crowds.

But all around there is the most astonishing poverty. There are beggars on every corner, pitiful and destitute, stranded copper-skinned girls with hungry clutching infants, their pleading eyes. Here the desperate, unknown world hits you right in the eyes, in the heart, this is not some carnival in New Orleans or Haight-Ashbury. Here on these grimy sidewalks is where death sits down next to life and impassively cuts the deck.

At one teeming intersection where several haphazard streets seem to converge, we are faced with a dream-like image. A large cluster of bright balloons floats above the throng, in surreal cadence with the frenetic energy. The multi-hued balloons bob up and down, on some invisible, guiding tether. The balloons jump in the air as if manipulated by some disembodied hand.

Staring at this bizarre sight, we laugh out loud. "That's unreal, man, no one's holding the string!"

"Come on, let's check it out. There has to be a cause!"

We make our way through the noisy crowd, plowing our way toward the phenomena. But the cluster of balloons weaves and bobs away, even as we pursue. The balloons leap away as if in jest, toying with us. We push onward, bumping bodies, laughing and mystified. Then the crowd parts open, and we come to an abrupt, eye-opening halt. A fireplug dwarf with saucer eyes grins madly up at us. He's festooned in a blue sequined suit and a red pork-pie hat. One stubby arm is thrust aloft, controlling the bright cloud of balloons. I gape into the little man's insanely friendly face, his irregular piano-key teeth, even as Bones mutters, "Are you fucking kidding me?"

"Amigos, my gringo amigos," the spangled dwarf cries, "my beautiful hippies! I was hoping you would notice and follow after me!"

He pumps his balloon arm up and down, beaming at us. "You like my balloons, hah, a good signal, no?"

Laughing, I say, "Yeah, you definitely caught our attention. What's your trip?"

"You mean," the dwarf whispers, "what can Pascualito do for you? I have been waiting. I know that you know that I know that I am the doorway to your wishes."

"Wait a second, man. You mean to say that you knew we were following you? We couldn't even see you."

"You must have eyes in the back of your head," Bones quips.

"Oh si, I do," affirms the dwarf, "I know everything that is happening on my streets. I knew you were there from three blocks away. The balloons are my eyes, floating high above all the other heads. The balloons tell me who is coming."

Taking in his rapid-fire bullshit, I ask, "Where'd you learn to speak such good English?"

The dwarf's mascara eyes are like pinwheels of lunacy. "In L.A. of course, mis amigos," he giggles, making his balloons dance in the air. "In L.A. I lived and played like you do. Before the bad-ass cops sent me home to recuperate."

"Then," Bones teases, "your balloons are your confidants? What do they tell you that we're looking for?"

"Ayy," the dwarf replies, rolling his eyes, "the sixty-four dollar question, no? No matter what it is you seek, consider Pascualito to be at your service."

"Hmm, that's cool. Because we want something special, something unusual, muy primo."

"But of course, si, of course you do!" beams Pascualito, sidling in between us. "You are daring gringo hippies and I am your friend! Tell me what you want, you can tell me. La mota, yes? I see it in your faces, you seek la mota! And I can take you right to her!"

Bones and I share an elated glance, then we all drift toward the wall, keeping our voices low, the dwarf nodding his bongo head. "So for real," I ask him, "you can do this? Tonight you can do this for us? We don't want just a few joints, man, we're after some quantity, maybe even a few kilos, comprende?"

"Oh si, I understand good," the little man says, pumping his arm, making his balloons dance. "And I can take you to the place where there is plenty to carry away with you. In fact, you will need a wheelbarrow. I will take you to La Mota Suprema!"

"Holy shit," Bones says to me, "we might have really lucked out. You feel like taking a chance?"

"You will not be disappointed in me, my amigos," insists the dwarf, kissing his stubby fingers. "I am here tonight to fulfill your hopes."

"All right, all right," I counter, "cuánto vale? How much for say a kilo? And no bullshit, only the really good stuff."

"Oh entiendo, only la mota suprema," Pascual beams up at me. "These people are mi familia, I am one of them, and I will vouch for you. That way you will be treated with the proper respect. But you will have to negotiate with the boss, he will make you the beneficial price. All I ask is that you give me ten gringo dollars to be your guide, then I will take you to El Jefe."

Bones and I consult each other, deciding to go for it. How can you refuse such spontaneous luck? Palming a ten spot into the dwarf's hand, I ask, "Is it far? How long will it take?"

"No, not far," he replies, tucking the bill into his blue satin sash. "But we must hurry. Already it is after dark and they will be shutting the gate. Follow me, hombres, vamos!"

The midget impresario turns quickly into a cobblestone side street, lofting his balloons, then makes a beeline into the Guadalajara under-ground. The bright neon glare of the boulevard fades, replaced by dim bulbs hanging above open doors, red lights, garish desultory whores smoking in the windows, calling to us as we pass. The dwarf moves fast, exchanging pleasant banter with the chiquitas, who all know him by his name.

"Pascualito, who have you brought us?" they cajole him, plucking at his jacket, gesturing for us, licking their plump red lips.

"No, no senoritas," the dwarf clucks, brushing them off. "Tonight we hurry on other business, no blow jobs for you tonight. We go to visit El Jefe!"

Bones responds to their advances with a lascivious grin, but doesn't dally. Up ahead the narrow street plunges into Stygian gloom, no street lamps at all. We go slower and traverse two muddy blocks in almost pitch darkness. I hear the dwarf's rapid breathing, smell the rank mud in the gutters, the barrio ahead shrouded in muffled silence.

Spooked, Bones demands, "Hey man, you said a little ways. Where are you taking us?"

"No no, do not lose your nerve," the dwarf admonishes, not stopping. "You are with me, Pascualito the magician. Just a little further, I promise you. You will have her tonight—La Mota!"

Stumbling through another dank block, Pascual leads us around a corner and stops in front of a massive wooden gate set into a high adobe wall. The gate is illumined by a feeble electric bulb, dangling from a cord that snakes over the adobe ramparts. The eerie scene reminds me of a 1920's movie set. Set into the wooden gate is another door, barely wide enough for one man at a time. Clutching his rustling balloons, our impish benefactor steps up to the door and pounds with his knobby fist.

"Ahora, now we wait," he says soto voce. "The watcher will come down and let us in."

An impatient minute passes. We hear footsteps, then a muffled male voice asking a question in Spanish. The dwarf responds in his theatrical lingo, repeating a phrase that sounds like a code. The door opens up a crack, revealing a man's shadowed face, taking us in at a glance. He swings the door open, saying in a gruff tone, "Rapidamente, vengan."

He cradles a double-barreled shotgun in the crook of his arm. We stare at the somber guard, then at the maniacal midget. "Yes, yes," Pascualito enthuses, "this is what you want! She is inside, the one you seek!"

As though caught in some kind of spell we step through the narrow passage. "You will introduce us to the boss, yes?" I remind him, stopping abruptly.

"No, that man will take you up to him," the dwarf leers. "I will wait for you here. Trust me."

Before we can object, the guard shuts the plank door and drops a crossbar into place, then motions for us to follow him. He leads us across a dark courtyard enclosed by high walls that we sense more than see, a courtyard of cobblestones, and on these cobblestones sleeping figures wrapped in blankets and ponchos, turning in dreams, coughing, silhouettes tossed on a charcoal canvas waiting for daybreak. We keep close to the cat-eyed guard, trying not to step on these moaning bodies. There must be dozens of them, collapsed in some kind of surreal slumber on the hard ground Who in the hell are these people, where do they come from?

We come to a high dim wall, the guard points to a narrow stairway attached to the adobe bricks. These stairs have no handrail, barely lit by another weak, naked bulb at the top. Up there, against the night sky, we can make out another rifleman gazing down at us. Fuck. Too deep now to back out, we both realize we have to climb those ominous stairs and brash it through.

The guard points with his shotgun barrel to the daunting stairs, muttering, "El Jefe está arriba alla, irnos."

Gathering my nerve, I go up and Bones comes after me, our left hands grazing the rough wall for a semblance of balance. On the roof, the rifleman holds a kerosene lantern in our faces as a young boy pats us down. It is is easier to see up here on the roof, not so tomb-like. The roof is narrow and flat, there are a few chairs and a round umbrella table. A low bungalow occupies the far side, not much bigger than a small garage. The glow of lamplight glints through its shaded window, another low-watt bulb flickers on the drab wall. The door is painted neon blue with black markings all over it.

Stepping back, the roof guard shoulders his rifle, saying, "Bien, ven comigo."

He takes us to the door, which is scrawled in indecipherable code, and knocks twice. A harsh voice comes from within, giving an order. A moment later, the door is flung open by a lizard-like man as tall as Bones who glares at us with indignation.

"Qué?" he hisses. "Por que esta aqui?"

The rifleman shrugs, saying, "La mota, el enano. Dos Norte Americanos."

"Ah, so you met our muy amable dwarf, Pascualito," the lizard man says in precise and sardonic English, baring his teeth. "And what makes you think you will find your wishes here?"

Taken aback by his disdain, we hesitate. The rifle guard drops his head and steps back into the shadows.

"Shut up, Pepi. Stop harassing them, you evil puta. Let them enter." These gruff words come from the low-lit room, spoken with blunt authority. Pepi spins aside, his eyes taunting us. Bowing slightly, he simpers, "Oh yes, entonces, my yankee amigos, do come into our penthouse and state your desires. The master declares."

"Pay no attention to him, or as little as possible," says the dark man who sits behind a littered, dimly lit desk. His shoulders are pushed against the wall behind him, his English is thick, heavily accented. A half-empty bottle of tequila is on the desk, a lamp with a green visor shade, and a long-barreled revolver like an after-thought. "He is a bitter whore who does not enjoy his life, so he vents his spleen on every stranger he meets."

El Jefe laughs at Pepe with a lewd fondness and Pepi glares back, a high tension spring on the edge of snapping. "But he is a smart cookie," the dark man adds. "He learned his linguistics in your country, where he also learned to obediently suck cock."

Pepi hisses, "You insult me in front of these gringos?"

Trying to ease the vibes, I open my hands and say, "Senores, we have come in the hopes of doing some business with you. That is our only intention. According to the little man with the balloons, this is the best place."

"Que business?" Pepi spits, bayoneting me with his eyes. "Hah, you know nothing about business here in Guadalajara, you long-haired faggot!"

"Shut your fucking hole," El Jefe growls, his coal black eyes like hollow pits. "Go back to your ironing or I will whip you in front of my guests."

Wincing, Pepi slinks behind an ironing board draped with white pleated shirts. In the yellow light of a bronze floor lamp, his hatred for us is palpable. He picks up an ancient electric iron as though he will throw it at me. Both of these men are smoking rank Mexican cigarettes, harsh smoke layers the claustrophobic room.

Forcing a smile, Bones says, "The carnival dwarf said we could buy la mota here, that it would be good and the price fair. My partner and I want to buy two or three kilos. Then, if it's a winner with our people back in Los Angeles, we'd like to set up a pipeline for more."

"A pipeline," the thick man, nodding his head hazed in smoke. "A pipeline siempre bueno, so long as there is something in it."

He fixes me with an ironic smile, a smile composed of shadows, a man of shadows. Then he snubs out his fag, saying, "Yes, the little man with the big funny head, he is quite the card, no? He is one of my sons."

I maintain eye contact with him, nodding slightly, my senses on full alert. His eyes are inkwells of irredeemable avarice. He laughs, almost a pant. "So you are my new associates, if Pascual brings you to me, everything is bien. You would like to smoke la mota, no?"

The lizard-man continues to glare at me, in the corner of my eye, dabbing at the shirt collars with a his hot, furious iron. I resolve not to ignore him, knowing he is dangerous.

"Sure, for sure," Bones says with his ingratiating smile, "lay some on us."

Pepi snickers, narrowing his eyes, a long pair of scissors now in his hand. Turning toward him, I say. "We are not your enemies, man. We're here to do some honest business."

He reacts as if stung, his eyes flaring, his lip quivering. "You think you are lucky because of where you are born, you fucking gringo? To me you are nothing!"

The dark troll behind the desk rises to his feet, silencing him with a deadly glance. Pepi lays down the scissors, trembling in palpable menace and shame.

Bones shoots me a what-the-fuck look. I say to the bossman, "Senor, we come here in good faith, to do some business. Like my friend says, we would like to negotiate a good deal with you and set something up."

I keep my eyes on him and my voice steady, but my awareness never leaves the lethal faggot coiled on my left.

"Si, but of course, yo tambien," El Jefe replies, his humorless eyes appraising us. Then he sneers at his minion, "Get out, you maricon. Go and wait outside while we negotiate like men."

Pepi ducks his head at once and slithers from the room as if his skin is on fire.

The shadow man spreads his enormous hands, leering with satisfaction "He will not bother us again. He is a sick runt who is deformed by his hatred of gringos. But he cannot help himself, and he has certain talents, so I take pity on him."

He turns to a wall cabinet and opens it, taking out a brown paper bag. Clearing phlegm from his throat, he rasps, "Here, la mota, muy excelente as you will see."

He dumps a dark green lump of twiggy weed on the desk, ugly at first sight, skunk weed. I know it for what it is, but pick some up, sniffing it. We make a show of appreciation, knowing we have to play our cards right. El Jefe scrutinizes us with glittering black eyes.

"Hmm, not bad," Bones opines, looking at me with a sly smile.

"Estoy de acuerdo," I say, nodding in appraisal. "It smells muy bien."

The dark heavy man grunts in satisfaction. "I can have three kilos for you in a half hour. But you need to sample it, no? You test it, so you can vouch for la qualidad."

I'm not sure whether he's playing some game or actually believes his ludicrous words. But to smoke any of this shit is the last thing I want to do. "Senor, the aroma alone tells us it is muy bueno. Besides, we don't have any rolling papers with us."

"Ah, that is no problema," says the dark man, coughing his syrupy cough. He tears a strip off the brown paper bag, crumples a leafy twig in his blunt fingers, laves it with his tongue, his eyes fastened on mine. His eyes gauge every nuance of our faces. He lights the joint with his Zippo, inhales manfully, then thrusts the repugnant turd at me. Sniffing the fumes, I take a meager puff, nodding judiciously, then pass it to Bones. It's hideous shit, I can't hold it for more than a few seconds. Bones takes a drag, chokes, but manages to keep his down a little longer.

"So, cuánto?" I say to our leering patron. "Es bueno, how much per kilo?"

"Ah, then you like it, que bueno," he says, his oily head gleaming in the lamplight. "Now you know how I like to operate. The junkie queer, he does not understand negocios, he only knows his lusts, he only loves what he hates. But some are meant to fall down, no? So others like us can walk on top of them. It is easy to trick such fools, it is the way things are. They are dogs who cannot eat except for what scraps come from our hand. That is the way things are. Those ones down there, sleeping on the ground, they are my dogs. All of them."

I meet his glittering eyes without emotion, showing nothing, but knowing I will kill to leave this suffocating room. But he only smiles, the dark man, lifting his eyebrows in recognition. I met him once long ago, this man of shadows, I met met him on a red-dirt road from my Texas childhood. I have never forgotten his sinister, passing presence, his predatory leer, and somehow I am not surprised that he is here.

For a moment neither one of us speaks, or even moves. Bones breaks the spell. "Okay then, how much will it cost us for the first few kilos?'

El Jefe tilts his perspiring face, disengaging from me. "I will charge you thirty-five dollars Americano for each brick. That is my special price since we are now amigos, so we can get things rolling."

The price is ridiculous, but I give an astute nod. "It's a fair price," I say. "I think we can do this thing, right, Bones? But let's make it an even one hundred for three."

"Esta bien, okay," El Jefe says, dropping the crude, unraveling joint into an ashtray. "You have the dinero to show me? Show me, and I will send my man. You will have your la mota muy pronto."

"No, senor, that is not possible," I shake my head. "Not tonight."

"Because we don't have those dollars with us," Bones says. "We don't carry much money when we wander the streets."

"Ah, comprendo." the dark man mutters, obviously displeased.

"And we didn't expect to be so fortunate tonight," I add, "to meet you like this."

He nods his heavy head, somewhat drunk on tequila, trying to gauge our words. "Si, you are both smart hombres," he says thickly, "that is good. But what then do you propose?"

Feeling my way, I reply, "The safest thing will be for us to drive over in the morning and park around the corner. Then we walk here and do the deal with you, cash on the table. We can work out the timing of our next deal too, maybe in about a month."

"We can get it all set up," Bones nods, "so it flows smooth as silk."

"Muy amable, if I can believe you," El Jefe mutters, whose name we do not know, nor does he know ours. He lights another Mexican cigarette, inhales deeply, the wheels turning in his head. "Esta bien," he says. "But what can you leave on my desk now, to show me good faith?"

There is no way around it, we know we have to pitch in to walk out. Bones shrugs, saying, "Well, we don't have much on us, I don't know."

Sensing that we have gained an edge, I say, "We'll leave you twenty American dollars tonight, in good faith. This is our down-payment on our new partnership with you."

I reach into my pocket and extract a pair of ten-spots, placing them on his desk. "Senor, this dinero says we will be here at nine en la manana, for three kilos de numero uno la mota."

El Jefe nods and grunts, scooping up the cash as if it belongs to him by the mere fact of his presence. "Okay, esta bueno I like the way you say our partnership, hah, si, we will make this pipeline, you muchachos and me. And fuck the rest of them para nada, hah ha ha!"

"Si, fuck the rest of them," I grimace "Money will flow across this desk, senor, and la mota, muchas la mota will flow back with us into California."

The bossman laughs his mirthless laugh, takes a pull of tequila, offers us some, then shakes our hands in a curt and tender grip. He leads us out the door and onto the dim rooftop, carrying in one hand a leather riding quirt. Pepi slouches at the umbrella table in the shadows, smoking, an expression of contempt on his face. Then he sees the leather quirt.

El Jefe gives the guard some concise instructions, then with a slight bow says to us, "En la manana." Turning to Pepe, he flicks him with the whip. "Look at you now, you wicked cringing puta. For insulting estos hombres, who are now my friends, I am going to punish you."

We follow the rifleman down the steep stairs, pick our way across the courtyard, over the comatose bodies, and wait as he unbars the door in the gate. We are shown out with a muffled, "buen noche". The naked bulb above the gate has been turned off, the street is pitch-black. The devious dwarf, Pascualito, is nowhere in sight. We stand stock-still for a moment, letting our eyes adjust. Then we retrace our steps through the gloom, hustling as fast as we can up the dark streets into the red light district. The whores are still there, crooning to us as we pass, but we ignore them. The neon boulevard is visible up ahead and we hasten toward its relative safety.

"Holy fuck, what a weird trip," Bones exhales, as we mingle with the street crowds, the shops vibrating with Mexicana musica and illusory promises.

"Man oh man, what an evil vibe! We're not going back there, Bones, nunca."

"Aiyee, and get a load of that putrid shit, not even worth ten bucks a key. But hey Jake, you were cool with that dude, I dug your action. You baited the hook and got us out of there."

"Yeah, but between him and the dwarf, it cost us another thirty fucking dollars."

"Right on man, let's stay clear of that shifty midget, he's bad news."

We stop on the bustling sidewalk and scan the area for hints of Pascualito. But he has vanished into the Guadalajara night, along with his cluster of balloons. We walk several blocks back up the boulevard toward our hotel, pausing every so often to make sure we aren't being tailed. We sit on a concrete bench eating salted peanuts and raisins, sipping bottles of mineral water. Finally at ease, we return to our decrepit, colonial hotel.

The old clerk mumbles, "Buenas noches", barely looking up from the newspaper that he reads with a magnifying glass. We take the creaking elevator upstairs, glad to be alone. Overcome by lassitude, we lie on the old iron beds and drowse off into the fitful slumber of those waiting to be hearkened. Hearkened, and blessed, and made whole again.

# Chapter 27

MORNING FILTERS IN through the tall streaked windows, carrying discordant street noises. The carnival dwarf seems almost like an apparition made of cobwebs. How could we have fallen for such bullshit? We wash our faces, eat oranges and bananas, then stroll into the Guadalajara sunlight. It's early and the exhaust fumes aren't too bad yet. At a small cafe, we treat ourselves to strong black coffee, scrambled eggs with onions, and buttered toast. Feeling quite protein-starved, we can only hope that the delicious eggs haven't been cooked in animal fat, and if so, that the power of the Mexican coffee will dissolve the lard.

Looking at the busy street, that whirlwind of Latino commerce, shielding my intuition, I say to Bones, "If we don't score today let's split and go over to the coast. I'd rather take our chances somewhere else."

Bones regards me with empathy. "Okay, I'm into that. This is pretty damned stressful."

"Hanging around this insane city, it's not what we came for."

"We can leave now, if you want. We should get out of here anyway after last night. There are some fishing villages over on the coast, like San Blas, surrounded by jungle and beaches that stretch for miles."

"Man, that sounds like the deal to me. San Blas, parrots and jungles, rolling surf."

"Okay, let's just go hang out at the Central Mercado for awhile, to see if we get lucky."

"Yeah, let's do it. Let's go find some good luck. Score some primo deluxe, then split."

AT A FRUIT stand outside the Mercado's main entrance we buy some fresh sweet pineapple slices. We sit and eat, alkalizing the nefarious grease of breakfast, watching the human parade come and go. And before long, lo, Marlon Brando comes sauntering along. The same brooding leather-clad hipster from yesterday, black studded jacket, engineer boots, black cap and bucket-cuff levis, a born rebel. We call out to him and he recognizes us, coming on over with a lop-sided grin, pleased to see us again.

"You two guys," he says in passable English, "I saw you on the street there, you are muy diferente Your long hair and style of clothes. I like it. From California, no?"

We affirm that we are indeed from Los Angeles, that wondrous place, and invite him to pay us a visit. "Ah," he exclaims, surprised, "that is my dream, to go live there. You are the first Californios that I meet. I might come and visit with you, verdad?"

"For true, you will be our guest when you come," I say, feeling a swift bond. "So now you have two friends already there, you can count on it."

Smiling broadly, he shakes our hands, and we show him the new-age soul-shake. Alejandro is his name. He has the Brando mannerisms down pat, carving out his identity according to American cinema noir. We find some chairs and sit down together, then we get down to serious business.

Alejandro listens to our request, furrowing his brow, his street-smart eyes attentive "Si, entiendo, la mota," he nods with confidence. "Si, that mota buena is around, You just have to be careful who you go to. My cousin es mi best conexión. He is honest and reliable."

"Hmm, that is good to hear, because last night we almost got royally screwed."

"Ah, que lastima. Who tried to mess with you?"

"The fancy dwarf with all the dancing balloons."

Shaking his head, Alejandro says, "That little midget is bad news. He is mixed up with con artists and devious hombres."

"Yeah, we figured that out fast. We barely got away. But what we'd like to know, can you help us?"

"Si, I can help you. La mota is a specialty for me, my cousin has mucho access."

"Man, that would be righteous beyond belief. And it is of good quality?"

Alejandro nods his handsome, duck-tailed head. "Si, esta muy bueno. But what that mean, that palabra you say. . . righteous?"

"Righteous, it means strong, muy bueno, very good," Bones says, "like between hermanos."

"Ah, then together we can accomplish this," Alejandro smiles. "My cousin Pablo's marijuana is only very good—number uno. If you want to see we can go to his house. It's a little ways but he is available."

We all shake again on this sudden new chance. The sheer serendipity of meeting this character is too much. We say yes, let's go, we want to score today! Alejandro explains that a bus ride of about an hour is involved, that will take us to the outskirts where his cousin lives. Our car will only attract unwanted attention in that poor barrio. We clamor aboard the next diesel-belching bus that comes along, finding seats in the back. We share stories with him of traveling on the road, and of the mythical mushroom mountains.

"On the road," he muses, his dark eyes shining. "By the famous beatnik, Jack Kerouac. I read parts of that book. I want to live like you live some day."

The crowded bus takes on a convoluted ride into the sunny, smog-choked Guadalajara suburbs At last, we get off in a barrio so run-down that you're surprised it hasn't been bulldozed. The corner park has fallen to ruin. Ninos play a turbulent game of futbol on a dirt-packed empty lot, exhorting each other. We walk with our new friend through a maze of streets, potholes, and sewer lines that reek in the heat, although these little casas are painted in bright pastels and most have vegetable gardens. This is place where a stranger should not meander alone, but it is Alejandro's home turf.

We go into a neglected adobe with a dusty couch in the front room, a spring bedstead with a thin mattress in the other room, and a three-legged table with a couple chairs in the kitchen. Nada mas, except for a few packing crates used as end tables. On one wall, a framed bullfight poster; the bull receiving the sword, the matador flashing his victorious red cape. Alejandro insists that we take seats on the sagging couch, then sits on a bamboo crate facing us. This used to be his house, he relates, a house shared with a woman who loved him until she ran off with a treacherous friend. Now, because of the memories, he no longer sleeps in this house but sometimes uses it for business.

Bones and I listen, commiserating, trying not to show impatience. No matter what you do in Mexico it seems to take more clock time, and we are already past noon. I'm hoping this deal won't take all day. I'd like to be on the road for the Pacific coast beaches before sundown.

"I'm sorry for your misfortune," I sympathize. "These love affairs, sometimes it's like walking on quicksand."

Alejandro shrugs, showing an impassive Brando face. "But I am better now without her. She had many bad habits."

He offers us a Lucky Strike, which we decline, then lights one for himself. "I apologize for the long bus ride," he says, exhaling. "But you can see for yourself that your car, the California plates, would be too obvious in this place, and these streets, they are fucked. The government makes many promises, but all the money goes in their bottomless pockets."

He goes to the doorless front door that is covered with a blanket, and calls a boy over from the burned-out park. He conveys some emphatic instructions and the kid runs off. "I have summoned my ally Pablo," he tells us. "He will bring us something bueno to smoke. Then you can decide for yourself."

So we wait in the dusty heat of the moldering house, enduring the eternal wait that all smugglers must endure. After awhile Alejandro's cousin shows up, carrying a slim rolled tube of newspaper. Pablo greets us warily but Alejandro puts us all at ease, declaring that we are all amigos here to do some honorable business. Pablo relaxes a little, his face tired and unshaven. He speaks only Spanish, in a quiet voice, glancing at Alejandro for interpretation as he communicates with us.

Alejandro listens with a slight frown, then says, "My cousin apologizes for his haggard appearance. He has been up all night handling the chaos of relatives. Muy malo. Life can be a bitch sometimes, no?"

Pablo smiles at us, a gleam of pride in his eyes, saying, "Aqui, mis amigos."

Opening one end of the newspaper tube, he pours out a couple ounces of golden-brown weed, no stems, very few seeds. It has a rich, pungent scent.

"All right," I murmur, crumbling a few buds in my fingers. "Bones, got any makings?"

Bones produces some linen Zig-Zags from his shoulder satchel; sets about rolling a fat tapered joint. It's a California-style number, thick as one's index finger. Smiling, he hands it to me. Pablo leans forward, deftly thumbing a cardboard matchbook, and lights it in one stroke.

Inhaling, I savor the flavor of the fine grass. "Ah, muy bien," I say, passing it to Bones. It doesn't give an instant wallop, but soon brings a bright, smooth high. Bones takes a lusty toke, then another, nodding his approval, then passes it around. Within minutes we are all grinning and laughing like old friends. For indeed, good marijuana makes brothers of everyone. Back in Los Angeles, we can make some good dough with this pot, no doubt.

Pablo tells us that esta excelente la mota is $25.00 a kilo up to ten kilos, $20.00 per key up to twenty-five, and above that the price is negotiable. Pablo's left eyelid has a slight tic, but he speaks in an even voice. Conferring briefly, we tell him we'll buy two keys now, for sampling, then set-up a regular buy with him and Alejandro for the coming months.

"That is a welcome arrangement," Pablo replies, "I'm sure we can make it work. But for now, I will need the money for the kilos upfront. I have to leave away from here in order get it."

Still leery from the devious tactics of the dwarf and the El Jefe, we hesitate.

But Alejandro reassures us, "You can believe him, he is my cousin. I will wait here with you, to guarantee everything is done right."

"Regreso en treinta minutos," Pablo says calmly, "no mas. It is the only way."

What is there not to like, we go for it. We all shake hands again, perspiring in this stifling room but cool in our marijuana buzz. We fork over two twenties and a ten to Pablo, who takes it with aplomb, meeting our eyes in kinship.

At the door he waggles his fingers, saying, "Trienta minutos, mas o menos," then leaves.

We settle into the heavy interior shade, hoping the sagging couch is not flea-infested, and polish off the pungent roach. A few fat flies begin to torment us, buzzing around our heads, the most despicable of insects. I really do not understand the creation of flies. Noxious creatures that appear out of nowhere, arising out of rancid garbage and piles of shit, loathsome maggots. What God in his right mind would make a maggot? Some say that flies are the spawn of Beelzebub and if that is true then Beelzebub must be a real being, a bewildering idea in itself. We smoke another joint and slip deeper into the torpid afternoon. Alejandro goes to the door, watching some ninos kick a soccer ball down the broken street.

"Goddamn little fiends," I gripe, waving the flies off, "trying to drink our sweat."

Bones sighs, "Aiyee, the flies, yes, they are repulsive. They've probably been feeding on the guts of a dead animal. Man, dig, I hope we don't get ripped off again."

"No, don't even think that, Bones, no, banish the thought. We can trust Alejandro. He is our friend and he believes in Marlon Brando."

"It's not him I'm worried about," Bones laughs. "No offense, Alejandro, but your cousin seems kind of strung out."

"He is just very tired," Alejandro admits, sitting back down. "His life is hard. His family is una problema."

"We have to take a chance to get somewhere," I say, feeling the creep of the minutes. "Cierto?"

"Si, we are amigos now," Alejandro replies, sitting cross-legged on the littered floor. "And I have done many transactions with Pedro."

"Is this how you make your living," I ask him, "dealing la mota?"

"No, not always, only sometimes. I do whatever I can to make the needed dinero." He rubs his thumb and forefinger together, the universal sign. "But you are different in my eyes from the other turistas. I mean, si, your long hair, your style, muy diferente, yet you are men, claro, you are men who do not fear the unknown."

Bones fingers the rudraksha beads around his neck. "Our long hair and our way of living, it's how we distinguish ourselves from the squares who live such programmed lives."

"The squares?" Alejandro says, trying to puzzle it out. "What do you mean?"

"The ones who live their lives," I say, "with their eyes half-closed, who pretend the problems in society are something other than what they are, God's will or some such shit, hoping something new will happen that will never happen because they keep acting in the same fucked-up ways. Cómo se dice, sleepwalkers? Sleepwalkers who make war on other witless morons and kill everything in sight in order to prove themselves right. No, we are not a part of that. We are not part of their world."

"Ah, I get it," Alejandro exclaims, nodding. "Like Viet Nam, yes, es horrible! That is not their country. How can your government pretend that is right?"

"Yeah, Viet Nam and all the other lying, political bullshit. Because they are liars, because they live and promote a giant ongoing lie. They wouldn't know the truth if it lit a bonfire in front of their faces. They try to hypnotize the people with their lies. But we are awake and we intend to stay awake. People have to love each other, not kill. We are all one family, nothing is more important."

Alejandro lights another cig, drawing deeply on it. "I like what you say," he says. "This change, then, this is what your movement is all about? This thing you hippies are doing?"

"We can only speak for ourselves. But yes, I think so. How do you see it?"

"Yes," Alejandro nods, "I do think so. War can never be the answer. War destroys everything that has been built with care."

"We want peace, not war," Bones says. "We want to make love, not war. That's our way. It's all about the choices we make, then staying true to those choices."

"The world rationalizes its bullshit constantly," I say. "Our governments deceive and lie constantly. But we don't live like that. We have to be truthful, stay true to ourselves."

Polishing off the delicious roach, his eyes shining, Bones says, "Aiyee, that's exactly right. Our purpose is to change this world and it's all about love."

Alejandro ponders these words, his face lit with wonder. "I would like to be part of your way someday," he says in a husky voice, his leather jacket creaking in the heat.

"Come to California, si, si, come up to L.A. and look us up. You are totally welcome, we are all hermanos now."

And although the three of us like each other immensely, a hard fact is dragging across our nerves. Pablo has not shown up nor sent any messenger. That irredeemable fucked-over feeling has begun to smother our optimism.

"Fuck, man," Bones mutters half aloud, "feels like another bogus trip going down."

Appealing to Alejandro, I say, "Amigo, what is happening? Where is Pablo? Can you check on him somehow?"

Alejandro is already on his feet, moving cat-like in his motorcycle stompers. He glances through the blanketed door. Taking his cap off, he swats at his leg, obviously frustrated.

"I don't know why he is taking so long."

"Dig brother, we're not blaming you. Maybe he had to go to some other place?"

"But I am responsible," Alejandro replies, embarrassed. "We wait here on my word, you have put up your money. And now he is late. But I will go find him, I know where he goes."

Flashing on the possibility that we might be stranded here, Bones grimaces at me, silently mouthing the word "fuck". Alejandro stands at the door, rummaging inside his jacket pocket. Looking at me, he takes out a worn .38 Special with a four inch barrel. The grips are taped together, the front sight has been broken off. Open-handed, he holds it out to me, butt first. I stare at the pistol, then into his frank eyes.

"Por favor," he urges me, "take mi pistola. It is worth very much dinero here in my city. This is my guarantee to return here to you. Por favor, accept it."

"No es necessario," Bones protests, shaking his head.

"It's okay, Bones, it's his way. It's a matter of honor, his gesture of trust."

Alejandro takes a red handkerchief from his pocket and wraps the revolver, then hands it to me. I heft the familiar old weight in my hand, then pass it to Bones over on the couch.

"I will regreso," Alejandro tells us, his handsome face troubled but determined. He goes out the blanketed door and into the hazy afternoon glare.

"Caramba," Bones mutters. "If the Federales catch us with this thing? We'd be fucked. People can't have pistols down here. It's against the law."

"I know. But that beat-up .38 is worth maybe two hundred dollars on the black market, quién sabe? Besides it's his prized possession. He'll be back for it."

"God, I hope so, man. I'm not grooving on these vibes. Something's gone out of synch."

And so we wait again, the inevitable waiting in the indifferent labyrinth of Guadalajara. One has no choice but to wait. I smoke a little more of Pablo's grass, putting my mind on cruise, mulling over the variables Would he have left this good weed here if he meant to rip us off? Now that he has his handful of dollars, who cares about a couple stray ounces? Is Alejandro somehow in on it, an incredibly clever ruse? But no, he has left us his gun. Bones closes his eyes and slumps, his chin sagging to his chest as daydreams take over. A savage dogfight erupts outside, barking and snarling, the cries of the ninos throwing rocks to break it up. The unreality of time drifts like the passion of smoke. I wait, my eyes open, making myself imperturbable to the pestering flies. Another fifty bucks leaking away on another misguided tangent. That makes seventy dollars in two days, bread we cannot afford to waste. We need to catch a good break, catch the chance that keeps eluding us. Maybe we shouldn't have tempted karma, karma has a way of dogging your ass. But no I dismiss these loaded thoughts. I'm not buying into the convenient karma cop-out. We live as warriors, not as wimps that whine and waffle. So I wait, sweat trickling down my armpits. Images come and go, dissolving like soapsuds. Bones stirs himself awake, his eyes composed. He gives me a rueful glance, resigned to another double-dealing subterfuge.

Alejandro comes through the door in a brooding, scowling mirage. I know at once that we have been betrayed, that he has been shafted by his own cousin. Or are we simply being conned? He sits down on the bamboo crate, his black leather jacket soaked with his sweat, confessing, "I could not find him, no one knows where he went. Then I demand of his wife to say what she knows. Finally she confesses she believes Pablo slides back into his bad old ways. She says he has not been the husband that she knows."

"Bad old ways? What the fuck, man. What are we talking about?"

Alejandro takes off his black cap, turning it in his hands. "Before, before our alliance, he had certain troubles. He had the awful habit of running with the devil's horse."

"Running horse," Bones echoes, looking at me with mournful eyes.

"Aw no, come on. Running what, Alejandro? You mean heroin?"

"Si, the heavy shit, narcoticos. He had stopped, he went clean, nada, for more than tres anos. But now she says he has fallen back into his weakness."

"Aw, goddamn the rotten fucking luck," I shout, "how could you not know?! He has gone and ripped us off for some smack!"

Alejandro spreads his hands, clutching his cap. "I swear to you I did not know, I thought he was just tired. He said he could not sleep because of the noise en su casa. But that was all bullshit, I see now, all a story, lo siento, lo siento. But I promise you I will find him tonight. He will buy his shit and get high, then cut the rest to sell to other junkies. So I will find him, I swear on my nina's soul, I will find him and get your money back."

He bolsters this furious promise by insisting that we hold his pistola as collateral, saying he knows his cousin's haunts and can track him down. "Every snake has his favorite hole, no?" He smacks his fist into his palm. "And I know where he prefers to go. If I am wrong, that gun is worth mucho más than fifty dollars on these streets. Just offer around."

"But is there no other way?" Bones implores, glancing at me. "We don't want any violent hassles."

"There is no other way," Alejandro shrugs. "You are my friends and we are men of our promise. If necesario I will take it out of my cousin's skin, porque he has shamed me."

We ride back into downtown Guadalajara on another slow crowded bus, brooding in our own thoughts. I like this man and hope we can smooth out this problem. I don't want this problem. I don't want to be ripped off. And if I'm going to smuggle, I want a flawless operation.

Back on the neon boulevard, Alejandro points to a restaurant that is one of his hangouts. "In that place they know me by name. En la manana, meet me there at nine o'clock, mas o menos. If I do not show, come back for the lunch hour. I will have your money. But if I cannot meet you for any reason, my pistola es su pistola. Just take it and go. Do not hang around asking questions. I do not trust much of anything these days."

We agree with a somber handshake. I know without a doubt that Alejandro has not deceived us. His eyes are honest and clear, his voice sincere. He believes he has fatally fallen in our esteem, he feels ashamed.

"We are still brothers," I say to him, tapping my heart with my hand. "This bullshit, the loss of fifty dollars or a gun doesn't change that. Just know that."

Bones says, "Jake tells it like it is, Alejandro. You are one of us. Our paths will cross again, come to L.A., we will help you. Our house is your house, always."

Alejandro's eyes shine with fierce gratitude. "You guys give me some real hope. I am glad that we meet. If my luck works out I will meet in the morning, or I will see you up there by Navidad. But remember, if I do not come en la manana, something goes wrong. Do not wait for me. Just drive away and do your thing in another place."

Alejandro turns and walks away, with the ominous tone of his last words. Shit could hit the fan, two gringo longhairs could get snagged in the chaos. And by now our entire Guadalajara trip now seems botched We have done nothing but lose good money, money to the dwarf, money to the junkie Pablo, and nothing to show for it but a handful of weed and some peyote buttons. I have an IQ of 158, but right now I feel like a fool. We spend the evening laying low, smoking Pablo's sucker's grass, eating bananas, raisins and peanuts, resolved to get our trip back on track.

In the morning we check out of the old hotel, lock our gear in the trunk, and before nine are at the rendezvous café drinking dubious cafe con leche. Already the flies are buzzing around, stalked by a gordita waitress with a flyswatter. She smashes a greasy one on the vinyl tablecloth, tittering with satisfaction. She comes over and refills our mugs, her eyes distraught and melancholy. The clock on the wall says nine-thirty. We ask her if an hombre named Alejandro in a black leather jacket has come in this morning? Barely comprehending our Spanglish, she says no, she hasn't seen no one, nunca, nada. When we ask if there's another place he likes to go, she says abruptly, "No sé, senores, no entiendo!"

Our appointment time has come and gone, no Alejandro. The fictional wall clock tell the story. We decide to leave, paying the waitress in peso coins, tipping her un poco. We walk toward the car, the streets already dense with diesel fumes and ricocheting noise. In a corner park, we sit on a concrete bench to sort out our thoughts.

Bones scowls, "Bad scene, bad trip, know what I mean?"

"Yep. I don't think we should stay, Bones. There's some kind of bad hassle we don't want any part of. Not only that, our luck's been rotten around here and the word's probably gone out on us."

"My instincts tell me you are one hundred percent right. Way too much fucking stress. Let's just chalk it up and drive over to San Blas, we can relax on those blue-sky beaches. Somebody over there is bound to be able to turn us on."

"Right on, and who knows? We might be able to trade that pistola for some righteous dope."

"Fucking A," Bones murmurs, glancing around, "I almost forgot about that. We've earned it."

"Okay then, let's split," I say. We get up and fall in stride. "Later for this dicey scene. We'll make it up to Alejandro when he comes to visit us."

"You think he'll actually come to L.A.?"

"Hah, after seeing what we've seen, wouldn't you?"

# Chapter 28

THE COUNTRY AROUND San Blas de Nayarit is green and lush, a montage of flowering jungle, banana palms, muddy serpentine rivers, clouds of flying parrots, and eternal humid summer. The gravel road into San Blas seems like a passage into another drowsing time-warp, though not so remote as Huautla de Jimenez. The village lies west of the Pacific coast highway, right on the water, its lagoon a safe harbor for a rag-tag fleet of shrimp and fishing boats. The village is shabby and worn, bearing no resemblance to the trendy Mazatlan resort further up the coast. Nestled in its time-warp, it's a perfect haven for low-budget ex-pats, wandering surfers and nomadic smugglers. No one bothers to ask you your business, yet everyone is glad to see you.

Everyone is glad to see you because San Blas is well off the beaten track, north of Vallarta, south of Mazatlan. The two or three run-down tourista hotels have mucho vacancies, with a handful of half-empty bars and restaurants. They're delighted to see you because you are new opportunity in this backwater town, friendly long-haired gringos always bring fresh cash.

In the sweltering heat we rest in a patio cafe across from the town plaza, home to pigeons, doves, parakeets, and a gurgling fountain. The old bronze statue of someone important lifts his noble head to the sky, supplicating heaven. Almost no one is around in this heat, they're all lying low. The big-bellied proprietor with his apron and luxuriant salt and pepper hair greets us like long-lost amigos, wandering hippies who look like half-starved. He doesn't bat an eyelash at our vegetariano requests, he hums with empathy, making suggestions in Spanglish. Within minutes, he brings us cold Carta Blancas and a platter of thick fragrant chips that he assures us has not been made with lard. His menu is an enticing piece of gustatory art. We can get fresh squeezed orange or pineapple juice, or a bowl of fresh watermelon and papaya for a song. Ah, the vibes are good. We're still a long ways from home and down to about one hundred fifty in cash, plus Alejandro's pistola, but we're flush with optimism.

The proprietor-chef brings us a heaping bowl of fresh guacamole garnished with green onions, jalapenos, fresh limes, and wedges of super-ripe tomatoes. It is a feast to wash away the insults of our wayward road. Guzzling the cold cervezas, we dig in with delirious gusto, chatting with our portly benefactor. He tells us where we can find decent cheap lodging, and of a dirt road that winds through the mangrove jungle to a secluded beach the vagabond surfers like. The ruthless sun beats down, but we sit shaded by the banana palms, indulging ourselves, destitute by American standards but rich, rich, rich with glorious life. Our loquacious host sits with us, telling of when he used to go out on the wing-netted shrimp boats. His caged songbirds are in full-throat, melodic and poignant in the sun-dappled ambiance. The only thing lacking here are hammocks. We feel certain we have come to the right place.

On the outskirts of this Mexican hideaway we find the cheapest place in San Blas, a motel that backs right up against a swamp lagoon. The sun-baked courtyard allows us to pull our car right up to the porch of the white-washed cabin. The tin roof cooks under the tropical sun, the single room has pale blue walls with a concrete floor, a kitchenette with no appliances save for a wooden icebox and a hot plate. We've already taken note of the town ice plant, only a few blocks away. There are two chairs and a table, two canvas sleeping cots with folded sheets, and a closet-sized bathroom with a toilet and a tin shower stall. These stifling quarters are vented by a single, small window fan.

From the porch we can see the brackish waters of the swamp about fifty yards off, but our windows and door are screened tight. The manager is a congenial man with a plump wife and three small daughters who giggle and hop about, fascinated by our appearance. He is delighted when we pay a week in advance and his wife brings us a ripe watermelon from her garden.

"Remember," Bones tells me, "when you shower here don't let any water get in your mouth or nose. It'll make us sicker than peach-pit dogs."

"Thanks for the reminder," I laugh, making a mental note to stock up on the green glass bottles of mineral agua when we go to fetch our block of ice.

In mid-afternoon, we take the sinuous dirt track through the green maze of jungle, splashing across muddy creeks and skirting mangrove thickets before coming out on a long pristine beach open to the sky and sea. There is not another human being in sight. The shoreline curves northward along the coast, and runs south another half mile to where it collides with a rocky cliff hanging with vines and bushes. An abandoned hotel under some palms sits all boarded up, a few palm-thatched palapas offer shade in the Mexican sun. Driving the long sand, we come across a pair of dirty VW buses with California plates near some fire-charred driftwood. The surfers themselves must be out on the waves, we see nor hear any trace of them. Bones and I sit on the dunes, smoking the last of Pablo's reefer, considering our chances. This is the place to be. There is no other place to be.

We drive slowly back into town in a blissful neglect of time. Flocks of parrots fly from tree to tree. We park on the plaza and amble through the stalls of the open-air mercado, vivid and aromatic with tropical fruit. We fill our jute bolsas with clumps of finger bananas, plump oranges, tender papayas delicious mangoes, stocking up on a case of bottled mineral water. Then sit in the shade of the patio cafe drinking perspiring bottles of Pacifica beer. The cordial owner brings us a clay bowl of garlic-spiced guacamole and chips to sample, on the house.

Patting his ample stomach, he observes wryly, "Even vegetariano puristas like yourselves must have sufficient protein, no? I will prepare some spicy frijoles for you."

The shadows of afternoon fall across the square, twilight is coming on. The bronze post lamps blink on one-by-one. The canaries and parakeets in the patio cage settle down. Somewhere nearby norteno music is playing on a radio, wistful and melancholy. The young men and women begin to show up, they promenade around the square moving in opposite directions. They walk with a friend or in small clusters. When they pass one another they smile and laugh, sharing a few shy remarks. But unless they are novio y novia, sweethearts, they rarely touch. This little parade around the square is how they meet and greet each other, check the vibes, every once in awhile a couple breaks off to sit together and hold hands. A few watchful women are around keeping an eye on the desirable Lolitas. This is courtship in slow motion, nothing like the uninhibited romance of free-wheeling California.

"Aiyee," Bones observes, "looks like a long time before you get laid."

Smiling, I say, "You can say that again. But it's beautiful, is it not? This is the old way."

Their shy flirtation has dignity and grace and it appeals to me. I've noticed that TV sets are quite rare in rural Mexico, and I wonder how long these rituals will last once the Boob Tube and its mindless bullshit hits the scene. Probably not too long.

In the gathering dusk we drive back to our swamp cabin, picking up a block of ice on the way. We load the upright wooden cooler with our luscious frutas and mineral water to chill. Night descends all at once in these lowlands, but brings little relief from the sweltering heat. A heavy, wet, suffocating blanket of tropical heat. Cicadas whir in the trees, creatures slither in the jungle vines, the swamp croaks with a million frogs. Hordes of mosquitoes whine against the screendoor, aroused by the scent of our gringo blood. The night steams, humidity drips from the walls of our lamp-lit room. We take turns rinsing off under the tepid flow of the rusting shower head, our lips sealed against the infamous microbes. But we are at peace. To be happy people don't need that much, not nearly as much as they imagine. They need only to be in love with the ever-now moment, to be enthralled with here and now, to let all things be new.

In the relative cool of early morning, we drink strong coffee negro at our friend's patio cafe, our senses humming. All this time south of the border has lulled us into a super-mellow cadence, but we realize we have to make some headway.

"If we run out of bread down here we're fucked," Bones says. "Who's gonna help us? We'd have to sell the car for whatever and take a bus home."

"I hear you, but dig, we have a plan. We just need to put it in gear and score."

"I don't want to be forced into selling my Merc," Bones grumbles. "I don't have a motorcycle back home like you do. You think those surfers could help us?"

"Maybe, yeah. Let's go back out there and say hello. Surfers are always heads, man."

The proprietor brings us mas coffee and a platter of sliced cantaloupe to balance off the homemade toast and butter. "Someone is here who wants to meet you," he tells us.

He introduces a young American named Artie who has been in San Blas all summer, about twenty-five, short and muscular, with a helmet of curly brown hair. Artie is open and talkative, someone you might meet anywhere. He tells us he came here to paint but ran out of paint, so now he's just drinking rum and smoking whatever pot he can luck into.

"Listen, man, dig," I confide, "I happen to have some primo-deluxe acid that I'll gladly trade for a good lid. If you know anybody? And if it's good weed, we might even pick up a pound or two."

Artie reacts as if miracle-struck. "Unbelievable," he laughs. "I was just telling someone the other day that I'd give my left nut for some good acid. Oh yeah, I can definitely line you up. But how good is it really? What do I need to do to score a few good hits?"

Bones leans in, saying, "Jake's acid is the best acid on the planet, man. Absolutely pure stardust. You'll trip out into cosmic bliss."

Incredulous, Artie promises to deliver for us if we'll hang with him for only a few hours. He even pays for our breakfast to underscore his confidence in the matter. "No worries, brothers," he affirms as we walk out. "Let's just go make some visits."

As it turns out, Artie knows every pothead in San Blas. But after making a few fruitless house calls, nobody home, no sé, not sure when he return, we all drive out to the deserted beach to find the surfers. Artie claims to know the surfers too, says he often gets loaded with them. We follow the winding dirt track through the jungle swamp, crossing the fer-de-lance streams, the air alive with tropical birds. Out on the pristine beach two of the surf brothers have come ashore to guzzle beer. A breeze comes in off the curling white breakers, tempering the rising heat, the sky a shining blue dome. We sit in the rustling shade of a tattered palapa, trading stories. These dudes have surfed their way as far south as Puerto

Escondido, now making their way back up to the Sea of Cortez, camping out in their buses. We wow them with our Huautla mushroom tales, passing around a thick number rolled from the remnants of Pablo's grass.

"So dig," Bones ventures, "what we'd like to know? Is there any decent weed around San Blas worth picking up on?"

"Oh yeah, definitely is," says the blond surfer, taking a hit, "and this nice weed, man, thanks. We ran out a few days ago."

Taking his thumb pass, his red-haired friend says, "Yeah, Trini should know where, this Mexican cat named Trini. Thing is, we gotta get word to him that we're looking. Otherwise he's like a ghost. But there's a person in town that passes the word along, then he shows up."

"Cool, man. How long you guys been hanging out here?"

"We been camping on this beach for almost one month. We love it, man. It's like we have the waves all to ourselves all day long."

"Hey, I know who you're talking about," Artie chimes in. "I spaced on him for a second. I think I even know where Trini lives."

"Right on," says the blond surfer, savoring the breeze-blown doobie, "except that his cousin's house in town. Trini lives way down in that jungle somewhere and keeps it secret. He's involved in all kinds of smuggling, like grass and parrots and whiskey. But if you go by that San Blas house, just say we want to see him out at the beach, and he'll show up."

"Like when?"

"Hah, like they say, tarde o temprano. But usually the day after tomorrow."

"All right," Artie beams, rubbing his hands together. "I'll go by there by myself, by myself is probably better. I'll go over there this evening."

"Cool, one thing," Bones says, "tell the cousin to tell Trini that if the merchandise is good, we might take two or three keys."

"Keys? Whooee, man," the flaxen-haired surfer laughs, "I dunno. Trini usually shows up with a handful of buds tied in a handkerchief. He travels light."

Bones and I share knowing glance. "That's okay," I reply. "Just let him know that we are very interested."

From my shirt pocket I take out an amber vial and tap out several snow-white tabs of Sandoz. With a half-smile, I say, "How long's it been since you boys tripped on some fine acid? And I mean super-fine. It's on the house."

Murmurs of keen enthusiasm arise and we put the deal in motion. I make sure that both surfers get a couple tabs apiece, with an additional two tabs each for their three buddies still out on the waves. Then, into Artie's hopeful palm, I drop four hallowed tabs of Albert Hoffman's finest. Bones looks on with a benign grin, rocking on his long haunches like a Sufi. Excited, they only half-listen to my warning about how strong Sandoz is, licking their chops. I split a tab in half in front of them, with my strong nails, to demonstrate.

"Now, just this little bit will put you into a super bright groove, with light and color effects, but not wild hallucinations."

"And if we want to hallucinate out of our skulls?"

"Drop that whole tiny tab and you'll be lit up for ten or twelve hours. You'll have a day on the waves you'll never forget."

"Es verdad," Bones laughs, "and don't swallow the whole thing unless you want to visit other realities."

We all clasp our sun-browned hands together under the Mexican sun. We are a strong, bright tribe, a new river of shining love. We are here for love.

Rising to my feet, I ask, "What time you say we should be back here?"

Stoned, the surfers ponder the question. Then the red-headed one says, "I'd say anytime in the afternoon, around the day after tomorrow. But probably before sundown."

"Hah ha ha, okay, will do. You mean if we can still keep track?"

"Exactly, man, hah ha ha, exactly. No one around here keeps a clock."

# Chapter 29

Nothing's the way you think it is; it's the way it seems, yet it's always different. Thing is, when you flash into this, it's tricky to see how it applies to your own act. But it does, it always does. We have to be alert. No one else is paying much attention to our wishes or desires. But with enough attention and intention we can usually create what we want.

The smuggler Trini is at the beach when Bones and I return, the only long-haired Mexicano that I've met. He looks like us and acts like us, he even talks like us. Trini confides that he lived in San Diego for a few years, and only came back home to San Blas about six months ago. His black hair hangs past his shoulders. He wears no shirt, only some ragged denims cut off at the knee. Barefoot, bronze and lean, he wades out of the surf to greet us, a green and yellow parrot on his shoulder. He has an effusive smile and speaks American lingo with flair, using words like "verve" and "hip" and "happening".

The surfers are all out on the rolling waves that boom in off the Pacific. We can hear them whooping it up, high and joyful on the translucent sunlight and transcendent Sandoz.

"They're all sailing on the primo lsd we laid on them," I tell Trini. "And you're welcome to some yourself, it's on us."

"Ah, very nice, but no, not right now," he smiles, spreading his arms to the sky. "I am high on all of this." The parrot on his shoulder bobs and chuckles in his ear.

"Hmm, I can dig that. I think we all have those aspirations."

Bones takes him in like a long-lost cousin, grinning broadly. We hunker down behind a shelter of driftwood logs and get to know each other. Trini is likable and forthright, mid-twenties, expressive and laid-back at the same time. He wants to know if we have any rolling papers, which, aha, it so happens that we do.

"Bueno, so this is what I have on hand," he says, unknotting a red bandana and spreading out some sticky, golden-brown buds. Ah, now here is the real goods! Bones rolls a nimble joint and we light up, sailing into a bright, laughing high almost at once. Trini insists that we take this bundle, his gift to us, since he understands we are after "the bigger fish".

"And these bigger fish can be caught?" Bones smiles, rocking on his haunches.

"Mucho bigger fish, potent and fragrancia," I say, hearkening to the boom of the surf, "maybe three or four kilos big."

Trini laughs, gazing at the beachcombers too, feeding his shoulder-stepping bird a few sunflower seeds. "Oh, that is available, no doubt. But for that amount I must discuss with my partner in town. We would have to take a boat trip down the coast, down there where it curves, and Conrad has the boat. But right now he is rebuilding his motorbike engine for the Guadalajara races, so I have to see if he can do it."

Rebuilding his racing motorcycle? Bingo, I think, natural affinity. This dude Conrad, Trini explains, is a German expatriate who's lived in Mexico for several years and likes to run in the winter flat-track races. Now, we have a Mexican hippie and a German expat biker to deal with, more our kind of people. We sit under the breezy palms, lulled by the roar of the afternoon breakers, the acid-head surfers still out on the waves, chatting with Trini, dipping into his stash of excellent jungle weed. Things are bursting with promise.

We agree to meet with him and his partner on the beach the next morning. Trini is enthusiastic, he wants to get this deal done. We offer to take him back into town but he wants to wait for his friends to come in off the ocean. So Bones and I drive back to our swamp motel and batten down the hatches against the hordes of insects. The saffron sun floods into the jungle bosque, flying blood-suckers rise out of the murky pools. They smell our gringo flesh, that exotic blood that is so delicious to a Mexican mosquito. But no problemo. We hunker inside our spare humid room, all but naked, sweating like natives, reading in the lamplight, taking an occasional toke.

In my New Testament leather pocket edition, St. Matthew, Jesus tells his wayward friends, "If thine eye be single, thy whole body be filled with light." Man, way out stuff!

Bones looks up from his lamplit shadows, my brother on the road, says, "How do you feel about this Trini deal? Think we can make it happen?"

"Think it looks better than anything we've had before. And he's got good vibes."

"Yeah, me too. Think we might strike it rich this time. This grass is righteous."

"And let's remember to take Alejandro's pistola with us, see if we can barter it."

"Yeah, I almost forgot, let's do it," Bones says. "That might be worth five keys."

"Five keys, hell yeah, maybe even ten. Who knows until we show the card?"

"Knock, knock, and it shall be opened to you."

"Knock, knock, yes indeed, we gonna fill those red, yellow and green bolsas."

IN THE MORNING we pass an impatient couple of hours waiting on the beach, watching the surf and listening to Artie's convivial rap. Artie was at our patio cafe for breakfast, so we brought him along. I'm in a restless mood, wanting to get a good deal done and back on the road to California. If things fall into place here, by this time next month we'll be flush with rich American greenbacks.

The cobalt sky sweeps westward over the endless, whispering ocean. The surfers are somewhere else. Their buses are huddled together on the sand a ways up the beach, the windows curtained. We figure that everyone has crashed from their wild acid escapade. Who knows how much they dropped, and what goes up must come down, always.

When Trini and Conrad finally show up they are in stark contrast to each other. Trini seems his open, ebullient self, in love with the moment, but his pal Conrad is a dour and skeptical man. Around Bones' age,

Conrad has a three-day growth and smells like he's been drinking all night. He dismisses my attempt to build some rapport on bikes, claiming he has a love-hate relationships with motorcycles. He only races dirt-track in the winter months to pick up some extra cash.

"Bikes are undependable as hell," he complains in guttural accent. "They leak oil, not to mention how shit is always breaking. You have to be insane to love a motorcycle, I'd rather have a used Mercedes any day."

Some people have "asshole" stamped on their forehead, you're wasting your breath trying to be friendly. When the talk turns to the illicit reason for us gathering here, Conrad doesn't even make eye contact. He sits facing away, staring moodily at the waves. He's a scrawny character, thin blond hair pasted to his head, but with muscles like wires. He wears dirty white canvas pants, a bleached yellow tee cut off at the midriff, and a worn pair of boat shoes.

"What you want," Conrad says in an annoyed tone, "means that him and me have to take a river trip through that fucking jungle with all the bugs and snakes." He makes a gesture down the curving green coast. "There's a plantation down there where we can do business. Everything is cash on the line."

"It's just like what I gave you," Trini says, seemingly perplexed by his partner's attitude. "It will take us one day there, one day to rest, and one day regreso."

"What day is this, anyway?" Bones muses to himself.

Artie laughs softly, saying, "It's Monday, Bones. Monday."

"Right on, right. I heard the church bells going off yesterday."

"So," I ask, ignoring the side-talk, "if we get this deal rolling, you would be back when?"

"We would be back on Thursday," Conrad says curtly, "if we don't get snake-bitten. Maybe around noon, mas o menos." He pivots on his bony ass, regarding me with pale eyes. "It depends how many kilos you want and how much cash you can front us. When I go there, it is always cash on the line. But we are always good for it. You can ask around."

My stomach tightens and I lift my eyebrows at Bones. We've heard this song before, we're tired of being scammed. "How much per key, say for five keys? What can we expect?"

"For that you can expect twenty-five dollars each, plus we need another twenty for the boat, food, beer, and petrol. Expenses."

Bones looks at me, liking the sound of it. I look at Conrad. "Pressed into bricks?"

Conrad laughs, almost a sneer. "Ask Trini how nice the last batch was."

"Si, it's true," Trini hastens to say. "Pressed into bricks, golden-green bricks, not much stems. It's what you call back in L.A. super-primo."

"Three days," I muse, nodding at Bones. "That sounds okay. But what about this?"

Bones reaches into his satchel and passes me Alejandro's handkerchief-wrapped revolver. Unwrapping the blunt-nosed .38, I display it. "How many keys can we trade for this Smith and Wesson?"

Conrad's eyes flare at the sight of the pistola. These hippies mean business. He inspects the unloaded revolver with the air of a mercenary, whereas the gun makes Trini visibly nervous.

"What do you hope to get for this?" Conrad asks, his eyes on the piece.

"You tell me. Several prime kilos at least," I reply. "We know what it's worth."

The German shoots Trini a speculative look, Trini nods. He says something definite in Spanish, including the words siete, possible ocho.

"Seven or possibly eight," Bones states, letting them know we dig the lingo.

"Maybe," Conrad grunts, non-committal. "We won't really know until we dicker. But I'll guarantee at least six good kilos. Maybe seven, quien sabe, but at least six. And I'll still need my twenty dollars American for expenses."

Bones and I are already in tacit agreement, but we consider. Bones strokes his beard. I take a long look down the coast. "Guarantee seven, and we've got a deal."

"Esta bien, yes," Trini declares, "we will agree." He stands up and jams his hands in the rear pockets of his cut-offs. "It's good business. So relax and don't fret while we're gone. I'll contact Artie as soon as we are back."

He turns and wades barefoot into the roiling surf, and I get the vibes that he's pissed at Conrad. Conrad is abrupt and almost disrespectful, whereas Trini likes to keep things friendly. But that is the pitfall in all partnerships, the clash in styles, no matter. The deal is a damned good one, I'm satisfied, and so is Bones. After all, the pistol only cost us fifty dollars and it's now currency for seven prime kilos that will make us rich. Trading Alejandro's gun is like playing with house money, and we're only out twenty bucks cash. We all shake on the deal, even the dour German, another deal struck in the opaque labyrinth of Mexico.

Next day, all but immobile in the smothering heat, we decide the waiting period will be ideal to ingest our still-green peyote buttons. The trick is how to do it, how to get high without puking our guts up. Raw peyote is extremely bitter, hard to swallow, and makes you sick on an empty stomach. Some people say to emulsify the buttons in a high-speed blender with fresh strawberries, but that's not possible in this swamp motel without appliances. Should we brew a tea steeped in jungle honey, or chop it fine with ripe watermelon and pineapple?

We mull it over. Finally, I slice the dense cacti buds into slivers with my Buck knife, licking the alkaloid residue on my fingertips. A shiver goes right down my neck. Then we lay the moist strips on the sun-baking roof of the car, certain that flies and ants will avoid this particular treat. I know that some birds will gorge on fermenting tree berries until falling-down drunk, but I have never heard of peyote intoxicated birds. Every couple of hours we turn the drying slivers over in the fierce San jungle sun.

By sundown, the peyote strips have turned into resinous curling chips. Taking the quart of fresh-squeezed orange juice that's been chilling inside the ice box, we force the bitter psychedelic down with gulping swallows. The radical combination of ingredients makes our stomachs heave and roil, verging on a calamitous barf. Barfing is the worst thing, a horrible way to ruin a good high.

We take turns under the tepid water in the shower stall, soothing our fervid bodies, waiting for something special to happen. Our queasy bellies won't stop gurgling, as if some tiny insidious beast has been set loose in our intestines.

It's almost an hour before the peyote actually hits us. When it does, the quicksilver effects flood with the howls of unseen jungle animals in the dusk, the croaking of millions of frogs, clouds of mosquitoes whining at the screens, and wet explosive farts popping from our asses with sweat bursting from our foreheads and armpits. The trapdoor to a hellish cesspool flies open and we're sucked down into the lurid devastation of our bowels. Our sensitive intestines dissolve in boiling floods of shit. We make frantic scampers to the toilet or lie curled in agony on our cots A hideous stench clings to the sweating walls of the humid room, the effluvium squirts from our assholes without cessation. I bang out the screen door gasping for fresh air, sagging into a rickety lawn chair, trembling, shrouded by biting insects driven crazy by their sudden good fortune. Aiyee, gringo blood! Mosquitoes by the thousands descend on me as my mind reels from demonic images and I can only hope this does not get worse. The frogs croak their dirge in the inky lagoon, the whining blood-suckers swarm over me. Swatting at them, tottering to my feet, I lurch back through the screen door. Bones shivers on the concrete floor, moaning, clutching his gut. A hot shitstorm erupts in my colon and I pitch toward the toilet and barely make it, letting loose, suffused in stench, in nameless regrets, fighting a mocking adversary. In the narrow window, above the echoing swamp, a pale moon is on the rise, a baleful moon if ever there was one.

The purgatorial night passes without a shred of rest, without sleep, without a moment's respite. The fiendish microbes breeding inside us tears our guts apart, leeches our strength and will, drains the precious fluids from our bodies as if being siphoned by some feces-sucking ghoul. It's inconceivable that one can shit so much, there's simply nothing left. Yet the foul diarrhea keeps coming through the pit of night as the gibbering peyote imps cavort in our psyche. Aiyee, this is what you call a bad trip, now I can't say I've never had one. We drain our bottled water in an attempt to counter the onslaught. Fever and madness creep through our ravaged bodies, teeth-chattering chills. It's impossible to think clearly for more than a few seconds at a time.

Somewhere in the no-man's-land of predawn morning I lapse into oblivion, only to start awake to see Bones dragging himself across the floor to the besmirched bowl. I crawl over to help him up on the seat, where he hunches and shivers and shits his life out. His feverish eyes implore me, but what can I do? We are doomed souls cast into a Satanic cesspool. Back on our cots we pass out like doused candles, only to wake again in gripping pain. The night fades into a merciless dawn that brings the rising heat of morning and still we shit, we shit, we defecate like demented wraiths as if this is our ultimate fate.

But as the sun rises above the window I realize with profound gratitude that the worst has passed. I sit up on my stained cot, put my bare feet on the cool concrete, and run my mind through my nether parts. Yes, praise God, the devastation has left me. Left me wrung and hollowed out, weak as a husk, spun like a dried thistle, but free from the torment.

Looking over at Bones' sprawled figure, I weakly laugh. "Jesus Christo, pardner, what a hellish night."

In a gesture that takes his last iota of energy, Bones lifts his pallid face, whispering. I can't make out his frail words. I will myself across the room to kneel beside his cot.

Taking his clammy hand, I ask, "What is it, Bones? What are you saying?"

In a dry rasping voice, he says, "I'm dying, Jake, I'm done for."

His bloodshot eyes peer into mine, his face gaunt and haggard. With a shock I realize that Bones might croak right before my eyes. "No, don't say that," I urge, "you'll be all right, man, you just gotta revive. You need fresh water, fresh orange juice maybe."

Hope flickers in his bleak eyes, his hand gives a pathetic tug. "Yes," he wheezes, "orange juice, I need jugos de naranja." Then, with spittle foaming on his lips, his head lolls back and he swoons away.

Stunned by the realization that my friend, my companion, lies here quaking on the edge of life, I struggle into my clothes and sandals. I force myself into the brutal sunlight with every nerve of my body flayed, walking the weak-kneed walk of the doomed toward the distant juice stand, carrying two empty canteens.

At the corner shop where the shelves are lined with cans of sugary fruit-flavored juices, I guzzle two pints of mineral water and feel instant renewal. I fill one canteen with good water, then push on to the fruit juice vendor on the plaza. Trembling, light-headed, I gulp a full quart of the fresh pulpy orange juice, then fill the second canteen with more orange juice. The wrinkled vendor eyes me with a melancholy fatalism. The gringo long-hair has overdone it, he is near his end. I rest in the shade of a banana palm for a few minutes, whispering to Bones to hold on, I'm coming, do not die on me. Then I stand up again and force my body into motion.

About half way back to the motel, pouring sweat, I have to step against a wall to make room for a green dump truck that's coming up the narrow street. There are men in the back of the truck calling out in loud voices. People are coming out of doorways, waving at the truck. Two men in straw hats up in the back are calling out, passing paper bags down to the people who are handing dinero back up.

"Manzanos, manzanos," the men sing out, "manzanos de las montanas!"

This milagro of perfect timing, of pure happenstance, strikes me with awe. The men in the truck are handing down bags and boxes of red mountain apples, the scent of ripe apples fills the air. The truck is piled high with apples trucked in from hundreds of miles to these coastal lowlands. The people are jubilant, anticipating with relish the crisp, delicious fruit. I wobble to the truck and exchange a handful of pesos with the grinning man for a sack of his sweet, holy apples. "Buenos dias," he says, "muchas suertes!"

Rich beyond belief, I lug home the apples and the juice canteens on shaky but determined legs. I believe in my luck, aiyee I do! I believe in my luck like the thighbone of Jesus!

Within the hour Bones is sitting up in his croaker's bed, sipping nectarous orange juice and cool water. Life flows back into his hollowed face, he regards me with grateful eyes.

"Jake, man, you have saved me. I've got to tell you, I felt death, I was wasted, I could feel my life running out. I thought I was a goner."

"Hah, but that is not to be," I reply, slicing the jovial apples for us to eat, "we just need to rejuvenate. That plantation weed will be here soon and we'll be good. But I agree, man, wow, that was an incredible shock. Jesus Christ, I almost shit my brains out."

# Chapter 30

B UT LO MALO, all is not bueno. On the third day when we return to the beach, feeling stronger, Conrad and Trini do not show up. The surfers have seen hide nor hair of them. We track Artie down in San Blas bar, but he has heard nothing. We wait, then wait some more, the grueling wait. We drive back to the wild, lonesome beach, hoping against hope we haven't been shafted. But pour hope in one hand and piss in the other, see which one fills up the fastest.

At last, on Saturday morning, Trini shows up in wretched condition. His left forearm hangs in a sling, a blood-stained bandage around his forehead. He limps over to us, describing the situation in an aggrieved voice. He and Conrad went down the coast to the remote farm. Another smuggler offered them two hundred cash for the .38 special and Conrad was all for taking the dough and fucking us over. "They are dumb green hippies, they are meant to be screwed! All we have to do is stay away for awhile, those longhairs will get tired and go!"

But Trini refused to double-cross us. He stood up to Conrad, demanding the pistol so he could honor our deal. The two violent men ganged up on him. "You can see what the fuckers did to me," Trini laments. "They hit me hard with the two by four and busted my arm."

Bones and I listen with squinting faces, eye to eye with Trini, burned again. Is he lying, or telling the truth? Someone obviously beat the shit out of him. He is unshaven, his hair tangled, blood-spattered and filthy. The treacherous German leers back at us in Trini's pleading eyes, and I knew he was an asshole. That gun was bad karma in itself. Now again, we've been ripped off—ripped off for the illegal pistola and another twenty dollar bill. Bones mutters that our planets must be afflicted, that we are under a bad sign, that he needs to cast a horoscope. But I know that Conrad meant to burn us from the get-go, and a bitter taste fills my mouth.

"The fucking pendejo attacked me with a board," Trini swears. "He bashed me on the head. Then he ran away and I could not even move for hours. That is why I am late coming here and I am sorry. I have come all the way by foot to tell you this terrible thing."

"Do you know where that motherfucker might be?" I want to know. "Where he goes? Where he hides?"

"He won't come back here until he feels you are gone. But I will go hunting him as soon as I rest. He has betrayed me and betrayed you, that bastard owes us!"

We leave it at that, for what choice do we have? Trini vows to track Conrad deep into the jungles if need be. He promises to report back to us within a week, but I doubt this will occur. After all, who are we to him? We are just strangers passing through, a black mark on his otherwise good reputation. He would just as soon that we write it off and leave.

Dejected and pissed, Bones and I return to town and wander around until we find Artie in a bar at the harbor, swilling cheap beer. Artie likes to draw the boats, he watches the fishermen unload their fresh catch of shrimp, redfish and dorado, making sketches. We take bar stools next to him, order cervezas, and tell him the rotten news.

We sit in brooding silence, peeling the labels off the beer bottles. The fans clack, the salt air washes through the open doors. Artie begins to grumble. "I've always detested that asshole Conrad. He looks down on everybody. But I figured you could count on Trini, he's always been solid. But looks like that kraut fucked him over too."

"I would love to pay Conrad back," I say, "if only I had the chance. Pay him back in spades."

Artie takes a thoughtful pull from his bottle, smacking his lips. He says, "I think you should pay that bastard back. And what's more, I'll even help you do it."

"Aiyee," Bones says, "what do you mean by that?"

Artie begins convulsing with laughter. He raps the old plank bar with his knuckles, saying, "Just so happens, I know where Conrad keeps his precious motorcycle."

"What the fuck, man," I mutter, "for real? You know where it is?"

We all lean our heads together, revenge in our eyes. "That asshole doesn't deserve any slack," Artie says. "He double-crossed everybody, even his partner Trini. He's got it coming."

Bones seems a tad ambivalent, but I have no misgivings. Scowling, I say, "Where's he keep that fucking bike?"

"It's in his casa, man, right in the front room, right here in San Blas. It's all in pieces right now 'cause he's rebuilding the motor. But it's right there for the taking. Only problem is the fat chick."

"What fat chick?"

"Denise, he lives with this fat Jewish broad named Denise, a real airhead. She rents the house year-round so she can hang around down here. And she lets Conrad stay for free and do his thing 'cause he bones her."

"Damn," smirks Bones. "So she is like the girlfriend? She guards his scene?"

"Yeah, she's sorta like the mother hen, you know? But dig, Denise is crazy for sex, she'll get it on with just about anybody with a hardon," Artie snickers. "And see, that's the trick. Someone has to pork her to get a shot at that bike. And it's not gonna be me, boys, uh uh, I'd rather beat off."

Aha! I lift my eyebrows at Bones, Bones the cocksman, who has never let blubber stand in the way of some hot pussy. Meeting my gaze, Bones gives me a nonchalant grin.

"You into this? I mean, you lay the bone to this Denise and I'll swipe the bike. How about it?"

"And I'll help you," Artie reiterates.

"Oh most definitely," Bones affirms, knocking back his beer. "I'm all in. We'll pull the rug out from under that bastard and lay the triple-cross all over him!"

We all indulge in a conspirator's laugh, as pure and bitter as burnt ashes. Clinking our bottles, we bend together and sketch our nefarious plans under the whirring overhead fan.


RIGHT AFTER DARK, Artie leads us to Conrad's house and we park on the narrow street. Denise answers the door, all friendly smiles, and Artie talks us inside with a couple of joints. Denise seems flattered to have three men drop by in surprise, but no, she doesn't have a clue where Conrad is. She thinks maybe in Guadalajara shopping for spare motorcycle parts. She's a repulsively obese brunette tanned a butter-nut brown, with laughing, flirtatious eyes. Artie whispers that she sunbathes nude on her patio with a foot-long dildo. Denise wears a orange paisley caftan that does not hide her pillow breasts, and Bones' eyes already shine with lust. We sit around in her red-tiled front room, her stick-figure artwork on the walls, sharing a potent joint. Bones ingratiates himself, laying on his jocular charm, and Denise laps it up like a cat in heat. Within minutes, she's leading him through the bead curtain into her art studio, to show him her latest painting. He gives me a lascivious wink as he disappears.

"There it is," Artie mutters, "over there. That's his baby."

Sure enough, over in an alcove, laid out in parts on greasy newspapers, Conrad's flat-track bike, a Bultaco 350 from the looks of it. The engine, sprockets, rims, chain, gears, frame and tank, completely disassembled. Conrad has put out an oily plastic basket to serve as a receptacle. Hah, with tip-toe stealth, we load the basket to the hilt with crucial parts, then haul it to the car trunk. For good measure I take the yellow gas tank too, tossing it into the rear seat. Back inside, we put our heads through the beaded curtain to see what's going down. In the pastel shadows, Denise moans, Bones snorts and shivers like a long-legged stud. We hear the heavy slap of sweaty flesh. Artie breaks into stoned giggles, yanks his head back and rushes for the front door, rushes into the night, laughing.

"Bones," I whisper into the dim room, "got to go, man. Deal is done!"

"Okay, yeah, okay," Bones gasps, "almost there, almost there!"

"What, what," Denise blurts in her befucked daze, clutching at him.

"No babydoll, it's all right," Bones croons "We gonna make it, we gonna come!"

Denise dissolves into urgent whimpering, her fat slapping, and I pull my head back. Best not to imprint certain images on your brain, no. I wait in the front room, pacing, impatient. Never hang around the scene of the crime, always split. My partner comes bursting through the bead curtain with a lewd grin, zipping up his slathered tool.

Pointing to where Conrad's bike used to be, I give a thumb's up, and we dash for the door. We pile into the Mercury and drive away in triumphant glee. Yes, it's true what they say, revenge is sweet, especially against a bastard like Conrad. If he wants his flat-tracker back he's gonna have to come across with the goods.

We stash all the bike parts in our motel room, thinking to negotiate hard when he shows up. The word will go out, sooner or later Conrad has to appear. Cough up the money, asshole, the pistola or all the kilos, if you want your Bultaco back. If he values his hot-rod bike even in the least, it's no contest. I figure the skulking ex-pat to be a weasel, and once confronted, the weasel will deliver. At least that is what I'm banking on and I'm not thinking past that.

But more listless days drift by under the punishing San Blas sun, our pocket dinero drib-drabbing away. The German stays away, taking no chances. We hear from Artie that Denise became hysterical when she snapped to the caper we had pulled. But her visa has expired, she doesn't want any stink with the local policia. It's Conrad's goddamn mess, let him fix it, she screamed at Artie, throwing a flower pot at him when he went back to negotiate the terms of ransom.

To be real, Bones and I are sick of these convoluted marijuana hassles. The cards seem weirdly stacked against us in our quest to score and smuggle dope. Sitting in the muggy cabin, running out of weed to even smoke, we talk over our lousy situation.

Swatting at flies, Bones proposes, "Why don't we give the bike to the motel manager? Maybe he could sell it. They're good people, they have ninos to feed."

"But dig Bones, sell the bike to who? What's he doing with all those motorcycle parts? It's a small village, word's bound to get around. We don't want to put him in a trick bag."

"Yeah, right on, see what mean. You think we could sell it on the road?"

"We'd have to cart that bike clear over to Guadalajara, or maybe up to Mazatlan, take it around to bike shops, it could get risky. Flat-tracking is a private club and were outsiders."

"Man, we're starting to run out of hang-around money and we're still a thousand miles from home. We've got to make a move."

"Yeah, I'm hip. And lugging all those stolen parts with us is asking for bad luck. Let's just ditch it in the swamp."

"You mean just throw it all away?"

"Yeah, fuck it. Fuck Conrad. Let's drive out in the jungle and throw the basket into the muck. Somewhere it'll never be found."

Bones breaks into a low-down chuckle, reaching out to tap my fingers. "Yeah, let's do it."

We take one of the aimless dirt tracks into the murky swamp, to where the road peters out into a brackish lagoon. Vines hang from the limbs mosquitoes rise, and some kind of monkey howls from the trees. One by one, we fling all of the bike parts into the black water. The yellow gas tank floats askew, a tell-tale signal. I hope someone finds it and tells the despicable German the bad news. Never in my life have I imagined doing what I'm doing to a motorcycle, but I watch the Bultaco gurgle out of sight with bitter-sweet satisfaction.

"I just hope what not accruing any bad karma for this," Bones reflects.

"No, fuck that noise, Bones. What goes around comes around. That asshole started it, we just finished it."

We make ready to head back to California, licking our wounds. We roll and repack our gear and stack it by the door, ready to load. We mosey around town and say our adios to our friends, having a few last beers. After a melancholy lunch at our favorite patio cafe, we drive out through the jungle to the wild and lonesome beach. The surfers are all gone, gone elsewhere in their quest for mystical waves. We drive down the long deserted beach to where the sand runs into a towering cliff that hangs with flowering jungle growth. The vines tumble down the rocky face, the waves boom and surge into the clefts.

Sitting on a driftwood log, we watch the burning sun descend into the vast Baja ocean. Things end, what can you do except keep on moving? Sitting here, rueful and contemplative, the sea rushing in and out of the rocks, we hear sounds on the cliff above us. Human voices, a donkey braying. Two stout mestizos emerge from the jungle bosque, one leading and the other prodding a burro down a steep path to the sands. They're in a jovial mood, hailing us when they spot us. With amused curses, they work their way down the precarious trail, their reluctant burro loaded with heavy canvas saddlebags. Parrots screech from the trees and take off into the eternal blue air. Curious, we wait for them at the bottom of the cliff. They come down and greet us like fellow gypsies, in Spanish dialect, saying, "Si, si, the woman said you would be here."

They reek of raw mescal, optimistic borrachitos, chewing on rustic hand-rolled cigars. They seem delighted to have found us, here with them on this magical beach. One of them takes an unlabeled bottle of amber booze from his paper sack, offering us a swig.

"Excelente, muy bueno," he declares, lifting his eyes and babbling a drunkard's praise to the heavens.

We laugh and shake our heads no, remembering our last wild fiasco with native moonshine. They shrug, then show us a couple dozen mescal bottles wrapped in palm leaves, strapped on the burro's back. I rub my sun-browned stomach to indicate its tender condition. But on an impulse, I ask, "Tiene la mota?"

"Ahh," they exclaim together, rolling their bloodshot eyes, "si, la tenemos!" Without further ado, they unflap one of the saddle packs as the burro flicks its long ears. The canvas pack contains a few dozen firmly rolled newspaper tubes.

"Miren," the trader murmurs, unwrapping one of the tubes. "Miren, amigos." He shakes the resinous gold-green buds into our cupped palms, our eyes bulging with incredulity. We inhale the rich, intense aroma, scarcely believing our luck – aiyee, it is la mota primo deluxe!

"Fuerte, muy fuerte," the traders affirm while we nod our heads, muttering, "Jesus, yes, si, está hermosa, fucking fantástico."

The immediate problem is that we didn't bring any Zig-Zags, there was no need, our own stash gone. We are hippies without rolling papers, even though this burro-borne weed begs to be smoked. Sunset begins to paint the vast Pacific sky and the waves boom into the clefts. The infernal mosquitoes gather around us, distracting us, making us swat and curse. The Mestizos laugh and offer us booze, and in truth, the mosquitoes show no interest in these sweating borrachos. Instead, they whine and hover around us, incensed by the aroma of our pure vegan blood, even as we ponder the gorgeous buds.

Flashing on that night in Guadalajara, I say, "Bones, the sack."

"Asi, asi," Bones replies, tearing a strip from the brown mescal sack. He forms a wrapper between his long fingers, I crumble one of the sticky buds into the channel, he rolls us a cigarillo. One trader extends his smoldering cigar, I toke the rustic joint to life, taking a couple of modest hits. Feeling it at once, I pass the number to Bones. He takes a deep, three-stage hit, filling his lungs with the jungle herb. The brown paper is harsh, but the marijuana essence is so rich that it leaves us in awe. An exquisite current spreads all through my nervous system. Smiling, I offer the joint to our Mexican benefactors, inviting them to partake with us.

"No, no," replies the burly one, "no para nosotros, muy loco, muy loco."

His cigar-chomping partner nods in agreement, taking another lusty swig of mescal. For you, for you, he laughs, we are all amigos now, por todo tiempo!

"As you wish," I smile, bowing, "we are California dopers, we will smoke it all!"

Savoring in another incredible hit, I pass the bomber to Bones, who inhales, holds it, inhales again, then exhales with a wheezing, "Holy fuck."

"Yeah, I know, unbelievable." We have had about three hits apiece, the weed is cosmic.

The sun sinks into the far western ocean in an orange molten ball, immersing itself in a horizon of fire. The infinite sky unfolds in curtains of scarlet and pink, gold and purple, in a wash of colors so flamboyant that it leaves you breathless. I stare at my hands and forearms, covered now by the feasting mosquitoes, yet I do not feel them, I don't even care. This invented idea we call time has stopped, the world has stopped, the ever-now moment reigns supreme.

"Whew, unbelievable," Bones murmurs, our fingers touching for a final pass, our faces transfigured, but we let the joint drop to the sands, unperturbed.

Watching us, the muchachos are beside themselves with mirth, congratulating each other. They swig from their whiskey sack, their eyes dancing at the prospect of gringo greenbacks. We laugh like brothers in this timeless sundown, on this magical beach, in the heave and boom of the waves, praising our lucky stars. As the light drains from the sky we dicker in Spanglish, in gestures, striking a deal for the newspaper bundles, maybe five kilos, mas o menos, for thirty-five dollars Americano, si, no mas, esta bueno, praise Jesus!

Shaking hands, we make arrangements to meet them again in two months. They tell us to contact a certain Indian woman who sells chili peppers at the San Blas mercado, say to her, "bolsa de mescalito", and hold up a specific number of fingers. Six days later our trader-amigos will arrive at this same beach with that number of kilos, same price, same qualidad, si, todo, totalmente la misma, siempre muy bien!

We part company grateful and elated, knowing we have all struck gold. The horizon on the Sea of Cortez has turned into a long reef of smoldering coals. Back in the City of Lost Angels we will get rich with this cosmic la mota! Great good fortune comes to those who dare and endure, so says the I-Ching.

Upon arising, we smoke a smidgen more of the magical weed just to confirm its mind-blowing potency. We stuff the Mexican newspaper tubes into our jute bolsas, stashing the bolsas in the trunk behind the spare tires, covered with an army surplus blanket. We pay our tab with the grateful innkeeper, giving him the beers left in the melting icebox. We eat raisins and peanuts and ripe bananas, drink coffee, count our remaining dollars, refrain from getting too stoned, then hit the road north. During the next couple days we grind up the long highway, sweating our way through Federale checkpoints under the sullen stares of machine-gun toting guards. They study our visas and pass us through, not once inspecting the car. We sleep on the empty desert beaches. We stay at a fleabag motel in Guaymas, not daring to use the moldy shower. We push north over the withering desert landscape into Tecate. Taking no chances, we stash our cargo under a mound of pale boulders on an empty mesa under a colossal August moon. Same night, we cross the silent border and drive on into Los Angeles. Our luck is good again, we believe. And in the heavens above an inscrutable roll of the dice is already deciding our fate.

# PART II

*"God is at no time hidden. He showeth himself at all times and in all places. God is in what is evil even as he is in what is good."*

~~Oscar Wilde

*"Life is only real then, when I Am."*

~~G. I. Gurdjieef

# Chapter 31

THE IGNOMINIOUS DETAILS of what happened at the border, how we were swatted like flies and thrown in the federal slammer, shadowed with oblivion, befriended by the notorious Rodriguez and his female lawyer, all that went down. But Bones is still in that horriible place. And I am back on the streets of Los Angeles. My life has become a surreal tangle of paranoid motion as I hustle up the money for my legal fees. My only goal is to get free and stay free – get free of the law, and stay free of the killing fields of Vietnam.

After my Mexico sojourn, I am in no shape to get an ordinary job. But freak that I am, I'm not without resources. I have the two fine Brit bikes, the race-tuned BSA Lightning, and the outlaw Matchless thumper. Stashed away in my rented Silverlake garage, shaded by Jacaranda trees, I have over 500 hits of acid, white tabs, purple barrels, orange sunshine, super-deluxe, ultra-primo. I'm facing some hard choices right now, no way around it. But one thing I can do is ride and deal, man, deal and ride, and always sleep with one eye open.

Every morning, or whenever I wake up, I have to squelch the impulse to flee. But how does one ever escape the Feds? They know who you are, your ID number, license plates, your fingerprints and addresses, and what you Probably look like. If you have the balls to make a run for it they never stop looking, even in other countries. I don't have the bread to disappear overseas anyway, and I don't want to spend my life on the lam. But I'm on the run now and money, fuck, money has become my driving obsession. I need to take care of Audrey Morgenson, my legal ace in the hole. She's not looking to get rich on my case, but she does require a steady infusion of cash. Bones is still in the San Diego Lockup, his sales-to-a-minor snafu an albatross around his neck. I'm back living with Veegee in the Silverlake storefront, like walking on marbles. Her sullen face, the unspoken blame, the I tried-to-tell-you-motherfuckers attitude, this I have to deal with everyday. And for me it's all about survival now.

The week after being released from the slammer I visit Audrey in her plush San Diego office, the padded leather chairs and mahogany furniture. I can only wonder where her money comes from, that allows her to play angel of mercy to delusional hippie fuck-ups.

"In light of what's happened to Bones," Audrey says, regarding me with her empathetic eyes, "we're going to handle your case differently. That means we're going to ask for a separate court date. Because, as a first-time offender, you are entitled to be tried under the Federal Youth Act which is a huge advantage for you."

"The Federal Youth Act? Never heard of it," I reply, feeling desperate for any advantage.

"It's a special federal provision that's in effect right now, to wit, you aren't twenty-one yet and you have no prior felonies. The Federal Youth Act all but guarantees that you'll receive automatic probation without any more jail time. That's providing you keep your act clean all through the trail process. Then, if you stay clean during the probationary period—no mishaps, no backsliding—you'll be completely exonerated. Your record will be expunged."

"Expunged?" I say, blinking in disbelief. "How so?"

"Wiped clean. They'll be no accessible record of your arrest or conviction except in the locked FBI files in Washington, D.C. In a few years, it'll be as if this border incident never happened."

"Are you serious? For real?"

"Yes, for real, Jake. If you play your cards right you'll come out of this deal clean as a whistle."

"Whoa, alright! What do I need to do? I mean, in court with you, how should I act?"

Audrey gives me a cryptic half-smile. "All right, let's look at that. A conservative judge could override the Youth Act if he takes a strong disliking to you. He could declare you a menace to society. That's why you have to show yourself to be a sincerely reformed citizen in court. Every appearance needs to reinforce that impression."

Reformed? I detest the implications of that word, the social control it implies, the subjugation of the individual, but swallowing, I say, "Okay, I understand. So what do you advise?"

"Let me be frank. The long hair and mustache has to go, it's much too reckless. Your hair needs to be no more than collar length, and always wear a clean shirt with a tie and a sport coat in court. You will need to come across as clean-cut. We're talking about your freedom here."

Goddamn. Smothering the revolt in my heart, I promise Audrey to change my appearance. Do I even have a sport coat or tie left in my outlaw wardrobe? Why do I have to pretend to be something which I am not? What happened to live and let live on the new American frontier? But living behind bars is not an option, I would perish in there. So I agree to do what I must do. I will cut my glorious hair, I will put on a contrite face to appease the skeptical judge.

"I'll do as you suggest, Audrey. Just tell me how to play this game right."

Audrey swivels in her chair, looking out the sun-flecked window at the San Diego skyline. After a moment, she says, "Did you ride your motorcycle down here?"

"Yeah, my BSA. It's a good day to ride, the ocean's beautiful and it's not too windy."

"Do you like to ride fast?"

"Sometimes, yes. But these days I'm keeping it pretty much around the speed limit."

"Jake Acree, I need to know if you are embroiled in any way in that second charge hanging over your friend Bones. It complicates his situation tremendously. Now he's facing not one felony charge, but two. If he's convicted on both charges he will most certainly be doing additional jail time."

"Jesus, that's horrible. Bones doesn't deserve to be in jail. He's totally peaceful."

Audrey looks me straight in the eyes. "That's not going to matter to the judge, if he's convicted of sales of narcotics to a female minor. The Los Angeles DA seems to thing they have him dead to rights, with a corroborating witness."

"Good lord, fuck," I mumble, then say, "Audrey, just know this, I had nothing to do with whatever that was. I didn't know that was going on. We had this rule, Bones and I, not to deal with kids."

"All right. So, no trailing arrest warrants trying to find you?"

"There's nothing else, no way," I say, hoping to God that I'm right.

"All right then," she says kindly. "Please be sure you keep it that way, Jake. Another false step like down at Tecate? You can forget all about the liberal provisions of the Youth Act."

I fork over a four hundred dollar down payment on my legal fees. Audrey advises me to enroll in a junior college as soon as possible, and to get a part-time job. She tells me these repugnant steps are essential to my well-being. My first trial date won't come on the docket for another three or four months—that's how busy the San Diego courts are sending non-conformists to hell, so yes, I'll have the time to adopt a make-believe persona.

"You'll need to show up in court with me at least two or three times," she informs me, "looking clean and contrite. But all we're really doing is pushing the trial date forward. The judge that I want on this case won't be available until after Christmas."

Realizing that I am but a pawn in this complex legal game, feeling quite helpless, I reiterate, "Audrey, whatever it takes, just enlighten me. Please keep me posted in advance."

"Oh I will, don't worry. But since you don't have a home phone, you'll need to call my office every Monday. That way you'll know if we have to meet."

Then Audrey Morgenson drops something on me that blows my mind. She takes off her glasses, rubbing the bridge of her nose. "Jake, do you suppose it's possible that someone knew what you and Bones were doing, and tipped off the border patrol?"

For a few seconds, I just stare at her. "Not possible, no, impossible. No one else had a clue, we were very careful. Why do you ask me that, Audrey?"

"Because," she replies, "we have certain reliable sources of information. And the tattle is that the Tecate border station was on the lookout for a car just like yours, and for two guys that matched your description. They even knew when to be on alert."

This information hits me like a lead fist. With sympathetic eyes, she takes a sip of her coffee. I look at her, my mouth agape, my thoughts reeling. We were fingered by someone close to us? But who, who even knew?

"Something to think about, isn't it? I want you to consider it, Jake."

"But who? It seems too impossible. I mean, we were . . ."

Letting my voice trail off, Audrey says, "Be careful who you confide in and what you say. And remember, the prosecution is still gathering evidence in this case."

The hundred or so mile ride back up the freeway passes in a blaze of conflicted thoughts. I had meant to visit Bones at the jail, but don't want to now with this new shit banging in my head. If it's true, what went down, who blabbed, who turned on us? Dawn knew next to nothing, and ditto with Donny. They only knew I might have some super-cosmic pot available before long, but still in Mexico. Only Veegee knew about our hidden border stash, and our intentions to smuggle it across. But it is unthinkable that Veegee ratted us out. Despite their hassles, she cares for Bones, she wants him back in her lusty bed. No, I cannot believe that she fingered us. So then was it Bones, running his garrulous mouth too much? Like goddamit maybe that same little teenybopper, who got herself pinched, then snitched him out?! Bones is a fool for sex, he drools for these air-headed Lolitas. The scenario plays out in my mind's eye like a leering movie. I race homeward on my 650 Lightning in the sunshine glinting off the blue sky sea, thoughts in turmoil, freedom like a tethered bird beating in my chest.

PARANOIA RUNS DEEP through my days and nights now, etching my consciousness, cutting right to the bone. I ramble from place to place, always on the move, hustling up cash and shuffling my deals. I no longer have the luxury of selling a few tabs to a group of sympatico friends, making just enough bread for my fun-loving expenses. Nope, the happy-go-lucky daydream has taken a hard right turn and now I have to move dozens and hundreds of hits at a time. I'm facing about 2500 dollars in legal fees, not a king's ransom, but for me plenty steep. And if for some reason this court doesn't lean my way, I need enough coin to split deep into Mexico. Because no matter what happens, I'm not going back inside that cage.

Paranoia swallows you like a stray dog devouring garbage. Moving acid in quantity means I must move in dicey scenes that I intuitively distrust. There's no shield in the underground bars and seedy hotels populated by hardcore dopers who may mix acid with narcotics but prefer heroin, or cold-blooded dealers who may look new-age but cut pure lsd with pcp to turn their profit. These are not my kind of people and not my world, and engaging with this lunatic fringe is a daily dose of flickering madness.

THE DAY I finally make the scene at my parent's house in Santa Monica, three weeks late for my birthday dinner, the bottom falls out. Even before I can explain express myself, standing in the door, my anxious blue-eyed mother takes one look at me, clasps her hands to her heart, and cries, "Oh lord, my son, lord, what have you done to yourself?!"

I am dumbfounded, blinking, at a loss for words. True, I haven't seen her in months, since before I left for Oaxaca, but her reaction to my presence startles me. Do I seem that tripped out? My eyes shine with a windblown light, my hair hangs halfway down my back, my body so lean on its raw food diet that I must seem like a sadhu on a motorcycle. But this is not a crime, this is only love. This is only what love does to you.

Taking my mother's hands in mine, I say, "I'm fine mom, really, I'm healthy, I'm okay. There's nothing wrong with me and I'm more aware than I've ever been. But unfortunately, I do have some bad news."

Aiyee, more bad news on my scorecard is not what my mother wants to hear. She was Florida born and raised in a conservative Presbyterian family. Her moralistic nature has always been at war with my amoral tendencies. She railed against my journey into psychedelics. She railed against my fascination with pagan motorcycles, Zen and Existentialism. When Dawn and I moved in together she declared we were living in sin and refused to visit us. My father would come and visit with us, sit, chat and drink beer with us, but not mom. Dawn took a real liking to my old man and he'd occasionally drop by the bar where she worked. A free-thinking iconoclast himself, he has always supported my Bohemian nature, saying I should decide for myself what's true and what isn't. But going against the grain meant war for my mother. Since the age of thirteen onward, when I declared that I was no longer going to church with her because it was full of hypocrites, we have been at fierce odds. But that is a game I no longer play with her.

Now, standing here in her Santa Monica kitchen, the flowering window boxes, I feel a tinge of remorse. Not for what I have done, but for being the cause of her suffering. This is no hunky-dory reunion. Explaining to my family, look, not to worry, but I just got busted on the Mexican border for smuggling dope, oh woe, oh fuck, my immoral ways have caught up with me. My mother's face sags into her hands in wailing lamentation.

Taking a ragged breath, I say, "Look, mom, try not to worry. I have a good lawyer who says the chances are real good I'll get straight probation. That means no jail time, so it's not that bad."

"But now you're a criminal," she cries, face blurred in tears. "Oh, how many times have I tried to tell you, but you wouldn't listen, you wouldn't listen, I knew it!"

What can I say? It's like a mallet falling on a block of southern intransigence. She only sees things her way. I almost ask if she saved me a piece of birthday cake, but refrain. She loves me, she only wants that I live up to her ideals for me. But those are her ideals, not mine. She sits there sobbing into her hands, making sure that I realize how much I have made her suffer.

My stoic, Bogart-like father goes over to comfort her, swaying a little on his feet. My old man showed me how to survive in the Colorado wilderness with a knife, a fly-rod, and a handful of wax matches. He's held top-security aerospace clearances at places like White Sands and Edwards AFB. He taught me to question everything and to believe nothing that I could not verify for myself. Rubbing her shoulders, he speaks to my mother in a gentle voice, reminding her that I'm the one with the real problem here. I lean against the kitchen counter, waiting for my moment. I could say that I'm sorry, but I'm not at all sorry. I'm only sorry that the motherfuckers caught me.

Yes, my father is somewhat drunk. He has a life-long fondness for good whiskey. He takes a drag on his Pall-Mall, studying me. Earlier this spring we stood out behind this same house, taking in the misty night. He offered me a swig from his pint of blended Canadian whiskey. I don't like whiskey, can't stand the smell of it. But smiling, I said to him, "Dad, I'll drink some whiskey with you when you drop some acid with me."

My old man responded with his rakish smile, saying, "Let me think that over, son. Let me consider that one."

Now, he stands with his hand on my crying mother's shoulder. "You think you can come out of this mess without any jail time? Your lawyer told you that?"

"Yeah, dad, there's a real good chance. This deal called the Federal Youth Act, no prior arrests. I just have to play my cards real straight."

Nodding, he says, like the friend he's' always been, "I imagine this could get rather expensive, son. At the moment I'm not in the best of shape. But I can rustle up just about whatever you need."

"Thanks, but I think I've got that covered. Don't even worry about that right now."

"But he'll have a criminal record for the rest of his life," my mother accuses, lifting her reddened eyes at me.

"Actually, mom, maybe not. That's what I'm trying to tell you. If things go right, if I clear probation without any mistakes, my whole record gets expunged."

"What's that mean, gets expunged?" my solemn brother Evan asks.

"Like it never happened. It gets legally wiped clean, erased."

"But it's still shameful, son, it's still wrong! If only you had listened this never would have happened!"

"Nonsense," I retort, "keep that moralistic nonsense to yourself." My mother has a penchant for making such declarations, it drives me up a wall.

"So what are you gonna do, man?" my brother intervenes, his eyes worried. "I mean, how're you gonna handle all this?"

"The best way I can," I say. But I know he wants to talk with me alone.

My father sways in center of the kitchen, then steadies himself. "Jake, keep me in the know on this, okay? I'll help anyway I can. Let's get together again soon." He steers himself into the hallway, towards his study, for some fresh fortification. He's glad that my situation isn't a total disaster, but he's heard enough for now.

I go over and kiss my mother on the blond crown of her head, murmuring, "I'm sorry, mom, truly I am. But I have to do what's right for me. It will all work out, just trust me on that."

"Oh, how can I trust you, son," she implores. "Trust you, trust you to go down the wrong path? Oh Jake, my Jake."

Impatiently, I bite my tongue this time. I suspect that most families are insane, mine is no exception. I look into my mother's blue eyes with kindness. Then I turn and gesture my kid brother out into the shaded backyard that's fringed with her gladiolus and iris beds.

"You know they're planning on going to Phoenix soon?" Evan tells me at once. "Dad's agreed to take some kind of engineering job over there with General Electric."

"No, how could I know that? I've been down in Mexico. So that lucrative deal he had with the aerospace headhunters went down the tubes?"

"Totally. That partner of his, Buzz, royally screwed him over again. He's not giving him his fair share, so the old man told Buzz to go fuck himself. You know dad."

I laugh softly, saying, "You mean he's not even going into to work these days?"

"Nope. He just stays home and drinks, sharpens his hunting knives and cleans his pistols, and broods. That's another reason mom's kinda hysterical. This bizarre trip of yours just put her over the edge."

"Well, fuck me," I say, feeling some of my parent's pain and frustration. "Then it's a good thing he got that new deal over in Arizona."

"Yeah," Evan says in a sorrowful tone. "But they'll be leaving out of here in just a couple of weeks, and I'm not going with them."

"Really? You serious?" I know how protective he is of his mom, even though they're in conflict too. She always wants it her way, which supposedly is the Lord's way, which of course is bullshit. Evan's enthusiasm for the Dylan records I've laid on him, combined with his disinterest in high school and delight in luminous grass has blighted the home front. But my younger brother is no idiot. We're all hanging in the shadow of a potential atomic disaster, governments gone insane, murderous wars, violated civil rights, so why be a carbon-copy?

"No man, no way I'm going to Phoenix with them," he says. "I'm not leaving this west coast scene, this is where it's happening. I'm gonna take a job at a paint store over in Culver City and rent a room somewhere around."

"Hey dig, hold on a minute," I say, thinking fast. "That sounds real good brother, but listen. I've got to clean up my act for this court situation, enroll in some classes at LACC., pretend I'm reformed for the judge. My smart female lawyer says that I've got to adapt. So how about this? When they move, why don't you come over and share a pad with me near the college? Lots of cool people around there, and it won't cost as much. And I'm sure you can find work around there, too. I see help-wanted signs in the store windows all the time."

Evan's hazel eyes light up. "Hey man, that would be fantastic, that would be far out. But what about Dawn? Aren't you two gonna live together anymore?"

"Umm, not right now. That wouldn't be good, not with my scene the way it is. Maybe later."

"Alright then, yeah, count me in. But what do you mean by that?"

"Well, I've got to get clear of this border hassle, obviously. My lawyer says I can do it as long as I keep my act clean. She's this brainy legal chick, a real crusader. But I've still got a load of dope, right? And I need to move it, I have to convert all of it into cash so I can pay her. That's number one."

"But aren't you just taking more risky chances?"

"I know what I'm doing, Evan. It's my main cash resource and it's a quick turn-around. But dig, it should all be done within a month or two. Then I'm clean. I'm signing up for the next quarter at LACC, and that'll also help me stave off the draft board. So things are going to work out. I promise you that."

"Okay, sounds good to me," Evan says, "yeah, I love the idea. It'll freak mom out but I don't really care. I'm sick of their endless squabbling. Dad's not going to quit drinking and she's not going to leave him alone. It's twisted."

"Yeah, I hear you. From what I can see just about all marriages get twisted."

We share a good strong Evan and me, we grew up together in the Texas post oak country. I need someone I can really trust and we're always solid, no matter what. Surrealistic Pillow, Highway 61 Revisited, Blond On Blond, the times dude they are a-changing. I fish a few joints out of my pocket and lay them on him. Evan lights one up right away and we savor a surreptitious smoke in our mother's backyard. I hear the solitary bird cheeping in the bushes, the little bird deranged by smog that never sleeps, who knows me, who knows who I am. When I listen closely I hear the sun roaring in my bloodstream. I hear the forgotten roar from the horizon of the earth. I reject all regrets. The only path worth taking is that road that makes your heart sing. There is no other risk worth taking.

# Chapter 32

Reluctantly, I bite the bullet and run a classified ad in the Los Angeles Free Press. The ad lists only my street address and the hours of 9:00 am until 12 noon for showing. Two days after I post the ad, a straw-haired biker with a far-away look shows up in a primer-gray pickup. He inspects my black Matchless Typhoon with a mechanic's hands, nodding with attention as I trip the compression release and kick the 600cc thumper over. He doesn't need to ride it, he claims, only needs to hear it, so I take him at his word. I let him Jew me down from my asking price of $400 to $350. The bike does need new pads in the front drums and a new rear knobby. The last few times I rode it, the front lever faded clear to the handle bar and I had to stand on the rear brake to bring it down. Resting his eyes on my BSA Lightning, he lifts his brows into a question mark.

"That one's not on the table," I tell him, appreciating his interest.

"I can see why," he remarks. "I'd never sell that Lightning, if I we're you. Hell, I'd never have sold that big Brit single. That can't be easy."

"It's not, believe me. But I need the bread, man. I've got some dope charges hanging over me and court's expensive."

He makes a clicking sound in his throat, saying, "Well, I'm wishing you the best of luck."

We load the black Typhoon into his truck, tie it down, then shake hands again. I watch him drive off with the first bike I've ever owned with a lump in my throat. It's all about what you love, and sometimes what you love comes down to nothing.

Going inside the brick storefront, I hand Veegee forty bucks on my rent, letting her know I'll be moving in about a month.

"You don't have to go, Jake" she says softly. "Please don't let my moods bother you. I'm gonna stand behind you and Bones, just know that. We'll all get past this."

"Thanks, Vee," I say, hugging her. "But I've got a lot of shit to handle and it could get intense. My brother's coming in from Santa Monica and we want to find a place a closer to the college."

"Listen to me, Jake. You can hide out here anytime you need, remember that. And in the meantime we're still sharing this pad."

Coming clean with Dawn is like falling through a distorted looking glass. Whatever hopes she had of me coming around to her version of things gets snuffed in the first moments of my confession. Frowning, biting her lower lip, she says, "So, this means that you're gonna go away? Like up shit creek?"

"No, Dawn, nothing like that. It's a first offense and apparently my age is in my favor. Some special deal called the Federal Youth Act. But it's going to cost me some bread, and it's going to be a tricky ride for awhile."

A shadow crosses her pretty face, she clasps her hands, studies her fingers. She is four months pregnant now and looks rounder and even more feminine. "I knew something bad was going to happen," she murmurs, "I felt it coming."

"And you know, I don't really need to hear that."

"But it's true."

"Look, I've got a good female attorney, she's very smart. She says what I'm looking at is two to three years probation and after that my record gets rubbed clean – as long as I stay clean. So yeah, it's a bummer, but it's not a total wipe-out. That's my good news."

Dawn regards me with pragmatic eyes. I know at once my carte blanche has been revoked. My acid dream girl is no longer present. "Well, I guess that's something at least," she says, "good for you. But you might as well know. I'm going to go back to Joliet to my mom's place, to have our baby. That's where I'll be in case you're interested."

Holding her hands, I say, "Dawn, I don't want you to vanish on me. I'm not going to disappear on you. I'm dealing with a hard situation but I'll do all I can to help you. Because I love you."

She sighs, then kisses my hand. "That means a lot to me, you bastard.

But I'm going to have a baby girl and you and me need to decide on her names."

"Come again? How do you know it's going to be a girl? Did your doctor say that?"

"No, I just know. I had a dream with my grandma and she showed me. She told me we should each pick a name."

The supernatural grandmother strikes again. I'd rather drop acid and go talk with trees and birds and rocks. But I say, "All right. You mean, what, like the first and last name?"

"No, I mean the first and middle name. I want her last name to be your name, if that's okay with you. And I'd like her first name to be Tia." Dawn graces me with her brown-eyed smile. "Now you choose."

"Wait, honey. Tia means aunt in Spanish. You want to call the baby 'auntie'?"

"I know, I don't care. I just love the sound of it. So you pick a name that goes with Tia."

When did she become so bossy? Naming unborn babies is not my thing but my intuition kicks in. I consider for a moment, then reply, "Velina. Tia Velina."

"Ohh, I like that," Dawn says, scooting closer to me. "Tia Velina, it's like a poem, okay. And can I give her your last name? Is that all right with you?"

"Yeah, actually I'd like that. You want to call her Tia Velina Acree? Far out. Except I'm not into getting married right now, so don't think that. I've got too much insanity to deal with."

Dawn gives me her wise-ass smirk. "What are you afraid of, anyway? It'd get you out of the draft, you know."

"I'll handle those robot assholes in my own way, babe. My conscientious objector claim is still pending, and there are other options. I'll leave the country if I have to."

"Same crazy Jake," she says, snuggling to me. "But you'll sign some kind of paper when the time comes?

"Yes, you have my word on it. When the time comes, just tell me what you need."

We pass some intimate time together, lifting our spirits. But I have the feeling this is the last time I'll see her for awhile. And three days later she takes a train from Union Station back to windy Chicago. She's gone, she's a precious refuge I no longer have. Aloneness and paranoia become my shadows, my ken, my riding companions. All I can do is keep my attention on what is right in front of me, nada mas, nothing more, and keep doing it until I'm free.

I TAKE THE most promising route back into L.A.'s underground drug culture: my old pardner, Donny Kubiak. Donny always has a focus on the doper underbelly, he gravitates to it. Motivated by what he calls "degenerate kicks", he wanders about in search of his twisted laughs. But no matter, each to their own. I know when I locate Donny, I'll find some action.

I roust Donny and his school chick Annie living in a dilapidated apartment building over in east Hollywood. They're delighted to see me, especially since I come with weed. I regale them with wild tales of the border bust, and Donny is back in my corner again. When Dawn and I first fell out there had been some jealous antagonism, but it's gone now.

"Christ, professor," Donny laughs, "you really fucked the pooch this time. You got too whacked out on acid, can't say I didn't warn ya. Now you got the law on your ass and you need some fast moolah. But no sweat, man, I can line you up."

Donny has changed in some vaguely perplexing way. He's saturated by a deep, beatnik doper vibe, more so than ever. The perverted appetites of L.A. act on him like a magnet. But he's unpretentious and fun-loving, as always. His idea of helping me is to introduce me to a sordid bag of Hollywood druggies that he's fallen in with, not that I'm bitching. I've put aside my mystic gypsy cape and put back on my hustler's sombrero. The name of this game is money.

We ride our bikes over to a seedy hotel on Melrose near Western. It's a dank warren of rooms rented by the week and month to wasted dopers, street dealers, thieves, hooker-models and washed-up alchie actors. Most of them are friendly enough, even welcoming in that way the lost embrace a fresh-faced stranger. One never knows who brings what gifts. But I soon realize that I am an anomaly in this motley pack. Being an acid-head biker with a recent smuggling bust gives me some cred, but these characters aren't really interested in acquiring multiple hits of premium acid. Other than a few random sales and the offer to pass the word, I strike out. No, these glassy-eyed denizens are heroin addicts, speed freaks, angel dust abusers and downer freaks. They suck on bongs from eyes open to eyes shut just to pass time between fixes. Decadence seeps from these fading walls, death hangs in the shadows, always ready to snatch another soul. After a few curious visits, I stay clear.

One afternoon, in a red-leather bar on Vermont that Donny likes to get tanked in, I meet a strangely erotic chick in her early thirties, Arlene. This Arlene takes a liking to me, she listens raptly to my talk about transcendental states and psychedelic esoteria. I'm hoping, of course, she has some cash that can fatten the wallet in my right boot. Donny is coming on to her, which she finagles with twinkling ease.

"I don't really care for acid myself," she murmurs to me, "it frightens me." Her hand rests on my thigh. "But, if this stuff is as good as you say, I know someone who'll go for it in a heartbeat. He's a film producer who loves to get high and he's loaded."

Arlene breathes in my ear, trailing her painted nails on my leg. She reminds me of one of those seductive 50's starlets, with strawberry blond hair, in her fetching short summer dress. Her creamy bare skin and silken legs, her plump lips and delicious cleavage, real juicy pinup material, Arlene's almost guileless eyes are china-blue, although her laugh is strange. Arlene's laugh has an off-key pitch that ends on a jangled note, as if she's practicing. Before long I suspect that this chick has at least one screw loose.

Donny treats her like one of the bar regulars, he's drooling to get under her skirt. But she tells me she only comes to this dive on occasion to slum a little. "This place makes me nervous," she confides, "because three times I've seen an undercover narc in here. I know who he is, too. My alchie art broker friend pointed him out."

"Fuck," I mutter, standing next to her stool, staring straight ahead into the mirror, "is he in here now?"

Arlene starts to giggle, then catches herself. "No," she says, pushing her thigh into my hip. "Why, does that make you feel nervous, Jake?"

"It might," I admit, feeling my way. "You could say I'm prone to a bit of instinctive paranoia."

"Hmmm. Why am I not that surprised?"

"I don't know, Arlene, you tell me."

"Because you're different from every other man in this place. And I don't mean just interesting. I mean, you're really different."

Donny, stoned and feeling left out, leers in. "Hey babe, if psychedelia is your thing this guy is the wizard of Oz. He's even connected with Leary's cosmic love tribe."

Giving Donny a sharp look, I say, "Hey man, that's bullshit. Don't exaggerate. But I have been known to trip now and then."

Arlene emotes a soft, husky laugh, then in my ear says, "You're friend's kind of a cute dumbbell, isn't he? He's been trying to pick me up for weeks, but he's not my type. I like bohemians who drive fast Jaguars and who don't confuse Matisse with the Maltese Falcon."

"Jaguars I don't do," I reply with a side-mouth grin, "but I do ride fast English motorcycles." This chick is right out of a film noir flick, and even though I'm celibate, she gives me a serious hardon. Donny drools over her swelling breasts for a few seconds, then turns to rap with the barmaid.

Arlene fans herself, waiting for me to say something.

"So, you were saying, you don't do any acid at all, no psychedelics?"

"No, it's way too wiggy for me. My tastes runs to other things, I'm kind of an old-fashioned girl. But if you have really good acid, I mean like super good? I have this friend who's always looking but keeps striking out on the inferior stuff."

For a moment, I say nothing. I just sit and gauge the vibes, turning the Coors bottle in my hands. "Well," she says, all but licking my ear, "can you or can't you?"

"Actually, yes, I can. Only the strongest, purest, smoothest acid on the planet. Sandoz or Owsley, you can take your choice. But I don't involve myself in dribbles and dabs."

"Wow," Arlene murmurs, pressing her unnaturally firm tit into my arm, "let's go outside where we can talk. I know this very rich guy. Let's go sit in my little red car."

We go through the back door and into parking lot and sit in her Fiat

Spyder. She tells me she's tight with a well-heeled film producer who's always on the lookout for high-grade dope. Arlene smiles playfully, enticing me with her starlet eyes, showing me her alluring thighs.

Trying to remain indifferent, I say, "And high-grade acid is getting harder to find all the time, yes, I know. More and more street shit around, cut with raw speed or angel dust."

"So bad," she says, lighting her Parliament, "and I hear it's truly horrible. People are ending up in psyche wards."

"Right on, and my point is, because pure acid is getting so rare—it's expensive. Mine happens to be ultra-pure, mostly pharmaceutical. And he's got to take at least a hundred hits at a time. No mickey-mousing around."

"Oh, don't worry," Arlene assures me, pushing my knee with her bare foot. "If it's what you claim he'll spring big for it. He's rolling in dough."

"Rolling in dough," I smile, loving the image then take from my pocket a cloisonne pill box. I show this come-hither little chick the minute treasures inside. Into her palm, I tap two Sandoz tabs and two purple owls, explaining what to do and what not to do.

"Free samples, so he'll know what he's getting into."

"Wow. How much will it be, or do you want to tell me that?"

"Of course I'm going to tell you. How else are we going to do business?"

"Okay, I just wanna be sure," she laughs, "you're the boss."

"It'll be five hundred dollars for the first batch of one hundred, either/or, mix and match, and four hundred dollars for the second batch. That's assuming he wants to score more. And the whole deal has to pass through you, Arlene. I don't need to meet him, I don't even want to. Oh, and by the way, I don't have a home phone."

"Hmm, you are a strange one, aren't you? And so beautiful."

"Fuck off, honey."

"No, I mean in the right way. You're a beautiful man. Here, I'm going to give you my number. So you can call me? Just give me a couple of days."

"Okay, no problemo," I say, wanting out of her little red car, away from her provocative body, as she scribbles on a matchbook cover. She smokes, but only takes three of four puffs on her cigs, then dabs them out.

Arlene slips me the number, batting her lashes, all but pushing her nipples through her chemise, showing me the tip of her tongue. I swallow hard. How long has it been since I've had a good, ball-churning orgasm? Way too long. This chick is a wet-dream in a Lolita dress.

"Can I ask you something?" she says, teasing her hair.

"Sure, why not. Ask me whatever."

"Well, back in the bar, we sat there for about an hour and you didn't even finish a beer. You just sat smiling and talking like you do, so I'm wondering. Are you tripping right now?"

I'm not going to tell her whether I am or not. I'm often cruising on a minor dose of acid, but it's none of her business. Instead, I point to my burgundy and chrome 650 Lightning, saying, "See that bike over there? That's how I get around, I don't use a car. I like to go fast and when I'm on that bike I don't drink. I'm not saying I never ride high, I just never ride drunk, because that's stupid. I know a guy who lost his leg wasted like on booze."

"So, it doesn't bother you that Donny's in there getting plastered? He's a real boozer, you know, and he rides bombed a lot."

"It's his life, and I'm not living his trip. I'm living my own."

"He keeps trying to fuck me but I won't let him. I tell him the only guy I wanna fuck is Jim Morrison when he's on stage at the Whiskey. Otherwise, I'm a good little girl."

"Far out," I laugh, "I'm sure that's true. Okay Arlene, dig, I really appreciate this. Let's see where this deal takes us."

Before I can ease out the door she leans and kisses me with her tempting lips, I know what her kiss says. Her moist kiss says I wanna take you home and suck your dick, let me.

"Later," I tell her. "I've got things to do."

We agree to meet at the same '50's red-leather joint later in the week. Arlene makes me feel intensely sexual, but I don't really trust her. Her coy, sex-kitten act turns me off. But if she can connect me with some rich acid-heads, I'll definitely play along for awhile.

WHEN WE GET back together a few nights later she looks rather frazzled, her pupils dilated. Over a scotch highball she complains she hasn't been sleeping well and that her ex has been harassing her. I coo a few sympathies, not really caring for the details, figuring she's probably on tranqs.

After a few minutes of chit-chat, I ask, "And how's our special project going?"

"Oh, unbelievably good," she gushes, needing approval, searching for an upbeat. "He tried the purple one and flipped out, he fucking loved it. I told him you said the white ones we're even better and he wants to know how soon—"

"Okay, don't tell me anymore in here. Let's just finish this drink and go outside."

Out in her red Fiat Spyder, I light up one of my custom joints Arlene sips it in dainty puffs, coughs, coughs again, fanning her face. Just as I'm about to coach her, she tells me, "No, really, I'm fine," and takes a long greedy hit.

"Ahhh, yesss," she says with a giddy laugh. "I actually needed that. Are you always this way, Jake, always the little touch of magic?"

"I'm always the way I am," I reply, surveying the parking lot, then smile. "Probably depends on the moon sign."

Arlene delves into her rhinestone purse and plucks out a fold of greenbacks. "Twenty-five twenties," she says proudly, "and he'll have four hundred, more next week. Said it was absolutely the best he's ever had and this boy is a connoisseur."

"Outta sight, Arlene, this is right on time. I've got some legal fees coming due and this helps. Thanks. But I'm not carrying anything on me. Can you follow me over to my place? It's actually not that far."

"Sure I can. And I heard about your bad little fracas at the border. I hope that female lawyer of yours knows what she's doing. Personally, I would never trust any chick to represent me."

Fucking Donny, Donny talks too much, but I let it slide. "Never mind that, Arlene, it's old news. You'll just need to follow me for a few miles over to Silverlake. Then wait a little bit while I go get it."

"A-ok with me," she flirts, "your wish is my command, maestro."

When we get to VeeGee's place, still my temporary digs, I leave Arlene smoking a roach in her Fiat while I make a run over the hill to my garage. Using a flashlight, I bag up a hundred tabs and a half-ounce of weed, and ride back. She tucks the goods under her driver's seat, her flimsy skirt riding up her sleek thighs, making sure that I get a good look.

"You actually live in there?" she asks me. "Gosh, it looks like an old store. Is that where you crash at night?"

"Yeah, most nights. But I'll be moving pretty soon. It's just one big room and I share it with my partner's girlfriend."

"Oh. And is your friend living there, too?"

"My friend?"

Arlene gives me a knowing smirk. "Yeah, you know, your friend who the girlfriend belongs to?"

"No, not really. Looks like he'll be away for awhile."

"Hmmm, that must be nice and cozy."

"Nothing like that, Arlene. Veegee and I are just roommates. Besides, like I told you, I'm practicing an esoteric form of yoga. Sex isn't in play for me right now."

"I remember you told me that, but it's hard to believe. A stiff prick has no conscience, right? Plus you're a magnet for chicks and you know it. How can a guy like you stay celibate?"

"Well, it's true, I am, take it anyway you want. For me, that's what's happening."

"Donny says you used to be an insatiable pussy hound. That you'd to fuck any pretty girl you could get your hands on."

"Hah, maybe, I don't know," I say in exasperation. "You've got a one-track mind. Wanting and doing are two separate things, right?"

"Okay, Jake, look, I'm sorry. I don't mean to be a such a silly bitch. I'm just feeling really tired and this pot has zonked me. I've had a tough couple of days, believe me. All I need is a friend and a place where I can rest for awhile. Would that be cool with you and roommate? I don't wanna nod out here in the car alone, holding, you know?"

I glance at the darkened window, covered with a Hindu bedspread. VeeGee is in there already asleep. Arlene is asking for a favor and she's been a real boon to me, taking chances to move my dope. Basically she's a good chick, just fucked up in her own peculiar way. She sits beside me with a forlorn air, it doesn't feel right to turn her down.

"All right, come on in and rest for bit. But listen, my roommate's asleep. She gets up and goes to work early in the morning. So we need to be really quiet."

"Oh don't worry I will, and thank you, Jake. You're a life-saver."

We steal inside the dim interior on cat's feet and I lead her over to my monastic pallet. We lie down side by side on the single mattress and pull a sheet over us. Almost at once, lulled by her feminine warmth, I start to drift away. Vivid splashes of purple light coalesce behind my eyelids. But as I doze off, Arlene whispers something ear and sits up in bed. She slips out of frock and entwines her smooth naked body around mine. Purring, she murmurs, "I just wanna be nude with you, I need to feel your skin. Don't worry, I'm not gonna rape you."

The pressure of her full, super-firm tits and her husky words confuse me. A dog is barking, up on the hill, we are somewhere, where are we? For a moment I'm back in the rainy night of Oaxaca, trying to light a candle. Who is this sleek, erotic creature moving down my body, undoing my zipper with her nimble fingers?

"Wait," I mumble, "stop. You need to stop."

"No way," she murmurs, and engulfs my leaping eager cock in her mouth and swallows me to the balls. She makes a sound in her throat, like she's just won the prize. I wrap my fingers in her strawberry curls, wanting to pull her off, but she bears down on me with her ravishing mouth. A moan escapes my lips, stunned by the sheer pleasure I have been denying myself, I stop resisting. Ahh, I give in, caressing her soft curls, caressing her adorable head. She takes me deep into the honeycomb of her throat, writhing with delight. I am hers now, she has me, and in a blinding thrill I explode in a geyser of molten spurts, spasms and demi-spurts as this wanton shakti sucks and swallows me to the root, not even flinching. Trembling all over, the pleasure now excruciating, I reach down and freeze her head with my hands.

"No, no more, fuck Arlene, no mas!"

She lifts her face, her lips sticky and wet, saying, "I can go all night for you, if you'll let me. I'll be anything you want me to be. I'll be your slave if you want."

I tumble back into the pillows, unable to respond. She slithers up beside me, her breath redolent with my rich, impeccable sperm. "You're really big," she whispers. "If you get any bigger I don't know what I'm gonna do."

Drained to the quick, my mind flickering over the ruins of my celibate master plan, I mutter, "Fuck, I don't even know what to say about this."

"What to say?" she coos in a self-pleased tone. "Well, how about an enny-weeny thanks for giving you such fabulous head?"

Turning my face to hers, aware that Veegee is surely awake and listening, I say, "Okay, yeah, thanks for sucking me off like that. But did it even occur to you that's not what I wanted? That maybe that's exactly what I really didn't want?"

"Oh like what," she retorts peevishly, "like your sainthood just got violated? Don't cop that attitude with me, fuck you. You loved it, you loved every second of it."

"You're not hearing me," I say, reaching out, grazing her skin. But she's turned her back. Sitting up, she pulls her frock over her head in one quick motion. "Oh well," she says, "I did my part. At least I didn't hold anything back."

"Look, Arlene, there's no reason to be uptight. It's just that I'm on a different trip—"

"Hubba hubba hubba," she says, pulling away, standing up, smoothing her dress down her thighs. "I guess I'll see you at the bar soon? To carry on with things not having to do with me swallowing your precious cum."

Arlene moves to the door, a succubus glowing with fresh life-force. "I must admit," she says in a lilting whisper, "you are yummy. See you around."

She slips into the night, leaving the door ajar. The dog has stopped yapping. I can hear the crickets outside. Her sportscar starts up, and she drives off. I get up and shut the door, sliding the bolt, then lie back down. What just happened? And does it mean anything at all?

"That woman is really odd," Veegee says from her antique brass bed. "I mean, that bitch is strange."

"Yeah, you got that right," I reply, "and sorry about all that, Veegee."

"Oh I didn't mind," VeeGee yawns. "Actually it was kind of entertaining. Life's a surprise. You only get hung up if you let yourself get hung up."

I make a sound of affirmation and she falls back to sleep within minutes, softly snoring.

Not for the first time, I wonder if Veegee could be the one who put the finger on us, out of spite, out of resentment for two-timing Bones, for being ignored by us? It's an unnerving thought, and I can't quite believe it. I only know that my life is getting stranger by the day, and I feel like there's some kind of target painted on my back.

# Chapter 33

RIDING MY BEASER down a hilly sidestreet I notice a for-rent sign on an unpainted post. Down the slope, there's a plank walkway leading to a gray clapboard house perched on the edge of the eroding bluff. The porch railing is draped with purple bougainvillea. I make a tight u-turn and put the kickstand down. Across the street, there's a dry field with a stand of tall Eucalyptus that shields a city water tank. Another street tees into this one, making a three-way intersection. From where I sit, I can look out over the smoggy L.A. basin towards the distant ocean. This area is off the beaten path and feels right.

I walk over the plank walkway to read the for-rent sign. "Front Studio Apt For Rent. $75.00 A Month, Utilities Included." I memorize the phone number, then walk past the window, looking in; the room is bare with eggshell walls. Further along the deck there's another apartment, at least twenty feet above the hillside on stilts. The eroding slope crumbles away below this ramshackle structure. I knock on the second apartment door, wait, knock again, no one answers. The window is covered with a sheet. Leaning over the weathered railing I take in the hillside, planted in Spanish Broom and red Hibiscus. A pair of chittering hummingbirds dart like dragonflies. I hear the Mexican doves calling from the trees over by the water tank. The noises of the city are muted here, with long views of the sunset coast. Los Angeles City College is no more than three miles away.

I try the studio-for-rent door and it opens. The place has that sharp, fresh paint smell. There's a front room ample enough for yogic meditation, a couch, a couple of chairs, coffee and end tables, and a mattress. Evan and I could make do with this layout. There's a bathroom with a shower tub, cracked tiles and peeling linoleum, but clean. The best room is the large kitchen with a fold-down table, gas stove, green fridge, and a rear storage room that houses the water heater. The old fridge rattles a little, the water heater burbles, but this is laid-back bohemian living on the cheap.

I take the steep path down under the plank walkway, down to where the backside of the structure has been covered with plywood all the way up the pilings. An unpainted door sags open to a basement carved into the slope, a cave-like room filled with old tools, paint cans, lumber, and miscellaneous junk. I find the light switch and flick on the bulb. There are nooks and crannies tucked up under the plumbing and dark floorboards. I can hide my stash up in here with no one having a clue, then shut my rented garage down. The felonious dope will be outside our actual living quarters, but within easy reach. It's the perfect lay-out.

I ride around until I find a corner payphone, dial the landlord, and arrange to meet. I've already decided to rent the place and move out of the old storefront. I feel certain that my brother Evan will be good with it. Borrowing Donny's '56 Ford hotrod, I transfer my stuff over in a couple of trips – my army pack stuffed with clothes, boxes and pine orange crates of boots, tools, camp gear, treasured books and notebooks, the typewriter, a few dozen 33 rpm albums and my portable suitcase Hi-Fi. Next, on a roll, I move Evan in from Santa Monica. We tie his single mattress onto the car roof and transport his belongings over the cross-town streets and into the hillside neighborhood. We order bottled water home delivery from Arrowhead, then, under the cover of night, I ride my stash over on my BSA and hide it deep in the funky basement.

Evan scores a job at the Orange Julius stand near Vermont and Hollywood. The friendly woman hires him on the spot. It's the perfect gig from five in the afternoon until midnight, providing steady cash and all the fresh-squeezed orange juice we can drink. Except for his sneaking lust for glazed donuts, Evan has more or less adopted my raw food diet. When I make my nocturnal rounds of the madman dives and doper haunts, sometimes I cruise by and we drain a quart of orange juice together. He tells me stories of the weird characters that populate this east Hollywood area, we snort and laugh. The only downer to this gig is that Evan has to cook greasy burgers on a grill, breathing through his mouth, fighting the dry heaves, but that's the hangup with all straight jobs. You're expected to do hideous work and pretend that's okay, no matter that you may be poisoning people. This fucked-up society is designed to coerce and manipulate you, and leech your soul into an ink-stained fingerprint. And people fight and justify and die for this ludicrous bullshit?

WAITING OUT THE shifting court dates down in San Diego, my life becomes an outlaw race by day, a glimmering hallucination by night. I replenish my psychedelic treasure trove on a regular basis, wanting nothing to do with a straight job. To be honest, I love living on the edge. I'm always able to put my hands on whatever I need whenever I need it. My constant roving around on a motorcycle is paying off, either through Arlene or this other dude I've met who restores and sells Alpha Romeos, and buys and resells hundreds of hits of my acid to his clients. I'm centered back in my celibate yoga discipline and Arlene has accepted this, sure that she'll get another chance when I'm weak. She's cunning and seductive, but the little bitch is moving a ton of acid for me in the safest possible way. She travels in various social circles and the psychedelic craze is in full swing. It pervades west coast culture, music, art and fashion, the unifying motif of new-age publications such as the L.A. Free Press and the San Francisco Oracle. All at once everyone wants to be high and hip, it's almost laughable. People are swallowing everything from morning glory seeds to baked banana peels to Datura thorn apples to get high. But I'm still in possession of the holy grail of psychedelics—the fabled Owsley purple barrels and the ultra-pure Sandoz, supplemented with the Orange Sunshine and the Windowpane coming from the Brotherhood of Eternal Love. My reserves fluctuate, but my Newport/Laguna connection is as good as gold. It's hard to swear off when you're having so much outrageous fun. And without a doubt the scene is changing.

Social tripping has become the favored high now, the mystical uses of Lsd pushed aside. Weekend hippies, day-tripping dilettantes, new-age libertines congregating in night clubs like the Whiskey or the Fillmore blow their wigs on psychedelic rock. They come together in spontaneous Love-Ins and Be-Ins in the city parks where thousands of people tune into love, peace, and happiness. It's an amazing social phenomena and seems mostly positive. Being on the drug-bust money hustle, my own use of psychedelics has changed. I rarely go for the deep, inward trip anymore, I can't afford to check out. I need to keep my senses focused, my wits together, moving hundreds of doses as anonymously as I can. I've cut back to a few mild, blissful doses a week, even trading my high-octane acid for liquid vials of mellow, watercolor mescaline. This way I stay high, cruising the crest, but without the cerebral flash-out. I glide all over town on my A65 Lightning in a groove, never hanging around long, avoiding the smack users, methedrine maniacs, and barbiturate droolers like the plague. I know who I am and who I trust, seeking those aware beings who have their act together.

But in reality, all acid heads often get caught in "that bizarre and hilarious moment," where things turn so weird that it defies explanation. I see many outrageous and deranging and implausible things. I stop at a famous Hollywood delicatessen for their delicious toasted bagel, cream cheese, slice of tomato and red onion, taking a bite, a swig of black coffee, looking around, to flash on the fact that the restaurant is filled with scarfing animal heads on human bodies – nervous coyotes, greedy baboons, lizards, pigs, poodles and quarrelsome parakeets. I stare at them in amazement, some stop eating and arguing and suspiciously stare at me. They seem to know that I know. My waitress peers at me with the face of a giant hamster. It's so astonishing I almost spew my half-masticated bagel all over the table. Laughing to myself, I wrap the bagel in a napkin, drop some bills on the table, and split on my bike.

One night as I cruise through the lamp-misted Hollywood streets, I see a red corvette roll through a stop sign and transmogrify into a slithering tube snake with a bizarre corvette snout. I idle at the red sign, all alone with my friend God, until the demented laughter subsides. One's face aches from laughing so much. In the wildflower phantasmagoria of every acid trip, there occurs at least one salient moment that sends you off into uncontrollable mirth. Every trip has that mythical peak moment. And in my mission to unload my bountiful stash, amusingly enough, a stash that I keep replenishing, I'm getting caught up in the madcap carnival of illusion and I can't pretend otherwise, nagged by the feeling that I'm putting off something very important.

I RIDE BACK home right around dusk, the neighborhood is tranquil and empty, as usual. I have never even seen a cop car in this area, it's the idyllic dopers retreat. I kickstand the Beaser on the sidewalk, carrying across the plank walkway a sack of bananas, avocados, rye bread and raw peanut butter. The weathered railing runs wild with purple bougainvillea, the doves call from the Eucalyptus hillside, and far to the west the ocean clouds a calligraphy of mauve shadows and orange brushstrokes. Our red and white windsock luffs from its tall pole, from inside I hear a Hindustani sitar raga.

The door is not locked, something I don't like. Evan is striding around the room glowing like a Christmas tree. Sandalwood incense, the plangent strains of a Ravi Shankar fill the room. My brother recognizes me, throws his arms wide in welcome. "Oh man, this acid of yours is incredible! I've been walking in India for hours, in the countryside, and talking to the yogi saints!"

I can only laugh in appreciation, this is Evan's first full-blown trip. A flood of inspired words rush out of him as I crumble a piece of oily Afghani hash onto the screen of our silver pipe. Listening, I have to ruefully admit that day-tripping doesn't compare to such mystical epiphanies. I've gotten caught up in the Alice-In-Wonderland phenomena out there, now my trips are less vivid, and more like a flickering movie I've already seen too many times. I resolve to go on an acid fast for awhile, then put the sacrament back into the psychedelic experience.

As we smoke the fragrant hash, we hear a sudden plop from the bathroom. Evan, who is on his feet with his pant legs rolled up because he has been wading in the Ganges River, goes and peers through the bathroom door. Pushing the round tip of his nose with his index finger, he says, "Incredible, there's a big hole in the bathtub wall. There's a black square hole going right into nothingness."

Suffused with the hash-hish, I go see for myself, and indeed, there is a dark hole in the plywood sheath that encloses the bathtub. One of the panels has popped out, about a foot square. Using a flashlight, I see some pipes and under the pipes the space falls away into the cave-like basement.

Making sure there are no black widows in the gap, we probe the bare sloping earth about eighteen inches below the hole. We fiddle with the square panel and find that with a little pressure it stays in. Aha, now I can move my canvas bag of goodies up from the basement and stash it right under this loose panel. No more comings and goings down the hillside that could arouse the suspicion of nosy cretins. My stash will be within arm's reach under the bathtub, but there still won't have any dope inside our living quarters. A cloak of serendipity falls around us.

ARLENE SIDLES IN and out of my life like an ocelot on the make. She's moving hundreds of hits of acid for me and refuses to take a single dollar for herself. She doesn't want money, she only wants to fuck me and I won't let her. The erotic energy between us is like a live wire, she seems to thrive on the constant arousal. But I stay up on my yogic high horse, keeping her at arm's length. I'm not giving into her audacious tricks again. I'm not going to ransom myself for another one of her soul-ravishing throat jobs.

Arlene claims that she's not this way with other men. She thinks I'm torturing her on purpose, with some kind of mad scheme. She comes around in the most provocative outfits, frilly frocks with low-cut blouses, bare-foot and braless in schoolgirl skirts with white unbuttoned shirts knotted at her navel. She shows up around midnight in garter belts and thigh-high stockings, tempting my rebellious, swollen, tormented hardon. Her generous mouth painted opulent red, her sultry eyes mascara temptations, the tip of her tongue teasing her lips. She has shaved her childless vagina, except for a petite blond tuft, and shows me, asking if I like her this way? Ayy, what a wild little game! But still, I hold myself aloof, and she keeps the game going by moving my dope. Arlene is the root cause of my disturbance, she mocks my spiritual aspirations, she hungers to give me lascivious head. She is my profane and utterly desirable and devious Lilith.

One late evening, across the street, below the city water tank, we sit in her red Fiat Spyder. She's complaining about how vain and self-absorbed most people are, nothing is straight on anymore. Everything you want has strings attached, life is bobby-trapped. Where did all the real people go?

"What real people? What gives you the idea that people are real? Since when?"

"Oh fuck you, Jake. You're strung out too, you just won't admit it. You are so narcissistic, don't deny it."

She goes on like this and I indulge her, she's just laid another three hundred dollars on me. I've almost got my lawyer paid up. Arlene squirms, puffing on the hash-laced number I've just rolled. Her breasts spill from her lacy chemise like suckable melons, her lips like lollipops, her mini-skirt riding up around her delectable thighs. If things were different, I sure as fuck would, but things are the way they are. Arlene always knows the score.

She wants me to initiate something, I can feel her impatience. I hum the refrain and quote her a few lyrics from Dylan's 'Desolation Row', a song that is a revelation for me. I believe that at any moment we can shatter the lock to our farce and set ourselves free.

Arlene studies me with a petulant expression. The shadows from the lamp-lit tree play across her nympho-angelic face. Playing with strands of her hair, she says, "You and your hippie-save-the-world shit, give it a rest. It all turns to nothing, don't you see that? You can't save people who don't care about being saved. Everyone's greedy, Jake, just flat-out greedy. They're in it for all they can get and it's fuck you, and fuck me, and fuck whoever. Nobody cares if you get screwed over. Lsd and yoga aren't gonna change that, and you never will."

I lift my eyebrows. Her voice has taken on a weird edge, like something unhinged trying to get out. "Time to get real, Arlene," I say. "You have no idea what's coming, even though you think you do. The times are definitely a-changing, that's as plain as day."

"Get real? You're such a ridiculous dreamer, you and all your mystical bullshit. That's not real, none of it means anything. And you know what? You need to give up that pansy-fantasy stuff and try some real drugs. Snort some blow, be a real man. Shove your thick dick down my willing throat, feed me cum and heroin."

Laughing in whorish delight, she reaches over to squeeze my cock. I swat her hand away, saying "Fuck off, Arlene. Coke? Is that your trip, cocaine? I've been wondering what makes you so strange, and why you never listen. Cocaine will kill you, baby. Cocaine will kill ya but they don't say when, cocaine's for horses, not for men. And not for anyone who wants to become self-realized."

"Oh fuck, what would you even know about it?" she retorts. "You don't know me, not even close. You think I'm this confused chick who's lost her bearings. That is so fucking hysterical! Oh I could open your eyes, Jake, give me one night my way and I'll open your eyes. I dare you, just give me one night my way!"

Feeling an eerie shudder down my spine, I say, "What are you babbling about, Arlene? You flipping out on me? Never mind. Just go on home."

"Oh man, you don't get it at all," she titters, "I'm not Arlene, I'm not that little cunt. You don't even know my real name."

Warning lights go off in my brain. Who is this broad? Watching me, Arlene begins to leer in a sly, deranged way. Clearing my throat, I ask, "Okey dokey, so you're not Arlene? That's sort of funny. Then who are you?"

"I'm Eileen, Jakie, Eileen, I'm the one who's really me. Arlene is just this namby-pamby slut that shares head-space with me. She's likes to run around doing favors for guys like you, sucking cock for approval. Isn't she pathetic? I let her play, oh yes I do, but she makes me throw up."

Arlene/Eileen, whoever this bitch is, bursts into a blood-chilling giggle, drawing her skirt up her thighs to her navel, giving me a perfect look at her shaven mons venus.

"All right, I think I got it, you're Eileen," I say, thinking Fuck, I'm dealing with a whacked-out bruja witch. "So what's your role in this intriguing scenario?"

"What's my role? Oh I'm the little cunt's boss, that's my role. She doesn't do anything without my say-so. And just so you know. I rule her silly precocious world."

"I see, far out. So she is like your obedient puppet?"

Ignoring my question, Arlene leans close to me, offering her ripe body. "And my game is to open your eyes like they've never been opened."

"Uh huh, of course it always takes two to tango."

She swirls her tongue over her coral lips. "Too bad you're so afraid."

"Well, to be honest, Arlene, Eilene, I think you're fucking insane, whoever you are." Putting my hand on the door lever, I say, "You've got way too many loose marbles."

"No, Jakie, no, I'm your hot little fox. I'm dripping wet for you. I'm the chick who gives you the best head you've ever had and swallows every drop and I know you want me to."

"What the fuck are you really after, Arlene?" I counter, weighing what she does for me against her obvious dangerous insanity. Seems like a good time to call the game over.

"Oh, that's simple. I want you to come over to my house in Lincoln Heights and take a trip with me. My kind of trip. Come do horse with me and let me suck you off. For at least one night let me change your world. Just let me have my way with you and I promise you'll never be sorry."

"Horse. As in heroin? Jesus Christ, now you want me to shoot up with you? You don't hear a single word I say, do you? That explains a lot. You are a crazy, junkie, bitch."

"Oh don't get mad, baby, I listen to you, really I do. But now I just want you to play with me, play my way. It's the grooviest thing you can imagine and I promise you'll thank me, you'll really thank me."

She's almost in my lap, trying to unzip me, my mewing slave, my shameless slut, my decadent lust, my oblivion. I shove her off and leap from the car. Taking a wild breath, heart thudding, looking into her sensual, resentful face, I say, "Listen to me, Arlene. Stay the fuck away from me from now on. Whoever, whatever you are, just stay-the-fuck-away-from-me. Our business is done. You got that?"

"You can't just push me away like that," Arlene shrills, "you hippie cocksucker! You'll be sorry!"

But I'm already walking off, her demented laugh in my ears as I walk over the planks to my door, glad that Evan is at the Orange Julius stand tonight, glad that I can be alone and slough off her vibes. A breeze is coming through the Eucalyptus above the city water tank, rustling the branches, rustling the dry weeds, fluffing the windsock, scattering portents into the darkness.

# Chapter 34

T HE SMOGGY HEAT begins to loosen its grip on the Los Angeles basin, the balmy light of Indian summer floats in off the ocean. This change brings a kind of peace to the frenetic city, although the shorter days makes me feel sad. The peerless days of summer I love the best, the long endless light. I would abide in summer for always if I could.

But in the interim, that space between what I would do and what I am doing, the bizarre shit keeps coming down. I take a few trips to San Diego for the required court appearances. I borrow a car for these trips so I can show up in a sport coat and tie, my hair trimmed to collar length. These tense moments result in trail postponements, and it's all in Audrey's hands. All I do is appear with a shaved face, clear eyes, and an earnest expression.

Bones has gotten out of jail on a substantial bond that was raised by unknown friends of his. I see him only once or twice at Veegee's place. Bones regards my beardless face and shorter hair as though I'm some kind of apostate. I don't bother to explain. If you're smart you get it, if you're obstinate you beat your head on the same old whipping post. These chance encounters are awkward, I feel judged by these protective friends of his who are not my friends, none of whom rode the border with us. Veegee lights sticks of rose incense, hoping that we'll reconcile. I did not visit Bones while he was in jail, and I had my reasons. But what's done is done and there's no going back.

One late night I run into him at an underground coffee shop near LACC, and he says to me, "You know, I've thought a lot about what went down. I had all that time in there and I couldn't figure out what went so wrong. When I got out I did some research. I recast our horoscopes for that exact three-day period, right? And whew, it blew my mind. You were under so much astrological stress that whole week that we had no business being anywhere near that border. You were being afflicted by a heavy-duty grand cross and a major hostile opposition. The catastrophe was inevitable."

"Really? That's your take on it?"

"Yeah, man, we never had a chance."

For a moment I just look at Bones, considering. I remember in vivid detail what happened. I remember what Audrey said, that chances are we had been fingered and betrayed by someone who knew too much. But I don't mention these things. Instead I say, "Bones, you can throw those horoscopes out the window as far as I'm concerned. They're just another form of brainwashing and limitation. The world fell in on us that day because you wouldn't listen and we weren't paying enough attention. Just that simple."

I wish him good luck in his own court case and walk into the night air, to kickstart my motorcycle. Hindsight is meaningless, hindsight can make any theory fit. Without present sight, without real insight, we are lost.

FEELING ISOLATED, BUT motivated by the impulse to find answers, to gain some measure of control, I prowl through the huge downtown library. In the metaphysical section, among hundreds of volumes on theosophy, zen, yoga, mysticism, Buddhism, and arcane occult philosophy, so many imposing tomes, one slim blue book stands out to me. The Psychology of Man's Possible Evolution. The author is an obscure Russian named P. D. Ouspensky who died in 1947. Taking a seat, I read a few pages, and the light goes on inside my mind. I read of an unknown system of Self-Awakening called The Fourth Way, originally taught by an Armenian mystic named George I Gurdjieff. Gurdjieff himself had learned the system from nameless masters deep within the Asian steppes and in Tibet before World War One, then brought the teachings from Russia into Europe.

For the next few weeks, I immerse myself in studying the radical Fourth Way teachings. Abstaining from acid and mescaline and even pot, I dive into Ouspensky's In Search of the Miraculous and Gurdjieff's Meetings With Remarkable Men, and it's like a door opens up inside of me. Gurdjieff taught this esoteric, hidden science in the 1920's and '30's, until his death in 1949. When he died, his body turned purple and stayed in an uncorrupted condition for over a month, at which time they buried him. His radical ideas about conscious human development have the same revolutionary impact on me that Dylan's lyrics had a few years earlier. Misunderstanding peels away like an old skin. My consciousness is set ablaze. This is what I've been hungering for.

I read aloud key passages from In Search of the Miraculous to Evan, who flashes on them too. Gurdjieff's singular Octave Theory and how the *law of random accident* rules the affairs of men like a blind scourge. The original intent of any plan is invariably deflected, by accidental events, in effect sabotaged, either by ourselves or someone or something else. The initial impulse gets deflected into counterfeit paths that often lead to disastrous consequences. Darkly funny as it seems, this clarifies for me what went wrong on the border. Whether we were ratted out or not, whether I was astro-cursed or not, the real problem was our lack of coherent awareness of the looming pitfalls. Like sleepwalkers, Gurdjieff points out, who cannot even hope to escape. Only the man who is awake can sidestep these disasters, can neutralize the whip of karma. Only the human being who has been awakened can actually shape events. Everyone else is at the mercy of bitter accident, to a maddening series of blunders, doomed to struggle under this unconscious spell called *Fate*, subject to endless war, tragedy, poverty and disease, living and dying like dogs, forgetting over and over what we only half-knew. This is what Gurdjieff called *"The Terror of the Situation."*

Aiyee, this radical philosophy hits me like the proverbial lightning bolt. These ideas make extraordinary sense to me, although I cannot say why. Evan and I study the Enneagrams, the aphorisms, and the self-remembering techniques that "G" recommended and passed on to Ouspensky and his other disciples. We read and ponder the enigmatic clues left by this strange who composed sacred dance music, who seemed to draw his teachings from the Central Asian shamans, the ecstatic Sufis, and from the magicians of Tibet. Catalyzed, I venture into G's 1200 page opus, *All And Everything, or Beelzebub's Tales to His Grandson.* This is my new road, there is no turning back.

At the apex of this mystic-intellectual frenzy, our studio apartment is littered with dozens of books opened to key, relevant pages. We tape "self-remembering messages" on our walls and mirrors in order to stimulate our awareness, to become one of the highly exalted. We take a voluntary, dope-free sabbatical because Gurdjieef himself advised that all mind-altering substances be set aside. The pearl of great price cannot be gained in that way.

No, the tricky process of one's conscious evolution from an ego-deluded sleepwalker into a super-conscious being can only occur when a unique energy has been accumulated. This energy, this prana, has to be produced inwardly and stored, then applied at specific gaps in one's progression of growth. If this is not done with the right knowledge, or done in a haphazard way, all the power stored is simply wasted, and once squandered, you slide back into semi-conscious ignorance and no lasting change takes place. The ego cannot prevent this, the ego can do nothing on its own. You are merely a bewildered buffoon, an automaton calling himself a human. Consciously-Directed Evolution is essential if one wants to escape such a worthless fate. But this can only be accomplished with the help of a Self-Realized Master – *A living, self-realized master is the key to transformation.* All the metaphysical studies, yoga practices, sacred mantras, meditation techniques, ardent prayer, will fall short without that direct initiation. But first a shock is needed, and that shock can come in many ways, including psychedelics.

Lights and bells go off in my head, insight flashes in my mind. This is why my own well-intended efforts to become superconscious have really come to nothing. I cannot sustain any transcendent awareness by myself, and the psychedelic boosters are transient. It's like I'm on a self-replicating spiral that goes up, then comes floundering right back down. Yet there has to be a way out of this mindless, carbon-copy, brain-washed society. Gurdjieff spoke lucidly about drugs and psychoactive plants. He said certain organic substances can provide man with a special chemical key that unlocks the door to a higher perception. But these higher-octave plants provide only fleeting glimpses, unstable flashing moments in another dimension of awareness. Without advanced training no permanent change is possible, all you are doing is rearranging the furniture. In fact, G asserts, the habitual use of psychoactive drugs can lead to permanent damage to one's neurological ability for real, transcendent growth. Aiyee, I read this with a certain grim apprehension, something inside me dodges and squirms. What is at stake here, if not super-conscious evolution? Perhaps the time has come for me to make some major changes.

Gurdjieff throws out a radical challenge that I can't ignore. Evan and I realize that we have chanced onto something of ineluctable value, and decide to put these it to the acid test. Breaking our three-week fast from psychedelics, we split one Sandoz tab and devote ourselves to the contemplation of Gurdjieef's extraordinary concepts. We close the books, giving our imaginations free flight. On the hi-fi, we stack long-play 33 rpm sitar and aoud ragas, to invoke the spirit of reverence as the pure psychedelic elixir infuses our nervous systems with its luminous force.

Using the kitchen wall as a spacious white canvas, we scribble the complex, multi-faceted, Fourth Way equations above the fold-down table, a kind of esoteric code that pours through our consciousness as the energy rises.

Revelation spills onto that wall, intricate flashes of insight, the miraculous conversion of life-force via pure diet, active meditation, self-observation, and sacred sounds that translates the pranayama into divine perception. The secrets of the Law of Octaves spill forth, unlocking to our perception, covering the wall in rarefied script, exposing the gaps of illusion, the transcendent self-revelation, God Is, God Is Ever-Present, This Thou Art. The wall becomes a hologram of irrefutable knowing, the links self-evident and brilliant, as if drawn by some supernatural intelligence.

After several hours of intense absorption in this metaphysical flow, we step back. We see It. We have have broken into the upper room and translated the evidence of a superior state of consciousness, of Being. We are deep into the miraculous investigation now, and not the same men who began.

"That's it," Evan says in awe. "There's no doubt, no doubt, Jake, can you dig it? And we can't ever forget. We can't let ourselves forget."

"You're so right, my brother," I say, "we can't ever let ourselves forget. Now we know, and we know what to do. Now it's up to us to make it real and keep it real, for always."

Evan goes into the front room and puts on some haunting flute music by Paul Horn. I sit there at the fold-down table, marveling at what we have accomplished. It's all there illuminating on the kitchen wall. I recall how my Laguna Beach chemist Charlie used to rave over his mad mathematical insights that he had scribbled all over a big black board while tripping on a thousand pharmaceutical micrograms. Charlie proved to himself the living existence of God, and now I laugh in profound empathy. That is exactly what Evan and I have done, here on this white wall. I know it will fade, this preternatural luster, but it's lucidly imprinted in my cerebellum now and I can find it when I need it.

Time has flown, the illusion of time, the fictitious cycle of the clock. We are deep into the night now, the hallow hours before dawn. There comes a knock at the door. Evan and I exchange a glance of disbelief, not ready for any intrusion into this sacred space. The soft knock comes again, along with a muffled, recognizable voice. Evan cracks the door, as I sit sphinx-like at the kitchen table. Bones Osgood stands there in the doorway, in a lambent, friendly aura. He greets Evan with a soul-shake, even as his eyes seek my own eyes across the room. We have been uneasy with each other since our border ordeal, a rift persists between us, our trust has not been rekindled.

But this remarkable moment feels different, his sudden manifestation in the exaltation of our Gurdjieffan acid trip. Evan told me that Bones had come by the Orange Julius stand, discussing new-age ideas. Maybe Evan had mentioned where we lived? Now he stands at my door, my companero of the Oaxacan high road. My essence does not hesitate.

Rising, I walk across the dividing space and we embrace. This man and I took a journey that few people will ever know. Evan watches is in silent respect, knowing every detail.

Looking into Bones' wounded eyes, I say, "Good to see you, my friend."

"I almost didn't find you," he smiles. "These streets around here are so convoluted, and it's dark. Then I spotted your motorcycle on the sidewalk and a light in the window, and I figured this had to be the place."

"Well, you're timing is far-out, Bones. We're just coming off the peak of this most amazing acid trip."

"Whew, yeah, wow, I can feel the vibes. Owsley or Sandoz?"

"Sandoz. Still have a little of that precious stuff left. We each dropped a full dose after fasting, you can imagine, eh? Come on in here, I want to show you something. Dig what Evan and I put up on the wall."

We all go into the kitchen and gaze at the hieroglyphics covering the white wall. "It took us, not really sure, hah, but maybe three or four hours to conceive all of that. That spontaneous formula verifies the living existence of God, right here, now, always present. But until we tap into the source-consciousness above and within us, and stay tuned in, random accident rules our lives. Anything can happen, like the shit that hit us at Tecate. Unless we're tapped in, our intentions are randomly sabotaged. But dig, this diagram reveals our potential to be divine, to become super-conscious, yeah, dig it. But to get there an ancient science has to be activated. It all works according to this concept called the Law of Octaves, here, right here, see it? that governs all human consciousness and growth. There are critical gaps – you could even say stumbling blocks – between the 3rd and 4th tones, right here, and here again between the 7th and 8th, where the next ascending octave takes off. But this is how seekers get tripped up, their initial intentions get deflected, confusion sets in, energy falters, and crazy fucking things happen. Sound familiar? Bones, that's how we got so messed up. Maybe if we had stayed up in Huautla? Maybe we might have made it through these gaps into another plateau of awareness, but who knows? Most people get side-swiped by their karma in these gaps."

"Far fucking out," Bones murmurs, staring at the wall, trying to piece it together with what he knows. "Man, you guys really flashed all the way out."

"Or all the way in, far, far in."

"Yeah, dig, Bones," Evan says, "we've been researching these Russian mystics Gurdjieff and his disciple Ouspensky. Incredible ideas, ideas you've never heard of before about the pathetic human condition. And this is the actual map of how we can consciously evolve into transcendent awareness."

"Aiyee, without any doubt," Bones quips, "the writing is on the wall!"

Bones flourishes one of his finely rolled joints. We light up and share a hit, then Evan turns back to his music. Bones serene eyes take in the cryptic equation on the wall in profound respect. We nod and confabulate, knowing it's all true—the cosmic flash-in, the curtain flung back, the irrefutable truth, but only for those who have made the trip. I don't want to talk about it much, words fritter away the revelation. I can already feel the energy dissipating, that special energy that enable us to "see."

Bones doesn't hang out long, sensing that we are still on a private frequency. We give him a few hits of acid and an Ali Akbar Khan record, then I walk outside with him. The faintest glint of dawn shows above the San Gabriels to the east. We lean on the railing side by side in the cool air, the street lamp enveloped in its corona of mist.

"I don't know what's going to happen," Bones says in a pensive voice. "Audrey says I should be ready to do at least a few months inside because of that sales-to-a-minor shit. What's weird is I still don't know who it was, or if that chick even exists."

I place my hand on his back. "You'll make it through it, Bones. This is an incredibly fucked-up world we live in, a world of injustice and stupidity, but you'll be okay. And I'll tell you this – I'm committed to finding another way. We've got to find another, better way through these flaws. And if that means tearing the whole rotten thing down and rebuilding it, then so be it. Rebuilding it with love."

"Right on, man, I hear you. And I'm thinking you're probably right about Huautla. For awhile there we had time stopped, you know? I wish I had just brushed those fleas off. We got off on that other track and really got out of synch."

"Ah, de nada, Bones, forget about it," I say, embracing him. "Let's just get our act together again. Let's get ourselves back into the sunshine, let's create a new world. I'm sorry I didn't come to visit you in jail. I will be praying for you, bro'."

"Me too, Jake, me too, for you," he says, his face shining, his eyes brave. "Keep it lit, my brother. Let's keep the faith lit."

"Oh I will, you know I will. You too, you too, my friend."

I watch as he walks over the plank ramp into the lamplight at the corner. He flashes me the peace sign, then drives off in a beat-up VW bug with only one headlight. I smile, knowing that he'll put that crate in good running order in no time. But I don't know when I'm going to see Bones again. Our cases have been split apart, we won't be meeting in court. We are caught in the cruel vortex of the system now, fending for ourselves, trying to scramble clear. It's a lonely feeling, knowing you're all on your own and dealing with the luck of the draw.

Coming off the acid flow, I lie down in that placid exhaustion that follows a full-bore flight, alone, Evan is sleeping. For awhile I drift between thoughts and images. Sometime after dawn, I go quietly back outside. The scarlet windsock hangs listless on its stave, radiant coral and golden clouds are crowning the distant San Gabriel mountains. I walk across the street, duck under the pipe gate, take the gravel path past the water tank and onto the dry slope beneath the tall eucalyptus. The scent of the dusty leaves permeates the air. I gather a batch of the tapered green leaves, meaning to rinse and dry them later for herbal tea. Back To Eden, we have to get back to Eden. I sit on the hillside in the rising sunlight, listening to the city, my heartbeat, the waking birds, the shadow of daybreak streaming toward the sea.

# Chapter 35

ONE MELLOW NOVEMBER morning I ride over and visit Donny and Annie in their always migrating apartment. I'm feeling more relaxed these days. I've sold off most of my illicit stash, the frenetic pace is easing. My first quarter at LACC is about to kick in and I've been approved for a work-study grant of $2000, plus a student loan of $2500. For the first time since the Tecate bust, without dealing, money will not be a challenge. I'm in the mood for some mindless, aimless fun, and there's no better fuck-off pardner than my old friend Donny Kubiak.

Donny and his chick Annie have been bouncing from pad to pad, living on the funds his doting mother doles out and on part-time jobs that Annie picks up, then soon quits. Annie has wanted a rambling, beatnik lifestyle ever since I first met her back on Chicago's northside, grooving to Dylan protest music. Now she's living that dream and her James Dean fascination with Donnie still flickers, although she's getting a tad burned out. But she's a loyal girl and that's the beautiful thing about most chicks. They stay close to you right through your changes and Donny is an unrepentant slob, hah. He has no ambition other than to stay stoned and seek perverse pleasure. He wants enough bread for a fat lid, some booze, cigs, cheap rent, hamburgers and onion rings, and gas for his bellicose Ford 429, but nada mas.

"Where there's dope, there's hope," remains Donny's devil-may-care motto.

"Don't you ever want to transform your scene?" I tease him. "Don't you want to realize something different, something unusual?"

"Naw, not really," Donny smirks. "I just want to be in my groove, man. I want to fly under the radar and do what pleases me. And it's better to be sort of average, you know? Because then, when you're average, more or less normal, you don't stand out. And when you don't stand out no one hassles you."

It's a weird philosophy but it's typical Donny. In fact, I laughingly call it the Kubiak "lazy doper anti-philosophy." A while back he sold his Norton 500 single, but now he has another bike. He finagled his mother into springing for a '63 Triumph TR6 on the promise that he would enroll in college in the spring, which he will not do. Such fey promises are like dollar bills to a reprobate like Donny, a currency of convenience. His TR6 has only one carb, no match for my race-tuned BSA, but still a tangerine and cream beauty. We all take a long, curving ride out Sunset to the beach. Annie clings to his back, stoned in her doper shades, her long hair sun-swept in the breeze.

The lovebirds are crashing in a run-down stucco building, a kitchen-ette studio with a double floor mattress, a black and white TV, transistor radio, three folding chairs and a folding card table. Greasy fast-food bags and beer cans litter the place, odious ashtrays, unwashed dishes, at least the windows are open. And I find them both in a strangely agitated state.

"Bad things are happening in this building," Annie tells me, her eyes anxious, hugging her pear-shaped breasts with clasped arms. We once got it on together on a snow-blown Chicago night with Coltrane, Sonny Rollins and Thelonius on the turntable, sharing a large straw-basket bottle of Chianti. Donny was off somewhere on one of his benzadrine and booze benders. That delicious little secret has always between us.

"What are you saying, Annie, bad things? What's going on?"

Donny taps his foot on the stained carpet, snapping his fingers to Sam and Dave, slouched on their mattress. His baby-blue eyes study me in a restless way. Donny probably wouldn't care that I had sex with Annie, he'd just figure that I owed him. But Annie doesn't answer my question. She makes a face, then looks over at her boyfriend.

"Well, fuck," Donny grimaces. "I made the mistake of getting high with some kids that live around here and now shit's coming down. I'm on the hot seat. One of them got popped for selling reds and yellow-jackets, stuff like that."

Smiling, I say, "You're an asshole, Donny."

"Maybe. But it's turned into a bad scene, Jake."

I consider this, knowing Donny like a dog-eared book. And I always know when he's lying.

"There were cops in the hallway this morning," Annie blurts, "asking people questions. I'm afraid he's gonna get sucked into it."

"For Christ's sake," I say, "man, you've got to know better. Reds, Seconal? Downers are for losers, Kubiak, don't tell me you're mixed up in that garbage."

"What, me? Hell no, come on, you know me better!" Donny darts his eyes back at Annie, then back at me, looking for support. "But you know I like to carouse around. Jake. Now I'm afraid one of those punks might point the finger at me, just to cover their own asses."

"Cause he's older," Annie adds, "so he's easy to blame. And he's always generous with his pot. They could lie and say Donny is the instigator."

"Huh, I dig it," I reply, piecing the scene together. "And just how old are these people? Are we talking juveniles?"

"No, not like that, eighteen, nineteen, more like," Donny mutters, slumping on the mattress beside Annie. "But just young and dumb, you know?"

Oh yeah, I do know, and he knows I know. Donny's been sniffing after some peach-fuzz pussy, while pretending otherwise to his girlfriend. Annie's actually quite intelligent, but she can be dumb as a brick. She has eyes, but sometimes she doesn't want to see what's what.

"What do you think we should do?" Annie pleads, her amber eyes beseeching me. She smooths her silky brown tresses down her breasts, hoping for, what? I don't know, maybe hoping that she still turns me on. She looks desperate and deliciously amoral.

"Okay, dig, both of you, you can't stay here, right? Not with the cops rooting around. You need to clear out of this place, disappear. Just pack your stuff, take the car and the bike, and split. What's so complicated?"

"We don't have anywhere to go," Annie whimpers, her eyes tearing up.

"What the fuck? Just go get a room somewhere, hole up for a week. Then get another place far away from here."

Leaning against her lazy boyfriend, Annie begins to sob. Poor pretty, frightened girl, quite sexy too. She's smarter than him but lets him make all the key decisions. That's their major hang-up.

"Yeah, I hear you, professor," Donny says, "but that's the problem. I'm down to my last twenty, flat busted till my old lady's next Western Union. You're right, we need to vacate this rathole pronto, but look." He fishes out his wallet and shows me his last two tens and a few ones. I know that Annie is between her musical chair jobs, so yeah, they're up against it.

"And that money wire's still a week away," Annie wails, "and we're afraid to ask for extra. His mom thinks Donny's got a regular job at the 7-11."

Hearing these words, I crack up. The idea of Donny having any kind of job at a convenience store is hilariously absurd. I laugh, pointing at him, tears welling out of my eyes, a deep funny-bone laugh.

"Yeah, Jake, fuck you," he laments, smothering his own laughter. "I shoulda been watching my p's and q's, I know that. And I realize you got your own heavy shit to deal with right now, but can you give us a hand? Just for a few days, until my bread gets here?"

"Yeah, I can and you both know I will, fuck off. You got gas in the car and the bike?"

"Damn straight. There's a half tank in the Ford and the trumpet's small change."

"Cool. Then let's bug out of here before the cops come back. You can crash at my pad, Evan will be good with that. Stay with us for a few days. Just pack an overnight kit, and in the morning come back and get your suitcases and other stuff."

Annie throws herself on me, clinging like a needy, sensual doll. "Oh thank you, Jake," she whispers, "I'll do anything for you, oh yes, please."

"I owe you one, man," Donny says, ignoring her, giving me a thumbs up. "I owe you a big one."

"De nada, brother, let's just get rolling. That story of yours makes me nervous."

Donny jives into motion, gathering up his dope and pipe and roach clip. "Annie," he snaps, "dammit, get some shoes on, pack a bag, you take the car, I'll ride the bike over with Jake. We gotta get a move on!"

"I'll wait outside for you. We'll all ride over together, an easy caravan. Hah, and tonight, we'll all get stoned just like in the old days."

"Sounds A-okay to me," Donny grins. "Like your man says, everybody must get stoned!"

AND WE ALL get royally ripped. We light the night up like the former care-free times, stoned and laughing, toking joints, smoking hash, drinking beer, listening to loud rock and jazz and soul that insulates us from the paranoia-driven world. Annie wants to know why my eyeballs are so bloodshot all of a sudden, and I reply, "That's why I only light up behind closed doors anymore. Something happened, some kind of psychosomatic allergy. But in the lugubrious eyes of Big Brother, I'm supposed to be reformed."

Har har har, Donny scoffs. "Too late, way too late. No, that will never happen."

We break into contagious laughter and it's good to be joshed. Annie sashays around in a blue halter top, her smooth naked belly teasing us, passing out chocolate-chip cookies. Seized by the munchies, we eat everything on hand and I remind myself to behave.

In the morning, we consume strong coffee, dates, and peanut butter toast, and sort out our plan. Donny wants me to ride with him to collect fifty bucks that someone owes him, which he wants to split with me. I let him talk me into riding with him on his Triumph, so he can show it off. Annie and Evan will take the Ford back to their studio flat and collect their belongings.

"Keep your eyes open over there," I advise Evan, "just get in and out, don't dally."

"Oh no sweat," he assures me, "I'm not even gonna sit down. I'll bet that we're back before you are."

Evan and I take a few minutes and go over our own apartment in detail, our paranoid ritual. We clean away the stems, seeds, roaches and pothead debris, dump it in a sack and toss the sack in a can down the street. Zig-Zag papers, loose weed, and hash are put back into my canvas stash bag, then tucked into our hidey-hole beneath the bathtub. Donny watches with impatience, as I tap the square panel back into place.

Walking to his curbside bike, he says, "You've become super-paranoid, professor. I've never seen you like this before."

"Yeah, that's true. But once you've been busted at the border, facing ten to twenty, thing's get real weird."

Donny primes the 650 carb, the TR6 fires on the second kick with a mellow rumble, I straddle the bench seat behind him. It's a beautiful morning in Los Angeles, where winter doesn't exist. The sun is a shining benediction, the sky a blessing overhead.

"I can dig it," Donny acknowledges, and takes off. The white and tangerine TR6 is smooth and balanced, very agile, although the acceleration is only so-so. At a stoplight, he tells me he's run it hard, that it doesn't overheat, which is something my BSA Lightning tends to do at high speed. And all these Brit bikes leak oil, there's not a damned thing you can do.

We cruise over into West Hollywood, an area with 1920's garden courts, dusty palm trees, and fading art deco facades. Donny tells me there's a rich chick who owes him the coin, that she's expecting him to come by.

"How do you know she's expecting you?"

"I called her yesterday on the pay phone, before you came over." Backing the Triumph into the curb, he says, "Piece of cake, professor. We'll be in and out in five minutes, then let's hit a strip club and swill some beer."

"Hmm, tempting man, but no, not this morning. Let's make sure everything's right Annie and my brother."

Donny frowns, then says, "Okay, that sounds right. But shit, man, what do you do for fun these days? Do yoga stands on your head?"

"Hah, funny man, funny. Smoke a little dope with friends? But to be honest, since the bust, I haven't had much easy-going fun. It's been one strange trip day after day. But I still love to ride, Donny. You could say that's my main fun, riding."

We walk up the steps of the white stucco building and down a long center hall. There's fresh air coming in through the propped-open rear door. Donny knocks on the last numbered door, waits, then knocks again. "Little chick's a real stoner," he mutters.

There's movement on the other side of the door, but no answer. Donny tries the glass door knob. The door is unlocked, he pushes it open about a foot. "Sherry, you in there, babe? It's me, Donny. Sherry?"

"Yeah, in here, over by the stove," a muffled female voice responds.

We walk in and go over to the kitchen arch. A young girl slumps on the floor in a yellow paisley frock, against the cupboards, her long brown hair covering her face like a dirty veil.

"I'm sorry, Donny," she mumbles, slurring her words. She's either drunk or loaded, I don't know what. And she's young, too young.

Glancing at me, Donny says, "Sorry? How so? Sorry for what?"

"They made me do it. I had no fucking choice."

Slapping Donny on the arm, I say, "Let's get the fuck out of here, man, something's not right."

But Donny stands there, frowning. "Sherry, what the fuck babe? What are you saying?"

"I'm so sorry," she sobs, sagging forward in utter defeat.

Abruptly, I turn for the door. "I'm outta here, bro. Wait for you outside."

But no sooner do I step into the main hall than a stout, dark-suited man bursts through the rear door, flashing a badge, barking, "LAPD, LAPD, Narcotics, freeze!"

At the same instant another man, much taller, in a blue sports coat and shiny black pants, comes rushing down the hall toward me with a drawn revolver, shouting, "Stop where you are! We are police officers, freeze, you are under arrest!"

Poleaxed, my hands go up in immediate reflex. The burly cop rushes past me into the apartment, barking orders. I hear Donny yelp, "What the hell!" I hear him slammed against the wall and the little chick lets loose an anguished wail.

My mind races at light speed, it's a trap, Donny's been set-up, and I've gotten snagged in it. I make myself stay calm as the tall narc spread-eagles me, frisking me down. I hear a curious door open, then close. He asks me to empty my pockets, I do so, thanking my lucky stars that I left the house this morning carrying nothing, no joints, no acid samples, nothing. I'm clean.

"Okay, turn around," the cop growls, stepping back and slipping his gun into his armpit holster. "I'm sargeant Maragos, LAPD Narcotics. We know who Kubiak is and we have a warrant for his arrest. He sold barbiturates to that under-aged girl and to her friends. Now, the question is, who in the fuck are you and why are you here?"

Thinking fast, I reply, "Sergeant, I'm just here by accident. My name's Jake Acree, I have no idea what's going on here. My friend Donny invited me to take a spin on his bike. And just for the record, I don't touch uppers or downers."

"Oh, is that so?" Maragos says, ushering me inside the apartment. He jerks his chin toward the kitchen where Donny is being read his rights. "But what are you doing here right now, to see that wasted little chick, with that bozo?"

"Like I said, Donny has this new bike. He invited me to take a ride, I hopped on. He said he wanted to swing by here and collect some money he was owed, that's all I know."

Maragos smirks at me. "You expect me to believe that weak-kneed bullshit?"

"Sargeant, it's the truth, what can I tell you? If I'd known he was dealing, I wouldn't be within ten miles of this place. I can't afford these problems."

"Oh is that right? Give me one good reason why I shouldn't cuff you as an accomplice. And you better fucking level with me, Acree."

The burly narc is on his squawking hand radio, I hesitate for a heartbeat, knowing it's all on the line. Another bust, I'm dogmeat. "Okay, I'll give you the reason," I tell him. "You mind if we step back back out into the hall? I'll give you the low-down on my situation. You'll see why I wouldn't be here if I'd had any inkling."

"All right, hotshot," Maragos replies, stepping back, unblocking me. "You go first and this better be good. And don't try any funny stuff on me."

"Sargeant, I have no intention of doing anything stupid. I just want you to understand."

Out into the center hall I lay it out for this mean-ass cop, knowing I have no choice. I tell him what went down at Tecate, the smuggling bust, my pending court case, my student-status at LACC, my reforming steps, the whole barbwired fandango. Maragos the Narc listens with a predatory, ferret-eyed interest.

"All of this will check out, sargeant, all you have to do is check. That's why I can't afford to be messed up in this shit, it'd mean jail time for me. How was I to know what Kubiak was doing?"

"But you hang out with him, right? You gotta know something, don't bullshit me."

"No, I don't really hang out with him. In fact, I haven't seen Donny in over a month until just a couple days ago. We're on completely different wave-lengths."

"Uh huh. That still doesn't tell me why you're together now. Why, on this run to collect drug money, are you with him? Where do I know you from? What are you, his supplier?"

"His suppler? Come on, man, get real. I detest downers, I detest narcotics, speed, all that crap. My whole thing has always been psychedelics, only acid and weed, and that's it."

"Only acid and weed," Maragos badgers. "And you were nabbed cold for smuggling kilos, right? Smuggling pot, marijuana, hard-core felony rap."

Before he can go on, the burly narc puts his face in the door. "Kubiak spilled the beans, he's shitting his pants. He and his girlfriend stayed at his house last night. That's where they disappeared to."

"Aha," Maragos sneers, "so that's where the little orphan Annie is! We've got a warrant for her, too. We tried to serve papers on them over at their apartment this morning. Oh what a tangled fuck-up we weave, right, Acree?"

Swallowing hard, I realize that Evan and Annie must have avoided these bastards by mere minutes. "Like I say, sargeant, I don't know what's going on. Donny's an old friend of mine from Chicago, both of them are. They asked if they could stay at my place while they looked for another apartment. I said okay."

Maragos studies my face, reeking of stale cigarettes. "Okay, listen up, hotshot," he says. "You take us over there so we can keep this nice and neat. We pop Annie, we pick up whatever belongs to them, and I'll let you walk. I don't have any reason to believe or disbelieve you. But I'm gonna check you out, you can count on it. And if I find any devious shit? You're going downtown with me."

Donny comes out the door in handcuffs, shadowed by the other narc. The young girl is blubbering on the couch. She ratted him out, she squealed, now she's getting a pass. Donny's shocked eyes meet mine – grim and trapped, no way out. An imperceptible nod passes between us.

"Whatever you say, Sergeant Maragos, I'll take you on over there."

# Chapter 36

ON THE DRIVE over to my place, Maragos carries on like a swaggering ego-maniac. He crows about how he's busting drug-addled hippies all over town. Donny and I ride in the backseat side by side, he's cuffed, head drooping, mumbling how his mother's gonna kill him. They haven't cuffed me, haven't even arrested me, I'm just their captive. Maybe they're hoping I'll turn snitch and join the other belly-crawlers, but no fucking chance.

"Fuck yeah," Maragos gloats, driving, as his partner chuckles in sardonic agreement, "bunch of wasted peace freaks, stoned, stupid, sitting ducks. It's all part of the masterplan."

We park in front of my hillside flat against the traffic, and at once my worst fear is realized. Evan stands there in the open door, lugging a big beige suitcase inside. He glances over at our blue unmarked sedan with a puzzled expression.

"Who's that?" Maragos demands, swiveling his predatory head.

"My kid brother Evan. He doesn't know shit. He's just doing everybody a favor."

They release me from the backseat cage, leaving Donny cuffed and red-faced. Maragos rushes across the plank walkway in his shiny black pants, flashing his badge. I hurry to keep up, the burly narc stomping right behind me. Evan stares at us, open-mouthed. Maragos launches into his intimidating spiel, but I'm able to give Evan a play-dumb headshake. "Everybody get inside," Maragos orders, "get inside, inside, dipshit."

We all crowd inside the studio front room. Annie stands there, clutching her hands in bewilderment. Maragos orders Evan to sit in a chair against one wall, me to sit on the couch across from him. He thrusts a warrant in Annie's shocked face, hitting her with a barrage of questions.

Mumbling meekly, "I knew it, I knew it," she dissolves into tears. The burly cop recites her rights, then leads her outside to their sedan paddy-wagon.

With a preening arrogance, Maragos says, "Like I said, dumb sitting ducks."

He grabs their two suitcases, growling, "Don't either one of you assholes move an inch." Then he hauls the luggage outside, calling out to his partner.

In that fleeting moment I communicate with Evan, who regards me with huge eyes. "Donny got busted for selling downers. Play it cool, you know nothing. You're just helping them move."

Maragos struts back through the door. "Hey, don't talk, motherfucker! Who gave you permission to talk? You only talk when I say so, Acree."

He begins to prowl the room in his sharkskins, lording it over us, enjoying himself. He picks up our books, fingering various intimate objects, a ceramic Buddha incense holder, a rosewood box containing tiny seashells that Dawn collected, my turquoise leather wrist band. "So uh huh," he mutters to himself, "all the usual hippie shit. Cheap Indian sheets on the wall, Oracle posters, fake Persian rugs, yogi books, all the faggot psychedelic crap."

Taking it all in with a look of disdain, he queries, "Tell me, Acree, if I tossed this place what would I find? What kind of dope you hiding in here?"

"No dope at all," I reply, "nothing. This place is clean."

But Evan's eyes go wide, and to my horror I notice that the hole under the bathtub is open. The panel has been removed, the black guilty gap in plain view. Annie must've given Evan some pot and he stuck it in there, but didn't seal it back up. Holy fuck.

"No dope, huh, no acid on ice," Maragos badgers, moving into the kitchen, poking into the fridge and freezer. He steps back into view, snatches a little brass pipe off the end table. Sniffing it, he says, "Eh, what's this boys? I smell hash, yeah, hash-heeesh. You realize I can scrape out enough residue to bust both your asses? So don't be fucking lie to me!"

"Look, sargeant," I implore, "I'm not saying I never smoke, okay? Because I do now and then. But what I'm saying is that because of what happened to me, I don't keep any dope around and my act is clean. I cannot afford anymore trouble."

"Fuck, don't make me laugh," Maragos retorts, "I can smell it, Acree, you're hiding something. You're not what you say you are." Turning on Evan, he says, "And what about you, punk? What's your story here? Show me your fucking I.D., you gonna lie too? You wanna get popped for a dirty pipe?"

"Look, officer," Evan protests, flustered but holding his own, "I don't even know what's going on. I thought we were giving Donny and Annie a place to stay for a couple nights. I've got a regular job over at the Orange Julius stand on Vermont, I don't even smoke pot and my brother's enrolled in college. Why are you coming down on us like this?"

"Oh well, mercy me," Maragos mocks, "you're just an innocent dummy?"

"I've been straight with you," I tell him, bringing the heat back on me. "I've laid out my whole situation for you. You can check it out, it'll all check out. What in God's name do you want?"

"Naw, cut the crap," Maragos says, his ferret eyes taking in every inch of the place. "You're hiding something. I heard about you, I know you from somewhere, don't try to con me."

He moves to the bathroom door, panic rises in my chest. "Hey, what's this?" he mutters, his back to me.

"It's our bathroom. What's it look like?"

"No, smart-ass," he snorts, coming round on me, "don't wise off to me. What's that hole under the tub?"

Shrugging, I reply, "It's a plumber's access. We keep having trouble with that drain. The guy said it's a mess under there."

"Oh yeah? Well, let's have a look, smart-ass." He gets down on one knee, peering into the dark hole, with a bloodhound instinct. Evan and I exchange a desperate glance. Crazed ice-pick images, wild solutions, flash through my head.

"Goddamn it," Maragos mutters, tentatively putting his hand in the hole, but only to his wrist. He probes, hesitates, draws back, mumbles to himself. The fact is that only fifteen inches below his hand, tucked against a pipe elbow, above the sloping dirt, is my stash bag. A short arm's length away, enough felonious acid, hash, and weed to send me away for years.

But Maragos the narc hesitates. I hear him mumble how he wishes he had a flashlight. Aha, I understand! I flash into his twisted, predatory psyche, I see into his head! The bastard is afraid of unseen bugs and spiders, of the lethal black widow that might be dangling in the gap! Sensing this, I pour all my concentration into the back of his Brylcreem'ed skull. I shoot lurid images of poisonous spiders and centipedes into his mind, praying under my breath. I share a wild-eyed glance with Evan. He bows his face, shuts his eyes, his palms turned upward in supplication. Deliver us from this beast, O Lord, deliver us from this fiend who would steal our lives!

Maragos squirms and draw back from the hole, muttering, "fuck it!" He scrambles to his feet, his snide face pale, dusting his knees, brushing his hands as if knocking off insects. He comes out, glaring at me. "You, you are now on my radar, Acree. You gonna slip up again, oh yeah you are, and I'm gonna be there."

I make an incredulous gesture, saying, "What is it with you, sargeant? I've told you everything, there's nothing more to tell."

He shrugs me off, glancing at his watch. "Anyways, right now, I'm taking your buddy and his chippie downtown to book their asses. But I'll be back around, hotshot, you can bank on it. You'll be seeing me again."

He struts out the door and strides up the plank walkway. Evan and I sit still, looking at each other, our eyes unwavering, ears cocked. We hear him pound over the ramp, hear the car door slam, we don't move until they drive off. Then we burst into jubilant laughter, we dance around the little house, a victory dance, because at least for now we have outwitted the evil ones!

After calming down, we check the street for any suspicious vehicles. I retrieve my stash and take it back down into the cave-like basement. I bury it under some old pipes and boards, promising myself to unload all my dope within the week. Maragos is hateful predator, he is to be feared. Then I take a bus across town to fetch Donny's stranded TR6 motorcycle.

DONNY AND ANNIE are bailed out of the slam within a couple of days. His mother bails them out long-distance, hiring a high-priced lawyer, then flies in from Chicago to take charge. She puts them up in a Los Feliz apartment, then hangs around to make sure they act right. I learn all of this about a week later, when Donny comes over to get his bike.

Rueful, eating chagrin, Donny says, "It's a bitch right now, man. My old lady hovering around, I can't even tap a six-pack, let alone get high. And now all of a sudden Annie is siding with her, saying we need to do a major clean-up."

"What, really? That's bizarre, man.Sounds like a tricky scene."

"No, no, things are just all fucked up with this bust. I dunno. But thanks for going after my bike, I was afraid it'd get stolen. I was hoping you'd get it."

"Glad to do it, man. I wasn't about to leave that pretty trumpet hanging out there."

I lay a few joints on Donny, saying, "Here, smoke 'em when you can, I'm unloading all my dope. What's your lawyer say about this scenario?"

"That's the good news, at least. He says it's a first time offense, plus it's my word against that airhead chick. All they actually got me for was possession of a half-dozen reds. The worst I'll get is probation for a couple of years, if even that."

"Could be worse, Donny. Could be a lot worse. And that Maragos is a bad-ass sonofabitch."

"Yeah, tell me about it. And listen Jake, there's something you need to know about him."

"He's a ruthless bastard, I already know that."

"Worse than that, he hates your guts. All the way downtown he's ranting about how he's gonna bust you, how he's gonna send you up for hard time."

"You kidding me?"

"No, no exaggeration. Said you were at the top of his shit list."

"But why? For God sake, what's his trip? He doesn't know me from Adam."

Furrowing his furry blond brows, Donny says, "Not sure, man, all I know he's got it in for you bad. He kept grilling us but we kept our mouths shut. Maragos thinks you're some kind of major dealer."

A chill shivers down my backbone. "Say what? Who does he think I am?"

"That's just it. From what I could tell, he thinks you're a main pipeline for psychedelics into Los Angeles. He kept saying you're a key player, he'd heard of you, he's gonna bring you down. Man, it was freaky, let me tell you. But anyway, please be on your toes."

I watch Donny as he rides off to his own trick bag, warning flags ripping through my mind. There's no doubt that I have made a mortal enemy in Maragos, one ruthless bastard. Keeping my word with myself, I sell the balance of my stash within a few days, at a discount. I set aside only thirty hits of pure Lsd and a half-ounce of Afghani hash for my own use, which I seal in a pint jar, wipe the jar clean of prints, and bury it in the dirt floor of the basement.

Dealing off my stash, I pass another week living on the freakish edge. I ride out in the mornings, assuming Maragos might be around, and make zig-zag patterns across town in case I'm being tailed. I figure they can't really track a fast bike as long as I keep moving through traffic, cutting away on side streets, always moving as I make my rounds. I don't return home until after dark, coming back into the neighborhood from different angles, scouring the streets for anything unusual. I ride with my day's stash tucked inside my left boot, ready to dash and rip it out and toss it. I've reached that clear-burning edge where paranoia is like a drug in itself. When I look in the mirror, I'm shocked by my somber, hawk-like visage. But I know that just one false step, and they'll come down on me like raving hyenas. It's not a matter of hating cops, hate has nothing to do with it. I am a lion of God and they are my sworn enemies.

Then late one evening, something extremely suspicious does happen. I ride down the street past the Eucalyptus trees, past the sere field and water tank, idling in neutral with my headlamp off. The streetlight at the tee-intersection is haloed in its misty penumbra, and I see by the light in our window that Evan is home. But my instincts flare. A dark sedan sits catty-corner from our door beside the fire hydrant. In the hazy light I make out two shadows in the front seat, their backs to me. Idling, I roll right up beside them, glancing inside. Two men in suits stare at me in total surprise, one's mouth open. I hear a muffled, "Aww shit," even as the driver fumbles at the ignition. These fuckers are cops, even though I've never seen them before. Rolling right on past, heart leaping in my chest, I drop the A65 Lightning into gear, tip a hard left at the tee intersection, then race off downhill through a maze of streets, never stopping, never slowing, just going, going, going. And in the night skies above east Hollywood and Silverlake police choppers ply the air, whop-whop-whop-whop, their prowling floodlights invading our sanctuary streets. But this is police-state California, this is war.

I swing back homeward in about an hour later, the scene seems back to normal. After doing my number down in the basement, I go in and tell Evan we're being staked-out by plain-clothes cops in a dark blue Dodge and they could be anyone, maybe even Feds. My brother, who's sitting reading Yogananda's 'Autobiography Of A Yogi', stares up at me with brooding eyes.

He leaps up, waving his hands like he's trying to chase off demons. "What are we gonna do, man? We can't live like this! This is insane, fucking insane! What are we gonna do?"

"No, I dig it man, I understand, calm down. And what we're gonna do is move. Yeah, in the next few days we're gonna get out of here when nobody's looking. We're gonna find another place back in these ambiguous side streets. So start packing."

Evan claps his hands in relief. "Cool, right on. Then I'll take a notepad and walk through the area on my way to work. I'll write down any info I see on the rent signs. And I'll come home a different way and do the same search."

"Perfect," I say, grateful for his response. "And I'll ride all over tomorrow, looking myself. We'll find a place and steal away under cover of night. And don't worry, all the dope is almost gone. We'll be clean and incognito in no time."

"Who are these fucking bastards?" Evan rants, gesticulating. "What gives them the right to hound people like this? We're not criminals, we're people, we're peaceful beings! How do they get off playing Jehovah?"

"It's the system, Evan, the system's rotten to the core. The system makes the obedient right and non-conformers wrong. The system lets egomaniacs like Maragos strut around like demigods, flaunting their bogus authority. Anyone who's different gets smashed. Anything they fear gets smashed. They make all these bullshit laws that turn people like us into criminals."

"But that's totally fucking wrong, dude," my kid brother howls, "that's a total lie! Who needs this fucking system? The system is Satanic!"

"Right on, I know it," I laugh, impressed by Evan's intensity. "And no doubt about it, the shit's coming down hard. It's a criminal war against free people, cracking down on people because they want to smoke an herb, they want to get high and explore new ways, busting people because they dare to live differently. Their only real god is greed and fear. Bombing the third world into the stone-age in their filthy, imperialistic wars. They're turning America into the new Roman empire. This whole evil machine has got to be stopped, you dig? We have to bring it down. It's crushing the love out of the entire planet."

"Yeah, man, I got it, I understand," Evan affirms, clasping my hand in a soul-shake, my brother on the shining path. We snake the hashpipe out of the hidey-hole, where it dangles on a clear nylon string in a tangle of pipes, already pre-loaded. We fire up the oily Afghani hash and calm ourselves down. There's something glorious about living on the outlaw edge, where you're responsible for your own true freedom. No one can take the truth of yourself from you. Fuck this counterfeit, robot society.

And in the morning I ride out, searching, alert as a wolf. Cruising the hilly streets, I come across a for-rent sign in a garden court back on a secluded cul de sac. It's no more than a half-mile from our studio flat, but a whole different vibe. The vintage stucco walls and stained red-tiled roofs, the step-up courtyard with flowering shrubs and lush foliage, even a few avocado trees. The hand-lettered sign says, "Two bedroom apartment, partly furnished, $125 month, damage deposit required. Garage available." I write down the phone number, then ride to the nearest pay phone and make the call.

The florid landlady meets me over the lunch hour. The place for rent is tucked in the back of the court, up a series of steps, sheltered by green plants. As advertised, it has two decent bedrooms, a chamber she calls a sewing-room, a spacious living room with an easy chair and a coral satin couch. The kitchen has better appliances, with a sturdy dining table and three chairs. Every room except the kitchen is carpeted. Compared to where we've been living, this place is a palace. Right out the backdoor, there's a row of single-car garages with wooden doors and hasp locks. The available garage is filled with old furniture and sealed boxes. Draped in her white caftan, the landlady says she'll clean it out and rent it for an additional $25.00 a month. I tell her that I don't own a car. I ride a motorcycle, and my brother walks or rides buses back and forth to his work.

"The garage is a nice extra," I agree, "I would like to get my bike in off the street at night. And just like it is, there's enough room for my bike and maybe a few more boxes."

"All right," she says, fanning her chubby face "and your point is?"

"Well, how much would you charge me to use it just like this? Just for my bike, and to store a few things."

Appraising me, she considers, then says, "Nothing, as long as you're willing to sign a six month lease and give me a hundred dollar security deposit. And you have to make sure that nothing gets lost or misplaced in this garage."

"Wow, that would definitely work for me. I'll keep it locked tighter than a drum."

Scrutinizing me from head to foot, she asks a series of direct and pertinent questions. Trying not to seem too eager, I answer patiently. Yes mam', my brother has a full-time job. Yes, I'm a full-time student on a work-study program at LACC. No, we don't do drugs, no mam', I am not a party freak, etcetera.

"I don't like turn-over with my tenants," she tells me with hopeful eyes. "That's how I'm able to keep the rents reasonable. It's a very peaceful complex. Are you sure you're not thrill seekers?"

"Oh no, not at all. My brother and I read a lot and we're both into meditation. This place is perfect for us. I'll be in school for the next two years, full-time, and my brother's the night manager at the Orange Julius. Partying is not on our agenda."

"No crazy girlfriends?"

"Nope, no girlfriends right now," I smile. "Just don't have time for one."

"Hmm, I find it hard to believe you don't have a girlfriend. But you do seem like an honest young man."

"I am honest, I am for sure, and so is Evan my brother."

"Okay, then I'll take a chance on you. I'll require the first month's rent and a hundred dollar cash deposit. I'll refund the deposit after the first six months. Is that agreeable?"

"Yes, mamm, that's totally agreeable. And when could we move in?"

"Meet me over here at noon tomorrow to sign the rental agreement, give me $225 plus a five dollar key deposit, and the place is yours. I'll have two sets of keys made for you. In the meantime, I'll take the sign down. Fair enough?"

Oh more than fair, dear lady, and may I kiss your fat hand? No, actually, I just shake her hand, give her two hundred dollars on the spot, then blaze over to the Orange Julius stand to share the news with my brother. He and I celebrate with a quart of fresh-squeezed jugo de naranja.

Two nights later, right around midnight, we disappear from the old pad like smoke on the breeze. We tote our stuff over the hill, on foot, to our new digs. Some raucous crows have bothered the neighborhood all day long, but now they sit in silence in the dark trees as we trudge past. It's relatively hard work, we make seven hikes back and forth carrying our gear. We leave behind most of the junk furniture, except for two coffee tables and a thatch-back chair. Nomads don't carry much, and nomads leave few traces. For the former landlord I leave a note taped on the fridge: 'Sorry about the epiphany on the wall. Keep the remaining rent, the furniture, and the $50.00 deposit. Thanks.'

Evan and I are jubilant as we settle in. Our new apartment is cocooned away from street, surrounded by flowering foliage, an avocado tree beside our red-tile porch, a mystic's sanctuary. We decide to transform the so-called sewing room into a meditation chamber, using one of the low tables that I lugged uphill on my head as an alter for candles, incense, and esoteric artifacts. We throw some tribal rugs over the shag carpets, hang some Indian bedspreads, tack up Oracle posters and Tibetan Mandalas to the eggshell walls. We can breath here, we can relax, we feel safe. Outside, in the world, reality is what it is, but in this refuge we can keep it all at bay.

# Chapter 37

MY DAY IN Federal Court comes at last, in San Diego, in early December. I stand convicted of the failure to pay import duties on illicit, unspecified contraband, a charge that carries a penalty of from two to ten years in jail. But Audrey Morgenson's lenient judge suspends the sentence and imposes three years of supervised probation on my humbled head. I listen with a contrite face as he reads the stark terms, but inside I'm dancing with gratitude. The prison gallows will not be my fate, and it's all the handiwork of my brilliant lawyer.

Audrey says to me, with a happy smile, "Merry Christmas, Jake. You know what you have to do. Stay in school and keep your act clean. And remember, you can't go into Mexico or even near that border. If you do and they find out, they can revoke your probation and put you behind bars. So play it by the book. Within a few years your slate will be wiped clean."

I thank her profusely, promising that I'll keep my part of the deal. I don't even mention the incident with Maragos, I don't want her to know. I mean to be done with this harrowing game of new-age outlaw, I've had enough.

In parting, Audrey says, "I hope I have no reason to see you again, Jake Acree. You have been one of my distinctive cases. And just know I'll be wishing you all the best."

"Thank you so much, Audrey, for what you've done and for trusting me. From the bottom of my heart, I won't forget."

Yet, I know that whatever is out there, it's still trying to bring me down. That predator who never sleeps keeps laying its traps. It knows that I'm still free and running around at will, and it hates that. This I have to remember at all times.

ABOUT TWO WEEKS after New Years Day, 1967, I get a summons by certified mail from the U.S. Justice Department. How they managed to locate my new address I have no idea. The letter instructs me to appear downtown at the Federal Building, on a certain date, for a final resolution of my Conscientious Objector's Claim. It's the final step of my moral challenge to the Vietnam war, a legal appeal that has been going on for almost two years. Now, at last, I'm going to talk to someone face-to-face about my stand against this criminal war being waged in the name of the American people ten thousand miles from home.

The morning I go to down to the Fed building, I put on my only clip-on tie, my only white button-down shirt, and my only rust-colored sport coat with dress slacks, pretty much the same disguise I wore during my court appearances. I walk over the hill and take the Sunset bus, trying to quell the knot of anxiety in my gut. I carry some paperwork with me in a an accordion file. There's a man raving on the bus. An imposing black man in drawstring pants and collarless red shirt and house slippers in the back of the bus.

"It don't matter what is wrong," the man rants, standing up, talking to no one yet talking to everyone. "It don't matter to them, cause you always wrong and they always right, uh huh, and if you look you see. If you stop the pictures they implant in you, stop the picture show even for a minute, you see, oh yes, yes you do, you will. You wrong and they right, and they gonna make sure you obliged to cooperate. Otherwise you declared a persona non persona and you gonna be erased. Dat man with the big erasure do the erasing, and apparently we just gonna bow our little black heads and our white heads and our yellow heads and our meek heads and just keep taking dat shit, ain't that right? Don't matter who gets erased or what gets nullified. Who got all da dollars? Ain't that right now, well, I'm asking you, ain't it? Ain't dat right?"

I sit there riveted by his words, oh, I listen to his growling voice. His dark eyes gleam, he detects the smile in the corner of my mouth, we share a prescient nod. The other people in the bus stare out the window or at their brainwashed newspapers, wishing he wasn't there, staring down into the hollow of their lives. But the truth stands there raving and burning on the downtown bus, no more, no less. I would love to ride all day with this beautiful, crazy man, oh I would, yes I would, but today I cannot.

The Federal building is a towering, bleak monolith. I take the silent elevator up to the eighth floor and check in with the U. S, Department of Justice. It feels so strange, standing here, in the lair of the monster itself. A prim, gray-haired lady takes me down a hall and into an office with windows that look out over the smudged city of fucked-over angels. And they are here, those same two men, waiting for me.

The large man in a navy suit sits behind a polished desk, nods, "Please sit there, Mr. Acree." He indicates a straight chair on the other side of the desk, angled toward him. Another man, ironed into a charcoal suit, sits on my side of the desk, facing me. Observing how things are set up, I sit down holding my document file in my lap. In the file are copies of all correspondence to and from the Selective Service System over the past two years, including copies of my recent conviction papers on Federal smuggling charges.

Wanting to state myself, I say, "I recognize both of you. You're the two guys who staked out my house that night. I came up on you on my bike with the headlight off."

"Yes," the man behind the desk acknowledges, "you did surprise us. However, what we were doing was within the authority of our investigation into your claim of conscientious objector status."

"You spy on people, on other Americans, without their knowing it?"

"If it's deemed necessary to gather pertinent information, yes, although we don't consider it spying. What we are after in these cases is the truth of the matter."

"The truth of the matter?" I say, with a tinge of irony. "And what truth would that be—whether I'm a peaceful or a violent individual, whether or not I'm a pretender? How can you tell that by spying on my house in the middle of the night?"

"Mr. Acree," the gray suit interrupts, "this is the concluding stage in your appeal for C. O. status. We would like to stay on course and not get off on a philosophical tangent. We have our job to do, a job that is well-defined by federal law."

"Although we do get," the man behind the desk says, "why you might be upset about being under surveillance. But if you have nothing to hide, you have nothing to worry about."

Nothing? They introduce themselves by name and rank. I think to myself, if they only knew the half of it, or do they know, just how much do they know? The vibes are tense, these are LBJ's war-hawk henchmen. Composing myself, I ask, "All right gentlemen, so why am I here today? What is it that you have to tell me?"

The gray-suited man addresses me. "You have written in one of your verbose letters, and I quote, 'I consider myself a front-line volunteer for a new America, for a new world where we do not make war on other people or invade foreign countries because they disagree with our political ideology. I consider myself an apostle of Christ, a follower of Buddha, a brother of Gandhi and Martin Luther King. I believe that love and peace, not violence, is only way to live. The only path I can walk is the path of peace. I believe that all patriotic wars are basically false, they exist only to destroy someone or some other nation that doesn't agree with you. These are my true convictions, my own true religion. I don't have to go to a church to practice this, because that church lives inside my heart.' "

He reads my words in a dispassionate tone, without nuance. "Do you recognize those lines?"

"Yes, of course. I wrote that. It's what I believe, it's how I try to live."

"Be that as it may, I'm afraid you have failed to convince us."

Swallowing, I say, "Oh really? And why is that?"

"Mr. Acree," the man behind the desk interjects, "you express yourself eloquently, I'll give you that. However, it's our appraisal that your claim to conscientious objection lacks sufficient merit, and for that reason it's been denied."

"Sufficient merit?" I retort, anger rising in my voice. Almost two years of wrangling with these people, down the drain. "What does that mean? Why can't you accept what I tell you about myself?"

Shuffling his papers, the blue suit says, "Let me put it like this: we acknowledge that Paul the Apostle underwent a miraculous transformation on the road to Damascus. However, we do not believe that this has happened to you. I'm sorry." He slides a document across the polished desk to me. There's some kind of official seal on it, as if that emblem decides my fate.

I think hard for a moment. Inside, I feel a calm, clear rage. "All right, I get it," I reply, "You sit up here and decide what's true and untrue about my life, although you know next to nothing about me. And then you expect me to just get in line? Do you ever stop to consider how absurd that is?"

"It's the decision of the United States government, Mr. Acree, *our government*, yours and mine."

"I don't confuse *your* government with the love I have for my country. What does that paper say?"

"The document before you," the gray-suit drones, "which you are required to sign, instructs you to report immediately to your local draft board for a physical examination, and possible assignment into the United States Army."

"That's not going to happen, gentlemen. Not today, and not any other day."

"I beg your pardon?"

For the space of a few heartbeats, no one speaks. I listen to my own chiseled thoughts. The two men exchange a complicit glance, they figuring they've got me pinned. They are my adversaries, and in the end it always comes down to this, you against the Lie. Who are you, when the Lie confronts you? But my war is not really with them. My war is with the soulless government that owns them, and I see no end in sight.

Shaking my head, I say, "I am not going to sign that paper, that has no authority over me. And you both need to be aware of something that alters this whole picture."

"And that would be what?" the blue suit asks tersely. The other man leans forward in his chair, making sure that I can see his shoulder holster.

"That would be this." Opening my accordion file, I pass the man behind the desk a copy of my San Diego court judgment.

"I've been convicted in a federal court of a major felony. Smuggling illegal, undeclared contraband across the border. I'm under a three year probation on the order of that court. There's my probation officer's name and telephone number. That's all the proof you need. You can confirm it for yourselves."

The man behind the desk ogles the document, speechless. His gray suited partner barks, "Are you telling us that you're a convicted felon? When did this take place?"

"If you mean when was I arrested, it happened back in September. I've been in and out of San Diego court rooms ever since. I'm surprised your investigation didn't turn that up."

The gray suit gives his cohort an incredulous look. The blue suit passes him the court copy, saying, "It appears to be on the level."

Rising to my feet, I say, "You'll find that it's all genuine. I'm under the control of the Federal court system, and yes, I am now a convicted felon. And in the eyes of the draft board that makes me unfit for military service, an automatic 4-F. Correct me if I'm wrong."

The man behind the desk regards me with morose eyes. "Why didn't you tell us this right at the beginning?"

"Because I wanted my C.O. claim to be honored, to stand on its own. But it wasn't. So this other thing became my ace in the hole. And just for the record, so you know, so you can write it down. I'll never fight in that evil, immoral, criminal war, and I mean never. Take a good look in the mirror."

# Chapter 38

S O YEAH, THE bizarre irony, it took me getting nailed at the border and convicted of a smuggling rap, to spring me from the killing fields of Vietnam. In effect, I've been granted at least a three year reprieve from the draft. To put this sequence of events on an imaginary wish list would be hard to do. I celebrate my freedom by dropping a blotter of orange sunshine in the hills above Malibu, thanking the spiritual presence that guides me. The shining path opens again. There is always a secret way over, around, or through, but you have to have the guts to take it.

Over at Los Angeles City College, the campus is alive with revolutionary energy, an enclave of long-haired freaks and free-spirited bohemians. I fall right in stride with my liberal arts classes, the trip is a breeze. People told me that college in California is mostly free because it's financed by the state. That sounded like a fairy tale, but now I see it's true. There is money for the asking, with few strings. I've scored a low-interest student loan that doesn't need to be repaid as long as I'm in school, plus an educational grant that comes to me through a work-study program. Within weeks, at this intriguing community college where the aromatic fumes of weed drift across the sunny quad, I have in hand a windfall of $4500 dollars. There's no tuition for my classes, the only thing I have to pay out-of-pocket are for my books. The work-study program only requires that I work fifteen hours a week around the campus greenhouse, tending the African violets and Coleus plants, and raking a few leaves. I mean, for real? I have to laugh to think this is how I'll be doing probation.

Dawn writes long, endearing messages to me. She writes picture letters in her fluid, childlike scrawl. What am I doing, when will I come, do I still care? I visualize her reading the National Enquirer, giggling over the preposterous stories. But her letters go right to my stranded, lonely heart.

She never asks me for money, but I send her what I can, knowing that she needs it. We talk long-distance about once a month, me hanging in a street-corner phone booth, her voice wistful in my ear. I have no idea of when we're going to be together again, but her voice fills me with a soft effulgence. "Me too," I affirm. "I want to be with you, too."

She's expecting a baby girl in late February or early March, and if that holds true then Tia will be a Pisces like her mother and her dead supernatural grandmother. It is too surreal for words. Will she be a clairvoyant too? I have never wanted a child and never even considered raising a family. When I stop to imagine it, it feels like a suit of clothes that will never fit.

To avoid confusion, I stay focused on what is immediately present, the flamboyant, multicultural, mini-skirted college. I take a palette of humanities courses—Existential Philosophy, Classical Philosophy, Latin American History, Asian Philosophy and Asian Art, Psychology and Political History, and a peculiar course called Aesthetics, which is described as "the study of the theory of the beautiful." But this intellectual hodge-podge is stimulating and I argue with some of my professors, challenging their pet notions. If reality is so cut and dried, why is the world so messed up? Because the design is inherently flawed, or because we passively accept it as it is, and shrug it off? Revolution is in the air, revolution/evolution, and anything is possible. When the grades come out I pull a steady stream of A's, the occasional B, nothing lbut ower. These scores make me smile, because I seldom ever crack a textbook. All I do before any test is read the opening and closing paragraphs of the relevant chapters, then consult my class notes. I listen to what each teacher talks about in class, then write down their favorite themes. Feed those ideas back to them in coherent words on the tests and you ring the bell.

THE FIRST TIME I meet with my probation officer, Mr. Camillo, we strike a rapport. Camillo is a perceptive, soft-spoken Mexican-American with a shrewd glint in his eyes. He has studied my file and knows all the details. He tends to listen more than he speaks. After asking me what I had been doing in Mexico in the first place, he listens with rapt attention. I give him a vivid sketch of of my perceptions there, highlighting the Oaxaca experience.

"That is very interesting," he acknowledges. "So am I right in assuming that you're serious about this transcendental approach to life?"

Surprised, I reply, "Yes sir, I'm completely serious. It's my day to day inspiration."

"Well, as long as you keep away from the psychedelics, there's nothing wrong with that," Camillo says. "That can keep you balanced and focused, along with your school, until you're in the clear. My job is to help you get into the clear. But to get there, and I'm going to stress this, you need to disengage from the drug scene totally. You need to stay away from those people and those negative possibilities. Because if you don't, and I know from hundreds of backsliders, you'll probably land in hot water again. Also, you must stay out of Mexico and away from the border zone, that's mandatory. You can't even leave the state without my approval. We need to be on the same page here."

"Yes sir, I understand what you're saying and I'm already taken some key steps. I've already let go of most of those old relationships, I'm done with that whole scene. I want a completely new experience. And just so you know, I'm sharing a place with my younger brother Evan and he's not into drugs at all."

Yeah, I'm laying on some bullshit but I have to set the right tone. Camillo regards me with a favorable light in his eyes. "These things are important, Jake. The power of associations either lift us or drag us down, it never fails. If you set your mind to this new direction, you'll steer a good course. And if you do that, I'll cut you loose early. I'll cut you loose early and your record will be sponged clean. The Federal Youth Act, pretty nice deal, huh?"

"Yeah, incredible deal, I feel like I got real lucky. And let me just say, mister Camillo, I'm not going to do anything to screw this up. You have my word on that."

He reaches across the metal desk and we shake hands. Strange as it sounds, we seem to have an affinity. Hesitating, I ask him, "When you say early, what exactly does that mean?"

Camillo smiles at me in an almost lethargic way. He's a semi-balding man around forty, in a beige polo shirt and olive green trousers. His eyes are skeptical but not unkind, his voice has a friendly quality. Clearing his throat, he says, "Let's just say not before two years, but sooner than three. And here's what I'll need from you. You report to me once a month and update me on what you're doing, how your classes are going, your situation in general. Now, every so often, I'm going to drop by your house unannounced so don't be surprised. Just keep things in order. I'm not going to go poking around in closets or drawers, that's not my style. But I have to write regular reports about you and I want to able to write good ones. That's how I'll justify cutting you loose from probation early."

As this news sinks in, I nod, saying, "All right, I'll do my part. But I'd like to have your okay to do something."

"And what would that be?"

"Well, now that my trial's over and done, would it be all right if I let my hair grow back out? I don't like it this short."

Camillo gives me a lop-sided grin. "No, I don't mind. You can grow it out again, but don't get too radical on me. Remember, my factual reports."

"Okay, I appreciate that and thank you. I appreciate your help. AsI said, I don't ever intend to ever go through this trip again. It's time to create a new life."

My probation officer tilts his head, making some notes on a legal pad, then looks up at me.

"Did you play cowboy when you were a kid, you know, with the six-shooters and cap guns and boots and hat?"

"Oh yeah, hah, I sure as hell did. Two silver pistols, the sombrero, little fancy boots, the whole bit. A Daisy lever-action bb rifle, then, later on, I got a single-shot .22. I grew up as a footloose kid with a dog on eighty acres in the Texas hilll country. Another world."

"Well, how about that," Camillo muses, "I don't know why but I see you that way. Okay cowboy, you do your part and I'll do mine. Together will get you out of this wayward trap."

DONNY GETS OFF his nasty little bust almost scott-free. His mother secures the best lawyer her money can buy and in two brief court appearances the charges are dismissed. Her wastrel son and potential daughter-in-law are turned loose with no more than a stern reprimand. Sergeant Maragos flew into a rage right in court and was warned by the judge to shut up or be fined for contempt. Donny's ass was saved by the fact that the cops had no eye-witnesses against him, and he'd had the crafty sense to deny everything. It came down to the mumbling teenybopper's word against his, and under the treatment of his slick lawyer her accusation fell apart. The possession charge was dismissed and Kubiak walked out of court like a fresh-faced schoolboy.

As Donny relates this to me, I wonder how some people manage to squirm out of every asinine jam. Clearly money plays a major part, a fact I am coming to bitterly resent. Because what happens if you don't have any? The system is twisted and corrupt, no one can deny it. The poor keep getting shafted, sent off to jail for a bag of pot or trucked off to war to die for the real swindlers. The brave are hunted down for their desperate acts of independence. People pledge allegiance to a patriotic, skewered fantasy. And by some kind of fucked-up logic we're supposed to cooperate with this scenario? Cooperate with what?

Maragos came up to Donny outside the courtroom and spat, "Okay, fool. You won this round but if you stay around L.A. I'm gonna ruin your world. And that goes double for your renegade pal, Acree. You both make me want to puke and I'm gonna take your asses down."

Maragos is insane, the hackles go up on the back of my neck. Donny's mother overheard this livid oath and turned pale. The blowback is that now she insists that he and Annie return to Chicago with her, otherwise she'll cut him off. Lazybones Donny has to agree, even though he knows this means she'll force him back into college classes.

"The whole sit-chee-ation is overseas, professor," he grumbles, as we polish off a six-pack on my avocado tree shaded porch. "She won't even let me ride my bike back, she's having it shipped by truck. She's got me by the short hairs, but what can I do? I've got to go along with the gig until I figure a way back out here."

"Sounds really messed up," I josh him, "but you're incorrigible, Donny. At least you'll have your Triumph to play with. How's Annie doing in all this?"

"Not too happy. I'm not sure if I mentioned this, but Annie's pregnant. Yeah, three months. And just like Dawn she's not gonna get an abortion. And my mother knows, so that really nails me to the wall."

"Wedding bells?" I quip, smothering a laugh. "Talk about the unpredictable. When we left Chicago together we didn't have the slightest premonition of what was coming. Except maybe for that old man on the road in the rain, the lunatic prophet. Maybe that was a warning. Shit just comes on like a freight train. And what is that? Is that karma or just plain bad luck?"

"I told you not to pick up that black kid. That dew-rag kid brought us bad luck."

"Oh fuck, man, that's such bullshit and you know it. That kid Malcolm never gave us any bad luck. What goes around comes around, so if anything that was beneficial."

"Yeah, well, who knows, but anyway. We've got your address and Annie and me will write. We'll visit Dawn and give you the low-down on the Windy City scene. You're still my best friend and we need to stay in touch."

"Right on, Donny. You know I'll write back. Hell, I'll write you a novela of the latest weird happenings, if I survive them."

We sit shoulder to shoulder, laughing, sharing a fat roach as the afternoon sun filters through the slatted windows, suspending time. "And Jake, whatever you do," Donny says, "watch out for that prick Maragos. He's one crazy sob and for he's got it in for you bad."

"I hear you, yeah. I hear what you're saying, thanks."

And I do hear. Maragos the narc will go out of his way to bust me, even if he has to invent a reason. And they wonder why some people under revolt.


SO THEY HEAD back to Chicago, Donny and Annie, with his string-pulling mother in control. Dawn is already back in Joliet expecting the baby anytime. Bones is locked up behind bars for at least six months, they stuck it to him hard. I'm the only one who's still free and I intend to stay that way. New Age California is deep in my heart and soul now. I can envision Dawn and I getting back together, but it won't be back in those atrocious, dim-bulb mid-western winters, and it won't be here in Los Angeles. We need to be somewhere up in the country, around avocado groves, stony washes leading downhill to the sea and uncluttered, unsmogged blue sky. Back to Eden, we need to get ourselves back to the promised land.

In the meanwhile, Evan and I groove on the flamboyant local scene. We get together often with two black cats named Ray Vargas and Lon Caheres, and a young truth-seeker named Aaron Gold from NYC. Sometimes we smoke a bowl, sometimes not, sometimes we drink red wine, then talk for hours about the teachings of Gurdjieff, Maher Baba, Yogananda and Krishnamurti. We congregate in their upstairs flat in a flophouse near campus, on fire, demanding real knowledge, real correlations, real meanings, dismissing conceptual restrictions of any kind. We strip bare the great writings of every epoch—Pythagoras, the Upanishads, Mark Twain, Gandhi, Alan Watts, Martin Luther King, Loren Eiseley, Herman Hesse, Ranier Maria Rilke, James Baldwin, Emerson and Thoreau, Jesus of Nazareth, Gautama, Lao Tzu, Kerouac and Ginsberg Langston Hughes and Henry Miller, wildly reciting, enthralled with the gyrations of our brilliant new friendships.

At these inspired meetings we swear fidelity to a new way. The world cries out for change, true change, not political or religious lip-service. Racism, ignorant delusion, war the greatest crime, poverty, all must be abolished, make love not war, be warriors of peace, strive for peace! We realize the only ones who can do it are us, those who gather in this passionate kinship. If we don't have the courage to make it happen it won't happen. Tear down every wall, every barrier, every clever cop-out, every reason no.

When we get tired of rapping in the cramped studio that Ray and Lon share, we bring out the congas, bongos and tablas and we drum and chant ourselves into a humming trance.

My friend Ray Vargas is a tall Afro-American, gifted with a smile, always talking with his hands, delighted at our remarkable accord. When we first me, he said, "You've been to some unusual places. Tell me something unusual."

I thought for a moment, then said, "Gandhi says an eye for an eye and the whole world goes blind. And I believe that."

Ray's profound eyes shone with tears as he exclaimed, "Yes, yes, yes!"

His friend Lon Caheres is a lean, intense man with moody eyes, who declares himself to be a reality-seeking agnostic. He says all his religious faith got ripped out of him in the bloody rice paddies of Vietnam. "I was lucky to make it out alive. And you're right, war is shit, unbelievable, stupid, meaningless shit. I survived, yeah, but to be honest I don't think God cared one way or the other."

But John takes to the ideas of Ouspensky and Gurdjieef like a man desperate for water. He immediately goes out and buys Gurdjieef's daunting 1200 page opus, 'All And Everything,' and begins to decipher every convoluted page. It makes perfect sense to Lon that the world is ruled by random, ominous accident and that human evolution cannot occur in mass political or religious movements, regardless of fervor, but only in small groups dedicated to pushing the borders of consciousness.

The New Yorker, Aaron Gold, is already involved with yoga meditation. Aaron sought out the giggling guru Maharishi Mahesh and got initiated into Transcendental Meditation. Now he practices for twenty minutes every day when he's not reading, drinking espresso or wine, rapping, or smoking pot. That approach strikes me as rather lightweight, but it's his trip, not mine. Aaron met and talked to Swami Satchidananda up in San Francisco, whose presence made an indelible impression on him.

"Swamiji has this unbelievable aura of peace," Aaron confides, squinting through the hashish smoke. "He said that until we start loving everyone and everything around us, and especially ourselves, that the world will not get better. The bad things will just go on happening, our own lack of love will guarantee it, along with all the greed and hypocrisy and the killing. He says this stuff in the most serene, gentle voice imaginable, and I totally agree with him."

My brother Evan, a bit shy and reticent by nature, does a lot of listening in these spirited meetings. He's been reading deeply into Yogananda's teachings. He listens, makes a comment now and then, getting his footing. He believes like we all believe that a new world is being born, being born in us, being born in and through our camaraderie and passion for a real honest-to-god change. Tear down anything that is in the way of that change, anything blocking it.

One afternoon, in that upstairs space filled with drifting sandalwood, radical books and congas, Evan starts talking about things Yogananda said before he died in 1952. Evan relates, "One of the things he told his followers, one of his incredible statements, was that you have to prepare yourself to do God's great work. And he meant all of us striving to become aware. Prepare yourself to do God's great work! Can you dig that? Can you dig the power and implications of that statement?"

"Mind-blowing," says Lon, whistling his teeth. "Absolutely mind-blowing. But what does that actually mean? I mean, all bullshit aside, assuming there even is a God, what would be God's great work? Work that we could do?"

Running with that, I say, "All right, yeah, what would that mean for each of us? Each of us, let's say one thing. God's great work, what does that mean? Ray?"

"Universal love, universal peace," Ray Vargas laughs, waving his long ebony hands, "that, it has to mean that, and I'm all in!"

"Right, right on," Evan tosses back, "and no more discrimination, no skin-color crap anymore—no more you count but you don't, you get some but you can't have any, you're saved but not you, you're fucked. No more of that because we're all from the same Divine Source! Otherwise it'll always be insane and the insanity won't ever end!"

"There is a fountain," I laugh, tears welling from my eyes, "there is, there is."

"Right," says Aaron, "there is a fountain and we always will be that!"

"Yes," laughs Ray, "one true human family!"

"Beautiful," cries Lon Caheres, "so if there is a God, then God's real work has to be to stop, stop these horrible murdering wars. Stop justifying it, stop fictionalizing it, stop pretending they're noble, just fucking stop! Because it's all a gigantic goddamn lie!"

Aaron leaps to his feet, declaring, "Stop all the war forever! Banish all war and aggression from the face of the earth! They say it can't be done but why not! We can do it! Let love and peace happen! We wouldn't even need all these weird laws then, we wouldn't need any religions or police forces!"

"And quit raping our mother earth," Ray intones, holding up Rachel Carson's prophetic book, "quit poisoning the land and air and water in the goddamned name of profit! Let's get back to the reverence, let's get back to righteous living!"

"Yeah, right on, absolutely!" We all join hands, jubilant, affirming the fervent wish that has set our lives ablaze.

"And how, how do we do this, my brothers? Remember, the masters all say, that if even a small portion of humanity wakes up, wakes up and stays awake, then those people can change the world."

"Change, the, world, I totally dig it."

"I'm in, I'm in, I'm all in."

"Me too. No holding back, no bullshit, no rationalizing."

"So am I, there's nothing I want more."

"Then we all know now," Ray Vargas says, his eyes welling with light. "That's it, we just clearly said it. There can be no slacking off."

"Holy fucking shit," John laughs, reaching for his congas. "I'm really starting to dig this trip, I'm starting to see it. Let's put a beat to it, man, let's give it some rhythm."

And so here it is again, simple and clear and direct. The living love, the impeccable truth, revitalizing the very atoms of our bodies. Teach the Way to one another, teach it to me and you, and share it with anyone who'll listen. Don't falter, don't slacken, and don't ever forget. We owe it to ourselves. We are the highly exalted, keep this knowing like the holy breath of life itself.

# Chapter 39

I N LATE FEBRUARY, in this new year of 1967, halfway across the continent on the Black River Reservation, our daughter is born, Tia Velina Acree. Dawn went up to her grandmother's old place in Wisconsin to have the baby, with the help of two midwives. She sends photos in the mail, the girl-child is fair-haired and light-eyed like me, an astrological fish like her. I write back to Dawn, praising her and the precious infant. I send a photo of Paramahansa Yogananda's calm and radiant face, penciling on the back, "Show Tia this picture. Keep it by her bed."

"Evan and I," I write to her, "are thinking about leaving L.A. Going up to the country somewhere above Santa Barbara, live in an old house on maybe an acre or so and grow our own organic vegetables, melons, sunflowers, practice cosmic awareness with the birds of morning. I've been reading Thoreau and Emerson, the back-to-the-land movement really resonates me. We're tired of all the city hassles, we want to move into something new. We'd like to start a self-sufficient earth commune, where others can come and meditate and join in. Think about this for all of us, Dawn. Because I love you. Something like this is what I imagine, out here in California."

I let her know that my heart is open, that I'm willing, but I don't want her to have any illusions about my direction. I have never even broached such an idea with her before.

She doesn't answer me head-on in her scrawled letters of simple sentences. She's playing all her cards one by one, hoping to get what she wants, and that's the way she is. I make it clear that my native hippie instincts aren't vanishing, just evolving into a more Utopian trip. Still, I have to laugh for us both. For all I know she might have a new boyfriend who digs the kids and has a regular job. Maybe she doesn't really like the idea of being the concubine of a fig-munching yogi celibate, and who could blame her/ Not me, that's for sure.

I am on fire to move ahead with my intense perceptions, to achieve the revelations, to become a super-conscious Being of Light. I don't want to waste any more time. My mentor Gurdjieff apparently did not leave a well-defined lineage, and Ouspensky completely copped-out on him at the end. Inn spite of my deep affinity for the Fourth-Way teachings, I have to admit that Gurdjieffan Awareness did not transmigrate into my three year old brain at the time of his death. One can fantasize, one can pretend, you can assume, but then you have to get real. The world is full of pretenders and I have no intention of joining their cult.

So, facing certain facts, and sensing my brother's affinity for esoteric yoga, we delve deeper into the teachings of Paramahansa Yogananda. Swami Yogananda founded the Self-Realization Fellowship in the 1920's, stemming from a lineage of revered masters, developed his teachings, then dropped his corporeal body in 1952. The SRF did not fall apart, in fact, it continued to grow. The keys to leadership eventually passed to his female disciple, Daya Mata. Some of his disciples left the inner circle after his physical death, but Daya Maya had been trained by Yogananda himself in the transcendental science of Kriya Yoga. She lives at the main SRF ashram atop Mt. Washington, and with any luck, Evan and I might be able to meet her and receive darshan. At some point in your spiritual awakening you've got to take a chance, and we are taking ours.

We read and reread Yogananda's incredible Autobiography of a Yogi. We go and talk with the monks and nuns over at the Sunset Boulevard meditation chapel, vegetarian restaurant, and bookstore. We sign up for the monthly discourses that were written by Parmahansa himself, booklets filled with his spiritual wisdom, counsel and everyday advice for vegan and celibate purists, special exercises to revitalize the body, creative affirmations, and unique meditation techniques. After two years of this discourse study, with relevant practice, you become eligible for initiation into the sacred Kriya method. Yogananda said that the ancient Sanskrit Kriya mantras are the most direct route to the realization of God-Consciousness. But there is one little gut-checking catch to our happy hippie free-style life. Like Gurdjieef had advised, you have to be willing to give certain things up.

Yes, indeed, and in order to get the Kriya tonal initiations, *you have to give up all mind-altering drugs*. Dig it—no hashish, no psychedelics, no weed, no nothing. Aiyee, this challenge that I already knew was on the horizon, is smack-dab in our faces. To be initiated into the higher techniques, we need to become clean. We have to relinquish the wild, carefree indulgences. A part of me wants to rebel, naturally, but some things can't be put off. The only question now is when.

We ease ourselves into this new scene, seeing how it fits, at first trying to straddle both worlds. During the week I go to my philosophy classes, do my greenhouse gig, then hang out in the coffee houses rapping with campus acid-heads, new-age artists, Che revolutionaries and beat mystics, listening to the omnipotent jukebox—Dylan and The Doors, Love, Janis and The Dead, Jeff Airplane, Coltrane and Miles, Cream and Hendrix and the Buffalo Springfield. I ride home on my beloved BSA, taking a spin through the sunny Griffith Park roads, more in love with freedom than ever. And in the evenings, I do a little text book studying, then get into my real studies – Yogananda and Gurdjieff, Buckminister Fuller and Maher Baba, along with researches into organic gardening by the moonsigns and, in general, how to beat the devil for the highest stakes. Evan comes home after his Orange Julius stint and studies with me, deep into the night. We don't talk that much, we don't really need to. There's nothing going on except the game of super-conscious awareness, of unlearning all the years of delusional, conditioned bullshit that's been pumped into us.

The Self-Realization Fellowship on Sunset and Vermont becomes our personal retreat. We start attending the weekend services at their meditation chapel, listening to the orange-robed monks and nuns read Yogananda's inspired writings. His teachings encourage an unwavering love of God and dedication to one's own self-realization, nothing else comes first. And of course there is an element of vivid madness in all of this. Yes, a leap of faith, a blind devotion, a trusting vulnerability that I'm ill at ease with. Still, we throw ourselves into the resonant chants and hymns to God and the Christ-Consciousness that Yogananda himself sang, accompanied by harmonium music. We sit through the silent meditation sessions on the hard folding chairs, immobile, focusing into the third eye chakra, battling our scampering thoughts, our skinny asses numb and aching.

But what is especially weird is how we stand out in these spiritual satsangs! We're the youngest ones in these friendly congregations and the only ones with obvious hippie roots. Most of these folks are much older, many have been around since Paramahansa was still in his physical body. They take us in with a kind of bright-eyed affection, as if we are neophytes to be petted and fawned over. Evan and I don't hang around after chapel, it feels too strange. But we know there's something going on in these heartfelt gatherings that we need to grasp.

After a few weeks of coming and going, we strike a spark with a large, gentle monk named Brother Mokshananda. He is a friendly man with a square head balanced atop his flowing, orange robes. Mokshananda makes personal time for us whenever we show up, taking us into the rose garden to answer our questions. He stutters a little, his face smiling with empathy. His huge, spatula feet stick out from beneath his robes. He tells us, "At first, I know, believe me I know, the devotional aspect seems very odd. But keep at it and you'll see, something in your heart opens and saturates you in bliss. Just know that you're not here by accident. Master called you, that's the only way it happens. So, if you find yourself feeling a tad confused, just come here and meditate and we'll talk. I see the light in your faces, and I know it's not easy, the ardent devotion that Master encourages. But it's all worth it a million times over, I promise you that. You'll see, you'll see."

One of the orange-clad sisters who works in the Indian cafe tells us that Mokshananda was one of the last individuals that Yogananda himself initiated into Kriya before dropping his body in 1952. We feel remarkably energized by his personal attention, even flattered. Doubts swarm into our thoughts, but we begin to feel that we have found a way that might work for us.

THE DAYS FLY along. All is good, although all is not yoga-swirled peaches and cream. I still consider myself a glory-bound hippie in disguise. On the weekends we let our Dionysian spirits run wild, leaping into the tribal rites happening in the green, pagan city parks. We deck ourselves in flowing bell bottoms and swaggering pirate shirts, colored glass beads and shades and headbands, and head over to Griffith or Elysian Fields for the free-spirited, spontaneous Love-Ins. San Francisco has its Golden Gate Human-Be-Ins, L.A. has its joyful Love-Ins. Sometimes we hop on my BSA and ride over to these celebrations, other times we walk down the flowering hill streets to east Sunset and hitch a ride. Everyone hitchhikes these days, it's just a matter of sticking your thumb out. Hundreds, thousands of flamboyant freaks gather together in the verdant meadows to make music with flute and drum, fiddle, guitar, hubcaps, sticks, coming together to dance and sing and get wondrously high.

It's a giant tribal peace ritual up and down the coast, clouds of wafting reefer, we're all here, we are the new-age community, all skin colors, all types and creeds, making love not war, high on pot, acid, mescaline, and just the sunshine itself. The rhythmic congregation of congas and bongos, wooden flutes and tin cans, guitars and saxophones rises and swells through the glorious afternoon. So many people laughing and whirling under the blue skies, the green trees, in the flowering grasses, giving themselves over to the sheer love of life. I cannot capture these unforgettable hours, though I wish I could. They are like intoxicating sticks of clean-burning incense on a breeze that can never be traced.

One weekend, at an astonishing festival of ten thousand freaks in Elysian Fields, promoted by an underground FM station, ripped to the gills on my last exotic tab of Sandoz, I am pulled up on the stage into a wild musical session. All at once I'm exposed to the world, yet I'm supposed to be flying under the radar. An ego-maniacal DJ who fancies himself some sort of cosmic ringmaster stalks around the stage in narcissistic pomp. I am so enthralled in the pure rush that I have trouble keeping rhythm with the tree of tambourines that a girl thrusts into my hands The radio poseur freaks, bugging his methadrine eyes at me, gesticulating, but I shine him on. He thinks he is the catalyst for this wild human Love-In, but in reality he is an animated prop. Right in front of the stage are thousands of people whirling and dancing in Bacchanalian glee, stoned, half-naked and delirious. Hopping on one leg, I shake the tambourines and chant like a dervish.

"Good Lord," I say to myself, in awe, "what have we created? Did we mean to do this?"

Getting into the voodoo rhythms, shaking the banshee tambourines, I keep hearing my name being called again and again, down in the raucous melee.

"Jake, Jake, it's us! Look, we're back, we're back, down here, Jake!"

And lo, right beneath me, in front of the massive vibrating speakers, to my amazement, stands Richard and Sarah from Huautla de Jimenez waving up at me. No, incredible, miraculous, how can it be! We shout out our greetings. I pass the tambourine wand to the dancing girl beside me, spread my arms, and leap into the riot of flashing, whirling humanity to embrace my friends.

"They drove us out," Richard shouts in my ear, "the Federales came and made all foreigners leave! We had to leave most of our things, they only gave us a few hours!"

"Fuck, the rotten bastards!" I cry, "it's the same everywhere! The bastards are obsessed with controlling our lives! They're drunk on power! We have to break free and create a new world! We have to create a new way to live!"

We huddle together in the ocean of sound, with crazy smiles, laughing like long-lost family. "We've only been back a couple weeks," Sarah tells me, "we've been trying to find you and Bones but no luck until, wow, here and now. Talk about serendipity!"

Ah, now I must deliver the bad news, the heavy news, the unholy message. Taking them away from the speakers, I confide, "I've got to tell you something. We got busted at the border, Bones and me, yeah, nailed for smuggling, a real bummer. Then Bones got hit with a second rap, selling a bag of grass to a minor. He's still in jail at the San Diego Federal Detention Center if you want to visit him. I had no priors, no other charges, so I lucked out with probation only. But I've got to tell you, things have been super-strange since that day."

"Oh my God," Sarah cries, tears flooding face. Richard's mouth contorts, "Fuck man, what did they do to you?"

"Nothing, except throw us in the cage and threaten us with twenty years to life. But we got a very good female attorney, she really helped us.

We're gonna both be all right, we're just not the same. Nothing's the same."

We're almost yelling to make ourselves heard. "Oh God, I relate," Richard shouts. "Our lives were turned totally upside down, and we have no plans! We're adrift. We wanted to stay down there but they wouldn't let us. They're afraid of people who are different, afraid that we'll stir up the peasants, I guess!"

"They're all power-crazed greedy motherfuckers," I rave. "They don't care about the people! We have to forget about them, forget about them and move on!"

The three of us share a blown-away laugh in the boom-blast, another embrace, then Sara digs into her Mazatec bag, She writes down my address and gives me their contact info, which I tuck in my shirt pocket. They are beautiful, smelling of rose oil and peace and primordial dreams, but we're almost crying. We know we've lost something so valuable, lost that rough paradise in the Oaxaca Sierra Madre. We hang together for awhile, in that wild celebration in Elysian Fields, then somehow I lose them. The swirling revelers push us apart and I lose track of them. My own rushing high has been scattered into a wind of exuberant pieces, and I wander through the fields of laughing, ecstatic acid-heads, the dancing believers, the dancing children of sky and water and earth. Making my way up the green hillside, I find a spot in the wildflower grass overlooking the panoramic meadows, cross my legs, and drink it in.

The psychedelic rock reverberates even up here on the hillside, and all around, semi-nude lovers lie tangled in the grass, clusters of happy pot smokers play with their dogs, Dionysian spirits reach for the infinite blue sky, music-makers and soothsayers and conga players, all the races of mankind reveling in the wine of freedom. It is an incredible vision and I know I will never forget it. There is no wrong in what I behold. But I am overcome with pangs of loneliness, missing her, missing our days together, her fresh scent and touch, her laughing brown eyes, her hair, her skin, her loving body. I am overcome with longing, it pierces right to my soul. The secret life of the heart cannot be denied, the soul must be satisfied even as it's ravished.

Looking out over the kaleidoscopic human love-in, these thousands of joyful under the sun and sky, I know my time for this is over. I have drained the glass, it's turned into an endlessly flickering movie that I have already seen. I am being called, being called very strongly into another life. My whole body resonates with this intuitive knowing.

I walk back down the grassy hillside and skirt the orgiastic musical celebration, and within minutes walk right into my brother Evan, who happens to be looking for me. Smiling, I recognize the luminous melancholy in his handsome face at once. We have come to a fork in the road, some transforming influence is separating us from this wondrous, free-spirited community.

"You about ready?" he asks me, his sensitive hazel eyes delving into mine.

"I am ready, my brother, I am. Let's be on our way."

# Chapter 40

I MANEUVER MY A65 BSA Lightning downtown through traffic to visit my probation officer. Any kind of riding is better than no riding, even through L.A. Traffic. Mr. Camillo greets me with a creased, overworked smile, asks me to sit down, offers me a paper cup of burnt coffee. I deliver the edited version of what I've been doing.

Slumping in his swivel chair, Camillo asks, "So tell me, anything else on your mind?"

Tasting the bitter dubious brew, I open up. "Actually there is an idea that I'd like to run by you. A kind of request. There's something unusual my brother and I would like to do, but I'll need your permission."

Camillo smiles, letting me know he has heard many other unusual requests. "Okay, shoot," he replies, "lay it out for me."

"All right, here's the deal. I'd like to get out of this L.A. scene. It's distracting, and it seems dangerous to hang around in. I mean, just through casual association I could get involved in something by accident. I have some friends and they're almost all liberals, they do what hippies do. What I'm saying is, L. A is getting more tricky for me all the time. I'd like to move."

Camillo gives me a sober nod, running his hand through his thinning black hair. "I hear you and I'm inclined to agree. It's not your best environment. But where would you go, assuming I gave the green light? And when would you want to do this?"

"I'd like to do it as soon as the current quarter is over at LACC, say in about a month. And where we'd like to go is about 200 miles up the coast, to the town of San Luis Obispo."

"Interesting. Why there, of all places?"

"Well, it's a laid-back town of around 30,000 people, but it has a college. It's surrounded by hills and open space and it's close to the ocean For us it would be like living out in the country. And it's right there on 101, so it'd be easy for me to come down and visit you once a month."

"That's true. And for me to travel to you, which I definitely would do to check out where you're living, and how you're doing."

"Yes, I understand," I say, acknowledging our formal relationship. "And see, by living there, that tranquil scene, we can get more into our spiritual studies. We can rent a place where we can do some organic gardening. We really want to grow our own food."

"Hmmm," says Camillo, lighting his Chesterfield. "Sounds pretty healthy, I agree. But you think you'll be able to find jobs around there? Do you know anyone living there?"

"Actually, yeah, we do. Evan and I have an older first cousin there named Lawrence. He's lived there with his wife for about seven or eight years now. She's an artist, he drives a Culligan water truck. Lawrence is into grass-roots politics, pretty much a straight and stable guy. I doubt he's ever smoked a joint in his life. We wrote him a letter sort of floating this idea, and he wrote back saying to come on up. This is the guy who taught me how to play baseball when I was five years old, back in Texas. Another good thing is he knows all the business people in San Luis, so we should be able to connect with jobs. I think this scenario would work out for me."

"All right, slow down, you don't have to sell me so hard. Frankly, I like the sound of it. You hanging around L.A. is not the best thing. I've heard that you made an enemy over in narcotics at the Hill Street District. That sergeant Maragos is nobody to mess around with and word is he's got it in for you."

Taken aback, I say, "Whoa, I had no idea that you knew about that. That run-in happened before I was even finished with the trial."

"Oh, I realize that. And I know that you weren't implicated for anything in that situation. But it underscores what you were just saying about this city. If you have a rap, you can get dragged back under just by hanging around. This sargeant Maragos? He's a predatory, hard-core narc. He's not above finding a way to even the score."

I've been nursing the delusional hope that Maragos would forget about me. Now, I think not. Swallowing, I say, "Then all the more reason for me to move on, don't you think?"

"Yes, I do think," Camillo replies, tapping a pencil against his knuckles. "Does your cousin in San Luis know that you're on probation?"

"No, he doesn't know. I can't see any point in confessing that. I'd rather move in there with a fresh slate."

"That's probably smart. You're not actually obliged to tell anyone that you're on probation, not even an employer unless they ask. If you were on parole, that's a different story. When did you say you want to leave?"

"Within a month, maybe two at the most. Just soon as classes and the exams are done. Give us a couple of weeks to get packed up, we're out of here."

"And how are you doing in your classes?"

"I'm passing everything with flying colors, glad to say. No problems."

Camillo takes a drag on his C-stick, regarding me with thoughtful eyes. "You're a smart young man, Jake. So yes, you have my permission to move on up to San Luis Obispo. Just be sure you stay alert while you're still here, and mind all your P's and Q's."

"You got it, Mr. Camillo, yes sir, I will, for damned sure. Thanks very much."

"No big deal. I'm here to help you become a rehabilitated citizen, hah, that's my job. And while we're on the subject—you know your bust down there at Tecate? How it all seemed like an accident?"

"Yeah, I remember it like yesterday, a really bad day. Everything just seemed to spiral out of control. Probably the worst day of my life."

"Right. Well, as it turns out, that was no accident, I've seen the files. The border patrol had been alerted to be on the look-out for couple of long-haired guys, driving the car you were driving, They even knew more or less when. They played it right by the book."

"Jesus goddamn," I mutter, staring backwards into the nebulous void of betrayal.

"Well, I wouldn't go that far, but I get your drift."

"But dig, Mr. Camillo, this isn't the first time I've heard that. My lawyer suspected the same thing, she said almost exactly what you just said. That some kind of double-dealing was involved."

"And your lawyer was one hundred percent correct. You we're fingered by somebody who was in the know, somebody under pressure, somebody in a bind. So be extra careful, Jake, until you are clear of this treacherous city."

"I will. Whew, I guarantee you I will be. And thanks for telling me."

"Glad to be of service." Camillo replies with his lethargic smile. "And be sure you come to see me again before you leave."

"One more time?"

"Once more will be enough. Then I'll come and visit you up there. It'll be a nice drive, give me a chance to get out of this smoggy end zone."

We shake hands warmly, me feeling grateful for this good and honest man.

THE ROSES OF dawn suffuse the skies over the San Gabriel mountains when I roll my BSA outside. I check the oil and tire pressure, feeling the chill, pulling on a faded brown leather jacket over my tee. The 650 Lightning comes to life on the second kick, I coast on down the alley at near-idle. It's early Sunday morning, almost no traffic, the best time to ride. I put the bike through its paces on the long streets as the sun comes up behind me. After a few miles I shoot onto the Santa Monica Freeway and get rapidly up to speed, wind flattening my hair, the cuffs of my denims flapping against my Wellingtons. The fine-tuned Brit bike starts to hit its stride, thrumming beneath me, the pipes blatting away on the fresh wind.

Far out over the sea, over the rooftops of Venice and Santa Monica, the sky is illumined by cloud-lit spears that descend from vast blue window panes. I race along the elevated highway for the coast, wanting that first glimpse of pewter-blue ocean and white cresting surf, a sense of glory rising in my chest.

The freeway empties down the palisades and onto the coast highway as I throttle down, then run north between the cliffs and the beachcombers, the spindrift misting my wrap-around shades. At the Sunset junction I resist the urge to veer up toward the SRF Lake Shrine, thinking not now, not today. I race on up Route One toward Malibu, playing a toe-tune on my gearbox, on this day of all days.

For awhile, I speed along on the near empty highway in the clear primal light, riding between the steep cliffs and the rocky shoreline, along the glinting horizon of sky and sea, house of sky, holy house of water, holy highway, me and my motorcycle. The road curves slightly inland, empty and free, clean as a whistle. I open the throttle and pray that they do not notice me today, O Lord, do not see me and do not catch me. The Beaser's pipes break into a resonating howl, the engine in third leaping past 80, racing to 90 as I bend forward over the tank, holding tight in the buffeting wind, eyes tearing behind my shades, hair tied back with turquoise-beaded rawhide, aiyee, I knick it into fourth at 95 and twist the hammer all the way open. The A65 Lightning booms past 100 with ease, needle bouncing to 105, 107, hovering around 110 as I hang in the wind blast, one with the spirit, fused, fear-free, fused in the sheer flying glory. Nothing else is like this, nothing else compares, and only a rider knows, only a rider can understand.

Gradually easing off, I bring the bike down into the 90's, mavelling at its primal ability, dropping into the 80's, then down to an easy 75, leaning into the curves along the shore, laughing with gratitude. I veer off at a canyon crossroads, a little store two gas pumps, ethyl twenty-five cents, top off the tank and take a break. The bike ticks and cools in the green shade of a tree as I sit on the ground, sipping a cold bottle of apple juice. I can't see the ocean from this spot, a rugged knoll intervenes, but I can hear it. The booming, rebounding sea clarifies my thoughts. I know what I have to do, I don't have to think about it.

A few cars pass on the two-lane coast road, the world is waking up. I stand and stretch, then walk over to my motorcycle to gauge the engine heat. A rider going south swings in from the highway, making a tight half circle, astride a black Norton twin. He crunches toward me over the gravel and stops, a lop-sided grin on his face.

"Hey man, whooee," the rider says, "an A65 Lightning with velocity stacks. Don't see many of those out here on the coast."

"No, that's true," I replay. "The dude I bought it from had gotten it in St Louis and rode it out here. Guess it scared him so bad he decided to sell it. But for me, it was love at first sight."

"Hell yeah, I can dig it. That BSA Lightning is one of the fastest street bikes going, maybe even faster than the top-end Bonnie. But tell me, you ever have any trouble overheating?"

"Yeah, sometimes I do. Especially when I wind it all the way out. I was really booking it coming up the coast and that's why I stopped here, to let it cool down a little."

"Booking it, huh? Like how fast?"

"The speedometer was pegged up over a hundred easy, pretty damned fast. Almost blew me off the seat."

My cohort gives me a conspirator's grin, and offers me his hand. His blond hair is cropped short, except for his sideburns. He's a hardcore rider, I don't even have to ask.

"Listen," he tells me, "I work for a motorcycle outfit up in Santa Barbara, Red Line Motorcycles. That's where I'm coming from, heading down to visit my sister in Long Beach. If you ever—well, you'll probably never let go of that motorcycle, Jesus Gawd, I wouldn't. But if you ever wanted to sell her? Come and visit us, I'm a bike mechanic at Red Line. We live and breath English bikes—Triumphs, Vellos, Nortons, Vincent, you name it. They'd give you more than a fair price for that 650 Lightning."

"Hah, thanks, man, I'll remember that. I had to sell a big Matchless single just awhile back. You never know what's gonna pop up out of the box."

"Yeah, ain't that the truth," the blond rider mutters, as if trying to erase some memory, then says, "and just so you know, it's your engine drive bearing."

"What is?"

"Your overheating problem. The side bearing is what causes it."

"Is that right? Damn, far out. Can that be fixed?"

With a cocky grin, he says, "Not sure if BSA has figured it out yet, but we took one apart. We've got a line on it. A little re-engineering is involved."

"Redline Motorcycles, you say? I may just ride up there and check you guys out."

"Anytime. The name is Mitch. Here's our card. We'd need your bike for a few days, but I'm sure we can set you up with a loaner."

"Righteous, man. I'm Jake. You might be seeing me some time soon."

We clasp hands in a strong soul-shake. He kicks his Norton over, eases his way across the gravel, waits for a couple cars to go by, then gives me a nod and revs his sleek Norton back onto the highway. Billowing clouds scud across the translucent sky above the Santa Monica hills, seagulls wheel and cry in the air. I straddle my bike and get going.

Cruising northward, I turn inland up a narrow canyon road that winds up over the high barren ridges, stunning views of the curving blue sea, then descends through steep hairpins into the San Fernando Valley. My exhaust pipes rumble behind me in a mellow cadence. I know that somewhere up ahead I'll hit 101 going back toward Hollywood. I am one with my bike, I am one. And I take a solemn vow to the earth and the sky and all the rivers that run, that I will ride again.

# Chapter 41

MY OLD FRIEND Jonathan Bender keeps showing up in my life like a bent reckoning of what not to be. Annoying and quirky, psychoanalyzed to his wits' end, Bender is like the dog chasing its own tail convinced that the elusive tip is the key to revelation. But he keeps showing up, so I figure there's some message and meaning involved You don't chase someone off just because they're crazy. If that were the case, I'd have chased myself out the back door long ago. No, Bender's stayed my loyal friend through all these crazy changes, and he's always welcome at our recluse sanctuary.

Bender gum-shoes around in the mystical vibes that permeate our place, he drinks it in. He reads every book I lay on him. He devours Yogananda's books, then Ouspensky, Gibran and Thoreau, the Bhagavad Gita, the challenges of Krishnamurti. Like a stubborn learner, he doubts, he parrots endless questions—how, why, who, what happens, what if, when, why not? It's the same old question relentlessly rephrased, the monkey mind on a roll. Turn off the internal chatter and observe, I advise, with an exasperated smile. I know it's not easy, but you're addicted to that begat, begat, begat bullshit and there are no answers on that merry-go-round. Turn off the inner chatterbox. If three hundred acid trips, sacred mushrooms and liquid mescaline have taught me anything, it's that—turn off the monkey mind, learn to look, listen, and grow aware.

Bender squirms in his chair, imploring me with a restless stare.

"That process of mentalizing always traps us, Jonathan. It doesn't go anywhere, doesn't really deliver anything. Our curiosity is insatiable but the mind can't free itself. As long as you chase your own shadow, you'll never get out of the trap."

"But," Bender protests, "I don't want to be a slave to any of that shit!"

"Me either, I hear you. You have to disengage, disentangle, switch it off."

"But how, man, how? Acid didn't do it for me, I don't know how."

"By following a method. By delving into the river of meditation, Zen breathing, the fourth way techniques, whatever works for you. It's not a contest. It's just a matter of finding what works. But nothing really changes until you start."

"So stop thinking about doing it or about how to do, and just do it. Right?"

"Right, that's all I know. Doing is what does it. Just do and do some more, keep doing, like your breathing."

"I wish I could believe like you do. I don't have your faith."

"Believe whatever you want. It's not really about belief or faith. It's about doing what you need to do in order to become what you want to be."

This conversation or some variation usually calms him down, eases his rubber-band anxiety. Bender vows to begin real meditation at once.

"I am going to try Vedanta this time," he declares, "I'll go over to that temple in Hollywood and learn the art of concentration."

"Cool, man, just do it. Go for it all the way and don't shilly-shally around."

"What do you think I should concentrate on?"

"Focus on something that doesn't make you worry. Try that."

But the chances are that he will dither around, he won't stay with it more than a week or two, then he'll hop to another trip. I've been knowing Jonathan for two years now, I know his traits. Chances are that he'll always be a window-shopper.

One afternoon, boosted by honey-sweet Turkish coffee, Bender tells me about his deplorable living situation. He's holed up in a rancid house with schizoid homosexuals, or so he insists, people that steal his money and love to torment each other.

"You don't want to visit me, Jake, trust me. These freaks are sick fucks, sick, sick weirdos."

"Then why in the hell are you staying there?"

"I didn't know it when I first moved in. I moved in and put my money down. They all seemed more or less normal. They rented me the master bedroom dirt cheap and I thought I'd lucked out. Then, dude, they turned sicko on me."

"Hah ha ha, Bender, you're twisted, you make your own luck. Tell me more. And remember, I may write all this down."

Energized, Bender confides, "Well, there's this crazy buzz-cut bitch with tattoos on her pudgy arms who owns the house. She shares it with these two wigged-out fags. The old one's in his fifties, a total gin head. He swishes around with this menacing face, pretending he can see inside your private thoughts. He never smiles, and never works, I don't how he gets his money. No wait, I do know. His younger pal or squeeze or whatever is a street hustler that the older one queered back in Omaha and brought out to L.A. I mean, this doped-up kid has mush for brains, you know? He's got carrot-colored hair and works out with dumb bells like that's his salvation, and he hates any non-queers he meets, like me. Of course he doesn't think he's a fag, but when I tell him he is it blows his mind, he turns crazy. He's the bastard who stole my money and my transistor radio, too. He goes out every night over on the strip and sucks cocks for cash, yeah, that's how they make it. They have the most hateful relationship you can imagine, always screeching at each other. It's driving me out of my gourd."

"Jonathan, have you lost your mind? You've got to get out of there, that's like living in hell! Doesn't that landlady even give a shit?"

"Yeah, not really, she lives in the back apartment, she's a lunatic fag-hag. She eggs them on while they're going at it, cackling, shaking her drunken blubber. You should see this shit, Jake, you ought to come check it out."

"No, I don't think so," I snort, "I'll pass. I've seen enough insane shit to last me for awhile."

"Yeah, and you're right, it's way too morbid. And I did complain to her, I did. But I caught her inhaling this powdery speed, you know, up the nose with a straw, what's it called?"

"Crystal meth, man. Really bad scene. You've got to split from there, you listening?"

"Oh I know, I dig it, it's like living in purgatory. When I bitched about the fighting she came after me with a hat pin, she tried to stick it right in my neck. No, I'm serious, she's insane. I had to barricade myself in my bedroom to get away."

"Jesus Christ," I say, shaking with laughter, "how do you get involved in this shit?" Bender starts laughing too, short barking hyena laughs, scrunching forward in his short sleeve white shirt and thin black tie. He's got an actual job now, selling men's shoes somewhere.

"I do have some messed-up karma, it's true, don't I? I'm trying to practice the meditations, but I'll never learn there. It's like living in an insane asylum."

"So just leave, make tracks, stop procrastinating!"

"I'm afraid I'm gonna get sucked under again, Jake. I'm worried."

"Bullshit. Just split, get away from that madness. Just go. You've got a paycheck job, go live in a cheap hotel for awhile."

Bender shakes his head. "No, I'm paid up for four weeks in advance and she won't give me my moolah back. So I'm gonna tough it out and save some cash. Then I'm gone, you can count on it."

"Another month, in that shit hole? Man, if you say so. But listen, I have an idea for you. How would you like to live here in this place? You keep saying how much you want seclusion and all."

"What, live here, in this pad? Are you kidding, with you and Evan? Fuck yeah, all the cool vibes, that would be the best! But where would I sleep? On the couch?"

"No, not with us, not exactly. But here's what's happening. We're moving up the coast to San Luis Obispo in about a month, yeah, we're moving to the country. We're gonna grow our own food and do the whole back-to-earth trip."

Bender stares at me, astonished. "You're putting me on."

"No, I'm not, this is for real. And this pad would be the perfect sanctuary for you, it'll be available. I'll put in a good word for you with the landlady. All I ask is that when we come down for a visit, I can stay here for a couple days."

"Oh fuck yes," Bender exclaims, his left eyebrow flaring upward. "I'll do it, I'd love to live here and you are my only real friend. And of course you can stay here, anytime. But you're actually gonna do that? I mean, back to the land, the retreat, the Rudolf Steiner bio-organic number?"

"Yeah, we're actually going to do it. We're committed We're getting out of this madhouse city and up to the country. And who knows, once we get our act together, Dawn might even come out with the baby."

"That would be so far out," Bender laughs, clapping his hands, "I'd love to see her again. But you're going to need cash, man. What if you can't get jobs up there in the boondocks? You say you're dealing days are done. What are you gonna do for bread?"

"That's true, I'm out of the dope scene, fini, that's in the rearview mirror. I'm moving into a whole new world of possibilities."

"But what about money? I mean, you don't even have a fucking car. How the hell you gonna move two hundred miles without a car?"

With a placating gesture, I reply, "It's no big deal, don't worry about it. We have a some saved and I have a plan to raise some extra cash. It'll come together. In the meantime, I'll get you set up with the landlady. She'll like you, you come across as clean-cut. Just don't start your psycho-babble with her."

"Oh I won't, I know how to play it. And Jake, man, my friend, thank you, thank you, this is just what I need! And my casa is su casa, always, always, anytime, just know that!"

Not wanting anymore of his frenetic vibes, I tell him I have some writing to do. We stand in the amber porch light beside the avocado tree. Not wanting to go, Bender implores me: "How do you do all these things? Tell me that, ever since I've known you. How do you take these leaps that you take, the way you do?"

"I'm just living my life, man. I'm not sure I know what you mean."

"Like the way you take these sudden risks—all the psychedelics, the Mexico trip, the border wipe-out, you, your fast motorcycles, now the yoga, you hold nothing back, you always go all the way. It totally freaks me out, I'd be a basket case. How do you do that?"

Bender looks like a haggard drunk in the amber light. But he's not drunk, he doesn't even drink. Who knows what kind of tranqs his shrink feeds him. Hesitating, I say, "I guess I just keep moving on, you know? As long as you keep moving you don't get stuck. You might get snagged here or there, but you don't get hung up. I swore off all guilt and shame, I don't indulge. Live your life – your life – and just keep moving on."

"I gotta write that down."

"Just try it. Give it an honest try. Because it works."

We part as friends because friends we are; this kinky oddball is the first person I ever dropped acid with. And that was only a couple of years ago, although it seems like lifetimes. Intensely vivid lifetimes exploding through a couple of swift-flying years, and so much has happened. And now, I really need to slow it all down.

# Chapter 42

RAINSTORMS KEEP ROLLING in off the wild Pacific, causing mudslides along the palisades, turning all the world green. Unusual amounts of rain, people are saying, for southern California, not that I mind the rain. I fell in love with the rains deep in the Oaxaca Sierra, in love with the moods that rain invokes. The storm-wet weather keeps me off my bike, making me catch buses or just walk to my classes. But this helps me strengthen my resolve to not put off what I intend to do. You can think while walking, there's always time. You don't think much on a fast bike unless you have a death-wish.

One twilight evening, I'm walking through the glistening streets after rain has blown through. The air is washed of the insidious smog, the jacaranda trees drip with light. An old Dodge panel wagon against the curb catches my eye, faded dark blue and rusted in spots. A hand-written sign is taped in its rear window: "1948, runs solid, radio works, good retreads, $200 firm, call etcetera."

I move all around the vintage truck, thinking it's the ideal vehicle to transport us up the coast. It's in decent shape, the price is right. There's a crack in the front windshield, but not too bad. Everything looks okay inside, three on the floor, frayed naugahyde seats, the speedometer tops at eighty. I stand there for a few minutes, thinking it over. Then I memorize the phone number.

On the walk home, I stop at a corner pay phone and call the owner. We agree to meet the following afternoon, so I can test-drive it. I ask him if the old Dodge burns any oil.

"No, none to speak of," the man says in a frank voice. "I've had it for over ten years and used to haul window display mannequins around in it. But now it just sits there. The motor's got over two hundred thousand on it, although I redid the top end about three years ago."

"Sounds interesting," I say. "What would you say is wrong with it, if anything?"

"Nothing much, it's just kind of old. It's a straight line six that uses about a quart of oil a month. Sometimes it'll pop out of third gear, but you just ram the shifter in back in and she goes right along. Still runs strong."

"And how about the brakes?" In my mind, I'm already buying this truck.

"Hell, the brakes don't even squeak. They work fine."

That night, I tell Evan about the '48 Dodge and how I'm pretty sure it's our ticket for the trek northward. It'll haul our orange crates of books and records, our mattresses, our kitchen and camp gear, our clothes, even a few sticks of furniture.

"How much for it?" Evan mumbles, filling one cheek with brown rice as he talks.

"About two hundred bucks. You want to come with me tomorrow to check it out?"

"No, I gotta work. Besides, you know cars and I don't. Buy it if you think it's right."

"I already think it's right, it's battered but has some style. Looks like one of those old farm delivery trucks. I just need to make sure it runs okay."

"Sounds pretty cool to me," Evan replies. "One thing, though—you think I can drive it okay? I mean, you'll be on your bike and I've got to follow you. So I just want to be sure it's not too complicated."

I smile at my kid brother, not showing all my cards. I don't think he's ever even had a driver's license. "No, it's a snap," I tell him. "You'll be able to drive it like a charm."

The next day I meet the amiable, balding owner, and we talk over the truck. He hands me the keys and I drive up and down and around the hilly Silverlake streets, checking the brakes, checking for odors, engine overheat. The panel wagon creaks and shudders but doesn't stall out, these old straight six motors are reliable. Bones and I drove one all over Mexico without a hitch. I know it won't do over sixty miles an hour but that will be okay for now.

When I drive back the owner is waiting, smoking his pipe, grinning. "Well, what do you think of the old buggy?"

"I think we've got a deal," I tell him, and fork over the two hundred smackers. He signs over the pink slip, scribbles a bill of sale, and we shake on it. I promise to take care of the registration transfer right away. It's a simple, clean way to do business. I drive the '48 Dodge panel wagon home feeling satisfied, knowing that Evan will be impressed. This rattling old truck has Vagabond written all over it.

Another wild, windy storm blows in off the Pacific, drenching the southland in inches of rain. Then the skies open into a peerless blue dome, and the radio reports a break in the storm pattern. Everything that happens, happens now, always, I remind myself. There is no point in putting off my solo action any longer.

I jump on the 101 on my 650 Lightning and race through the gap in the Hollywood Hills into the long San Fernando valley, maneuvering through the mid-morning traffic. The storms have cleansed the atmosphere, a blessing to anyone running on two wheels. Riding up 101, I keep the bike in the comfort zone around 75 mph, now and then hitting a delirious burst of speed. But I keep it in check this time, and keep myself on purpose. The purple ice plant slopes and tall palm trees zip past. Up above Van Nuys, the highway opens up and I race along the long blue surfline, hugging the sweeping curves, then shoot up the slot through Carpenteria and Montecito. I veer over into the right lane and throttle down coming into Santa Barbara, ready to make my signifying gesture. The ride from my place in Silverlake to Redline Motorcycles has taken me a couple of hours, long enough to reconcile myself.

They turn out to be righteous dudes, they welcome me as a friend. And around noon on this bright spring day, we strike a deal. I sell my BSA A65 Lightning for $900 cash, $400 less than I paid for it, but the price is fair. The bike needs new tires and brake pads. I've put nine thousand miles on it in fifteen months, and part of that time it was cached in a garage. I've ridden it swift and hard, with a purpose, without regrets. Selling it to these dedicated riders is not that hard. Going home without my ride, not being able to race the sunset down the wind-swept coast, that's the hard part.

From Santa Barbara I take a Greyhound back to Hollywood, and a city bus home from the station. I feel consoled by the fact that we now have enough money to make the move, to not have to scramble for jobs. We have the bread to look around, find a cottage, to put in an organic vegetable garden with melons and sunflowers. This is the first time I've been without a bike since I was seventeen, Evan will be blown away. But our mystical quest now needs be honored above all else.

Looking out the window of the Greyhound, I marvel at our courage, where we end up is anybody's guess. But I know we have to follow that road of truth, that shining path, into the endeavor of who we are.

# Chapter 43

F AITHFUL JONATHAN BENDER comes over on the weekend to help us load the '48 Dodge panel wagon. We don't have room to carry much, so Bender inherits a worn love seat, some end tables, and a bronze floor lamp that blinks on and off. Evan gives him one of our favorite Spanish guitar records and I give him the keys to our garden court retreat.

"Remember, both of you," he insists, "this pad, my house, man, it's your house, always, anytime. Just know that."

"Thank you, man," I smile, "you're a good friend. And keep the faith, keep it lit."

"Do you think we can ever tell the future?" he suddenly asks. "I mean, for real, how can we know what's going to go down? Or are we just always in the dark?'

"Hah, funny you should mention that," I say, "I've been thinking about that. I didn't used to think could, but here's what I think now. Whatever we're doing today, as in right now, that's what creates our tomorrow. There's a direct and intimate connection. I mean if we just look past our wishful thinking, what we're doing now foretells our future. That's our crystal ball."

ALL THAT HAPPENS, happens now. We pull out of Los Angeles on a shining April day in 1967, my brother and I, high on our newfound freedom. We chug over the hills and into the San Fernando Valley, trucking north on the 101 freeway. The Dodge panel wagon won't do much more that fifty-five, a snail's pace for me, but I'm not complaining. I'm on my way into the unknown again, and nomads are happy as long as they keep moving. The old truck rattles and shakes, the noise from the tractor engine fills the cab, but not so loud that we can't talk. I am forced into the far right lane, being passed by everyone. But an anthem of light fills our chests and spins out behind us.

Up past Santa Barbara, edging inland from the surf-washed coast, we climb into the green, rain-drenched hills. The engine strains and groans on the steep grade, the floor shift pops out of third gear back into neutral. No matter how I try and jam the lever back into third, pumping the clutch, it won't go. Damn, we are grinding along on fleet 101 in second gear, shuddering along at no more than forty miles an hour.

Evan shoots me a nervous glance. "Whoa, you think this old crate's gonna make it?"

I smile at him. I look at him with the eyes of sky, of rain, of love and stormlight, I tap the metal dash with my fingers. "Yeah man, one way or another, we're gonna make it. We might be riding a donkey all the way to San Luis, looks like, but we are going to make it."

Laughing and encouraged, we buckle in for the remaining hundred or so miles up to San Luis Obispo, ignoring the blaring horns, taking in the rolling countryside and Irish green hills. We are travelers, riding on a wave of brilliant change. The strangest thing about this world is that no sooner do you find what you're looking for, than you seem to lose it. But you have to keep moving forward with gratitude. The new world is being born in us and through us and for us. We will make it manifest by our undaunted courage. We will stop the murderous wars, the horror, the bloodshed. We will stop the money-grubbing bastards who profit from misery. We will bring to their knees the devious politicians who grovel at their feet. Yes, we will, yes we will. You cannot drown the love that burns inside and you cannot smother the truth. This revolution burning in the heart of man is for always. And I tell you now and I tell you for always, you have not heard the last from us. Om Shanti.

*"In the midst of winter, I found there was within me, an invincible summer."*

~~Albert Camus

## The End